New Library of French Classics
HENRI PEYRE, SERIES EDITOR

❂❀❖❀❂❀❖❀❂❀❖❀❂❀❖❀❂❀❖❀❂❀❖❀

Our judgment on literature, like those on the music, the painting, the thought of past ages, stands constantly in need of revision. With some laziness, many of us have accepted an arbitrary choice made by teachers or critics of an earlier generation, which declared only certain novels by Stendhal, Balzac, Flaubert, Zola, or by German, Russian, Spanish novelists, to be "masterpieces" and passed off other works as "minor."

The present series is intended to reconsider such archaic choices. Our age has reassessed the fiction of the eighteenth century, once placidly ignored, and that of seventeenth-century France, and rediscovered many a tale of the Renaissance.

A number of less well-known novels of the nineteenth century touch us more than many of the more celebrated volumes by Balzac or Flaubert, by Dickens or Turgenev, conventionally acepted as most fit for schoolboys. After all, Balzac wrote many other novels than EUGÉNIE BRANDET *and* LE PÈRE GORIOT, *and in the eyes of good judges, maybe better ones. Stendhal is not all enclosed in* LE ROUGE ET LE NOIR. *Zola is at least as original in* LA FAUTE DE L'ABBÉ MOURET *as he is in* NANA, *and a much greater poet and portrayer of love in the first of those two novels. Even in our own century, novelists who have been neglected by translators and publishers may well appear to a later generation equal to others who have been temporarily acclaimed outside of France.*

The purpose of this series is to bring some of those half-neglected yet highly significant novels from French literature to American readers. The translators are persons of established competence both as masters of the French language and as talented writers. The novels should afford psychological insight, social criticism and enjoyment to those who may discover them in their American version, and, in the poet's words, "give grace and truth to life's unquiet dream."

HENRI PEYRE

Already published:

AXEL
by Villiers de l'Isle-Adam

THE SIN OF FATHER MOURET
by Emile Zola

Other translations in preparation:

LE VESUVE
by Emmanuel Roblès

L'AGE INGRAT
by José Cabanis

LE PAYSAN DE PARIS
by Louis Aragon

L'INSURGE
by Jules Vallès

BEATRIX

by
Honoré de Balzac

Translated by Beth Archer

PRENTICE-HALL, INC.
Englewood Cliffs, New Jersey

Designed by Janet Anderson

CONTENTS

696558

BEATRIX

꘎꘎꘎꘎꘎꘎꘎꘎꘎꘎꘎꘎꘎꘎꘎꘎꘎꘎꘎꘎꘎꘎꘎

*To Sarah** On a clear day, along the shores of the Mediterranean where once the elegant empire of your name extended, the sea occasionally discloses under the veiling of its waters a sea flower, masterwork of Nature. The lace of its netting tinted with purple, sepia, pink, violet, gold; the freshness of its living filigree; the velvet of its texture—all whithers as soon as curiosity extracts it and exposes it on the beach. So would the sunlight of publicity offend your pious modesty. Therefore, in dedicating this work to you, I must silence the name that would ennoble it. But concealed by this half silence, your splendid hands may bless it, your sublime forehead may bend dreamily over it, your eyes filled with maternal love may smile at it, for in it you will be both present yet hidden. Like that jewel of marine flora, you will remain on the pale silken sand where your lovely life flourishes, hidden by a wave that is transparent only to a few friendly, discreet eyes.

I would have liked to place at your feet a work in harmony with your perfection, but since that was impossible, I knew I might gratify one of your instincts by offering something to protect.

De Balzac

* Countess Emilio Guidobone-Visconti, née Sarah Lowell. The Viscontis were a Milanese family whose importance, particularly in the 14th century, extended as far as Genoa and Pisa. Balzac had a prolonged amorous and financial relationship with this intriguing Englishwoman who repeatedly lent him money and was rumored to have borne him a son.

N.B. All notes throughout text are the translator's.

BEATRIX
OR
LOVE
IMPOSED

PART ONE

A
PATRIARCHAL
FAMILY

I A TOWN IN BRITTANY France, and particularly Brittany, still has a few towns that are totally outside the social currents which have bestowed on the 19th century its particular character. Lacking reliable communication with Paris, barely linked with the sub-prefecture or provincial capital of the district, these towns watch modern civilization go by like a parade—they are amazed by it but do not cheer it; and out of fear or indifference, remain faithful to their old ways whose imprint they still carry. Anyone wishing to travel around as an archaeologist of society, observing man rather than stone, could recapture the age of Louis XV in some small Provençal village, that of Louis XIV in the heart of Poitou, and of still more ancient times deep in Brittany. Most of these towns are now bereft of any splendor which historians, concerned more with facts and dates, do not even mention, but which still survives in memory, as in the case of Brittany where the national character allows nothing relevant to it to fall into oblivion. Many of these towns were the capitals of some small feudal state, county, or duchy, conquered by the kingdom or divided up by heirs lacking a male descendancy. Disinherited from active life, these heads became arms, and arms deprived of nourishment wither and vegetate. Over the last thirty years, these portraits of former ages are beginning to fade and disappear. While working for the masses, modern industry progressively destroys works of art that had been as personal for the buyer as for the creator. Nowadays, we have *products;* we no longer have *works.* Monuments play the greater part in these phenomena of retrospection, while for industry, monuments are stone quarries, or saltpeter mines, or cotton storehouses. In a few more years, these unique towns will be transformed and remain visible only in the iconography of literature.

One of the towns where the most accurate physiognomy of feudal ages can still be seen is Guérande. The name alone evokes a thousand memories in the minds of painters, writers, and thinkers who may have ventured as far as the coast where this magnificent feudal jewel lies, proudly commanding the sand flats between the sea and the dunes, and which is like the apex of a triangle at whose other angles lie two no less remarkable jewels—Le Croisic and the town of Batz. Aside from Guérande, only Vitré in the center of Brittany, and Avignon in the south, have retained their medieval appearance intact to the present day. Guérande is still encircled by mighty walls; its broad moats still filled with water; its battlements unbroken, its loopholes unencumbered with weeds, its square and round towers unshrouded by ivy. There are three gates whose portcullis rings are still visible; one can enter only by passing over a drawbridge of iron-clad wood which though no longer raised, could be. The municipality, when blamed for having in 1820 planted poplars along the moats to shade the avenue, replied that a hundred years earlier the beautiful long esplanade of the fortifications on the dune side, which look as though completed yesterday, had been converted into a mall shaded by elms where the townspeople strolled.

The houses have undergone no change; there are neither more nor fewer than before. None of them have felt on their façade the architect's hammer, the whitewasher's brush, or been weakened by the weight of a superstructure. All of them have kept their original character. Some, resting on wooden pillars forming galleries under which pedestrians circulate, have floors that creak but do not break. The shopkeepers' houses are small and squat, faced with slate shingles. The now rotted woodwork was mostly used for sculpting figures above the windows. Along the beams, they project above the pillars as grotesque faces, extending at the angles into fantastic beasts, animated by the great concept of art, which at that time imbued inert matter with life. These antiquities, resistant to everything, provide painters with the ocher tones and mellowed lines that their brushes enjoy.

The streets are still the same as four hundred years ago. However, since the population has declined and social activity is less intense, a curious traveler eager to explore this town—as impressive as a full suit of ancient armor—can wander, though not without a certain melancholy, along an almost deserted street whose stone windows have been cemented over to avoid taxation. The street ends at a postern closed off by a stone wall above which grows a cluster of trees, elegantly placed there by the hands of Breton nature—among the most luxuriant in all of France. A painter or a poet might stop to savor the silence that clings to the new-looking vaulting of this postern, to which no sound comes from the life of this peaceful town, and from which the fertile countryside appears in all its splendor through the loopholes, once occupied by crossbowmen and archers, that are like the panoramic windows of some belvedere. It is impossible to walk there without being reminded at every step of the customs and habits of the past; every stone bears witness to them; even the ideas of the Middle Ages have survived on the level of superstition. Should a gendarme pass by in his braid-trimmed hat, his presence is a shocking anachronism. But it is most unusual to come upon any sign of modern life. There is hardly any trace of modern dress, and what little has been accepted by the inhabitants has somehow been adapted to their unalterable ways and unchanging physiognomy. The central square is filled with wonderfully contrasting Breton costumes that artists come to sketch. The whiteness of the smocks worn by the *paludiers*—the salt workers in the marshes—contrasts vividly with the blues and browns of the peasants, and with the authentic and sacredly preserved head-dresses of the women. These two classes, along with the jacketed seamen in their patent leather hats, are as distinct from one another as the castes of India and continue to recognize the differences that separate the bourgeoisie, the nobility, and the clergy. Here, everything is still neatly divided. The planing tool of the Revolution found the masses too rough, too hard, to smooth down—it would have been dented if not broken. The immutable character bestowed by Nature on her zoological species is here to be seen in man.

In short, even after the revolution of 1830, Guérande still remains outside of time, profoundly Breton, fervently Catholic, silent, withdrawn, inhospitable to new ideas.

Its geographic position may account for this phenomenon. This lovely town overlooks the salt marshes whose salt is known throughout Brittany as the salt of Guérande, and is considered by many Bretons to be responsible for the excellence of their butter and sardines. Its only communication with present-day France is by two roads: one leading to Savaney, the district to which it belongs, and continuing to Saint-Nazaire; the other leading to Vannes, thus connecting it with the Morbihan. The district road provides the overland route, and Saint-Nazaire the sea route to Nantes. The overland route is used only by the bureaucracy of the district. The faster, more frequented route is via Saint-Nazaire. Now between this town and Guérande there is a stretch of at least six leagues that is not served by stagecoach, and for good reason: there are hardly three passengers a year. Saint-Nazaire is separated from Paimboeuf by the mouth of the Loire which is four leagues wide. The delta of the Loire makes steamboat navigation fairly hazardous, and by way of further complication, there was no dock in 1829 at the cape of Saint-Nazaire. This is an area of slimy rocks, granite reefs, and gigantic boulders providing a natural defense for its picturesque church, and compelling travelers to hurl themselves and their possessions into rowboats when the sea was rough. In calm weather, they were obliged to walk across the reefs to the jetty then under construction. Such obstacles, hardly an encouragement to lovers of travel, may still exist. To begin with, bureaucracy moves slowly; in addition, the inhabitants of this region—jutting up like a molar on the map of France and contained between Saint-Nazaire, Batz, and Le Croisic—are fairly well adjusted to these difficulties that prevent the access of strangers.

Flung out at the edge of the continent, Guérande thus leads nowhere and attracts no one. Content to remain unknown, the town concentrates on itself. The market for the immense production of the salt marshes, providing the treasury with no less than a million francs a year, is in Le Croisic—a peninsular town whose link with Guérande is across the moving sands that erase by night the path traced by day, or across the inlet, requiring boats, that provides Le Croisic with a port and intrudes on the sand. This charming little town is thus the Herculaneum of feudalism minus the shroud of lava. It exists without being alive, and with no other justification for existence except that it was not demolished.

Should you arrive in Guérande from Le Croisic, having crossed the expanse of salt marshes, you would be much impressed by the sight of this immense fortification, apparently quite new. Its picturesque setting and the unsophisticated charm of its environs when arriving from Saint-Nazaire, are no less captivating. All around, the countryside is exquisite—flowering hedges, honeysuckle, boxwood, roses, lovely shrubs. One might think this an English garden designed by some great artist. This blooming spot, so natural, so little cultivated, suggestive of the unexpected charm of a bed of violets or lily-of-the-valley in a forest glen, is framed by a Saharan desert bordered by the ocean—a desert without a tree, a blade of grass, a bird, where on a sunny day the white-clad salt workers scattered across the marshes look like Arabs in burnooses. Thus Guérande, with its lovely inland scenery, its desert bounded on the right by Le Croisic and on the left by Batz, resembles nothing that the traveler sees elsewhere in France. These two extremes of nature, united by the last vestige of feudal life, are indescribably striking. The town has the same effect on the soul as a sedative has on the body; it is as soothing as Venice.

There is no public conveyance except a wagoner who transports in his rickety wagon travelers, merchandise, and even letters, from Saint-Nazaire and back again. Bernus, the driver, was the factotum for the entire community in 1829, coming and going as he pleased, known by the whole countryside, running everybody's errands. The arrival of a carriage is considered a major event—whether a lady passing through Guérande on her way to Le Croisic, or some aged invalids come to take salt-water baths which, around the rocks of this peninsula, are said to be superior to the baths of Boulogne, Dieppe, or Les Sables. Peasants come in on horseback carrying their produce in sacks. They come into town, as do the salt workers, to buy the jewelry peculiar to their caste which is given to all Breton brides-to-be, and the white linen and other fabrics for their clothing. Within a radius of ten leagues, Guérande has remained the illustrious Guérande where the historic treaty * was signed, the key to the coast, exhibiting no less than Batz a splendor now lost in the darkness of time. The jewels, cloth, linen, ribbons, hats, are all made elsewhere. But for the buyers, they are still from Guérande. Any artist, and even one who is not, passing through Guérande, experiences the same desire one feels in Venice and too soon forgotten to end the rest of his days in such peace and silence, strolling in good weather from one gate to the other along the mall that encircles the town on the sea side. At times, the image of this town returns to haunt the temple of one's memory: she enters crowned with her towers and decked with her walls, trailing her flower-strewn gown, waving the golden cape of her dunes, exuding the intoxicating scents of her delicious briar paths scattered with flowers, dwelling in your mind like a gorgeous woman seen by chance in some distant land who remained lodged in a corner of your heart.

* In 1365, a treaty was signed following the battle of Auray by Charles V of France, granting Jean de Monfort the ducal crown of Brittany.

II L'HÔTEL DU GUAISNIC Near the church of Guérande stands a house that is to the town what the town is to the country—a perfect image of the past, a symbol of something great now destroyed, a poem. This house belongs to the noblest family of the region, the du Guaisnics, who at the time of the du Guesclins were as superior to them in fortune and antiquity as the Trojans to the Romans. The *Guaisqlain* (also spelled formerly *du Glaicquin*), which became du Guesclin, are descended from the du Guaisnics. Old as the granite of Brittany, the Guaisnics are neither Franks nor Gauls; they are Bretons, or to be more precise, Celts. They were probably Druids, in some remote time, gathering mistletoe in the sacred forests and making human sacrifices on the dolmens. It is futile to speak of what they were. Today this race, fully equal to the Romans without demeaning themselves to become princes, who wielded power long before Hugues Capet's ancestors were even heard of, this family of unalloyed strains has an income of about 2,000 francs a year, the house in Guérande, and the little castle of du Guaisnic. All the estates belonging to the du Guaisnic barony, the oldest in Brittany, are leased to farmers and bring in about 60,000 francs in spite of inadequate cultivation. The du Guaisnics are still the owners of their lands, but since they can not reimburse the capital left in their hands two hundred years ago by the tenants, they cannot touch a penny of the income. They are in the same position as the kingdom of France toward its *engagistes* before 1789. Where and when could the barons find the million francs that their farmers paid them? Before 1789, the fiefs held by the du Guaisnic castle, which is perched on a hill, were still worth 50,000 francs. However, the National Assembly voted to abolish the tax on leases and sales formerly paid to the lords. Given the circumstances, this family, now insignificant in France, would be an object of ridicule in Paris; in Guérande, it is the symbol of Brittany. In Guérande, the Baron du Guaisnic is one of the great barons of France, one of the men above whom there is but one other—

the King of France, formerly elected their chieftain. Today, the name du Guaisnic, full of Breton connotations, whose origins are explained in *Les Chouans ou la Bretagne en 1799,* has undergone the same changes as the name du Guaisqlain. The tax collector, like everybody else, spells it Guénic.

At the end of a dank, somber alley formed by the gabled walls of neighboring houses, one sees the arch of a gateway high enough and wide enough to allow the passage of a horseman, which suggests that at the time of its construction carriages did not yet exist. This arch, supported by two jambs, is entirely made of granite. The door, of oak as fissured as the bark of the trees that provided the timber, is studded with enormous nailheads that create a geometric pattern. The arch has a molding that displays the du Guaisnic shield as clear and sharp as though just sculpted. This coat of arms would delight an amateur of heraldry by its simplicity testifying to the pride and antiquity of the house. It is the kind invented by the crusaders of Christianity for the purpose of recognizing one another. The Guaisnics have never quartered it; it has remained pure, like the royal shield of France which experts discern in heart point or quarters among the oldest escutcheons. This is how it can still be seen in Guérande: *gules in a hand proper manched ermine holding a sword argent in pale,* with the stupendous motto, FAC! What an impressive thing! The baronial coronet surmounts this simple blazon whose vertical lines, raised in relief to represent the gules, are still clear. The artist has conferred on the hand an indescribable quality of pride and chivalry. With what force it holds the sword that was brandished by the family only yesterday! Indeed, should you go to Guérande after reading this tale, you cannot avoid being thrilled on seeing this shield. Even the most hardened republican would be moved by the fidelity, the nobility and the greatness hidden at the end of that alleyway. The du Guaisnics did well yesterday; they are prepared to do well tomorrow. *Do* is the great word of chivalry. "You did well in battle," were the words of highest praise bestowed by the constable, that great du Guesclin who for a time succeeded in ousting the English from France. The depth of the sculpture, protected from all inclemencies by the broad margin that forms the rounded projection of the arch, is in keeping with the spiritual depth of the motto that rests in the soul of this family. Anyone who knows the du Guaisnics would find this detail moving.

The open doorway reveals a rather large courtyard; on the right are the stables, on the left the kitchen. The house is built of hewn stone from cellar to attic. The façade on the courtyard has a twin staircase whose gallery bears vestiges of sculptures effaced by time, but an antiquarian's eye can still distinguish the major segments of the hand holding the sword. Beneath this lovely gallery, framed by molding now cracked in many places and polished with wear, there is a little enclosure formerly occupied by a watchdog. The stone balustrades are disjointed, and weeds, tiny flowers, and moss have sprung up through the cracks and between the steps of the staircase which, though displaced by time, have not lost their solidity. The door must once have been most handsome. As far as one can judge from the remains, it was designed by an artist of the great Venetian school of the 13th century, and displays a curious combination of Byzantine and Moorish elements. It is crowned with a circular projection overgrown with vegetation that varies according to the season from pink to blue, yellow to brown. The door of studded oak opens onto a vast hall leading to another door with a similar gallery going down to the garden. This hall is marvelously preserved. The wainscotting is chestnut and the walls above are hung with magnificent embossed Spanish leather whose gilt is peeling. The coffered ceiling was painted and gilded, but the gilt is now barely visible. It now looks like Cordovan leather, but one can still perceive a few red flowers and green leaves. A cleaning might restore the paintings which are similar to those that decorate the ceilings of the house of Tristan in Tours, and which would prove that those ceilings were re-done or restored during the reign of Louis XI. The carved fireplace is enormous and contains wrought-iron andirons of exquisite workmanship. It could hold a cord of wood. The furniture in this hall is all oaken and bears the family arms on the chair backs. Hung on the walls are three English muskets suitable for hunting or warfare, three sabres, two game bags, and various equipment for hunting and fishing.

Alongside is the dining room that communicates with the kitchen by a door cut into a corner turret. This turret, following the design of the courtyard façade, corresponds to another one in the other corner containing a circular staircase that leads to the upper floors. The dining room is hung with tapestries dating from the 14th century, as indicated by the spelling of the inscriptions on the pennants beneath each figure. However, since they are written in the primitive language of the fabliaux, it is impossible to transcribe them into contemporary language. These tapestries, splendidly preserved in those places where the light has not hit them, are framed in carved oak now black as ebony. The exposed beams of the ceiling are each decorated with a different leaf design. The cross beams have a painted facing along which runs a garland of golden flowers on a blue ground. Standing face to face are two old buffets whose shelves, polished by the cook Mariotte with Breton stubbornness, hold—as they did in the days when the kings of 1200 were as poor as the du Guaisnics in 1830—four old goblets, an antique tureen and two saltcellars of chased silver, a number of pewter plates, and many jugs of blue and green stoneware, decorated with arabesques and the du Guaisnic arms, with hinged pewter lids. The fireplace has been modernized, proving that this room has been used by the family during the last century. It is of stone carved in the style of Louis XV, surmounted by a mirror in a beaded gilt frame. This contradiction, unnoticed by the family, would upset a poet. In the center of the mantelpiece covered in red velvet, there stands a tortoise-shell clock inlaid with brass, and on either side a candelabrum of curious design. A large square table on twisted columns stands in the middle of the room. The chairs of turned wood are covered with needlepoint. A single-legged table, carved to represent a vine stock and placed before the window looking onto the garden, holds a strange lamp. This lamp consists of a globe of ordinary glass, a bit smaller than an ostrich egg, held in a candlestick by a glass knob; the wick, twisted like a worm in a tube, is fed by nut oil from the globe. The window looking out on the garden, like the one on the courtyard, both in corresponding positions, has stone mullions and hexagonal leaded panes, and is hung with draperies and tasseled valances of red silk shot with yellow, an old fabric once known as brocatelle.

On each of the two floors of the house, there are only two such rooms. The first floor serves as living quarters for the head of the family; the second was formerly intended for children. Guests were housed in the attic rooms, and servants lived above the kitchens and stables. The sloping roof with its leaded gables has been opened on the garden and courtyard sides to contain a magnificent ogival dormer, almost as high as the ridge of the roof, with delicate consoles whose carvings have been eaten away by the salt air. Above the sculpted arch of this 4-mullioned window a weathercock still creaks.

A precious detail, utterly simple but interesting to the archaeologist, should not be overlooked. The turret containing the circular staircase rounds off the corner of a large gabled wall lacking any opening. The stairs descend through a small arched doorway down to a gravel stretch separating the house from the enclosing wall that backs the stables. This turret is repeated on the garden side by a five-sided tower ending in a cross vault that supports a belfry instead of the conical dome of its twin. This is how those elegant architects provided variety in symmetry. These twin turrets are joined, on the first floor only, by a stone gallery decorated with prowlike forms bearing human heads.

This exterior gallery carries a balustrade constructed with great elegance and refinement. From the top of the gable, beneath which is one oblong loophole, a stone ornament is suspended resembling the canopy above statues of saints in church portals. Both turrets are pierced by lovely ogival doorways leading onto this terrace. This is what 13th-century architects extracted from what in today's houses is a cold bare side wall.

Can you not envision a lady walking along this balcony in the morning, looking beyond Guérande at the sun as it burnishes the golden sands and shimmers on the ocean's surface? Do you not admire this wall with flowered finials, completed at either end by turrets that seem almost fluted—one unexpectedly rounded off like a swallow's nest, the other displaying its charming gothic doorway with the sword-bearing hand? The other gable of the Hôtel du Guaisnic adjoins the neighboring house. The harmony so carefully sought by the master builders of that period is preserved in the courtyard façade by the turret that corresponds to the one with the spiral staircase—or *vis,* as it was called then—that connects the dining room with the kitchen; it ends at the first floor and is crowned by a perforated dome that surmounts the blackened statue of Saint Calixtus.

The garden is sumptuous for such an ancient construction. It is about half an acre, with trees espalier-trained along its walls. It is divided into vegetable beds bordered by quenouille-trained fruit trees that are tended by a manservant named Gasselin who also grooms the horses. On the far side of the garden is a bench shaded by an arbor. A sun dial stands in the middle. The paths are graveled. The garden façade has no tower corresponding to the one alongside the gable. This is compensated by a fluted column that must once have borne the family standard since it terminates in a rusty iron socket with scraggly weeds now growing out of it. This detail, in keeping with the surviving sculpture, proves that the manor was constructed by a Venetian architect. This elegant standard-bearer is like a signature left by the art of Venice, by the chivalry and refinement of the 13th century. Any remaining doubt would be dispelled by the nature of the decorations. The trefoils of the house of du Guaisnic have four instead of three leaves. This discrepancy betrays the Venetian school corrupted by its trade with the East whose half-Moorish architects, little concerned with Catholic symbolism, provided the trefoil with a fourth leaf, whereas Christian architects remained faithful to the Trinity. In this instance, Venetian fantasy proved to be heretical.

If this house kindles your imagination, you may wonder how it is that such miracles of art are not repeated today. Nowadays, great houses are sold, demolished, replaced by streets. No one knows whether his generation will maintain the ancestral home through which each member passes like guests at an inn. When building a house in the past, one worked for, or at least believed in, the posterity of the family, hence the beauty of those houses. Faith in oneself produced marvels as great as faith in God.

As to the disposition and furnishings of the upper floors, they can only be surmised from the description of the ground floor, and from the habits and characteristics of the family. For the last fifty years, the du Guaisnics have only received guests in the two rooms already described which, like the courtyard and the external aspects of the manor, exude the spirit, grace and simplicity of noble old Brittany.

Without this topography and description of the town, without this minute portrayal of the house, the remarkable characters of this family might be less comprehensible. The frames have thus preceded the portraits. It may then be concluded that things dominate people. There are indeed monuments whose influence is apparent on those who live near them; it is, for instance, difficult to be irreligious in the shadow of a cathedral like Bourges. One is also less likely to fall short of one's destiny when all around, images remind one of that destiny. This was the view held by our ancestors, now abandoned by a generation that no longer has either signs or distinctions, and whose way of life alters with every decade. Are you not prepared to meet the Baron du Guaisnic, sword in hand, or else dismiss all this as untrue?

✱↬✦↬✱↬✦↬✱↬✦↬✱↬✦↬✱↬✦↬✱↬✦↬✱↬✦↬✱↬✦↬✱↬✦↬✱↬✦↬

III THE BARON During the early days of August, 1836, when this scene opens, the du Guénic family still consisted of Monsieur and Madame du Guénic, Mademoiselle du Guénic, the elder sister of the Baron, and an only son aged twenty-one named Gaudebert-Calyste-Louis, following a family tradition. The father was named Gaudebert-Calyste-Charles. Only the last patron saint was variable. Saint Gaudebert and Saint Calixtus were always the protectors of the du Guénics. The Baron du Guénic left Guérande as soon as Vendée and Brittany took up arms; he fought alongside Charette, Cathelineau, La Roche-jaquelin, Elbée, Bonchamps, and the prince de Loudon. Before leaving, he sold all his worldly goods to his elder sister, Mademoiselle Zéphirine du Guénic, by a stroke of genius unique in revolutionary annals. After the death of all the heroes of the West, the baron, whom only a miracle had saved from sharing their fate, refused to yield to Napoleon. He fought on until 1802, the year he was almost captured, returned to Guérande, and from Guérande went to Le Croisic where he set sail for Ireland—a faithful partner to Brittany's traditional hatred of England. The people of Guérande feigned ignorance of the baron's existence; in twenty years there was not a single indiscretion. Mademoiselle du Guénic collected the revenues and transmitted them to her brother via fishermen.

In 1813, Monsieur du Guénic returned to Guérande as casually as though returning from a holiday in Nantes. During his stay in Dublin, the old Breton despite his fifty years became enamored of a charming Irish girl, daughter of one of the noblest and poorest families of that unhappy land. Miss Fanny

O'Brien was then twenty-one. The baron came home for the documents needed for his marriage, went back for the wedding, and ten months later, at the beginning of 1814, returned with his wife who gave birth to Calyste the very day Louis XVIII entered Calais, which accounts for the name Louis. At that moment, the loyal old Breton was seventy-three, but the partisan wars against the Republic, his hardships during five crossings on the open sea, his life in Dublin, had all weighed heavily on him; he looked more than a hundred. In no previous age had any Guénic been more in harmony with this ancient manor, built in the days when court was held in Guérande.

Monsieur du Guénic was an old gentleman tall in stature, straight as a rod, gaunt, sinewy, and lean. His oval face was lined with thousands of wrinkles causing arched fringes above his cheekbones and eyebrows, making him resemble the old men so appreciated by Van Ostade, Rembrandt, Miéris, and Gerard Dow, whose portraits require a magnifying glass to be fully admired. His features seemed almost sunken under his many lines, produced by a life of exposure and by his habit of surveying the countryside in sunlight, from sunrise to sunset. Nonetheless, a careful observer could still discern those imperishable features of the human face that continue to communicate even when the eye sees little more than a death mask. The firm contours of the face, the curve of the brow, the severity of the lines, the sharpness of the nose, the structure of the frame that only wounds can alter, expressed unselfish boldness, limitless faith, unquestioning obedience, incorruptible fidelity, unwavering love. In him the granite of Brittany became incarnate. The baron had lost all his teeth. His lips, once red but now purplish and supported only by the strong gums that chewed bread his wife carefully softened in a damp napkin, withdrew into his mouth producing a grimace that was both menacing and proud. His chin seemed to be reaching for his nose, but one saw in the character of that battered nose the signs of his energy and Breton endurance. His complexion, marbled with red that showed through the wrinkles, indicated a violent, sanguine temperament, well suited to endure the fatigues that no doubt saved him from many an apoplectic seizure. His head was crowned with hair as pale as silver that fell to his shoulders in curls. His face, for the most part extinguished, glowed with the brilliance of black eyes that shone from the depth of their brown orbits, casting the last sparks of a generous and loyal soul. His eyebrows and eyelashes had fallen out. His skin, dried out and stiff, made shaving so difficult that he had been obliged to grow a fan-shaped beard. The feature a painter would most have admired in this old Breton lion, with his broad shoulders and sinewy chest, was his hands—splendid soldier's hands, broad, thick, hairy hands such as du Guesclin must have had, hands that grasped the sword only to relinquish it, like Joan of Arc, on the day when the royal standard floated from the cathedral at Reims; hands that had often been bloodied by the thorns of the underbrush in the Bocage, hands that had held the oars in the Marais to ambush the "Blues," or in the open sea to permit Georges' landing; hands of a partisan, a cannoneer, an infantryman, a leader; hands that remained white though the elder branch of the Bourbons was in exile; on looking closely, one could see a few recent marks that indicated the baron had at one time joined MADAME in the Vendée—today, this fact can be admitted. Those hands were the living proof of that noble motto which no Guénic had ever failed: *Fac!* *

---

* These are all allusions to the Wars of Vendée which were civil wars that began in the western provinces of France in 1793. The "Whites" were the monarchists; the "Blues" the republicans. Georges Cadoudal was one of the partisan leaders who organized a plot against Bonaparte and was caught and executed in 1804. MADAME was the name given to the Duchesse de Berry who in 1832 attempted to raise up the whole of Vendée against Louis-Philippe, but failed and was imprisoned.

His brow attracted attention because of the golden tints at the temples that contrasted with the brown of the shallow brow that his balding had enlarged enough to bestow even greater majesty on this splendid ruin. This physiognomy—somewhat materialistic, but how could it be otherwise—like all the Breton faces around the baron suggested a savage quality, a primitive calm that resembled the impassivity of the American Indian, a certain quality of stupidity originating perhaps from the complete repose that follows extreme fatigue, revealing the pure animal underneath. Thought was rare on this face; it was evidently an effort. It resided more in the heart than in the head and culminated more readily in deeds than in ideas. However, on examining this splendid old man with sustained attention, one might guess at the mystery behind this fundamental opposition to the spirit of his age. His beliefs and sentiments were, so to speak, inborn thus dispensing him from any need to meditate. He had learned his duties through the act of living. Institutions and religion did his thinking for him. He and those close to him were thus able to reserve the mind for action, without dissipating its energies on such matters as they considered useless but that others deemed significant. His thinking, which he drew from the heart, like his sword from the scabbard, had the same radiant candor as the ermine-sleeved hand on his coat-of-arms. Once this secret was guessed, everything became clear. One understood the profundity of decisions that resulted from thinking as clear, precise, candid, immaculate as ermine. One understood the sale of all his property to his sister, before the war, which implied every risk—death, confiscation, exile. The beauty of character of these two old people—for his sister only lived through and for her brother—can not possibly be understood by the selfish mentality that the uncertainty and instability of our present day have engendered. An archangel summoned to look into their hearts could not have discovered a minimal trace of egoism.

In 1814, when the parish priest of Guérande suggested to the baron that he go to Paris to claim his due, the old sister, other-wise avaricious where the family was concerned, exclaimed: "For shame! Should my brother stretch his hand out like a beg-gar?"

"One would think I had served the king out of personal mo-tives," answered the baron. "Furthermore, it is for him to re-member. And besides, this poor king is bothered enough by all those people who harrass him. Were he to give away all of France piece by piece, they would still ask for more."

This loyal servant, so devoted to Louis XVIII, received the rank of colonel, the Cross of Saint Louis, and a pension of 2,000 francs.

"The king remembered!" he exclaimed on receiving the offi-cial papers.

No one tried to disillusion him. The whole affair had been arranged by the Duc de Feltre according to the lists of the Vendée armies, among which he found the name of du Guénic with other Breton names ending in *ic*. And so, to thank the king, the baron held a siege at Guérande in 1815 against the battalions of General Travot; he had decided never to surren-der that fortress. When finally he was forced to evacuate it, he fled to the woods with a band of Chouans who remained armed until the second return of the Bourbons. Guérande still cher-ishes the memory of that last siege. If all the Breton partisans had joined in, the war provoked by this heroic stand would have inflamed all of Vendée.

It must be admitted that the baron was completely illiterate, as illiterate as a peasant: he could read, write and do a bit of arithmetic; he was versed in warfare and heraldry; but outside of his prayer book, he had not read three books in his lifetime. His clothing, not without interest, was invariable and consisted of stout shoes, woolen hose, green velvet breeches, a woolen waistcoat, and a high-collared redingote on which he wore the Cross of Saint Louis. An admirable serenity lay over his face which a somnolence—forerunner of death—seemed to be preparing over the last year for eternal rest. These constant slumberings, more frequent with every day, in no way disquieted his wife, his blind sister, or his friends, whose medical knowledge was hardly extensive. For them, these sublime pauses of a blameless but weary soul could easily be explained: the baron had done his duty; that was all there was to it.

Within this manor, the major concerns were over the destinies of the dispossessed royal family. The future of the exiled Bourbons and of the Catholic church, the influence of political innovations on Brittany, were the exclusive preoccupations of the Baron's family. No other interest interfered except for the deep attachment of all for the only son, Calyste—the heir, the only hope of the great name of du Guénic. The old Vendéen, the old Chouan had experienced a few years earlier a kind of rejuvenation when training his son in those violent sports that are fitting for a gentleman who at any moment can be called upon to wage war. From the time Calyste was sixteen, his father accompanied him in the marshes and the woods, teaching him the rudiments of warfare in the pleasures of hunting, preaching through his own example of resistance to fatigue, steadiness in the saddle, sureness of aim whether the game was on the ground or in the air, fearlessness when jumping hurdles, and inviting his son to danger as though he had ten children to spare. And so, when the Duchesse de Berry arrived in France to conquer the kingdom, the father took off with his son in order to make him exercise the motto of his escutcheon. The baron left during the night, without informing his wife who might have weakened his decision, leading his only son to battle as though to a fair, followed by Gasselin, his sole vassal who trotted gaily after. The three men were gone for six months, sending no news to the baroness who never read the *Quotidienne* without trembling from line to line, or to her aged sister-in-law, heroically unbowed, whose brow never furrowed while listening to the reading of the newspaper. The three muskets suspended in the great hall had thus recently been in use. The baron, who decided the insurrection was hopeless, left the campaign before the battle of La Pénissiére—otherwise, the house of du Guénic would doubtless have come to an end.

One dreadful night, the father, son, and servant arrived home after having taken leave of MADAME, and surprised their friends, and the baroness and aged Mademoiselle du Guénic who, through the highly developed sense of the blind, recognized the steps of the three men in the alleyway. The baron looked at the circle formed by his anxious friends around the little table illumined by the antique lamp, and said in a faltering voice, while Gasselin replaced the three muskets and sabers, the following words of feudal simplicity: "Not all the barons have done their duty." Then, after kissing his wife and his sister, he sat down in his old armchair and ordered supper for his son, for Gasselin, and for himself.

Gasselin, having placed himself to shield Calyste, was wounded in the shoulder—a thing so normal that the ladies barely thanked him. Neither the baron nor his guests indulged in curses or invectives against the victors. This reticence is one of the traits of the Breton character. In forty years, no one had ever overheard a word of contempt from the baron's lips against his adversaries. It was for them to carry out their task and for him to do his duty. This kind of deep reticence is an index of immutable will. That final exertion, those flickerings of a dwindling energy, were the cause of the baron's feebleness at that moment. The new banishment of the Bourbons, ousted as miraculously as they were restored, left him in a state of bitter melancholy.

At about six in the evening when this story begins, the baron, who always finished dinner at four o'clock, had just fallen asleep while listening to his wife read the *Quotidienne*. His head rested against the back of his chair beside the fireplace on the garden side.

✦❥❉✦❥❉✦❥❉✦❥❉✦❥❉✦❥❉✦❥❉✦❥❉✦❥❉✦❥❉✦❥❉✦❥❉✦❥❉✦❥

IV THE TWO WOMEN Seated on one of the old chairs in front of the fireplace, beside that gnarled trunk of an ancient tree, the baroness was that type of adorable creature which can only be found in England, Scotland, or Ireland. Only there are such girls born: milk-fed, golden-haired, with ringlets that seem curled by the hands of angels, for a heavenly light shimmers through them as they are tossed by the air. Fanny O'Brien was one of those sylphs, strong in tenderness, invincible in misfortune, sweet as the music of her voice, pure as the blue of her eyes, of a refined, elegant beauty, and blessed with skin silken to the touch, caressing to the eye, that neither brush nor words can describe. Still beautiful at forty-two, many a man would have considered it a stroke of luck to marry her on seeing the splendors of this warmly tinted August filled with flowers and fruits, refreshed by celestial dew. The baroness held the newspaper in a dimpled hand with upturned fingers and nails cut squarely across as on ancient statues. Half reclining in her chair, without awkwardness or affectation, her feet outstretched to warm them, she was wearing a gown of black velvet, for the wind had been cool during the last few days. The closefitting bodice molded her magnificent rounded shoulders and splendid breasts that the nursing of her only child had in no way spoiled. She wore her hair in the English fashion, with ringlets falling along her cheeks and a simple twist held at the back of her head by a tortoise-shell comb. Her hair, unlike those nondescript shades of blond, glowed in daylight like filigrees of burnished gold. The baroness braided the little hairs that grew wildly at the back of her neck and are a sign of nobility. This tiny plait, lost in the mass of her carefully upswept hair, allowed the eye to follow with delight the flowing line of her neck and shoulders. This little detail indicated the care she always took in her grooming. She was eager to please the old baron. What a charming and touching attention! When you see a woman displaying in her home the coquettry that is inspired in other women by very different motivation, you may be sure she is as noble a

25

mother as she is a wife; she is the joy and flower of the household; she has understood her feminine duties; her soul and her sentiments are as elegant as her appearance; she is beneficent in secret; she knows how to love unselfishly; she loves her neighbors as she loves God—for themselves. And so it would seem that the Virgin in paradise, under whose protection she lived, rewarded her chaste girlhood and saintly life at the side of this grand old man, by surrounding her with a kind of halo that protected her from the ravages of time.

Plato would doubtless have celebrated the alterations in her beauty as so many added charms. Her complexion, once so white, had taken on the warm pearly tones that painters so adore. Her broad, well shaped brow tenderly reflected the light that played on it like shimmering satin. Her eyes, of a turquoise blue, shone under their light velvet brows with gentleness. Her drooping lids and sensitive temples suggested a kind of mute melancholy. The pale skin beneath her eyes and at the bridge of the nose was touched with the blue of tiny veinlets. That nose, with its slender, aquiline shape, had something regal about it that recalled the nobility of her origins. Her mouth, pure and finely drawn, was further embellished by a natural smile dictated by her inexhaustible good humor. Her teeth were small and white. She had gained some weight, but her slim hips and slender waist in no way suffered. The autumn of her beauty thus offered a few overlooked but still blooming flowers of spring, and all the burnished riches of summer. Her nobly rounded arms, her smooth lustrous skin, had acquired a finer texture, and the contours of her body had achieved their plenitude. Finally, the candor of her face, serene and faintly pink, the purity of those blue eyes that a sharp glance would have offended, expressed the inalterable sweetness, the infinite tenderness of an angel.

On the other side of the fireplace, the baron's octogenarian sister, like her brother in every way but dress, sat in an armchair listening to the newspaper while knitting a stocking—a handiwork for which sight is unnecessary. Her eyes were veiled with cataracts which she stubbornly refused to have operated despite her sister-in-law's entreaties. She alone knew the secret of her stubbornness: she explained it as a lack of courage, but it was in fact to save 25 louis which would have made a dent in the household budget. Nevertheless, she would have enjoyed being able to see her brother. These two old people provided a splendid background for the baroness' beauty. What woman would not have appeared young and beautiful between Monsieur du Guénic and his sister? Mademoiselle Zéphirine, deprived of sight, was unaware of the changes her eighty years had effected in her face. Her pale hollow face, reduced to a death's-head by the immobility of the blank eyes, and made almost menacing by the three or four protruding teeth, had deep eye sockets mottled with red, and a few whitened signs of virility growing on her chin and upper lip. Her cold, tranquil face was framed by a little brown hood, quilted like a counterpane and edged with a percale ruffle, that was tied under her chin with perpetually soiled ribbons. She wore a skirt of heavy cloth over a quilted petticoat—a veritable mattress stuffed with louis d'or, with pockets sewn to a belt that she took off every evening and put back on in the morning like a garment. Her bodice was corseted in a short jacket worn by all Breton women, of the same cloth as her skirt, and trimmed with a tightly pleated collar whose washing was the subject of her only quarrel with her sister-in-law; she would have changed it only once a week. Extending from the large padded sleeves of this weskit were two dessicated but sinewy arms at the end of which fidgeted two reddened hands that made the pale arms look like poplar wood. Her hands, contracted into claws from the habit of knitting, were like a perpetual motion machine; the marvel would have been to see them stop. From time to time, Mademoiselle du Guénic would pull a knitting needle out of the bosom of her dress, poke it between her bonnet and her hair, and scratch her white head.

A stranger would have been amused by the unconcern with which she stuck the needle back into her dress without the slightest fear of hurting herself. She was as straight as a tower. Her perfect posture could be attributed to one of those senile vanities that prove how essential to life pride is. She had a gay smile. She too had done her duty.

As soon as Fanny saw that the baron was sleeping, she stopped reading. A ray of sunlight shot across the ancient room from one window to the other, dividing it into two by a band of gold that made the almost black furniture gleam. The light caught the carvings of the ceiling, fluttered over the cabinets, spread a shining cloth over the table, and cheered this somber room with the same luminous gaiety that Fanny's voice produced in the old woman's heart. Soon, the sunbeams took on the reddish tones that by imperceptible gradations arrive at the melancholy shades of twilight. The baroness fell into deep meditation, one of those total silences that her aged sister-in-law had noticed during the preceding fortnight and had tried to explain by herself without ever asking any questions. She nonetheless examined the reasons for this preoccupation in the manner of the blind who read, as it were, a black page with white letters, and whose soul rings with every sound like an oracular echo. The old lady, for whom the darkening hour had no importance, continued to knit. The silence became so heavy one could hear the click of the needles.

"You have just dropped the newspaper, my sister, but you are not sleeping," said the old woman perceptively.

Night fell. Mariotte came to light the lamp, placing it on the square table in front of the fire. She then got her distaff, her hank of yarn, a little stool, and sat down to spin, as she did every evening, in the recess of the window looking out on the courtyard. Gasselin was still out making his tour of inspection; he looked in on the baron's horses, saw to it that all was in order in the stable, gave the two fine hunting dogs their evening meal. The happy barks of the two animals were the last sounds to rouse the echoes hidden among the somber bastions of the old manor. Those two dogs and two horses were the last vestiges of chivalric splendors. Someone with imagination, seated on the steps outside, abandoning himself to the poetry of the images still inhabiting this house, might well have been startled by the barking dogs and neighing horses.

Gasselin was one of those stocky little Bretons—thickset, black-haired, olive-skinned, slow-moving, taciturn, stubborn as a mule, and like a mule always following the path laid out for it. He was forty-two and had been with the family for twenty-five years. Mademoiselle had hired him when he was fifteen after learning of the baron's marriage and probable return. This servant considered himself one of the family: he had played with Calyste, loved the family's dogs and horses, had spoken to them and caressed them as though they were his own. He wore a short jacket of blue duck with little pockets that flapped over his hips, a vest and trousers of the same material in all seasons, blue hose and hobnailed boots. In very cold or wet weather, he put on a goatskin, commonly worn in this region. Mariotte, who was also past forty, was an exact feminine counterpart. Never was a pair better harnessed together—same complexion, same build, same bright black eyes. It was incomprehensible that they never married; perhaps it would have been incestuous, they were so like brother and sister. Mariotte earned ninety francs and Gasselin a hundred, but a thousand crowns would not have tempted them away from the du Guénic household. Both of them were under the orders of the old lady who, from the time of the Vendée wars to her brother's return, had taken over the management of the household. So that on learning her brother was bringing a mistress to the manor, she became very upset at the thought of losing the scepter of the household and having to abdicate in favor of the Baroness du Guénic, whose first subject she would have been.

Mademoiselle Zéphirine was pleasantly surprised to discover that Miss Fanny O'Brien was a girl born to a high station who was considerably repulsed by the details of running a poor household, and like many noble souls would have preferred a dry crust of bread to the best meal of her own preparation. She was capable of accomplishing the most taxing duties of motherhood, able to endure any necessary privation, but lacked the courage to face routine housekeeping. When the baron, in the name of his timid bride, begged his sister to look after the household, the old spinster kissed the baroness as she would a sister. She adopted her, adored her, overjoyed to be able to continue her reign of the household which she managed with incredible rigor and economy, relaxing it only for such special occasions as the confinement and diet of her sister-in-law, and for whatever pertained to Calyste, the child adored by all. Even though the two servants were accustomed to this severe regime and required no orders, taking their masters' interests more to heart than their own, Mademoiselle Zéphirine always saw to everything. Since her attention was never distracted, she was the kind of person who knew without checking the height of the pile of walnuts left in the loft, and how much remained in the stable oat bins without digging her wiry arm into them. Attached to her belt was a boatswain's whistle which she used to call Mariotte by one blast, and Gasselin by two. Gasselin's great joy lay in cultivating the garden and raising beautiful fruits and vegetables. He would have been bored without this garden for he had very little to do. In the morning after grooming his horses, he polished the floors and cleaned the two rooms on the ground floor; he had so little tidying up to do after his masters, he devoted himself to the garden where not a weed or harmful insect could be found. From time to time, Gasselin could be seen transfixed, bareheaded in the hot sun, staring at a field mouse or at the June bug's dreadful larvae. He would then run with the joy of a child to show his masters the animal that had kept him busy for a week. On fast days, he delighted in going to buy fish in Le Croisic where it was cheaper than in Guérande. And so, never was there a family of greater unity, greater mutual understanding or greater coherency than this saintly, noble family. Masters and servants seemed made for each other. In twenty-five years, there had never been any difficulties or disputes. The only anxieties had been over the minor ailments of the child, and the only terrors had been caused by the events of 1814 and 1830. If the same things were invariably done at the same hours, if the foods were determined by the regularity of the seasons, this monotony —like that of nature which is varied by the alternatives of cloud, rain and sun—was lightened by the affection that reigned in all their hearts and was all the more fruitful and beneficial in that it stemmed from the laws of nature.

When twilight had passed, Gasselin entered the room and respectfully asked if his master had any further need of him.

"After prayers you may go out or go to bed," answered the baron rousing himself, "unless madame or her sister. . . ."

The two ladies nodded in agreement. Gasselin knelt down on seeing his masters go to kneel at their chairs. Mariotte also knelt to pray at her stool. The venerable Mademoiselle du Guénic recited the prayer. When she ended, a knock was heard at the door. Gasselin went to open it.

"It is doubtless monsieur le Curé," said Mariotte. "He is always the first to arrive."

In fact, everyone recognized the priest of Guérande by the sound of his steps on the resonant stairs.

✤↱✤↱↱✤↱*↱✤↱*↱✤↱*↱✤↱*↱✤↱*↱✤↱*↱✤↱*↱✤↱

V THREE BRETON SILHOUETTES The priest respectfully greeted the three du Guénics with those words of unctuous amenity that priests always have ready.

"Are you by chance distressed or unwell, baroness?" he asked.

"Thank you, no," she replied.

Monsieur Grimont, a man of about fifty, of medium height, encased in his cassock beneath which peered two heavy shoes with silver buckles, displayed above his collar a plump face, for the most part fair though tanned. His hands were plump too. His perfect abbot's head reminded one simultaneously of a Dutch burgomaster because of the coloring and smoothness of complexion, and of a Breton peasant because of the straight black hair and vivacious brown eyes that nonetheless reflected sacerdotal decorum. His cheeriness, like that of all people whose conscience is pure, tolerated joking. There was nothing disquieting or forbidding about him, as in the case of priests whose power or mere existence is threatened by their parishioners and who, in Napoleon's great words, instead of being the moral leaders of the people and the natural justices of the peace, are considered enemies. Even the most unbelieving of travelers, on seeing Monsieur Grimont stride through the town, would have recognized him as the sovereign of this Catholic community; even this sovereign, however, humbled his spiritual authority before the feudal supremacy of the du Guénics. In this room he was like the chaplain in his lord's castle. In church, when giving the benediction, his arm always extended first toward the chapel of the du Guénics, whose armed hand and motto were sculpted on the keystone of the vaulting.

"I thought Mademoiselle de Pen-Hoël had already arrived," said the priest kissing the baroness' hand as he sat down. "She is becoming unpunctual. Could the fashion for dissoluteness be spreading? I see that Monsieur le Chevalier is at Les Touches again this evening."

"Do not speak of these visits in front of Mademoiselle de Pen-Hoël," the spinster softly explained.

"Ah, mademoiselle," replied Mariotte, "can you stop the whole town from gossiping?"

"And what do people say?" the baroness asked.

"Young girls, old gossips, everybody in fact, thinks he is in love with Mademoiselle des Touches."

"A young man as attractive as Calyste is only following his vocation by making himself loved," said the baron.

"Here is Mademoiselle de Pen-Hoël," Mariotte said.

The gravel in the courtyard was just then heard crunching under the prudent steps of this person who was accompanied by a servant carrying a lantern. On seeing the servant, Mariotte carried off her spinning to the great hall where she could chat with him by the light of the resin candle that she burned at the expense of the stingy, rich old maid, thus economizing her masters' candles.

Mademoiselle de Pen-Hoël was a thin, dried-out old maid, yellow as the parchment of an ancient scroll, rippled as a wind-swept lake, with gray eyes and large buck teeth, hands like a man's, fairly short with a slight curvature of the spine, and probably humpbacked. But no one had ever been curious enough to analyze her perfections or imperfections. Dressed like Mademoiselle du Guénic, she displaced an enormous quantity of skirts and petticoats when looking for one of the openings in her dress that allowed her to reach into her pockets. The strangest clinking of keys and coins resounded among those folds. On one side, she always kept the metal paraphernalia of all good housekeepers, and on the other her silver snuff box, her thimble, her knitting, and other sonorous utensils. Instead of Mademoiselle du Guénic's quilted hood, she wore a green hat that she probably donned when inspecting her melons; like them, it had paled from green to yellow. As to its shape, Paris fashion after twenty years has revived it under the name of *bibi*. This bonnet was put together under her own eyes by her nieces' hands. It consisted of green florence purchased in Guérande, and a body that was renewed every five years in Nantes, for she accorded it the duration of a legislature. Her nieces also made her dresses, cut from unvarying patterns. This old spinster still carried the crutch-handled cane fashionable at the beginning of Marie Antoinette's reign. She stemmed from the highest Breton nobility. Her blazon carried the ermines of the ancient dukes. The illustrious Breton house of Pen-Hoël ended in her and her sister. Her younger sister had married a Kergarouët who, despite the disapproval of the region, added the name Pen-Hoël to his own, thus calling himself the Vicomte de Kergarouët-Pen-Hoël.

"Heaven has punished him," the old spinster used to say. "He only has daughters, and the name of Kergarouët-Pen-Hoël will die out."

Mademoiselle de Pen-Hoël had an income of about 7,000 francs from her properties. Of age for the last thirty-six years, she herself administered her holdings, inspecting them on horseback and revealing in everything she did the firm character common to humpbacks. She was of an avarice that was admired over a radius of ten leagues and nowhere met with the slightest disapproval. She kept one maid and this little man-servant. All her expenses, not counting taxes, amounted to less than a thousand francs a year. For that reason, she was the object of much flattery on the part of the Kergarouët-Pen-Hoëls, who spent the winter in Nantes and the summer on their estate near the banks of the Loire below the Indret. It was known that she intended to leave her fortune to the niece of her choosing. Every three months, one of the four young ladies, of whom the youngest was twelve and the eldest twenty, came to spend a few days with her.

Long a friend of Zéphirine du Guénic, Jacqueline de Pen-Hoël, who was raised in adoration of the du Guénic greatness, had formulated since Calyste's birth the project of transmitting to the young chevalier all her wealth by marrying him to one of her nieces. She planned to buy back some of the best du Guénic properties from the *engagiste* farmers. When avarice sets an aim for itself it ceases to be a vice; it becomes the instrument of virtue; its excessive privations become continual sacrifices and ultimately, a grandeur of purpose is revealed beneath its pettyness. Perhaps Zéphirine was an accomplice to Jacqueline's secret. Perhaps too, the baroness—totally immersed in her love for her son and her fondness for his father—suspected something when seeing the calculating perseverance with which Mademoiselle de Pen-Hoël brought along her favorite niece, Charlotte de Kergarouët, aged fifteen. Surely, the priest was in her confidence, since he advised the old spinster in the wise investment of her money. But Mademoiselle de Pen-Hoël could have had three hundred thousand francs in gold (the assumed value of her savings), or ten times the property she actually possessed; the du Guénics would never have permitted any gesture on their part to lead the old maid into thinking they were interested in her fortune. With admirable Breton pride, Jacqueline de Pen-Hoël willingly acquiesced to the supremacy affected by her old friend Zéphirine and the du Guénics, and always appeared honored by any visit condescendingly paid her by the daughter of Irish kings and by Zéphirine. She even went so far as to hide the sacrifice she consented to every evening at the du Guénics when allowing her little servant to burn an *oribus*—the name of that gingerbread-colored candle used in parts of western France. And so, this rich old spinster was a paragon of nobility, pride and dignity.

At the very moment that you are reading her portrait, the Abbé Grimont has made it known through an indiscretion that on the evening when the old baron, the young chevalier, and Gasselin took off with their sabers and muskets to join MADAME in Vendée—to Fanny's great horror and the Bretons' great joy—Mademoiselle de Pen-Hoël had placed in the baron's hands the sum of ten thousand gold francs, an immense sacrifice, supplemented by another ten thousand francs resulting from a tithe collected by the priest, which the old partisan was to offer the mother of Henri V,* in the name of the Pen-Hoëls and the parish of Guérande.

In the meanwhile, she treated Calyste with the airs of a woman secure in her rights over him; her plans authorized her

* Henri V, Henri de Bourbon (1820-1883), son of the Duc and Duchese de Berry, (his mother was known as MADAME), was the legitimate pretender to the throne.

surveillance of him, not because she was narrow-minded in matters of gallantry (she had the indulgence common to ladies of the *ancien régime*), but because she abhorred revolutionary mores. Calyste might have won her admiration for any adventures with Breton ladies, but he would surely have lost it by manifesting what she called the novelties of the day. Mademoiselle de Pen-Hoël, who would have unearthed money to appease a dishonored girl, would have thought Calyste degenerate if she saw him drive a tilbury, or heard him speak of going to Paris. Had she caught him reading impious magazines or newspapers, there is no telling what she might have done. To her, new ideas meant reversing the order of crop rotation, disaster in the name of improvements or new methods, in short, the eventual mortgaging of property as a result of experimentation. For her, prudence was the true means of amassing a fortune. Wise administration consisted of accumulating buckwheat, rye, and hemp in one's silos; of awaiting an increase in prices at the risk of appearing to corner the market; of obstinately hanging on to one's grain bags. Through remarkable luck she often hit on good markets, which only confirmed her theories. Though she was taken for shrewd, she was nevertheless unintelligent. What she did have was the orderliness of a Dutchman, the prudence of a cat, and the persistence of a priest, which in a region enslaved by habit was tantamount to profound intelligence.

"Will Monsieur du Halga be with us this evening?" she asked, removing her woolen mittens after the usual exchange of pleasantries.

"Yes, mademoiselle," replied the priest, "I saw him walking his dog on the mall."

"Good!" answered the old maid. "Then our game of mouche will be animated this evening. Yesterday we were only four."

At the mention of mouche, the priest got up and went over to one of the sideboards. He took out of a drawer a small round wicker basket, ivory chips turned yellow as Turkish tobacco through twenty years of use, and a pack of cards as greasy as those used by the customs officials in Saint-Nazaire who bought fresh packs only twice a month. He then distributed the chips necessary for each player, placing the basket next to the lamp in the center of the table, with the eagerness of a child and the gestures of someone accustomed to performing this little task. A loud official knock resounded through the silent depths of the old manor. Mademoiselle de Pen-Hoël's little servant went solemnly to open the door. After a moment, the long lean body, methodically clothed to suit the weather, of the Chevalier du Halga, former flag captain of Admiral Kergarouët, was silhouetted against the half-light that still fell on the landing outside.

"Enter, chevalier," cried Mademoiselle de Pen-Hoël.

"The altar is laid," said the priest.

The chevalier was a man of delicate health, who wore flannel for his rheumatism, a black silk cap to protect his head against dampness, a spencer to guard his precious torso against the sudden gusts that cool the air of Guérande. He always went armed with a goldheaded cane to chase away the dogs that paid their undesirable court to his cherished bitch. This man, as fastidious as a lady-in-waiting, completely undone by the slightest annoyance, barely audible to preserve the little voice he had left, had once been among the most intrepid, most knowledgeable officers of the Royal Navy. He had been honored with the esteem of the Bailiff of Suffren and with the friendship of the Comte de Portenduère. His valiant conduct as Admiral Kergarouët's flag captain was legibly written across his wound-scarred face. To look at him no one would have recognized the voice that dominated the storm, the eye that scanned the sea, the indomitable courage of the Breton sailor. The chevalier did not smoke or swear; he had the softness and gentleness of a girl. He fussed over his bitch, Thisbé, with the solicitude of an old lady. In this way, he encouraged the highest opinion of his defunct gallantry. He never mentioned those surprising deeds that had amazed the Comte d'Estaing. Although he carried himself like an invalid, walked as though on eggs, complained of the coolness of the breeze, the heat of the sun, the dampness of the fog, he exhibited white teeth set in red gums that belied his supposed invalidity, and a costly one at that for it consisted of eating four copious meals a day. His frame, like the baron's, was spare and indestructibly strong, covered with parchment-like skin, glued to his bones like the hide of an Arabian steed that shimmers over its muscles in sunlight. His coloring had retained a swarthiness acquired during his trips to the Indies from which he brought back not a notion, not an anecdote. He had emigrated, lost all his fortune, then acquired the Cross of Saint-Louis and a pension of two thousand francs which was legitimately his and which was paid out of the fund for wounded veterans. His slight hypochondria, which led him to invent a thousand ailments, was easily justified by his hardships during the emigration. He had served in the Imperial Russian Navy until the day Tzar Alexander decided to send it against France. He resigned and went to live in Odessa near the Duc de Richelieu, with whom he later returned and who arranged for the pension fully deserved by this glorious wreck of the ancient Breton navy. On the death of Louis XVIII, at which time he returned to Guérande, Chevalier du Halga became the mayor of the town. The priest, the chevalier, and Mademoiselle de Pen-Hoël had developed the habit, over the last fifteen years, of spending their evenings at the du Guénics, where a few other distinguished citizens of the town and country were also frequent visitors. Anyone could easily recognize the du Guénics as the leaders of this rural Faubourg Saint-Germain, into which no official of the new government has ever penetrated. For the last six years, the priest invariably coughed at the critical words *Domine, salvum fac regem.* That was where politics still stood in Guérande.

VI. An Ordinary Evening *Mouche* is a game played with five cards in each hand and one face up on the table. The turn-up determines the trump. At each deal, the player is free to play or pass. If he passes, he only loses his initial stake, for as long as there are no penalties collected in the basket, each player contributes a small sum to the ante. If he plays, he is obliged to make his trick, which is then pro-rated according to the bet. If there are five sous in the ante, the trick is worth one sou. The player who fails to make his trick is *à la mouche;* he then owes the entire sum of the ante, which is added to the pool on the next deal. The *mouches* owed are marked down; they are paid into the basket in diminishing order, the greater before the lesser. Those who decline to play turn in their cards after the deal and are out of the game. Cards may be exchanged for as many cards from the deck as desired, but by order of the deal, so that the first two players to receive cards can use up the deck between them. The turn-up belongs to the dealer, who is the last to receive cards. He may exchange it for one of the cards in his hand. There is one terrible card that trumps all the others; it is called *Mistigris* and is the jack of clubs. This game, though extremely simple, is not devoid of interest. The natural cupidity of man is stimulated by it, as are diplomatic subtleties and the talent for reading facial expressions.

At the du Guénics, each player took twenty chips worth five sous, which brought the ante to five liards—a major sum in the eyes of these people. Assuming a great run of luck, one could win as much as fifty sous, an amount that no one in Guérande spent in an entire day. Mademoiselle de Pen-Hoël consequently went into the game—whose simplicity in the annals of card playing is surpassed only by war—with the passion of a hunter after big game. To risk one liard for the chance of winning five, hand after hand, constituted for the old hoarder a major financial operation which cost her as much nervous tension as is expended by an avid speculator on a bullish stock market. By diplomatic agreement dated September 1825, when Mademoiselle de Pen-Hoël lost 37 sous, the game ended whenever a player wished, after losing ten sous. Etiquette would not allow a player to suffer the chagrin of having to watch a game without participating. However, all passions have their casuistry. The chevalier and the baron, those two seasoned politicians, found a way to get around the agreement. When all the other players wished to continue a particularly exciting game, the valiant Chevalier du Halga—one of those prodigal bachelors whose affluence stems from their reduced expenses—always offered ten chips to Mademoiselle de Pen-Hoël or to Zéphirine when one or both of them lost their five sous, on condition of reimbursement should they win. An old bachelor could permit himself this gallantry toward the old maids. The baron also offered ten chips to the spinsters, under the pretext of continuing the game. The two misers always accepted but not without urging, in keeping with the manners of old maids. In order to allow themselves this extravagance, the baron and the chevalier had to be winning, otherwise their offer would have seemed offensive.

An evening of mouche became highly successful when one of the Kergarouët girls was visiting her aunt—plain, unhyphenated Kergarouët, for in Guérande no one in the family had succeeded in being called Kergarouët-Pen-Hoël, not even by the servants who had been given strict orders on that subject. Mademoiselle de Pen-Hoël spoke to her nieces about the game of mouche to be played at the du Guénic's as a rare pleasure. The young lady was on strict orders to be amiable, which was easy enough when she saw the handsome Calyste, who was adored by all four Kergarouët girls. These young people, brought up in the midst of modern civilization, were unconcerned over five sous and paid one *mouche* after another. As a result, there were some pools that went as high as one hundred sous, with *mouches* ranging from two and a half to six sous. Those were evenings of great excitement for the blind old maid. Tricks were called hands in Guérande. The baroness tapped her sister-in-law's foot as many times as the number of tricks she was certain of making. To play or not to play, when the basket was full, involved interior monologues in which cupidity struggled with fear. They asked each other: "Will you play?" suffering envy toward those whose cards were good enough to tempt fortune, and despair when it was necessary to pass.

If Charlotte de Kergarouët, generally considered a bit wild, was lucky in her daring and her aunt was unlucky, on returning home she would be treated to a cold rebuff and a few corrective lessons: her character was too willful; a young person should not challenge people many times her age; she had an insolent way of taking the basket or starting the bidding; the manners of a young lady required more reserve and modesty; one did not laugh at another person's bad luck, and so on.

The perennial jokes, repeated a thousand times a year but always enjoyed, turned around the kind of harnessing to give an overloaded basket. They spoke of harnessing oxen, elephants, horses, mules, dogs. After twenty years, no one noticed these repetitions; the same stale joke always elicited the same delighted laugh. This was also true for those words that disappointment over the loss of a full basket dictated to those who had fattened it without any profit. The cards were dealt with mechanical slowness accompanied by murmured comments. These dignified aristocrats were so exquisitely petty that they doubted each other's honesty. Mademoiselle de Pen-Hoël almost invariably accused the priest of cheating when he took in a full basket.

"How strange! I am never accused of cheating when I lose," the priest would then reply.

No one ever laid down a card without profound calculations, sly glances, wry comments, and clever, often ingenious, remarks. The hands, as one can imagine, were spiced with local news and political discussions. The players often spent half an hour engrossed in conversation, their cards fanned out against their stomachs. Following such a pause, if the basket was found to be short a chip, everyone maintained he had placed his. It was generally the chevalier who made up the difference, having been accused by all of contemplating the buzzing in his ears, of thinking about his head or his manias and of forgetting to put in his chip. When the chevalier finally made his contribution, Zéphirine or the wily hunchback would be seized with remorse—they imagined they were responsible for the missing chip; they weighed the possibilities, they doubted, but after all, the chevalier was rich enough to afford such a bagatelle. Often, the baron lost his bearings in the game whenever the conversation turned toward the misfortunes of the royal family. Sometimes, the game turned out surprisingly for the players, all of whom counted on the same winnings. After a certain number of hands, when each player had made up his initial stake, they went home because of the lateness of the hour, without profit or loss but not without excitement. On such frustrating occasions, the game itself came under attack: it had not been challenging. The players accused the game as natives beat the moon's reflection in the water when the weather is bad. The evening was judged as dull; they had worked hard for precious little. When the Vicomte and Vicomtesse de Kergarouët first visited Guérande and spoke of whist and boston as more interesting than mouche, they were encouraged by the baroness, who was vastly bored by mouche, to explain these games. The whole group participated eagerly but not without protests against such innovations. However, it was impossible to make them understand these games which, after the Kergarouët's departure, were dismissed as algebraic puzzles of overwhelming difficulty. Everyone preferred his beloved mouche, his sweet, delightful little game. Mouche triumphed over modern games as did all old things over new in Brittany.

While the priest was dealing the cards, the baroness asked the Chevalier du Halga the same questions about his health that she had asked the day before. The chevalier made it a point of honor to have some new ailment each day. Though the questions were always the same, the former flag captain had the singular advantage of being able to vary his replies. Today, his floating ribs were bothering him. The most remarkable thing about this worthy officer was that he never complained of his wounds. He was prepared for anything serious, he fully understood such things; but the products of his fantasy—the pains in his head, the hounds that devoured his stomach, the bells that rang in his ears, the thousand other lunacies—upset him terribly. He considered himself incurable, and with all the more reason, since doctors know no remedies for nonexistent maladies.

"Yesterday I thought you were concerned about the pain in your legs," said the priest with great seriousness.

"It moves around," replied the chevalier.

"From the legs to the floating ribs?" asked Mademoiselle Zéphirine.

"Doesn't it stop somewhere along the way?" asked Mademoiselle de Pen-Hoël, smiling.

The chevalier bowed gravely with a negative gesture of considerable humor, proving that in his youth the old sailor had been witty, loving, and loved. His fossilized existence in Guérande may well have concealed a host of memories. When he stood on the sunlit mall, planted stupidly on his heron's legs, looking at the sea or at his dog's games, he may have been reliving the earthly paradise of a memory-filled past.

"So the old Duc de Lenoncourt has died," said the baron, recalling the passage in the *Quotidienne* at which his wife had stopped reading. "The king's privy councilor did not tarry long before joining his master. I shall soon follow them."

"My dear, what are you saying!" said his wife, gently rapping his calloused, bony hand.

"Let him talk, dear sister," said Zéphirine, "so long as I am above ground he cannot go below. He is younger than I."

A gay smile flitted across the old maid's lips. Whenever the baron dropped a remark of this kind, the players and visitors looked at each other anxiously, distressed by the sadness of the King of Guérande. The people who had come to see him said as they left, "Monsieur du Guénic was sad. Did you see how he dozed?" And the next day, the whole town chattered about the news. "The baron is failing!" was the opening line of every conversation in every household.

"How is Thisbé?" asked Mademoiselle de Pen-Hoël of the chevalier when the cards were distributed.

"That poor little thing is like me," replied the chevalier. "She has a nervous disorder. She constantly raises one paw when running. You see, like this."

By bending his arm as he raised it to imitate his dog, he afforded his hump-backed neighbor a full view of his cards. She was curious to see whether he had trumps or *Mistigris*. He had never before succumbed to any ruse.

"Oh!" cried the baroness, "the tip of Monsieur le Curé's nose has just gone white. He surely has *Mistigris*."

The pleasure of having *Mistigris* was so intense for the priest, and the other players as well, that the poor man was unable to hide it. In every human face there is one spot that betrays the secrets of the heart, and these people, accustomed to observing each other, had succeeded after all these years in discovering the priest's weak spot. When he had *Mistigris,* the tip of his nose turned white. Everyone then took care not to play.

"You had guests today," said the chevalier to Mademoiselle de Pen-Hoël.

"Yes, one of my brother-in-law's cousins. He surprised me with the announcement of the remarriage of the Comtesse de Kergarouët, formerly a de Fontaine. . . ."

"One of Grand-Jacques' daughters!" exclaimed the chevalier, who during his stay in Paris had never left his admiral's side.

"The countess is his heiress. She has married a former ambassador. My visitor also told me the most extraordinary things about our neighbor, Mademoiselle des Touches, so extraordinary I can hardly believe them. If Calyste knew, he might not be so assiduous in his visits to her. He surely has enough good sense to notice such monstrous things."

"Monstrous?" asked the baron, roused by the word.

The baroness and the priest exchanged a glance of complicity. The cards were dealt afresh; Mademoiselle de Pen-Hoël held *Mistigris*. She was unwilling to continue the conversation, but was happy to conceal her joy behind the general stupefaction caused by her remark.

"Your card, Monsieur le Baron," she said impatiently.

"My nephew is not one of those young men who enjoy monstrosities," said Zéphirine, poking through her hair.

"*Mistigris!*" cried Mademoiselle de Pen-Hoël, neglecting to answer her friend.

The priest, who appeared to be informed about the entire relationship between Calyste and Mademoiselle des Touches, did not enter the jousting lists.

"What is so extraordinary about her?" asked the baron.

"She smokes," answered Mademoiselle de Pen-Hoël.

"That's very healthful," said the chevalier.

"And what about her estates?" asked the baron.

"Her estates she devours," retorted the old maid.

"Everybody has lost, everybody has to pay a *mouche!* I have the king, the queen and the jack of trumps, *Mistigris* and a jack," cried the baroness. "The basket is ours, my sister."

This hand, won without even being played out, undid Mademoiselle de Pen-Hoël who promptly lost all interest in Calyste and in Mademoiselle des Touches. By nine o'clock, the only ones remaining in the room were the baroness and the priest. The four old people had gone off to bed. As always, the chevalier accompanied Mademoiselle de Pen-Hoël as far as her house, located on the central square of Guérande, commenting along the way on the skill of the last play, their respective good or bad luck, or the consistently delighted way in which Mademoiselle Zéphirine stuffed her winnings into her pocket, for the old lady could no longer control the reactions on her face. The baroness' apparent preoccupation was the major subject of their exchange. The chevalier had noticed how distracted the charming Irishwoman seemed. At the door of her house, after her little servant had gone in, she replied confidentially to the chevalier's speculation on the baroness' unusual manner, in words pregnant with meaning.

"I know the reason. Calyste is lost unless we marry him off at once. He is in love with Mademoiselle des Touches—an actress!"

"In that case, send for Charlotte."

"My sister will have my letter tomorrow," said Mademoiselle de Pen-Hoël, taking leave of the chevalier.

One can judge from this perfectly ordinary evening the upheaval provoked within the households of Guérande by the arrival, sojourn, departure, or even the passing through of a stranger.

❋⥼❀✛❋⥼❀✛❋⥼❀✛❋⥼❀✛❋⥼❀✛❋⥼❀✛❋⥼❀✛❋⥼❀✛❋⥼❀✛❋⥼❀✛

VII CALYSTE   When no further sound was heard from the baron's room or from his sister's, Madame du Guénic looked at the priest who was pensively toying with the chips.

"I see that you have finally come around to sharing my concern over Calyste," she said.

"Did you notice Mademoiselle de Pen-Hoël's primness tonight?" the priest asked.

"Yes," the baroness replied.

"I know," continued the priest, "that she has the best of intentions toward our dear Calyste. She loves him as though he were her own son, and his performance in Vendée at his father's side, and MADAME's praise for his devotion, only increased Mademoiselle de Pen-Hoël's affection for him. She will leave her entire fortune to whichever of her nieces Calyste chooses to marry. I know you have a much richer match for your beloved Calyste in Ireland, but it is wiser not to put all your eggs in one basket. In the event your family does not assure Calyste's future, Mademoiselle de Pen-Hoël's fortune is not to be disdained. You will always be able to find a wife for the dear boy with an income of seven thousand francs, but you may not be able to find a fortune accumulated over forty years, or properties as well managed, well built, and well repaired as hers. That impious creature, Mademoiselle des Touches, has made quite a mess of things by coming here. Now we know about her."

"My goodness, what?" asked the baroness.

"Oh, she's a harlot, a trollop," exclaimed the priest, "a woman of very questionable repute, active in the theatre, consorting with actors and actresses, squandering her fortune in the company of hack writers, painters, musicians, the devil's own cohort! To write her books, she assumed an alias by which she is said to be better known than by her own name of Félicité des Touches. A perfect charlatan, who has not set foot inside a church since her first communion except to look at sculptures or paintings. She has spent a fortune decorating Les Touches in the most indecent manner, to make it into a Moslem paradise where the houris are not women. More good wine is consumed during her stay here than in all of Guérande during an entire year. Last year, the Bougniol sisters took in as lodgers some bearded men, suspected of being Blues, who used to go to her house and sing indecent songs that would make a virtuous girl weep with shame. This is the kind of woman our young chevalier adores at the moment. If that creature, this very evening, wanted one of those infamous books in which today's atheists denigrate everything, our young man would saddle his horse himself and gallop off to Nantes to get it for her. I wonder whether Calyste would do as much for the Church. In addition, Breton though she is, she is not a Royalist. If it came to fighting for the Cause, and Mademoiselle des Touches, or Monsieur Camille Maupin as I now remember she calls herself, wanted Calyste to stay with her, he would let his old father go off alone."

"No!" said the baroness.

"I would not like to put it to the test. You might suffer too much," replied the priest. "The whole town is topsy-turvy over Calyste's passion for this amphibious creature who is neither man nor woman, smokes like a hussar, writes like a journalist, and at this very moment has staying with her the most venomous of all writers, according to the postmaster, that middle-of-the-roader who reads all the newspapers. Even in Nantes people are talking about it. Just this morning, a cousin of Kergarouët, who wants Charlotte to marry a man with an income of 60,000 francs, came to see Mademoiselle de Pen-Hoël, and for seven hours dizzied her with stories about Mademoiselle des Touches. Here it is a quarter to ten and Calyste is still not home. He is at Les Touches and may not come back before morning."

The baroness listened to the priest who had inadvertently substituted monologue for dialogue. He was looking at this member of his flock, reading the anxiety written all over her face. The baroness blushed and trembled. When the Abbé Grimont saw tears fall from the beautiful eyes of this dismayed mother, he was moved.

"Be assured," he said consolingly, "I will see Mademoiselle de Pen-Hoël tomorrow. It may not be as great an evil as it sounds. I will find out the whole truth. Furthermore, Mademoiselle Jacqueline trusts me. After all, Calyste is our pupil, and will not let himself be ensnared by the demon. He has no desire to disturb the harmony within his family or to upset the plans we are making for his future. So do not cry. All is not lost, dear madame. A single error is not vice."

"You have only supplied me with details," said the baroness. "Was I not the first to notice the change in Calyste? A mother keenly feels the pain of being reduced to second place in her son's heart, or the grief of no longer being alone in his heart.

This phase of a man's life is one of the agonies of motherhood, and even though I was prepared for it, I did not think it would happen so soon. Then too, I would have wished him to take into his heart at least some fine, noble creature, rather than a histrion, a faker, a woman of the theatre, a writer accustomed to simulating emotions, an evil woman who will deceive him and make him unhappy. She has had affairs . . . ."

"With many men," said the Abbé Grimont. "Yet this miscreant was born in Brittany! She is a disgrace to her birthplace. On Sunday I shall preach a sermon about her."

"Heaven forbid!" exclaimed the baroness. "The salt workers and peasants might attack Les Touches, and Calyste, who is Breton and worthy of his name, might come to harm, for he would defend her as though protecting the Blessed Virgin."

"It is ten o'clock. I shall bid you good night," said the Abbé Grimont lighting the wick of his lantern, whose polished glass and gleaming metal bespoke the meticulousness of his housekeeper. "Who would have thought, madame," he continued, "that a young man nurtured by you and raised by me in Christian ethics, a fervent Catholic, a child as untarnished as a lamb, could plunge into such iniquity."

"But can one be so sure?" asked the mother. "And how could any woman avoid falling in love with Calyste?"

"One needs no more proof than the length of that sorceress' stay at Les Touches. In the twenty-four years since she came of age, this is the longest she has ever stayed. Fortunately for us, her appearances here were always brief."

"A forty-year-old woman," said the baroness. "I had always heard in Ireland that a woman of this age is the most dangerous mistress a young man can have."

"On that point I am completely ignorant," replied the priest. "In fact, I shall die in my ignorance."

"Alas, I too," said the baroness naively. "I wish now that I had had the experience of love so as to observe and advise and console Calyste better."

The priest did not cross the charming little courtyard alone. The baroness accompanied him to the gate hoping to hear Calyste's footsteps on the streets of the town. But all she heard were the heavy, prudent steps of the priest that grew fainter in the distance and came to a halt when the parish house door was shut, clanging out through the silent town. The poor woman went back in, disconsolate at the thought that the whole town was aware of what she had assumed she alone knew. She sat down, relit the wick of the lamp after cutting it with a pair of old scissors, and took up the needlepoint that she worked on while waiting for Calyste. She deluded herself into thinking that this would oblige her son to return sooner and spend less time with Mademoiselle des Touches. This strategy of maternal jealousy was quite useless. With each day Calyste's visits became more frequent, and each evening he came home later. The previous day, he had not returned home until midnight. The baroness, lost in motherly contemplation, pushed and pulled her needle with the busy fingers of people who think while doing manual work. Anyone seeing her bent over in the lamplight, beneath the century-old paneling of the room, would have admired this sublime picture. Fanny's skin was of such transparency that one could read her thoughts on her forehead. Stung by the curiosity that seizes innocent women, she wondered what diabolic secrets these daughters of Baal possessed to bewitch men so completely that they forgot their mother, their country, their self-respect. She went as far as to wish she could meet such a woman in order to judge her fairly. She estimated the damages that the new spirit of the age—so pernicious to young souls, in the priest's opinion—could inflict on her only child, until then as honest, as pure, as an innocent girl whose fresh beauty could have been no fresher than his.

Calyste, that magnificent scion of the oldest Breton race and the noblest Irish blood, had been carefully raised by his mother. Until the moment she placed him under the priest's tutelage, she was certain that no indecent word or thought had soiled her son's hearing or thinking. His mother, having nourished him with her own milk and thus twice nourished him with her blood, was able to present him in virginal innocence to the pastor who, out of veneration for this family, promised to give him a complete and Christian education. Calyste was given the instruction of the seminary where the Abbé Grimont had been a student. The baroness taught him English. A mathematics teacher was found, not without difficulty, among the clerks in Saint-Nazaire. Calyste was consequently unaware of modern literature, or of the progess and contemporary advances in science. His education had been limited to the geography and circumspect history taught in girls' finishing schools, and to the Latin and Greek of seminarist studies, along with classical literature and a selected number of French writers. When at sixteen he began what the Abbé Grimont called his "philosophie," or final year, he was as innocent as when Fanny first gave him over to the priest. The Church was as maternal as the mother. Without being bigoted or ridiculous, this cherished boy was a fervent Catholic. For this son, so handsome, so pure, the baroness hoped to arrange a happy, obscure life. She anticipated the legacy of some two or three thousand pounds sterling from an old aunt. This amount, added to the present fortune of the du Guénics, would enable her to find for Calyste a wife with some twelve or fifteen thousand francs. Charlotte de Kergarouët with her aunt's fortune, or a rich Irish girl, or any other heiress, were all the same to the baroness. She was completely ignorant of love, and like all the members of her circle, viewed marriage as a means toward establishing a fortune. Passion was unknown to these Catholic souls, these elderly people exclusively concerned with their salvation, with God, the King, and their fortune. One can hardly be surprised, therefore, by the gravity of the thoughts that accompanied the wounded feelings in this mother's heart, whose whole life was motivated by her son's interests as by his affection. If the young couple followed sound advice, the second generation of du Guénics, by living parsimoniously and economizing as one knows how to in the provinces, would be able to redeem their lands and reconquer the splendor of affluence. The baroness hoped to live long enough to see that dawn of luxury arise. Mademoiselle du Guénic had fully understood and adopted this plan which was now being threatened by Mademoiselle des Touches.

The baroness shuddered as she heard midnight strike. She imagined all sorts of horrors during the hour that followed, for the stroke of one was still resounding and Calyste was not yet home.

"Could he be spending the night?" she wondered. "It would be the first time."

At that moment, Calyste's footsteps rang out in the alleyway. His poor mother, in whose heart anxiety gave way to joy, ran to open the door.

"Oh mother darling," he cried with embarrassment, "why are you waiting up for me? I have a key and a tinderbox."

"You know perfectly well, my child, that I could not possibly sleep while you are out," she said kissing him.

When the baroness returned to the room, she looked at her son trying to surmise from the expression on his face the events of the evening. But as always, this caused in her an emotion that habit did not weaken and that all loving mothers feel at the sight of the masterwork they have wrought, an emotion that momentarily clouds their vision.

Except for his father's black eyes bursting with energy and brightness, Calyste had his mother's lovely blond hair, her aquiline nose, adorable mouth, turned-up fingers, soft coloring, delicate fair complexion. Although he looked a bit like a girl disguised as a man, he was of herculean strength. His muscles were as supple and powerful as steel coils, and the uncommonness of his black eyes in a fair face was not without charm. His beard had not yet sprouted, which is said to be a sign of longevity. The young chevalier was wearing a short coat with silver buttons of the same black velvet as his mother's gown, a blue foulard, handsome gaiters, and gray trousers. His snow-white forehead seemed to bear the marks of great fatigue. However, it was only the weight of his sadness. His mother, incapable of suspecting the pain that wracked his heart, attributed this sudden change to happiness. Calyste was nonetheless as beautiful as a Greek god, and totally without conceit: to begin with, he was used to his mother's admiration, and then he was little concerned with a beauty he knew to be useless.

"Those beautiful smooth cheeks," she mused, "with rich young blood coursing through their myriad vessels, are now another woman's, and that girlish forehead too. Passion will crease it with countless anxieties, and dim those bright eyes that shine like a child's." This bitter thought gripped her heart and spoiled her pleasure.

It may seem remarkable to anyone who knows the cost of living that in a family of six, obliged to live on three thousand francs a year, the son had a coat and the mother a gown of velvet. It happened that Fanny O'Brien's aunts and rich relatives in London stayed alive in the memory of their Breton kinswoman by sending gifts. A few of her sisters, having made wealthy marriages, were sufficiently interested in Calyste to want to find him an heiress knowing him to be as handsome and noble as their beloved expatriate, Fanny.

"You stayed at Les Touches even later than yesterday, my darling," said his mother with emotion in her voice.

"Yes, mother dear," he replied with no further explanation.

The curtness of the reply hurt the baroness who postponed an explanation until the next day. When mothers are besieged by such anxieties as the baroness felt at that moment, they all but tremble before their sons, intuiting the great emancipating effects of love. They understand what this emotion will deprive them of, but at the same time take some pleasure in knowing their sons are happy. It is as though a battle raged in their hearts. Although this implies that their sons are now adult and self-sufficient, real mothers do not relish this tacit abdication, preferring their children little and needing protection. Perhaps that is the secret of a mother's predilection for the weak, deformed, or helpless among her children.

"You are tired, my sweet, go to bed," she said controlling her tears.

A mother uninformed of all her son's activities thinks all is lost, if that mother loves and is loved as much as Fanny. Perhaps any mother would have been as miserable as Madame du Guénic. The patient striving of twenty years could easily be annulled. This human masterpiece of noble, prudent, religious education could be destroyed. The happiness of his future life could be ruined forever by a woman.

❋❖❖❋❖❋❖❋❖❋❖❋❖❋❖❋❖❋❖❋❖❋❖❋❖❋❖

VIII ANXIETIES AUGMENTED The next day, Calyste slept until noon. His mother would not allow him to be wakened and Mariotte served this spoiled child his breakfast in bed. The inflexible and almost monastic rules governing mealtimes yielded to the caprices of the young gentleman. Whenever anyone wanted to coax Mademoiselle Zéphirine's keys away from her for anything outside of mealtimes, which would have required interminable explanations, one had only to pretend it was for a whim of Calyste. Around one o'clock the baron, his wife, and his sister were assembled in the hall, for they dined at three. The baroness had picked up the *Quotidienne* again and was finishing the reading for her husband who was always a bit more attentive before meals. Just as Madame du Guénic was about to end, she heard her son's footsteps on the floor above and put down the paper saying, "Calyste is probably dining at Les Touches again. He has just finished dressing."

"So long as the child is enjoying himself . . ." said the old woman taking out her silver whistle and blowing it.

Mariotte came by way of the turret, appearing at the door

that was masked by a portiere of the same silk as hung at the windows.

"You called?" she said. "Is there something you wish?"

"The chevalier is dining at Les Touches. You need not prepare the sea trout."

"But we know nothing as yet," said the baroness.

"You sound annoyed, dear sister. I can tell from your voice," said the old blind woman.

"Monsieur le Curé has learned some disturbing things about Mademoiselle des Touches who, for the last year, has produced a considerable change in our Calyste."

"In what way?" asked the baron.

"Why, he reads all kinds of books."

"Ah ha!" said the baron. "So that is why he has been neglecting his hunting and his horse."

"She leads a reprehensible life and writes under a man's name," the baroness continued.

"A battle name," said the old man. "I was called *l'Intime,* the Comte de Fontaine *Grand-Jacques,* the Marquis de Montauran *le Gars.* I was a great friend of Ferdinand, who was as determined as I not to surrender. Those were the good old days. There was a lot of shooting but we nevertheless managed to have some fun from time to time."

These military reminiscences that substituted for paternal concern upset Fanny for a moment. The priest's confidences and her son's lack of them had prevented her from sleeping.

"Suppose Monsieur le Chevalier were in love with Mademoiselle des Touches, what would be so terrible about that?" asked Mariotte. "The hussy has thirty thousand francs a year and is beautiful to boot."

"What are you saying, Mariotte?" exclaimed the old man. "A du Guénic marry a des Touches? The des Touches were not even our squires at a time when the du Guesclins considered it a signal honor to be allied with us."

"A woman calling herself by a man's name—Camille Maupin!" exclaimed the baroness.

"The Maupins are a very old Norman family," said the old man, "and bear gules with three . . . ." He stopped short. "But she cannot be a des Touches and a Maupin at the same time."

"Her theatrical name is Maupin."

"A des Touches could never be an actress," he said. "If I didn't know you Fanny, I'd think you were out of your mind."

"She writes plays and books," the baroness added.

"Books?" he asked, looking at his wife with as much surprise as if he had learned of a miracle. "I have heard that Mademoiselle de Scudéry and Madame de Sevigné wrote, which is not what they did best. For such wonders one had to have Louis XIV and his court."

"Will you be dining at Les Touches, monsieur?" Mariotte asked as Calyste came in.

"Probably," he answered.

Mariotte was not curious. She was one of the family. She left the room without trying to hear the question Madame du Guénic was about to ask of Calyste.

"You are going to Les Touches again, my dear?" she said, stressing the *my*. "Les Touches is not a decent, respectable house. Its mistress leads a wild life and will corrupt our Calyste. Camille Maupin has made him read all kinds of books, and she has had all kinds of adventures! And you knew all this, you naughty boy, while we did not even tell our old friends."

"The chevalier is discreet," replied his father, "a virtue of the past."

"Too discreet," said his jealous mother, noticing the blush creep up her son's cheeks.

"Dearest mother," said Calyste kneeling at her feet, "I did not think it necessary to publicize my defeats. Mademoiselle des Touches, or Camille Maupin if you wish, rejected my love eighteen months ago at the time of her last visit here. She very sweetly made fun of me saying she could be my mother. A woman of forty who loved a minor was committing a kind of incest, and she was incapable of such depravity. In short, I was crushed by her endless teasing, for she has a divine gift of wit. Then when she saw me shed hot tears, she consoled me by nobly offering me her friendship. Her tenderness is even greater than her talent, and she is as generous as you are. Now it is as though I were her son. When I learned on her return here that she is in love with another man, I resigned myself to this fact. Do not repeat the calumnies that are spread about her. Camille is an artist, she has real genius, and she leads one of those exceptional lives that cannot be judged by ordinary standards."

"My child," said the pious Fanny, "nothing can dispense a woman from conducting herself as the Church teaches. She fails in her duties toward God and toward society by abjuring the gentle faith of her sex. A woman who merely goes to the theatre has already sinned. But to write impieties repeated by actors, to run around the world first with an enemy of the Pope and then with a musician *—ah, Calyste, you will not find it easy to convince me that such behavior implies acts of faith, hope or charity. Her fortune was given by God to do good. What does she do with it?"

Calyste suddenly stood up and looked at his mother. "Mother, Camille is my friend. I cannot hear her spoken of in this way. I would give my life for her."

"Your life?" said the baroness, looking at her son with terror. "Your life is our life."

"My handsome nephew is saying all kinds of things I cannot understand," exclaimed the old blind woman gently as she turned to him.

"Where did he learn these things? At Les Touches?" said his mother.

"But mother darling, she found me as ignorant as a fish."

"You knew all that was necessary by knowing the duties that

* Allusions to George Sand's lovers: Lammenais and Chopin respectively.

religion teaches us," replied the baroness. "Ah, that woman will destroy all your noble, holy beliefs."

The old maid stood up and solemnly extended her hands in the direction of her dozing brother.

"Calyste," she said in a voice that came straight from the heart, "your father never opened a book, he speaks Breton, he risked his life fighting for the king and for God. Educated people were responsible for all the evil, and learned gentlemen abandoned their native land. Learn then, if you wish!"

She sat down and resumed her knitting with the nervous haste dictated by her inner excitement. Calyste was struck by the Phocionic ring to her pronouncement.

"Oh my angel, I have the premonition that some harm will befall you in that house," said his mother brokenly, as tears began to fall.

"Who is making Fanny cry?" exclaimed the baron, suddenly awakened by the sound of his wife's voice. He looked at his sister, his son and at the baroness. "What's going on?"

"Nothing, my dear," the baroness answered.

"Mother," Calyste whispered into her ear, "it is impossible to explain these things now, but this evening we can talk. When you know the whole story you will bless Mademoiselle des Touches."

"Mothers are not given to cursing," replied the baroness, "and I could hardly curse the woman who truly cared for my Calyste."

The young man said goodbye to his father and left. The baron and his wife rose to watch him go through the courtyard, open the door and disappear. The baroness did not resume her reading; she was too upset. In a life as peaceful and harmonious as theirs, the brief exchange that had just taken place was tantamount to a quarrel in another family. Though somewhat relieved, her anxiety was far from dispelled. Where would this relationship, which could involve Calyste's life and imperil it, ultimately lead him? And what reason could she possibly have for blessing Mademoiselle des Touches? These two questions were as serious for her simple soul as the most violent revolution for a diplomat. Camille Maupin had unleashed a revolution in that gentle, placid family.

"I am very much afraid that this woman will ruin him for us," she said taking up her paper.

"My sweet Fanny," said the old man roguishly, "you are far too angelic to understand such things. Mademoiselle des Touches, so they say, is black as a crow, strong as a Turk, and forty years old. Our dear boy was bound to be attracted by her. And so he will tell a few perfectly honorable white lies to cover up his happiness. Let him enjoy his first illusion of love."

"If only it were some other woman . . . ."

"My dearest Fanny, if this woman were a saint, she would hardly be receiving your son."

The baroness went back to her newspaper.

"I'll go to see her myself," said the old man, "and I'll give you a full report."

These words can only be savored in retrospect. After reading the biography that follows, can you possibly imagine the old baron at grips with this famous woman?

The town of Guérande, which for the last two months had been observing Calyste, its pride and flower, go off every day, morning or evening, and sometimes both, to Les Touches, was convinced that Mademoiselle Félicité des Touches was passionately enamored of this young man and that she exercised some kind of black magic over him. More than one girl or young woman wondered what rights an old woman had to exert such absolute power over an angel like Calyste. When Calyste crossed the main street on his way to the gate that leads to Le Croisic, more than one pair of eyes followed him.

It has now become necessary to explain the rumors that were circulating about the person Calyste was going to visit. These murmurs, swelled by Breton gossip, envenomed by general ignorance, had finally reached the priest. The Tax Collector, the Justice of the Peace, the Chief of Customs in Saint-Nazaire, and other literate people in the region, had provided the Abbé Grimont with no reassurances by telling him of the bizarre life of the authoress hidden behind the name of Camille Maupin. She had not yet eaten any children, she did not kill slaves like Cleopatra, she did not have men thrown into the river, as the heroine of the Tour de Nesle was falsely accused of doing. But as far as the Abbé Grimont was concerned, this monstrous creature, part siren, part atheist, incarnated the immoral joining of female and philosopher, and flaunted every social law invented for constraining or exploiting the weaknesses of the gentle sex.

PART TWO

A
FAMOUS
WOMAN

I The Childhood of Mademoiselle des Touches Just as Clara Gazul * is the feminine pseudonym of a man of talent, and George Sand the masculine pseudonym of a woman of genius, so Camille Maupin was the mask that for a long time hid a charming girl of the finest Breton blood named Félicité des Touches—the woman who was causing the Baroness du Guénic and the good parish priest of Guérande such anguish. This family has no connection with the des Touches of Touraine, to which the Regent's ambassador belongs, a man more famous today for his literary than for his diplomatic talents. Camille Maupin, one of the few famous women of the nineteenth century, was long taken for a genuine male author because of the virile beginning to her career. Everyone is now familiar with the two volumes of plays, unsuitable for staging, that were written in the style of Shakespeare or Lope de Vega, published in 1822, and that created a minor literary revolution at a time when the burning question of Romanticism versus Classicism was raging in the newspapers, in literary circles, and in the Académie. Since then, Camille Maupin has produced a number of plays and a novel, which have not belied the success of her first publication, too soon forgotten.

To explain the chain of circumstances that achieved the masculinization of a young girl, how Félicité des Touches became a man and an author, why unlike Madame de Staël she remained free and is thus more readily forgiven her celebrity, would doubtless satisfy a great deal of curiosity, and justify one of those monstrosities that occur in humanity, whose glory is enhanced by its rarity. In twenty centuries one can barely count twenty great women. And so, because of her great influence on Calyste, even though she only plays a secondary role here, and because of the role she played in the literary history of our time, no one will regret having stopped for a longer look at this figure than current literary fashion would allow.

* Prosper Mérimée's pen-name as a playwright.

Mademoiselle Félicité des Touches became an orphan in 1793. Her property thus escaped the confiscation which her father or brother would probably have incurred. Her father died on the tenth of August, struck down on the palace steps defending the king he had served as major of the Palace Guard. Her brother, a young corpsman, was massacred at Les Carmes. Mademoiselle des Touches was two years old when her mother died of grief a few days after this second catastrophe. On her deathbed, Madame des Touches placed her daughter in the care of her sister, a nun in the convent of Chelles. This nun, Madame de Faucombe, prudently took the orphan to Faucombe, a sizable estate near Nantes which belonged to Madame des Touches, where she settled with three sister nuns from the convent. During the last days of the Terror, mobs from Nantes came and destroyed the château, seizing the nuns and Mademoiselle des Touches who were thrown into prison under the slanderous accusation of having received emissaries from Pitt and Cobourg. The Ninth of Thermidor liberated them. Félicité's aunt died of fright. Two of the nuns fled France. The third entrusted Félicité to the child's nearest relative—Monsieur de Faucombe, a maternal great uncle who lived in Nantes—and then joined her companions in exile.

Monsieur de Faucombe, an old gentleman of sixty, had taken a young wife to whom he left the management of his affairs. He concerned himself exclusively with archaeology—a passion, or better still, one of those manias that enable old men to believe in their vitality. The education of his ward was left entirely to chance. Scarcely looked after by her young aunt who devoted herself to the pleasures of the Empire, Félicité grew up as a boy. She kept Monsieur de Faucombe company in his library reading whatever pleased her. She thus acquired a theoretical knowledge of life and, lost all intellectual innocence while remaining virginal. Her intelligence drifted among the impurities of knowledge while her heart remained pure. Her learning became extraordinary, encouraged by her passion for reading and aided by an excellent memory. By the time she was eighteen she was as erudite as young authors today ought to be before they start writing. Her prodigious reading did more to control her passions than life in a convent, which only inflames the imagination of a young girl. The child's brain, stuffed with information that was neither digested nor classified, dominated the child's heart. Such intellectual depravity without any effect on physical chastity would have amazed philosophers or observers, were anyone in Nantes capable of suspecting the significance of Mademoiselle des Touches. The effect was in inverse relation to the cause: Félicité had not the slightest penchant toward evil; she apprehended everything through her mind and abstained from all experience. She enchanted the old man and aided him in his work; she wrote three of the good gentleman's books which he took for his own, for his spiritual paternity was equally blind. Such exhausting work, so out of keeping with the natural development of a young girl, took its toll. Félicité fell ill, her blood became feverish, her lungs seemed threatened with inflammation. The doctors ordered horseback riding and social distractions. Mademoiselle des Touches became a very able horsewoman and recovered in a few months. At eighteen she appeared in society and made such a sensation that in Nantes she was always referred to as "la belle demoiselle des Touches." However, the adoration she inspired left her unimpressed for she had achieved it through one of those imperishable motives in women, however superior they may be. Offended by her aunt and her cousins, who made fun of her interests and mocked her standoffishness, assuming her to be lacking in social graces, she decided to become coquettish and flippant, a woman in short. Félicité had expected some manner of intellectual intercourse, of flirtations in keeping with the level of her intelligence and studies. She was disgusted by the platitudes of the conversation, the stupidity of the gallantry, and above all was shocked by the aristocracy of the army, which at that time held complete sway. She had, of course, neglected the arts of the salon. On seeing herself inferior to the puppets who played the piano and were admired for the love songs they sang, she wanted to become a musician. She returned to her isolation and began to study relentlessly with the best teacher in town. Since she was rich, she sent for Steibelt * to perfect her skills, which amazed the entire city. This princely behavior is still talked about in Nantes. The maestro's sojourn cost her 12,000 francs. She later became an accomplished musician. In Paris, at a later date, she studied harmony and counterpoint, and wrote the score for two highly successful operas, without the audience ever discovering her identity. These operas are ostensibly authored by Conti, one of the greatest artists of our time, but this circumstance has to do with her sentimental history which will be clarified later. The mediocrity of provincial society bored her so deeply, her imagination was so filled with grandiose ideas, that she soon deserted the salons after reappearing in them long enough to eclipse the other ladies by the radiance of her beauty, to savor her triumph over the other musicians, and to make herself adored by the few cultivated people. Then, having demonstrated her abilities to her cousins and driven two lovers to despair, she returned to her books, to her piano, to Beethoven, and to her old guardian, Faucombe.

In 1812 when she was twenty-one, the archaeologist handed over to her the accounts of his trusteeship. From that year on, she undertook the administration of her fortune which consisted of a revenue of 15,000 francs from her father's estate, Les Touches; 12,000 francs from the lands of Faucombe, which increased by a third when the leases were renewed; and 300,000 francs in savings accumulated by her guardian. Félicité had gained nothing from provincial life besides an understanding of money and that talent for wise administration which perhaps reestablishes the balance between the economy of the provinces and the in-

* Steibelt was a German pianist who enjoyed great favor in Paris.

creasing movement of capital towards Paris. She withdrew her 300,000 francs which the archaeologist had kept invested in the estate, and placed them in the National Debt at the time of the disastrous retreat from Moscow, thereby gaining an additional income of 30,000 francs. With all her expenses deducted, she was still left with 50,000 francs a year to be invested. At twenty-one, a girl of such strongheadedness was the equal of a man of thirty. Her intelligence had acquired great breadth, and her critical habits allowed her to judge people and things, arts and politics, with lucidity. As of then, she intended to leave Nantes, but old Faucombe fell ill with the malady that finally caused his death. She was like a wife to the old man, nursing him for eighteen months with the devotion of a guardian angel, and closing his eyes at the very moment when Napoleon was wrestling with Europe over the corpse of France. She therefore postponed her departure for Paris until the end of the struggle.

Being a Royalist, she hastened to Paris to be present at the return of the Bourbons. She was welcomed by the Grandlieu family, to whom she was related. Then the catastrophes of March 20th occurred leaving everything for her in suspense.[*] She was able to view at close range this last image of the Empire, and admire the Grande-Armée as it arrived in the Champ-de-Mars, as though in a Roman arena, to salute its Caesar before going to its death at Waterloo. Félicité's noble soul was captivated by this magical spectacle. The political agitations, the magic of this theatrical performance in three months that history has named The Hundred Days, filled her thinking and protected her from all passion, in the midst of an upheaval that scattered the royalist society in which she had made her début. The Grandlieus followed the Bourbons to Ghent, leaving their house to Mademoiselle des Touches. Félicité, unwilling to see herself in a subordinate position, bought for 130,000

[*] The date of Napoleon's return to Paris, from which Louis XVIII fled the day before.

francs one of the handsomest houses on the rue du Mont-Blanc, which she moved into when the Bourbons returned in 1815, and whose garden alone is today worth two million. Accustomed to looking after herself, Félicité soon became familiar with a way of life usually considered the exclusive privilege of men. In 1816, she was 25. She was ignorant of marriage, understood it only intellectually, judged it in terms of cause rather than effect, and saw only its inconveniences. Her superior mind rebelled against the abdication with which a married woman begins her life. She highly prized her independence and felt only disgust for the cares of motherhood. These details are necessary to explain the anomalies that characterize Camille Maupin. She had known neither her mother nor her father, she was her own mistress from childhood on, her guardian was an elderly archaeologist, chance placed her in the realm of science and imagination, and in the literary world, instead of circumscribing her within the limits of the meaningless education given to women, and the maternal teachings regarding dress, hypocritical decency, and the man-hunting techniques of her sex. And so, long before she became famous, one could see at a glance that she had never played at being the little doll.

Toward the end of 1817, Félicité des Touches noticed not so much the withering of her beauty as the first signs of fatigue. She understood that this beauty would deteriorate as a result of her obdurate celibacy. She wished to preserve her beauty for she valued it highly. Science had taught her that nature places a term on her creations, which perish as readily from disuse and from abuse of her laws. She remembered her aunt's macerated face and shuddered. Forced to choose between marriage and passion, she opted for freedom; she was no longer indifferent to the homage paid her.

At the time this story begins, she looked almost exactly as she had in 1817. Eighteen years had passed over her lightly. At forty, she could easily pass for twenty-five, and so a portrait of her in 1836 shows her as she looked in 1817. Those women who know in what conditions of temperament and beauty a woman must live in order to resist the ravages of time, will understand how and why Félicité des Touches enjoyed so great a privilege by studying a portrait that requires the most brilliant shades of the palette and the most ornate frame.

→☙→→☙→*→☙→*→☙→*→☙→*→☙→*→☙→*→☙→*→☙→*→☙→*→☙→

II PORTRAIT Brittany presents the curious problem, as yet unresolved, of predominantly dark hair, dark eyes and dark skin in a country so close to England and with a climate so similar. Is this problem related to the great question of race or to unobserved physical influences? Scientists will one day study the causes of this singularity which disappears in the neighboring province of Normandy. Pending solution, the bizarre fact remains that blonds are most uncommon among Breton women, almost all of whom have the flashing eyes of southerners. However, instead of the greater height and sinuous lines common in Italy and Spain, they are generally short, compact, full-figured and solid, except for the upper classes which have mixed with the aristocracy.

Mademoiselle des Touches, a fullblooded Breton, is of ordinary height. She is in fact shorter than she appears, but is given the benefit of the difference because of the structure of her face which heightens her. She has that complexion characteristic of lovely Italians that appears to be olive by day and fair by night and seems to be living ivory. Daylight gleams on such skin as though on a polished surface. A violent emotion is necessary for the palest flush to creep into those cheeks which then disappears almost immediately. This quality lends a primitive impassibility to her face. This face, longer than oval, resembles some beautiful Isis of the Egina bas-reliefs. It has the purity of a sphinx's head polished by the heat of the desert, caressed by the flaming Egyptian sun. Thus the color of the skin is in harmony with the precision of the head. Thick, black hair falls in plaits along the back of the neck like the double-banded headdress of the statues at Memphis, admirably following the general severity of the lines. The forehead is full and broad, flared at the temples, highlighted by the planes that catch the light, ridged like that of Diana the huntress—a forehead that bespeaks strength and willfullness, silence and calm. The vigorous arch of the eyebrows extends over two eyes whose fire glows at times like the light of a fixed star. The white of the eye is neither blue-tinged, nor red-veined, nor pure white; it has the warm tones of bone. The pupil is circled with orange; it is bronze ringed with gold, but a living gold and an animate bronze. It is a pupil with depth, not like some eyes that seem opaque and reflect the light like the eyes of cats or tigers. It does not have that terrible fixity that causes sensitive people to shudder. This depth has its infinity just as those mirror-like eyes have their absolute. The gaze of an observer can easily lose itself in that soul which contracts and withdraws as rapidly as it flashes from those velvety eyes. In moments of passion, Camille Maupin's eyes are sublime. The gold of her glance sets the white ablaze, and the whole eye seems to flame. But in repose, it is dull; the torpor of meditation often makes it look stupid. When the light of the soul is absent, the lines of the face become sad as well. The lashes are short, but thick and black as ermine tails. The lids are shadowed and traced with red capillaries which grants them both grace and strength, two qualities hard to find together in a woman. There is not the faintest line or puckering around the eyes. Here too, one is reminded of the time-mellowed granite of Egyptian statuary. The cheekbones, though gently rounded, are more prominent than in other women and complete the general effect of strength expressed by the face. The nose, straight and narrow, has obliquely cut nostrils passionately dilated to reveal the luminous pink of their delicate lining. This nose beautifully follows the line of the forehead; it is perfectly white all the way to the tip which is endowed with a kind of mobility that performs wonders when Camille is indignant, angry or rebellious. It is particularly that part of the face, as Talma noted, that expresses the anger or irony of great souls. Immobile nostrils indicate a certain frigidity. Never did the nose of a miser quiver, it is as pinched as the mouth; everything in his face is as sightly shut as the rest of him. The mouth, arched at the corners, is a vivid red, filled with the living, pulsating scarlet that endows the mouth with its many seductions, and reassures the lover who might be put off by the majestic severity of the face. The upper lip is thin; the groove that joins it to the nose arches it like a bow, which gives particular emphasis to her disdain. Camille need do very little to express her anger. That pretty lip is bordered by the full red edge of the lower lip, wonderfully kind and loving, that Phidias might have modelled as the rim of an open pomegranate, which is indeed its color. The chin is firmly set, though a bit heavy, expressing resolution and providing the splendid termination of a royal if not divine profile. It must be added that the upper lip, below the nose, is lightly shaded with a most charming down. Nature would have erred by not placing that soft fuzz there. The ear is delicately convoluted, a sign of many hidden refinements. The chest is broad, the bosom small but adequate, the hips slim but graceful. The slope of the back is magnificent and more reminiscent of a Bacchus than of the Venus Callipyge. It is here that one can see the nuance separating most famous women from the rest of their sex; in this region of the lower back they bear a vague resemblance to men. They have neither the suppleness nor freedom of movement common to women destined by nature for motherhood; their stride is not broken by a gentle undulation. This observation is bilateral, for it has its counterpart in men whose hips are feminine; such men are shrewd, cunning, false, and cowardly. Instead of a hollow at the nape, Camille's neck forms a rounded contour connecting the shoulders to the head without any sinuosity, an unmistakable trait of strength. This neck in certain movements has marvelous athletic curves.

The shoulders, superbly rounded, seem to belong to a female colossus. The arms, vigorously molded, ending in wrists of English delicacy and pretty dimpled hands embellished with pink, almond-shaped, deeply set nails, are of a whiteness which suggests that the firm well-proportioned body is of quite another tone from the face. The cold stern carriage of the head is contradicted by the mobility of the mouth, the variety of expressions, and the sensitivity of the nostrils. However, despite its exciting prospects, which to the uninitiated are fairly invisible, there is something disturbing about the tranquillity of this face. It is a face more melancholic and serious than graceful, marked by the sadness of perpetual meditation. Mademoiselle des Touches listens more than she speaks. Her silence and the deep scrutiny of her thoughtful glance are unsettling. No truly cultivated person has ever looked at her without being reminded of Cleopatra, that diminutive brunette who almost changed the face of the world. But in Camille, the animal is so perfect, so complete, so leonine, that a man with anything of the Turk in him regrets the placing of so great a mind in such a body, and would have it all woman. One is afraid to discover the weird corruptions of a diabolic soul. Are her passions not colored by the coldness of analysis and pragmatism of thought? Does this woman not judge rather than feel? Or still more frightening, does she not feel and judge at the same time? Since there are no limits to her mind, must she stop where other women stop? Does this intellectual power enfeeble the heart? Does she have charm? Can she condescend to the many tender little acts with which women delight, engross, and divert the men they love? Would she not destroy an emotion that did not measure up to the infinity of her grasp and contemplation? Who could fill the chasms of those two eyes? One is afraid to find in her some wild, untamed quality. A strong woman should be no more than a symbol; she is frightful to see in reality. Camille Maupin is to some degree the living image of Schiller's Isis, hidden deep within the temple, at whose feet the priests used to find the dying gladiators who had dared consult her. The adventures held by everyone to be true and not denied by Camille herself, confirm the questions posed by her appearance. Perhaps she enjoys this kind of slander? The nature of her beauty has not been without influence on her reputation, just as her fortune and position have maintained her in society. Any sculptor wishing to make a fitting statue of Brittany would do well to copy Mademoiselle des Touches. This sanguine, fiery temperament is the only kind to withstand the action of time. The constantly nourished tissue of this skin that seems varnished is the only weapon nature has given women to prevent wrinkles, which in Camille's case are further inhibited by the impassivity of her face.

❋↷☙↷❋↷☙↷❋↷☙↷❋↷☙↷❋↷☙↷❋↷☙↷❋↷☙↷❋↷☙↷❋↷☙↷❋↷☙↷

III THE BIOGRAPHY OF CAMILLE MAUPIN In 1817 this charming woman opened her house to artists, famous writers, men of learning, and journalists toward whom she was attracted by her tastes. Her salon was similar to that of Baron Gérard, in which aristocracy mingled with celebrities, and to which the elite of Parisian ladies came. Félicité's family and fortune, augmented by her inheritance from her aunt who had been a nun, aided her in the attempt to create her own circle, a difficult undertaking in Paris. Her independence was one of the reasons for her success. Many ambitious mothers dreamed of having her marry their sons, whose fortune was in disharmony with the splendor of their coats of arms. A number of peers of France, enticed by her annual income of eighty thousand francs and seduced by the magnificently furnished house, brought some of their more cantankerous and demanding female relatives there. The diplomatic world, always in search of intellectual diversions, came there and liked it. Mademoiselle des Touches, surrounded by such diversified interests, was able to study the various comedies which all men, even the most distinguished, are led to play by passion, avarice and ambition. She soon saw the world as it is and was indeed happy not to experience too soon the total love that takes possession of a woman's mind and faculties and inhibits her reasonable judgment. Generally speaking, a woman feels, takes pleasure, and judges in successive order, giving rise to three distinct ages, the last of which coincides with the sad period of old age. For Mademoiselle des Touches the order was reversed. Her youth was encased in the snows of science and the cold of contemplation. This transposition further explains the strangeness of her life and the nature of her talent. She was observing men at an age when women see only one man; she despised what they admired; she discerned lies in the flatteries they accepted as truths; she laughed at the things that saddened them. This contradiction lasted for a long time but came to a dreadful end: she was to experience her first love, in all its youth and freshness, at the moment when women are condemned by nature to renounce love. Her first affair was kept so secret it was never known by any one. Félicité, like all women trusting in the good sense of the heart, was led to deducing the beauty of the soul from the beauty of the body; she was infatuated with a face and discovered instead the vacuousness of a lady-killer who saw in her just another conquest. It took her some time to recover from her disgust and from this absurd relationship. Her suffering was detected by another man who consoled her without ulterior motives, or at least knew how to conceal them. Félicité thought she had found the nobility of heart and mind that had been lacking in the dandy. This man was one of the most original minds of the time. He himself wrote under a pen name and his first books proclaimed him a lover of Italy. Félicité was obliged to travel or else perpetuate her only remaining lacuna. This sceptical ironical man took Félicité to discover the homeland of the arts. This pseudonymous celebrity can be considered the teacher and creator of

Camille Maupin.* He put Félicité's vast knowledge in order, increased it through the study of the masterpieces that abound in Italy, gave her that subtle and ingenious, epigrammatic and profound quality that characterizes his own talent, always a bit unorthodox in form, that Camille Maupin modified by the delicacy of feeling and naive touch innate in women. He inculcated her with the taste for English and German literature and made her learn both languages during their travels. In Rome in 1820, Mademoiselle des Touches was abandoned for an Italian. Barring this misfortune, she might never have become famous. Napoleon called misfortune the midwife of genius. That event inspired in Mademoiselle des Touches a permanent distrust of mankind which accounts for her strength. Félicité died and Camille was born. She returned to Paris with Conti, the illustrious musician, for whom she wrote the libretti for two operas, but she was left without illusions and became, unknown to the world, a kind of female Don Juan with neither debts nor conquests. Encouraged by her success, she published her two volumes of plays which from the very outset placed Camille Maupin among the ranks of anonymous celebrities. She recounted her deceived passion in a beautiful little novel, one of the masterworks of the period. This book, a dangerous example, was ranked with *Adolphe,* a horrible lamentation whose counterpart is to be found in Camille's novel. The delicacy of her literary metamorphosis is still not fully appreciated. Only a few subtle minds discern the inherent generosity that in a man exposes him to criticism and in a woman saves her from fame by allowing her to remain unknown. In spite of her desires, her fame grew daily as much through the influence of her salon as through her witticisms, the fairness of her judgment, the solidity of her knowledge. She was considered an authority, her epigrams were repeated, she could no longer resign the duties

* The portrait is unmistakably of Stendhal, although there was no such relationship between Stendhal and George Sand.

invested in her by Paris society. She became an accepted exception. The world yielded before the talent and fortune of this strange creature; her independence was recognized *de facto* and *de juris;* women admired her intellect, men her beauty. Her behavior, in fact, conformed to all the laws of society. Her friendships appeared to be purely platonic. There was furthermore nothing of the "lady author" about her. Mademoiselle des Touches is as charming as any woman of the world, at the right moments feeble, indolent, coquettish, fashion-conscious, enchanted by the trivialities that delight women and poets. She understood full well that after Madame de Staël, there was no more room in this century for a Sappho, and that Ninon could not exist in Paris without great lords and voluptuous court life. She is the Ninon of the intellect; she adores art and artists; she alternates from poet to musician, from sculptor to novelist. She is noble and generous to the point of gullibility, so given is she to pity the unfortunate and disdain the fortunate. Ever since 1830, she moves in a circle of chosen friends who love and esteem each other deeply. As far removed from the fracas of Madame de Staël as from political struggles, she pokes fun at Camille Maupin as the younger brother of George Sand whom she calls "her brother Cain," for that more recent glory has dimmed her own. Mademoiselle des Touches admires her successful rival with angelic indulgence, and without jealousy or hidden bitterness.

Up until the moment this story begins, she had the happiest existence that can be imagined by any woman strong enough to take care of herself. From 1817 to 1834, she came to Les Touches five or six times. Her first trip took place in 1818, after her first disappointment in love. The house at Les Touches was uninhabitable. She sent her steward off to Guérande and took his lodgings at Les Touches. She had at that time no inkling of her future success; she was sad, saw no one, and wished in some way to contemplate herself after that great disaster. She wrote to one of her friends in Paris regarding the furniture necessary to decorate Les Touches. It arrived as far as Nantes by boat, was then transported by barge to Le Croisic, and from there carried with considerable difficulty across the sands to Les Touches. She brought artisans from Paris and settled in at Les Touches which she found extremely attractive. She wanted to be able to meditate on the vicissitudes of life as though in a private convent. At the onset of winter she left for Paris. The little town of Guérande was immediately aroused by diabolical curiosity. The only subject of gossip was the oriental luxury of Mademoiselle des Touches. The notary public, her steward, gave out passes to visit Les Touches. People came from Batz, Le Croisic, Savanay. This curiosity within two years brought in the enormous sum of seventeen francs to the gatekeeper and gardener. Mademoiselle des Touches returned to Les Touches only two years later, on her return from Italy, and came by way of Le Croisic. For some time no one in Guérande knew she was there with the musician Conti. Her subsequent appearances did little to excite the curiosity of the town. Her overseer and the notary were the only ones to know the secret of Camille Maupin's glory. At that moment, however, the contagion of new ideas had made some progress in Guérande and a number of people became aware of the double existence of Mademoiselle des Touches. The postmaster began receiving letters addressed to Camille Maupin, Les Touches. Finally, the veil was torn off. In a region so profoundly Catholic, backward and filled with prejudices, the strange life of this illustrious woman was bound to provoke gossip that terrified the Abbé Grimont. In the minds of such people she appeared monstrous; a life such as hers could never be understood by them. Félicité was not alone at Les Touches; she had a guest. This guest was Claude Vignon, a contemptuous, arrogant writer who, though limited to criticism, had managed to impress the general public and literary circles with his superiority.* For the last seven years, Félicité had been re-

* Evidently modeled after Gustave Planche, both physically and temperamentally.

ceiving this writer—as she had a hundred other authors, journalists, artists, celebrities—all the while knowing his inflexible character, his indolence, his penury, his negligence and his disgust with life, yet nevertheless, to judge by her treatment of him, desirous of having him for a husband. Her behavior, which was incomprehensible to her friends, she explained as ambition and the fear of aging. She wanted to devote the rest of her life to a superior man for whom her fortune would provide a stepping stone and who would continue her position in the literary world. She therefore carried off Claude Vignon to Les Touches as an eagle carries off a kid in his claws, to study him and come to some major decision. But she was deceiving both Calyste and Claude; she had not the slightest interest in marriage. She was experiencing the most violent convulsions that can befall a nature as strong as hers; she found herself the dupe of her own mind, seeing life illumined too late by the sunlight of love, as radiant as it is in twenty-year-old hearts. And now, here is a picture of Camille's "convent."

❋↬⊛↱❋↬⊛↱❋↬⊛↱❋↬⊛↱❋↬⊛↱❋↬⊛↱❋↬⊛↱❋↬⊛↱❋↬⊛↱❋↬⊛↱

IV Les Touches A few hundred steps outside Guérande the ground of Brittany ends and the salt marshes and dunes begin. One goes down to this desert of sands left like a margin between the sea and the land by way of a plunging road that has never seen a carriage. This desert consists of sterile sand, irregularly shaped pools bordered by mud ridges in which the salt is cultivated, and the little inlet that separates Le Croisic from the mainland. Although geographically Le Croisic is a peninsula, it can be considered an island given the fact that it is only attached to Brittany by the sandbanks that connect it with Batz—arid, moving sands, extremely difficult to cross. At the point where the path from Le Croisic to Guérande branches onto the road on solid ground stands a country house surrounded by a large garden noteworthy for its twisted, tortured pines—some of them umbrella pines, others bare of branches, all revealing their red trunks where the bark has been stripped away. These trees, victims of storms, surviving despite winds and tides, prepare the soul for the strange and awful spectacle of the salt marshes, and the dunes that resemble an immobile sea. The house, rather well built of schisty stone and mortar held in place by granite bands, has no style whatever; it presents the eye with a blank wall pierced by the regular openings of the windows, which on the ground floor have small panes and on the upper floor large panes. Above the upper floor the lofts extend under an enormous raised, twin-gabled roof with two large dormers on each slope. Under the angle of each gable, a window looks out of its Cyclops eye, on the west toward the sea, on the east toward Guérande. One façade of the house faces the road to Guérande, while the other faces the desert at the end of which stands Le Croisic, and beyond it the open sea. A streamlet escapes through an opening in the garden wall, crosses the path to Le Croisic which runs alongside, and disappears in the sand or in the saltwater lagoon produced by the intrusion of the sea, and ringed by the dunes and marshes. A short driveway, built on this break of the land, leads from the path to the house. One enters through a large doorway. The courtyard is surrounded by rather modest rural buildings— a stable, a coach house, the gardener's cottage which stands beside the farmyard, used more by the gatekeeper than the mistress. The gray shades of this house harmonize beautifully with the scenery it surveys. Its park is the oasis of this desert which the traveler enters by way of a mud-thatched customs shed. This house, without lands, or rather with lands situated around Guérande, received an income of 10,000 francs from the marshes, and the rest from tenant farms scattered around the mainland. This is the fief of Les Touches which the Revolution deprived of its feudal revenues. Today, Les Touches is an estate, but the marsh workers continue to speak of the *Château* and would call the owner the *Seigneur* if it were not a woman.

When Félicité began restoring Les Touches, she was careful, being the artist that she is, not to alter the desolate exterior that gives this lonely building its prison appearance. Only the gateway was embellished with two brick columns that support a balcony under which a carriage can pass, and the courtyard was planted.

The arrangement of the ground floor is the same as most of the country houses built a hundred years ago. This house was evidently built on the ruins of some little castle that perched there like a link connecting Le Croisic and Batz with Guérande, and lording over the marshes. A peristyle was constructed at the foot of the stairs. One enters first into a large paneled anteroom, in which Félicité placed a billiard table. This is followed by a vast salon with six windows, two of which, on the gabled end, are doors that lead to the garden down some ten steps which correspond to doors on the other side of the salon leading to the billiard room and the dining room. The kitchen, at the other end, communicates with the dining room by a pantry. The staircase separates the billiard room from the kitchen which had a door opening into the peristyle, but which Mademoiselle des Touches had closed off and another opened onto the courtyard. The height of the ceiling and spaciousness of the rooms enabled Camille to decorate this ground floor with noble simplicity. She avoided any overdecoration. The salon, entirely painted in gray, is furnished with antique pieces in mahogany and green silk, white calico draperies edged in green, two consoles, a round table; in the middle of the room, a square-patterned rug; on the mantlepiece a clock representing the sun chariot between two Empire candelabra; on the wall above, an enormous mirror. The billiard room has gray calico draperies trimmed with green and two divans. The dining room furniture consists of four large mahogany sideboards, a table, twelve mahogany chairs with horsehair seats, and some splendid Audran engravings in mahogany frames. From the middle of the ceiling hangs an elegant light fixture such as one finds above the staircases of great houses and two lamps. All the ceilings, with exposed beams, were painted a wood color. The old wooden staircase with its broad railing is completely covered with green carpeting.

The first floor had two apartments separated by the staircase. Félicité took the one with the view on the marshes, the dunes and the sea for her own use, and arranged it into a little sitting room, a large bedroom, a dressing room and a study. On the other side of the house she managed to create two apartments, each with a sitting room and a study. The servants have their rooms in the attic. The two guest suites were at first decorated with only the bare essentials. The artistic luxury ordered from Paris was reserved for her own rooms. In this somber, melancholy dwelling that looks onto a somber, melancholy landscape she wanted to create an artistic fantasy. The little sitting room is hung with beautiful Gobelin tapestries in marvelous carved frames. The windows are draped in heavy, old-fashioned fabrics—deep-pleated red and gold brocade with regal fringe and tassels worthy of the most splendid papal throne. The room is furnished with a cabinet purchased for her by her agent which is today worth seven or eight thousand francs, a carved ebony table, an ivory-encrusted desk from Venice with countless drawers, and a collection of fine Gothic pieces. There are all the finest paintings and sculptures that one of her painter friends was able to select at antique shops whose dealers, in 1818, had no inkling of the value these treasures would later acquire. On the tables, she placed exquisite Japanese vases of remarkable design.

Her bedroom is a perfect replica of the style of Louis XV, down to the last detail: the exact canopied bed of carved wood painted white, surmounted by flower-strewing cupids, the headboard padded and upholstered in brocaded silk, the canopy decorated with four clusters of feathers; the walls hung in genuine Persian cloth, with silk valances, tassels, and bows; the fireplace in rocaille work; the ormulu clock flanked by two large vases of early blue Sèvres mounted on gilded copper; the mirror in a similar gilded frame; the Pompadour dressing table with its lace skirt and mirror; all the curved pieces: the duchesses, the chaise longue, the little love seat, the fireside chair with a quilted back; the lacquered screen, the draperies of the same silk as the chairs, lined in pink satin and hung with weighted cords; the Savonnerie rug—in short, all the elegant, expensive, sumptuous, delicate trappings among which the lovely ladies of the 18th century indulged in amorous pursuits.

In contrast to the Louis XV fineries, the study, completely modern, is furnished with handsome mahogany furniture; the bookcases are filled. The room could serve as a boudoir, it has a divan; it is bursting with charming feminine knickknacks attracting the eye with their modernity: books with locks, handkerchief and glove cases, picture lampshades, statuettes, Chinese objects, writing cases, a few albums, paperweights, and all kinds of currently fashionable paraphernalia. The curious visitor notices with worried surprise the presence of pistols, a waterpipe, a riding crop, a hammock, a pipe, a hunting rifle, a blouse, a tobacco pouch, an army knapsack—a bizarre collection that typifies Félicité.

Any sensitive being coming into this house would be struck by the singular beauty of this landscape that extends its savannas beyond the grounds of the estate—truly the last vegetation of the continent. Those dismal squares of brackish water separated by narrow white paths on which the white-clad marshmen walk to rake the salt, collect it and put it into bins; that expanse of saline vapors that keeps birds away and inhibits all plant life; those sands whose sterility is only relieved by a stubborn little plant with pink flowers and by the wild dianthus; the salt lake, the sand dunes and the view of Le Croisic, a miniature town arrested in mid-ocean like Venice. And finally, the immense Atlantic that edges the granite reefs with its foamy frills making their weird forms stand out more sharply—this spectacle that stimulates the mind while at the same time saddening it, an effect invariably produced by the sublime which awakens a nostalgia for the unknown, glimpsed by the soul at exasperating heights. These savage harmonies are only fitting for great minds and great sufferings. This rippling desert, where on occasion the sun's rays reflected by the water and the sand whitewash the town of Batz and flow over the roofs of Le Croisic glaring unmercifully, could occupy Camille for days. She rarely turned toward the deliciously refreshing views, toward the groves and flowering hedges that decked Guérande like a bride with flowers, ribbons, veils, and festoons. She was suffering at that moment from terrible unknown agonies.

✻✲✢✻✲✢✻✲✢✻✲✢✻✲✢✻✲✢✻✲✢✻✲✢✻✲✢✻✲✢✻✲✢✻✲✢

V Two Loves As soon as Calyste saw the weathervanes of the two gables above the bushes of the driveway and the tortured heads of the pines, the air seemed lighter to him. Guérande was a prison for him; his life was in Les Touches. Who could fail to understand the attractions there for an innocent young man? A love not unlike Cherubino's, that had been for him an infatuation with the idea of love before transferring itself to the woman, could easily survive Félicité's inexplicable refusal. This emotion, which is more the need to love than the act of loving, had certainly not escaped Camille Maupin's inexorable analysis, which was doubtless the reason for her rejection —a subtlety that Calyste could not have understood. In addition, the marvels of modern civilization seemed all the more wondrous there in their contrast to the rest of Guérande, where the poverty of the du Guénics appeared to be opulence. Spread out before the bewildered eyes of this young ignoramus, who knew nothing but the moors of Brittany and the heaths of La Vendée, were all the Parisian wonders of a new world; even his ears heard an unknown, resonant language. Calyste while there listened to the accents of a most exquisite music, the amazing music of the 19th century, in which melody and harmony are equal rivals and vocal and instrumental music have achieved unheard of perfection. He saw examples of the most prodigious painting—the French school which is Italy's heir today, the Spanish school, the Flemish school—in which talent has become so commonplace that our tired eyes and senses, sated with mere talent, cry out for genius. He read there works of the imagination, those amazing creations of modern literature that produce their maximum effect on unjaded sensibilities. In short, our 19th century appeared to him in all its glory, with its criticism, its efforts at renewal in every domain, its tremendous endeavors, almost all of them on a level with the giant who rocked the century's infancy in the cradle of his flags, while singing hymns to the accompaniment of the canon. Initiated by Félicité to all this grandeur, which may perhaps escape the attention of its promoters and craftsmen, Calyste was able to satisfy at Les Touches the craving for the marvelous that is characteristic of his age, and that naive admiration, the first love of adolescence, that is so impatient with criticism. How natural it is for the flame to rise! He listened to that delightful Parisian wit, that elegant satire which revealed to him the French mind and awakened in him a thousand ideas that had been slumbering in the torpor of his family life. For him, Mademoiselle des Touches had become the mother of his intelligence, a mother he could love without guilt. She was so good to him: a woman is always adorable to a man in whom she inspires love, even when she does not seem to return it. At that moment, Félicité was giving him music lessons. Everything for him was intensified, animated by a light, a spirit, a quality which were supernatural, indefinable, strange—the spacious rooms on the ground floor rendered even more spacious by the ingenious landscaping of the park, the stair wall decorated with masterworks of Italian patience, carved wood, Venetian and Florentine mosaics, ivory and marble bas-reliefs, curios ordered by medieval magicians, and that intimate apartment, so seductive, so voluptuously artistic. The modern world with its poetry contrasted violently with the somber, patriarchal world of Guérande, setting up two opposing systems. On the one side, the myriad effects of art; on the other the unity of primitive Brittany. No one will wonder then why the poor boy, as bored as his mother by the subtleties of mouche, trembled whenever he entered the house, rang the bell or crossed the court. It is to be pointed out that such apprehensions no longer trouble mature men, inured to the irritations of life, surprised by nothing and prepared for everything.

On opening the door, Calyste heard the piano and thought Camille Maupin was in the salon, but when he entered the billiard room, the music no longer reached him. Camille was doubtless playing on the little spinet that Conti had brought her from England and that was in the upstairs sitting room. Calyste progressively slackened his pace as he climbed the stairs, whose thick carpeting completely muffled the sound of his steps. He recognized something extraordinary in this music. Félicité was playing for herself, carrying on a conversation with herself. Instead of going in, he sat down on a Gothic bench with a green velvet seat that stood on the landing beneath a window handsomely framed with carved wood, walnut-stained and varnished. Nothing was more mysteriously melancholy than Camille's improvisations which made one think of some *De profundis* cried out to God from the depth of the grave. The young lover recognized a prayer for love out of despair, the tenderness of resignation to grief, the sighs of contained anguish. Camille had been amplifying, modifying, creating variations on the introduction to the cavatina, "Grâce pour toi, grâce pour moi," which is practically the whole of the fourth act of *Robert le Diable*. She suddenly began singing this aria in a heart-rending manner, then broke off. Poor Camille Maupin! Totally without vanity, the lovely Félicité let him see her face bathed in tears, took out her handkerchief, wiped them away and said simply: "Good morning." She was ravishing in her morning attire. On her head she wore one of those red velvet nets currently in fashion, from which a few gleaming clusters of her black curls escaped. A short redingote, creating the effect of a modern Greek tunic, revealed sheer cotton trousers with embroidered cuffs above the most exquisite red and gold Turkish slippers.

"What's wrong?" Calyste asked.

"He hasn't come back," she replied, standing at the window looking out over the dunes, the inlet, and the marshes.

The reply accounted for her outfit. Camille was expecting Claude Vignon and was fretful as a woman is when her pains are unrewarded. A man of thirty would have understood that, but Calyste saw only Camille's unhappiness.

"Are you worried?" he asked.

"Yes," she replied with a melancholy this boy could not fathom.

Calyste suddenly started walking out of the room.

"Where are you going?"

"To find him," he replied.

"Dear boy," she said, taking him by the hand and holding him at her side as she gave him one of those tender looks that for young hearts are the handsomest of rewards. "Are you mad? Where would you find him along this wild coast?"

"I will find him."

"Your mother would be beside herself with worry. And furthermore, I want you to stay. Truly I do," she said, drawing him down on the sofa. "Do not let me upset you. These tears you see are the kind that give women pleasure. There is in us a faculty that men do not possess, that of abandoning ourselves to our emotional nature by pushing our sentiments to the extreme. By imagining certain situations and letting ourselves go we arrive at tears and sometimes even more serious conditions, real disorders. A woman's fantasies are not games of the mind, but of the heart. You came at just the right moment. Solitude is not for me. I am not fooled by his desire to be alone on his visit to Le Croisic and its rocks, Batz and its sands, and the salt marshes. I knew he would devote several days to it, not just one. He wanted to leave us alone. He is jealous, or more precisely, he is playing at being jealous. You are young and you are handsome."

"Why didn't you tell me? Should I stop coming here?" asked Calyste, unsuccessfully holding back a tear that fell on his cheek and touched Félicité deeply.

"You are an angel!" she exclaimed. Then she gaily sang the *Restez* aria from *William Tell* to eliminate all trace of seriousness from this magnificent reply of the princess to her subject.

"In this way," she continued, "he wanted to make me believe that his love for me is greater than he really feels. He knows how much he means to me," she said looking at Calyste closely, "but he may feel humiliated at finding himself inferior to me in this. Perhaps he has also become suspicious about you and hopes to surprise us together. But even if he is only guilty of wanting to seek the pleasures of this excursion in the wilderness without me, of wanting to keep me out of his walks, outside the ideas inspired by these spectacles, and of making me dreadfully worried, is this not enough? I am no more loved by this great brain than I was by the musician, by the wit, or by the officer. Sterne was right: names signify something, and mine is the cruelest joke. I shall die without finding in a man the love that I bear in my heart, the poetry I have in my soul."

Her arms lay limp, her head rested against the cushion; her eyes, dull with concentration, stared at a pattern in the rug. The suffering of superior minds has something grandiose and imposing about it, and reveals the immense expanses of soul that the mind of the spectator expands even further. Souls like these share the privilege of royalty whose misfortunes affect an entire people and ultimately the whole world.

"Why did you . . ." said Calyste unable to continue.

Camille Maupin's beautiful hand was placed burning over his own and eloquently interrupted him.

"Nature altered her laws for me by granting me five or six more years of youth. I rejected you out of egoism. Sooner or later age would have separated us. I am thirteen years older than he, and that is quite enough."

"You will still be beautiful at sixty!" Calyste heroically exclaimed.

"May God hear you!" she replied smiling. "Furthermore, dear child, I want to love him. In spite of his insensitivity, his lack of imagination, his cowardly indifference and the invidiousness that devours him, I believe there is greatness under those rags; I hope to galvanize that heart, save him from himself, and make him need me. Alas, I have a clairvoyant brain and a blind heart."

Her lucidity toward herself was frightening. She was suffering, and simultaneously analyzing that suffering, just as Cuvier and Dupuytren explained to their friends the fatal progress of their disease and the oncoming stages of death. Camille Maupin knew herself emotionally as well as those two scientists knew themselves anatomically.

"I came here expressly to evaluate him. He is already bored; he misses Paris. I told him, he misses criticism. He has no author to tear apart, no system to undermine, no poet to torment, and is unwilling to give in to any abandon here that might lighten the burden of his mind. Alas, my love is evidently not real enough to relax this brain. In short, I do not inebriate him! Why don't you get drunk with him tonight. I shall say that I am not well and remain in my room. Then I shall know whether I am mistaken or not."

Calyste blushed cherry red from brow to chin and his ears flamed.

"Oh my God!" she exclaimed, "here I am corrupting your girlish innocence without even realizing it. Forgive me, Calyste. When you are in love, you will discover that one becomes capable of setting the Seine on fire just to satisfy the slightest whim of The Loved One, as the fortune tellers say." She paused.

"There are some arrogant, rational minds that proclaim when they have reached a certain age, 'If I had my life to live over I would do exactly the same.' I, who do not consider myself weak, say 'I would be a woman like your mother, Calyste.' To have a Calyste, what joy! Had I married the greatest fool, I would still be a humble, submissive wife. And yet, I have committed no crime against society; I have only harmed myself. Alas, dear boy, a woman can no more be alone in a civilized society than she can in a primitive one. Affections that are not in harmony with social or natural laws, affections that are not obligatory, shrink from us. If I am to suffer for the sake of suffering, I may as well be useful. What do I care about the children of my Faucombe cousins who are no longer Faucombes, whom I have not seen in twenty years, and who furthermore have married merchants! You are a son who cost me none of the pains of childbirth. I shall leave you my fortune and you will be happy, at least in that sense, through me, dearest treasure of beauty and grace that nothing must spoil or wither."

After speaking these words in a solemn voice, she lowered her eyelids to prevent him from reading her eyes.

"You have never wanted anything from me," said Calyste. "I shall return your fortune to your heirs."

"Child!" said Camille in a low voice, as the tears fell to her cheeks. "Can nothing save me from myself?"

"You have a story to tell me and a letter to show . . . ," the generous lad said to distract her, but he did not finish, for she interrupted him.

"You are right. Above all one must keep one's promises. It was too late yesterday, but it would seem we have all the time in the world together today," she said in a tone both charming and bitter. "And while fulfilling my promise, I shall sit in such a way as to look at the path leading to the cliff."

Calyste placed a large Gothic armchair in that direction and opened the window. Camille Maupin, who shared the oriental tastes of her illustrious female colleague, brought over a magnificent Persian narghileh that an ambassador had given her. She filled the bowl with patchouli, cleaned the mouthpiece, perfumed and fitted the quill tube that she only used once, lit the yellow leaves, placed the handsome instrument of pleasure with its long-necked base of blue and gold enamel beside her, and rang for tea.

"If you would like a cigarette . . . ? Oh dear, I always forget that you do not smoke. Purity like yours is so rare. It seems to me that to caress the satin down of your cheeks one would need the hand of Eve fresh from the hand of God."

Calyste blushed and sat down on a stool. He did not see the deep emotion that made Camille blush.

✳↩☯↪✳↩☯↪✳↩☯↪✳↩☯↪✳↩☯↪✳↩☯↪✳↩☯↪✳↩☯↪✳↩☯↪✳↩☯↪

VI MARQUISE BÉATRIX "The person from whom I received this letter yesterday, and who may be here tomorrow, is the Marquise de Rochefide," Félicité said. "After marrying off his elder daughter to a Portuguese nobleman who is permanently settled in France, old Rochefide, whose family is not as old as yours, wanted to arrange a marriage for his son that would ally him with high nobility, in order to obtain for him the peerage he was unable to obtain for himself. The Comtesse de Montcornet pointed out to him a certain Mademoiselle Béatrix-Maximilienne-Rose de Casteran, younger daughter of the Marquis de Casteran who wanted to marry off his daughters without a dowry in order to reserve his entire fortune for his son, the Comte de Casteran. The Casterans, it would seem, stem directly from Adam's rib. Béatrix, born and raised at the Casteran castle in the Orne district, was, in 1828 at the time of her marriage, about twenty. She was known for what you provincials call eccentricity, which was merely a superior mind, great enthusiasm, a taste for beauty, and a degree of artistic cultivation. Take the word of a poor woman who has gone all the way in these directions, there is nothing more dangerous for a woman; by following such inclinations, one reaches the point at which you see me, and which the marquise reached . . . an abyss. Only men have the walking stick necessary for remaining upright on these precipices, a strength that we lack and that makes monsters of us if we do possess it. Her old grandmother, the dowager of Casteran, was delighted to see her marry a man to whom she would be superior in lineage and intellect. The Rochefides were in every way acceptable; Béatrix had only to congratulate herself on the match. And the Rochefides were similarly pleased with the Casterans, who through their alliances with the Verneuils, the d'Esgrignons, and the Troisvilles, obtained the peerage for their son-in-law in that last great batch of peers made by Charles X and later annulled by the July revolution. Rochefide is not very bright; he nevertheless started out by having a son; however, since he mercilessly inflicted himself on his wife, she soon had enough. The early days of marriage are as perilous for dull minds as for burning passions. Rochefide, in his dullness, mistook his wife's ignorance for frigidity and classed Béatrix, who is very fair, as a cold, lymphatic woman. From then on he led a bachelor's life in utter security, trusting to the marquise's frigidity, her pride, her self-respect, and the grandiose style of life in Paris which surrounds a woman with countless barriers. You will know what I mean when you visit Paris. Those who hoped to profit from his mindless complacency told him: 'You are a lucky man. You have a cold wife whose only passions will be intellectual. She is content to be admired; her fantasies are purely artistic; her jealousy, her desires will be appeased if she can have a salon for the brightest minds around. She will have debaucheries of music and orgies of literature.' And the husband lapped up these jokes with which Parisians take in fools. However, Rochefide is not just an ordinary fool: he is as vain and proud as a man of intelligence with the difference that intelligent people anoint themselves with modesty and become cat-like; they caress you in order to be caressed. Whereas Rochefide is a great big conceited pig who admires himself in public and is always smiling. His vanity wallows in the stable and feeds noisily as it slurps its forage out of the trough. He has the kind of faults that are known only to people who can judge them in intimacy, faults that are only apparent in the shadows and mysteries of privacy, while in society and to the world at large the man seems charming. Rochefide must have been unbearable as soon as he felt his privacy threatened, for he has that kind of petty, hidden jealousy that becomes brutal when taken by surprise—cowardly for six months, murderous the seventh. He thought he was deceiving his wife and feared her—two reasons for tyranny the day he should discover his wife was charitable enough to seem indifferent to his infidelities. I am giving you this analysis of his character in order to explain Béatrix's behavior. The marquise had the greatest admiration for me; however, from admiration to jealousy there is but a step. I have one of the most remarkable salons in Paris; she wanted one of her own and tried to woo my circle. I am not given to retaining those who would leave me. She had those superficial people who are friends to all out of idleness and whose aim is to leave a salon as soon as they have entered it; but she did not have the time to establish a society. At that time, I thought her devoured by the desire for any manner of fame. She nonetheless has a certain breadth of spirit, a regal pride, ideas, and a wondrous facility for perceiving and understanding everything. She is equally conversant with metaphysics and music, painting and theology. You will see in the mature woman what we saw in her as a bride. However, she has a certain tendency to affectation, too often giving herself airs of knowing esoteric things like Chinese and Hebrew, or questioning hieroglyphics, or expounding on the papyrus used for wrapping mummies. Béatrix is one of those blondes who would make the fairness of Eve look black. She is as slim and straight as a candle and as white as a communion wafer. Her face is long and pointed; her complexion is highly changeable, one day pale as percale, another tawny and mottled as though her blood had carried dust during the night; her brow is magnificent though a trifle too audacious; her eyes are a pale sea green and float in the white of the eyeball under weak brows and indolent lids. She often has dark rings under her eyes. Her nose, which describes a quarter circle, is pinched at the nostrils and highly refined, though impertinent. She has an Austrian mouth, the upper lip being fuller than the lower which has a contemptuous droop. Her pale cheeks are colored only by some violent emotion. Her chin is fairly heavy; mine is not slim, and I probably should not tell you that women with heavy chins are exigent in love. She has one of the most beautiful figures I have ever seen; a back of dazzling whiteness that used to be very flat but has since, it would seem, developed and filled out. Her bosom, however, has not been as fortunate as her shoulders, and her arms have remained thin. She has, in addition, a grace in her bearing and in her manners that redeems whatever defects she may have, and provides a splendid background for her beauty. Nature has given her that princely air that cannot be acquired, that suits her and immediately reveals the noblewoman, in perfect keeping with her narrow though most deliciously rounded hips, her perfectly shaped foot, and that luxuriant growth of angel's hair that Girodet's brush so often painted and, that looks like waves of light. Without being faultlessly beautiful, she can, when she wishes, make an unforgettable impression. Were there any occasion for Béatrix to wear the costume of the period when women wore pointed bodices laced with ribbon that rose up from the padded fullness of their heavily pleated brocade skirts, their faces framed by starched ruffs, their arms concealed under slashed sleeves with lace ruffles from which the hand protruded like a pistil from a calyx, and combed their tightly frizzed hair over a jewel-netted chignon, then she would have the edge over any of the ideal beauties of that time."

Félicité showed Calyste a good copy of Miéris' painting, in

which a lady in white satin, holding a sheet of paper, stands singing with a Brabant nobleman while a Negro pours old Spanish wine into a footed glass and an old housekeeper arranges some biscuits.

"Blonds," she continued, "have the advantage over most of us brunettes in their enviable variety: there are a hundred ways of being blond and only one of being dark. Blonds are more feminine than we; we dark Frenchwomen look too much like men. Well then," she added, "don't fall in love with her on the basis of the portrait I have drawn for you, like some prince in the *Arabian Nights*! It's too late for that, my dear. But console yourself, with her it's first come first served."

These words were said advisedly. The admiration expressed on the young man's face was stimulated more by the painting than by the painter whose intention had missed its mark.

"In spite of her blondness," she continued, "Béatrix does not have the softness of her coloring; her lines are severe, she is hard and elegant; she has the face of a dry point engraving, yet one might say there is a tropical heat burning inside her soul. She is an angel that flames and dries up. There is a hunger in her eyes. She is best seen full face; in profile her face looks as though caught between two doors. You will see if I am mistaken. Here now is what led to our friendship: for three years, from 1828 to 1831, Béatrix judged men, things, events, life, from the heights of her intellect while enjoying the last festivities of the Restoration, wandering from salon to salon, going to court, and gracing the costume balls at the Elysée-Bourbon. She was kept fully occupied. That first dizzying encounter with the world prevented her heart from awakening; it was still numb from the first cruelties of marriage: a pregnancy, a child, and the whole claptrap of motherhood that I dislike. In that respect I am not a woman. I find children unbearable, they cause endless pain and constant worry. I find that one of the great benefits of modern society that we were deprived of by that hypocrite, Jean-Jacques, is our freedom to be or not to be mothers. If I am not alone in thinking this, I am alone in say-ing it. During the upheaval of 1830-1831, Béatrix went to her husband's country estate where she was as bored as a saint in paradise. On her return to Paris, the marquise judged, and per-haps correctly, that the revolution which appeared to be purely political in the eyes of some people was to become a moral rev-olution as well. The world to which she belonged, having been unable to reconstruct itself during the unexpected triumph of fifteen years of the Restoration, was going to give way to the battering ram of the middle class. She had understood Monsieur Lainé's prophetic words, 'The kings are departing.' * This opin-ion, I think, was not without influence over her conduct. She participated intellectually in the new ideas that pullulated for three years following the July Revolution like horseflies in the sun, and that turned many a lady's head. However, like all noblemen, while finding these innovations superb, she wished to safeguard the nobility. Seeing no further place for excep-tional individuals, seeing the high nobility resume the same mute opposition it had maintained against Napoleon—which was its only possible role in an epoch of action and deeds, but which in a moral epoch is tantamount to abdication—she pre-ferred happiness to silence. After things calmed down a bit, Béatrix met at my house the man with whom I had hoped to end my days, Gennaro Conti, the great musician of Neapolitan origin but born in Marseilles. Conti is a very gifted man, and has great talent for composition although he can never be first-rate. Without Meyerbeer and Rossini, he might have been con-sidered great. He has one advantage over them—he is to the voice what Paganini is to the violin, Liszt to the piano, Taglioni to ballet, and a successor to Garat, of whom he reminds those who ever heard him. It is not just a voice, my dear, it is a soul. Whenever that singing corresponds to certain ideas, certain in-describable moods in which a woman finds herself at times,

* Vicomte Lainé, a minister under the Restoration, spoke these words at the time of the July decrees.

then she is lost on hearing Gennaro. The marquise fell wildly in love with him and took him from me. It was extremely provincial, but perfectly fair. She gained my esteem and my friendship through her behavior toward me. She thought I was the kind of woman who defends her possessions; she did not know that in my opinion the most ridiculous thing in such a position is the very act of fighting. She came to see me. This woman, proud as she is, was so enamored that she revealed her secret to me and made me the arbiter of her fate. She was enchanting; in my eyes, she remained both a woman and a noblewoman. I must tell you, my dear, women at times are nasty; but they have a secret greatness that no man can appreciate. And so, as a woman on the brink of the old age that awaits me, I may as well make my testament: I can tell you that I was faithful to Conti, that I would have remained so until my death, although I knew him only too well. He is charming on the surface and detestable deep down. In matters of the heart, he is a charlatan. There are men, like Nathan of whom I have already spoken to you, who are charlatans on the outside and honest underneath. Such men lie to themselves. Perched on their stilts, they think they are on their feet and perform their tricks with a kind of innocence. They are born comedians, braggarts, as extravagantly constructed as Chinese vases; they are perhaps capable of laughing at themselves. What is more, they have generous natures which, like the splendor of Murat's regal garments, expose them to danger. Conti's deceitfulness, on the other hand, will never be known to anyone but his mistress. In his art, he has that celebrated Italian jealousy that led Carlone to assassinate Piola, and that cost Paisiello a stiletto wound. This dreadful envy is hidden behind the most gracious affability. Conti does not have the courage of his vice; he smiles at Meyerbeer and flatters him when he would sooner dismember him. He knows his weakness and gives himself airs of strength, and is so vain that he pretends to sentiments that are the furthest removed from his heart. He passes himself off as an artist who receives his inspiration from heaven. For him, art is something sacred and holy. He is fanatical; he is sublime in his contempt for the world of society; he has an eloquence that seems to stem from deep conviction. He is a prophet, a demon, a god, an angel. And even though forewarned, Calyste, you will be taken in by him. This Latin, this tempestuous artist, is as cold as a fish. According to him an artist is a missionary, art is a religion that has its priests and should have its martyrs. Once he has gotten started, Gennaro reaches the most disheveled pathos that any German philosophy professor ever disgorged on an audience. You may admire his convictions, but he believes in nothing. When elevating you to the skies with his singing that seems to be a mysterious fluid seeping love, he looks at you ecstatically, but is measuring your admiration. 'Am I really a god for them?' he wonders, at the same time saying within himself 'I ate too much spaghetti.' You think he loves you and in fact he hates you without your knowing why. But I knew. He saw a woman the day before, took a fancy to her, and insulted me with feigned love, hypocritical caresses, and made me pay dearly his enforced fidelity. He is insatiable in his need for adulation, he mimics and mocks everything; he can feign joy as easily as grief, and succeeds admirably. He is charming, is loved, and elicits admiration whenever he chooses. When we parted he hated his voice, yet he owed more of his success to his voice than to his talent as a composer. He would rather be a man of talent like Rossini than a performer of the caliber of Rubini. I had made the mistake of becoming attached to him, and was prepared to bedeck this idol indefinitely. Conti, like many artists, has a taste for luxury; he enjoys his comforts and his pleasures; he is vain, elegant, fastidious. And I humored all his whims, and loved his weak and wily character. I was envied, and at times I smiled bitterly. I valued his courage; he is brave, and it is said that bravery is the only unhypocritical virtue. On one occasion during a trip, I saw it put to the test when he risked the life most precious to him. Yet in Paris, I have

97

seen him commit what I would call mental cowardice. My dear, all these things I knew. I told the marquise, 'You do not know what kind of abyss you are stepping into. You are the Perseus of a pathetic Andromeda, you are liberating me from my rock. If he loves you, so much the better, but I doubt it; he only loves himself.' Gennaro's pride was in seventh heaven. I was not a marquise, I was not born a Casteran, I was forgotten in a day. I offered myself the bitter pleasure of delving deep into that character. Certain of what the end would be, I wanted to watch Conti's deviousness. My poor boy, in one week I witnessed horrors of sentimentality and ghastly charades. I shall tell you no more about it; you will see him here. However, since he knows I know him, he loathes me now. If he could stab me in perfect safety, I would not exist for two more seconds. I have never said a thing to Béatrix. Gennaro's ultimate and perpetual insult is that he believes me capable of communicating my awful knowledge to the marquise. He has become increasingly anxious and pensive, for he places no trust in any one. For my benefit he still plays the role of the unhappy lover, miserable because he left me. You will find in him an all-pervading cordiality; he is tender and chivalrous. In his eyes, every woman is a madonna. You have to live with him a long time before penetrating the secret of that false good humor and discovering the invisible dagger of his subterfuges. His convincing manner would beguile God. You too will be ensnared by his feline seductiveness and will never believe in the deep-seated, rapid calculation of his inner thoughts. Enough of him.

"I carried indifference to the point of receiving them at my house. The result of this was that the most perspicacious of societies, Parisian society, knew nothing of this intrigue. Although Gennaro was drunk with pride, he doubtless needed to play a part for Béatrix; his dissimulation was exquisite. I was surprised, for I expected him to demand a showdown. It was the marquise who compromised herself after a year of happiness that had been subjected to all the vicissitudes and all the hazards of life in Paris. She had not seen Gennaro for a few days, and I had invited him to dinner at my house where she was to come during the evening. Rochefide suspected nothing, but Béatrix knew her husband so well that, as she often told me, she would have preferred the greatest misfortunes in life to what awaited her with that man if he ever gained the right to despise her or torment her. I had chosen the evening when our friend, the Comtesse de Montcornet, normally receives. After coffee had been served to her husband, Béatrix left the room to change, even though she never began dressing for the evening that early. 'Your hairdresser has not yet arrived,' Rochefide commented on learning the reason for his wife's departure. 'Thérèse can comb me,' she replied. 'But where are you going at this hour, you can hardly go to Madame de Montcornet at eight o'clock?' 'No,' she said, 'but I thought I would hear the first act at the Opera.' Voltaire's interrogating bailiff of Huron is a mute compared to an idle husband. Béatrix fled the room to avoid being questioned further, and did not hear her husband reply, 'In that case, we shall go together.' He meant no harm by this; he had no reason to suspect his wife, and she had so much freedom! He made a point of never constraining her; it was a matter of pride for him. Furthermore, nothing in Béatrix's conduct was open to reproach by even the severest critic. The marquis had no precise idea of where he wanted to go, perhaps to his mistress. He had dressed before dinner and had only to take his hat and gloves, when he heard his wife's carriage roll up under the awning of the courtyard steps. He went into her room and saw she was ready, but utterly bewildered at seeing him. 'Where are you going?' she asked. 'Did I not tell you I was accompanying you to the Opera?' The marquise repressed the exterior signs of her extreme annoyance, but her cheeks flushed a deep red as though she had put on rouge. 'Well then, let us be off,' she said. Rochefide followed her without noticing the emotion her voice betrayed; she was consumed by a wild anger. 'To the Opera,' her husband called out. 'No!'

Béatrix cried, 'to Mademoiselle des Touches. I have something to tell her,' she added when the door was closed. The carriage took off. 'If you wish,' Béatrix continued, 'I can drop you off at the Opera and go to her afterwards.' 'No,' said the marquis, 'if it is only a matter of a few words, I can wait in the carriage. It is half-past seven.' If Béatrix had said to her husband, 'Go to the Opera and leave me alone,' he would have obeyed her quietly. However, like any intelligent woman, knowing herself guilty, she was afraid of arousing his suspicions and resigned herself. When she decided to leave the Opera and come to my house, her husband came along. She walked in red with anger and impatience. She came up to me and whispered in my ear, with an expression of total calm, 'My dear Félicité, I am leaving tomorrow with Conti for Italy. Please ask him to make his arrangements and be here with a passport and coach.' She then left with her husband. Violent passions require freedom at any cost. For the last year, Béatrix had been suffering from constraint and the infrequency of their meetings; she considered herself permanently attached to Conti. Consequently, I was hardly surprised. In her place, with my character, I would have done the same thing. She opted for this complete break simply because she had been crossed in the most innocent way; she was forestalling one misfortune by an even greater one. Conti's joy appalled me; only his vanity was involved. 'That's what I call being loved!' he said to me in the midst of his transports. 'How many women would give up their lives, their fortunes, their reputations like this!' 'Oh yes, she loves you,' I said to him, 'but you do not love her!' He became furious and made a scene. He perorated, argued, described his love by saying he had never thought it possible to love so much. I remained impassable and lent him the money it turned out he needed for the trip which had taken him by surprise. Béatrix left a letter for Rochefide and took off for Italy the next evening. She remained there two years. She wrote to me a number of times. Her letters are enchantingly friendly. The poor dear became attached to me as the only woman who understands her. She says she adores me. The need for money finally drove Gennaro to writing a French opera; he did not find in Italy the same financial opportunities that composers have in Paris. Here is Béatrix's letter. Now you will be able to understand it, if at your age one can already analyze matters of the heart," she said handing him the letter.

At that moment Claude Vignon came in.

❋↝✧↝❋↝✧↝❋↝✧↝❋↝✧↝❋↝✧↝❋↝✧↝❋↝✧↝❋↝✧↝❋↝✧↝❋↝✧↝

VII CLAUDE VIGNON This unexpected apparition left Calyste and Félicité speechless for a moment—she out of surprise, he out of a vague uneasiness. The very high forehead of this young man, bald at thirty-seven, seemed shadowed by clouds. His tight judicious mouth expressed cold irony. Claude Vignon is an imposing figure, despite the precocious dilapidation of a once magnificent face, now livid. Between the ages of eighteen and twenty-five, he looked somewhat like the divinely beautiful Raphael, but now, his nose—the feature in the human face that changes the most—has become pointed; his face has become sunken under mysterious hollows, his contours have taken on a puffiness; his complexion is unhealthy with leaden grays predominating in the tired skin, though no one knows the fatigues of this young man, aged perhaps by bitter solitude and the abuses of cerebration. He scrutinizes the minds of others with neither purpose nor system, the pickaxe of his criticism constantly tearing down, never constructing anything. His is the weariness of the laborer, not the architect. His pale blue eyes, once brilliant, have been veiled by unknown suffering, or dimmed by mournful sadness. Dissipation has shadowed his eyelids as though with a charcoal smudge. His chin, incomparably distinguished, has grown fleshy without nobility. His voice, not very sonorous to begin with, has grown weak; it now lies somewhere between hoarseness and complete extinction.

The impassivity of his splendid head, the fixity of his gaze conceal an irresoluteness, a weakness that is betrayed by a witty sardonic smile. This weakness affects his actions but not his mind. There are signs of encyclopedic comprehension on this forehead, and in the mannerisms of this face that is both child-ish and haughty. One detail might explain the eccentricities of his character. The man is quite tall and already slightly bent, like all those who carry within them a world of ideas. These great long bodies have never been noteworthy for their stamina or creativity. Charlemagne, Narses, Belisarius, and Constantine, in this regard, have been noteworthy exceptions. Certainly, Claude Vignon offers many mysteries to unravel. To begin with, he is both extremely simple and extremely subtle. Al-though he is as susceptible to debauchery as a courtesan, his mind remains unfaltering. This intelligence, capable of criti-cizing art, science, literature, politics, is incapable of governing his outer life. Claude contemplates himself in the vastness of his intellectual dominion, and neglects his appearance with the indifference of a Diogenes. Content to penetrate every-thing, to know everything, he has contempt for material things; however, attacked by doubt the moment it comes to creating, he sees all the obstacles without being enchanted by any of the beauties, and by dint of weighing the means, he remains, arms hanging, without ends. He is a Turk of the intellect, drugged by meditation. Criticism is his opium, and his harem of already written books has disgusted him with any works that wait to be written. As indifferent to little things as to big ones, he is obliged, by the very weight of his head, to succumb to de-bauchery if only to abdicate for a few minutes from the fatal power of his omnipotent analysis. He is far too occupied with the wrong side of genius, and you may now understand that Camille Maupin would have liked to right him. This was a fascinating task. Claude Vignon thought of himself as a great politician as well as a great writer. But this unpublished Machiavelli laughs up his sleeve at ambitious people; he knows everything he will ever know; he instinctively measures his future against his faculties; he sees himself as great; he squarely faces obstacles; he penetrates the fatuousness of parvenus; he loses confidence or loses interest, and lets time slip by without getting down to work. Like Etienne Lousteau, the journalist, like Nathan, the famous playwright, like Blondet, another journalist, he comes from the middle class to which we owe the majority of our great writers.

"How did you come?" Mademoiselle des Touches asked him, blushing with pleasure or surprise.

"Through the door," Claude Vignon drily replied.

"Of course," she exclaimed, shrugging her shoulders. "You are hardly the man to come in through the window."

"Climbing through a window is a kind of medal of honor for women who are loved."

"Enough," Félicité said.

"Am I disturbing you?" asked Claude Vignon.

"Monsieur," said the innocent Calyste, "this letter . . . ."

"Keep it; I am asking nothing. *At our age, such things are not in need of explanation,*" he said mockingly as he interrupted Calyste.

"But monsieur . . ." Calyste said indignantly.

"Calm yourself, young man. I am extremely indulgent in matters of sentiment."

"My dear Calyste . . ." said Camille trying to interject.

"Dear?" said Vignon interrupting.

"Claude is joking," Camille continued, addressing Calyste, "and he is wrong to do so with you who know nothing of Parisian banter."

"I did not know I was joking," Vignon replied with seriousness.

"What road did you take back? For the last two hours I have not ceased looking in the direction of Le Croisic."

"You were not *always* looking," Vignon replied.

"You are intolerable with your teasing."

"I, teasing?"

Calyste stood up.

"You are not uncomfortable enough here to want to leave," Vignon said.

"Quite the contrary," replied the furious young man, to whom Camille offered her hand which he kissed rather than shook, leaving on it a hot tear.

"I would like to be that little lad," said the critic as he sat down and took the mouthpiece of the houka. "How he will love!"

"Too much! For then he will not be loved enough in return," said Mademoiselle des Touches. "Madame de Rochefide is coming here."

"Fine!" said Claude. "With Conti?"

"She will stay on alone, but he is bringing her."

"Have they quarrelled?"

"No."

"Play me a Beethoven sonata; I do not know anything of his music for the piano."

Claude began filling the bowl of the houka with tobacco, all the while examining Camille more carefully than she realized. A horrible idea possessed him; he thought he was being duped by an honest woman. This was certainly a novel situation.

***

VIII Béatrix's Letter Calyste, as he went away, gave no further thought to Béatrix de Rochefide or to her letter; he was furious with Claude Vignon for his indelicacy and pitied Félicité. How was it possible to be loved by that sublime woman and not adore her on bended knees, not believe her on the strength of a glance or a smile? After having been a privileged witness to Félicité's anguished wait, having seen her stare out toward Le Croisic, he was filled with the desire to dismember that cold pallid spectre, whose riddles—the great talent of newspaper wits—he had not understood, as Félicité pointed out. For him, love was a human religion.

On seeing him in the courtyard, his mother could not withhold an exclamation of joy, and at once old Mademoiselle du Guénic whistled for Mariotte.

"Mariotte, here is our boy, put on the trout."

"I have already seen him, mademoiselle," replied the cook.

His mother, somewhat disturbed by the sadness that showed on Calyste's face, though never suspecting it was caused by Vignon's ill treatment of Félicité, took up her tapestry work. The old aunt pulled out her knitting. The baron offered his armchair to his son, and strode up and down the room as though to loosen up his legs before taking a stroll in the garden. No Flemish or Dutch painting has ever shown an interior of such brown tonalities or faces of more harmonious softness. That handsome young man dressed in black velvet, that mother still beautiful, those two old people framed by that ancient hall, expressed the most moving domestic harmony. Fanny would have liked to question Calyste, but he had already withdrawn from his pocket the letter from Béatrix, which might well cause the destruction of all the happiness this noble family enjoyed. While unfolding the letter, Calyste's vivid imagination conjured up the marquise dressed as Camille Maupin had so fancifully described her.

Letter from Béatrix to Félicité

Genoa, 2 July

I have not written to you, dear friend, since our stay in Florence, but Venice and Rome have taken all my time, and as you know, happiness plays an important role in life. One letter more or less is hardly of concern to either of us. I am a bit tired. I wanted to see everything, and when one is of a nature not easily sated, the repetition of pleasures re-

sults in lasitude. Our friend has had great success at La Scala, at the Fenice, and lately at the San Carlo. Three Italian operas in eighteen months! You cannot say that love has made him lazy. We have been wonderfully well received everywhere, but I would have preferred silence and solitude. Is that not the most fitting way of life for women living in utter contradiction of the rest of the world? This is how I thought it would be. Love, my dear, is a more demanding master than marriage, but how sweet to serve him! Having offered up to love my entire life, I did not know I would have to see the world again, even in glimpses, and the attentions I was surrounded by were just so many insults. I was no longer on equal footing with women of highest quality. The more deferentially I was treated, the greater my sense of inferiority. Gennaro did not understand these subtleties. But he was so happy, I would have been ungracious not to sacrifice these petty vanities to something as great as the life of an artist. We women live by love alone, while men live by love and by action, otherwise they would not be men. However, women in my position suffer major disadvantages that you have managed to avoid. You have remained great in the eyes of the world which had no hold over you; you retained your freedom of choice, I have lost mine. I speak here only of matters relating to the heart, not to society which I have totally sacrificed. You could be coquettish and willful, have all the graces of a woman in love who grants or refuses anything she wishes. You preserved the privilege of caprices, even on behalf of your love and the object of that love. In short, still today you are under your own jurisdiction while I no longer have the freedom which one always enjoys asserting

in love, even when that passion is eternal. I do not
have the right to quarrel lightheartedly, which means
so much to us, and rightly so—is this not our way
of probing the heart? I have no threats available to
me, my powers of attraction must now be gained
through limitless obedience and sweetness, I must
make my impression through the magnanimity of
my love. I would sooner die than leave Gennaro, for
my only remission is the sanctity of my love. Between social dignity and my private little dignity, a
secret between me and my conscience, I did not
hesitate. If I have any moments of melancholy—like
clouds passing across an azure sky—that we women
tend to give in to, I stifle them; they would seem to
be regrets. Good Lord, I have so well understood
the extent of my obligations that I have armed myself with unlimited indulgence. So far however, Gennaro has not aroused my over-sensitive jealousy. In
fact, I really do not see how that darling, wonderful
genius could possibly fail me. Sweet angel, I am like
those devout believers who converse with their God;
is it not to you that I owe my happiness? And so you
can be sure I often think of you. At last I saw Italy
as you saw it, and as one should, illuminated by love
as it is by its brilliant sun and its masterpieces. I am
sorry for those people who at every step are moved
by the admiration that Italy inspires and have no
hand to clasp, nor a heart into which they can pour
their exuberant emotions which grow deeper as the
exuberance subsides. These last eighteen months are
all of life to me, and my memory will gather splendid fruits. Did you not also have the desire to remain in Chiavari, to buy a palace in Venice, a cottage
in Sorrento, a villa in Florence? Do not all women
in love fear the outside world? And was it not rea-

sonable that I, forever cast out of that world, should want to bury myself in some gorgeous landscape, in a mass of flowers, facing a lovely sea or an equally beautiful valley like the one you see from Fiesole? But alas, we are poor artists, and money brings the two bohemians back to Paris. Gennaro does not want me to miss the luxury I have renounced, and is returning to Paris to rehearse a new work, a grand opera. You understand as well as I do, my lovely angel, that I cannot set foot in Paris. At the cost of my love, I would not wish to encounter one of those glances, whether from a woman or a man, that would make me feel homicidal. Yes, I would hack to pieces anyone who honored me with his pity, or shielded me with his protection, like that adorable Châteauneuf who, under Henri III I think, spurred her horse to trample the Provost of Paris for just such a thing. I am therefore writing to tell you that I shall soon be coming to see you at Les Touches, and to wait in that charterhouse for our Gennaro. You see how daring I am with my benefactress, my sister? It is because the magnitude of my debt will never lead me, as it does others, to ingratitude. You have so often spoken of the hardships of the overland route, that I am going to try to reach Le Croisic by sea. The idea came to me upon learning of a little Danish vessel, already carrying marble, that is stopping there to put in salt on its return to the Baltic. This way I avoid the fatigue and the expense of traveling by coach. I know that you are not alone and am very happy about it; I felt remorseful in the midst of my happiness. You are the only person with whom I can be alone and without Conti. Will it not be a pleasure for you too to have near you a woman who understands your happiness without being envi-

ous? So then, 'til we meet. The wind is fair, I send
you a kiss on leaving.

~~~~~~~~~~~~~~~~~~~~~~~~~~~~~~~~~

IX THE FIRST CONFIDENCE "So then, she too knows how
to love," Calyste thought to himself as he folded the letter
sadly.

This sadness flashed into his mother's heart as though some
light had illumined an abyss. The baron had just left. Fanny
bolted the turret door and came back to lean against the chair
her son was in, in the pose of Dido's sister in Guérin's painting. She kissed his forehead saying, "What is it, my dearest
Calyste, that makes you sad? You promised to explain the
frequency of your visits to Les Touches, and according to you,
I ought to thank its mistress."

"Yes indeed," he said, "she proved to me, my darling mother,
the inadequacy of my education at a time when noblemen
must acquire a personal distinction if they are to resuscitate
their names. I was as removed from my times as Guérande is
from Paris. She has in a sense been the mother of my intellect."

"It is hardly for that that I will bless her!" said the baroness,
her eyes brimming with tears.

"Mama," exclaimed Calyste on whose forehead the hot tears
fell, two pearls of maternal grief, "Mama, do not cry, for only
a short while ago, I wanted to render her a service by racing
through the whole district, from the shore of the custom house
to Batz, and she said, 'How worried your mother would be.'"

"She said that? Then I can forgive her many things," said
Fanny.

"Félicité has only my best interests at heart," Calyste continued. "She often refrains from saying those sharp, equivocal
things that artists let slip, in order not to shake my faith that
she knows is unshakable. She has told me of the life in Paris led
by a number of young men of high nobility coming out of their

province as I might from mine, leaving families without fortunes, and achieving great fortune by the power of their will
and intelligence. I might do what the Baron de Rastignac has
done; today he is in the ministry. She has been giving me piano
lessons, she teaches me Italian, introduces me to a thousand
new social secrets that no one in Guérande even suspects. She
was not able to give me the treasure of her love, but she does
give me the treasures of her vast intelligence, her wit, her
genius. She does not wish to be a pleasure, but rather a light
for me. She does not offend any of my beliefs; she has faith
in the nobility, she loves Brittany, she . . . ."

"She has changed our Calyste," said the old blind woman interrupting him, "for I understand nothing of these words. You
have a solid house, my beloved nephew, old relatives who adore
you, good old servants; you can marry a fine little Breton girl
who is religious and pure and who will make you happy. And
you can reserve your ambitions for your oldest son who will be
three times richer than you if you know how to live quietly,
economically, humbly and in the peace of the Lord, so as to
redeem our family's estates. It is as simple as a Breton heart.
You too will be a rich gentleman, perhaps not as rapidly, but
more solidly."

"Your aunt is right, my angel, and she is as concerned with
your happiness as I am. If I do not succeed in arranging your
marriage with Miss Margaret, the daughter of your uncle
Lord Fitz-William, it is almost certain that Mademoiselle de
Pen-Hoël will bequeath her fortune to which ever of her nieces
you desire."

"In addition, there may be a few francs right here," said the
old aunt in a mysterious low tone.

"Marry at my age?" he said looking at his mother with one
of those expressions that weaken a mother's reason. "Am I to
go without those beautiful, wild passions? Will I never tremble,
palpitate, be afraid, be assuaged, lie down under implacable
eyes and be able to placate them? Must I never know unfettered

beauty, the soul's fantasy, the clouds that shadow the azure of happiness which the breeze of pleasure disperses? Will I never wander along those winding paths damp with fresh dew? Will I never stand under a flowing downspout without noticing it is raining, like the lovers in Diderot? Will I never hold a burning coal in the palm of my hand, like the Duc de Lorraine? Am I never to climb a silken ladder, or hang from a rotting trellis without bending it, or hide in a closet or under a bed? Will I discover nothing more of women than conjugal submission, and of love only the even glow of its lamp? Must my curiosity be sated even before it has been aroused? Must I live without having experienced the ravages of the heart that heighten a man's powers? Must I become a wedded monk? No! I have tasted of the Parisian apple of civilization. Don't you see that by the very chaste, ignorant ways of this family, you have stoked the fire that consumes me, and I would be destroyed without having worshipped the divinity I see all around me, in the green leaves as in the sun-burnished sands, in all the beautiful, elegant women depicted in the books and poems I devoured at Camille's? Alas, of such women there is but one in Guérande, and that is you, my mother! Those blue birds of my dreams come from Paris, they emerge from the pages of Lord Byron, of Scott—they are Parisina, Effie, Minna. They are the royal duchess I saw on the moors, across the heather and the broom, a sight which sent the blood rushing to my heart."

The baroness saw all these things with more clarity, more beauty, more vividness than art can provide for the reader; she saw them in a flash, all tumbling from his glance like arrows from an overturned quiver. Without ever having read Beaumarchais, she, along with many other women, thought, "What a crime it would be to marry off this Cherubino."

"Oh my sweet child," she said, taking him in her arms and kissing the beautiful head that was still hers, "marry when you wish, but be happy! It is not for me to torment you."

Mariotte came in to set the table. Gasselin had gone to walk

Calyste's horse which he had not ridden for the last two months. The three women, the mother, the aunt and Mariotte, with instinctive feminine shrewdness, were in agreement over how to entertain Calyste when he dined at home. Breton parsimony, consolidated by habits and memories dating from childhood, attempted to vie with Parisian civilization, so faithfully reproduced only two steps from Guérande, at Les Touches. Mariotte tried to distract her young master from the artful preparations of Camille Maupin's kitchen, just as his mother and his aunt tried to outdo each other in attentions that would ensnare their child in the nets of their affection and make all comparison impossible.

"Ah, Monsieur Calyste, you are having a sea trout tonight, and snipe, and crêpes, such as can only be eaten here," said Mariotte with a sly look of triumph, as she prided herself on the whiteness of the tablecloth—a veritable snowfall.

After dinner, when his old aunt took up her knitting, and the priest and the Chevalier du Halga returned in expectation of their game of mouche, Calyste returned to Les Touches, on the pretext of giving back Béatrix's letter.

❋⤙۞⤚❋⤙۞⤚❋⤙۞⤚❋⤙۞⤚❋⤙۞⤚❋⤙۞⤚❋⤙۞⤚❋⤙۞⤚

X A Moment of Happiness Claude Vignon and Mademoiselle des Touches were still at the table. The great critic had a weakness for good food, a vice that Félicité willingly gratified knowing how indispensable a woman makes herself by such complaisance. The dining room, completed only a month earlier, indicated the susceptibility and rapidity with which a woman espouses the character, profession, passions, and tastes of the man she loves or would like to love. The table reflected the sumptuousness that modern luxury and the improvements of modern industry have bestowed on service. The du Guénics, with their impoverished nobility, had no notion of their adversary, nor the fortune required for jousting with silverware repaired in Paris, china considered good enough for the country, fine linens, vermeil, knickknacks on the table and a highly skilled cook—all brought from Paris by Mademoiselle des Touches. Calyste declined the liqueurs offered from one of those magnificent cabinets inlaid with precious wood that look like tabernacles.

"Here is your letter," he said with innocent ostentation, looking at Claude who was sampling a glass of Martinique rum.

"Well then, what do you say?" asked Mademoiselle des Touches, as she tossed the letter across the table to Vignon who began reading it, alternately raising and setting down his glass.

"How lucky the women of Paris are, they all have men of genius to adore and be adored by."

"In that case, you are still a country bumpkin," Félicité said laughing. "Is it possible you have not understood she already loves him less, and . . . ."

"That is evident," said Claude Vignon, having only read the first page. "Can one see anything about one's own position when one is really in love? Can one be as subtle as the marquise? Can one calculate or distinguish? Dear Béatrix is attached to Conti out of pride; she is condemned to love him no matter what."

"Poor woman!" said Camille.

Calyste was staring at the table and no longer saw anything. The lovely woman in the fantastic costume traced by Félicité that morning had appeared to him in an aura of light; she smiled at him, gesturing with her fan while her other hand emerged from the lace ruffle of a red velvet sleeve, its chaste whiteness against the ample folds of her splendid gown.

"Now that would be just the affair for you," said Claude Vignon to Calyste with a sardonic smile.

Calyste was offended by the word *affair*.

"You mustn't give the dear boy any thought of such an intrigue. You don't realize how dangerous such jokes can be. I know Béatrix, and she has far too much pride for such a thing. Furthermore, Conti will be here."

"Aha!" said Claude mockingly, "a little twinge of jealousy?"

"Do you really think so?" said Camille proudly.

"You are more perspicacious than a mother," Claude teasingly replied.

"But it hardly seems possible," said Camille gesturing toward Calyste.

"Nonetheless, they would be well matched. She is ten years older than he yet it is he who would seem to be the girl."

"A girl, monsieur, who has twice seen battle in Vendée. Were there twenty thousand such girls . . . ."

"I was praising you," said Claude Vignon, "which is considerably easier than shaving you."

"And I have a sword for beards that are too long," replied Calyste.

"And I have a talent for epigrams," said Claude smiling. "Come now, we are Frenchmen, the affair can be arranged." Mademoiselle des Touches gave Calyste a beseeching look which calmed him down.

"Why is it," said Félicité to end the debate, "that young men like my Calyste always begin by falling in love with older women?"

"I know of no sentiment more genuine or more generous," replied Vignon. "It is the consequence of the adorable characteristics of youth. And besides, how could mature women end their lives without this love? You are young and beautiful, and will remain so for twenty years, so one can discuss this in your presence," he added with a knowing glance at Mademoiselle des Touches. "First of all, the semi-dowagers who attract young men know far better how to love than young girls. A young man is too much like a girl to find her appealing. A passion like that borders on the myth of Narcissus. Aside from that, there is, I believe, a mutual inexperience that keeps them apart. So that the reason which accounts for a young woman's heart being understood only by a man whose competence is concealed behind a real or feigned passion, is the same, allowing for differences in nature, as that which makes a mature woman more seductive to a boy. He instinctively feels he will succeed with her and the woman's vanity is deeply flattered by his pursuit. It is also perfectly natural that youth should seek ripe fruit, and the autumn of a woman's life offers splendid luscious ones. Are such things insignificant—those glances at the same time bold and reserved, languishing when necessary, gleaming with the last rays of love, so warm, so gentle? And that practiced elegance of expression, those magnificent shoulders so ripe and golden, those ample curves, those full, undulating contours, those dimpled hands, that succulent skin, that radiant brow bursting with emotional abundance, that beautifully groomed hair parted to reveal delicate lines of white skin, and those necks with their superb folds, those provocative napes displaying all the resources of art to reveal the contrast between the hair and the flesh tones, to accentuate all the spiciness of life and love? Even brunettes take on blond tones, the amber shades of maturity. Then too, these women, in their smiles and their words, disclose their knowledge of the world: they know how to talk, they will lay the whole world before you to make you smile, their pride and dignity are sublime, they can emit cries of despair to rend your soul, and make farewells to love that they can rescind and that revivify passion; they become young again just by varying the most absurdly simple things. They constantly seek redemption from their coquettishly proclaimed downfall, and the inebriation of their triumphs is contagious. Their devotion is absolute: they listen to you, they love you, they grasp love the way someone condemned to death clings to the minutest detail of life, they are like those lawyers who make every kind of plea in their briefs without boring the jury, they utilize every means; in short, there is no knowledge of total love except through them. I do not think one can ever forget them, any more than one forgets what is great or sublime. A young woman has a thousand distractions; these women have none. They no longer have conceit, or vanity, or pettiness; their love is the Loire at its mouth—immense, swelled with all the affluents, all the deceptions of life, and that is why . . . my lass is mute," * he said noticing Félicité's ecstatic expression as she gripped Calyste's hand, perhaps to thank him for having been the occasion of so singular a moment and so ceremonious a tribute in which she could see no pitfall.

For the remainder of the evening, Claude Vignon and Félicité were sparkling with wit, recounting anecdotes and describing Parisian life to Calyste who was completely taken with Claude, for wit is especially seductive to people of feeling.

"I would not be surprised to see the Marquise de Rochefide arrive here tomorrow, along with Conti who is doubtless accompanying her," said Claude at the end of the evening. "When I left Le Croisic, the sailors had spied a Scandinavian vessel."

These words colored the cheeks of the impassive Camille. That evening, Madame du Guénic again waited until one o'clock for her son, without understanding what he could be doing at Les Touches, since Félicité did not love him.

"He must be in their way," this adorable mother thought to herself. "How can you have had so much to say to each other?" she asked on seeing him come in.

"Oh mother, I have never spent a more delightful evening. Genius is a very great, a sublime thing! Why did you not give me genius? With genius, one ought to be able to choose among women the one woman one loves and who is necessarily yours."

"But you are beautiful, my Calyste."

"Beauty is meaningful only in women. Furthermore, Claude Vignon is beautiful. Men of genius have luminous foreheads, eyes that flash with lightning, and I, miserable fool, I only know how to love."

* Allusion to the famous line from Molière's *Médecin malgré lui,* "et voilà pourquoi votre fille est muette."

"It is said that this is enough, my angel," she said kissing his head.

"Is that true?"

"So I have been told, though I have never experienced it."

"I will love you for all those who would have adored you," he said.

"Dearest child, I'm afraid it is your duty; you have inherited all my emotions. And so do not be rash. Try to love only noble women, if you must love."

❋↷✦↴❋↷✦↴❋↷✦↴❋↷✦↴❋↷✦↴❋↷✦↴❋↷✦↴❋↷✦↴❋↷✦↴❋↷✦↴❋↷✦↴❋↷✦↴

XI THE FIRST MEETING What young man, bursting with unfullfilled love and suppressed vitality, would not have had the glorious idea of going to Le Croisic to see Madame de Rochefide land, in order to examine her incognito? Calyste greatly surprised his parents, who knew nothing of the arrival of the lovely marquise, by taking off early in the morning without breakfast, and only heaven knows how fast he took off! It was as though some unknown force were aiding him; he seemed light as air. He skirted the walls of Les Touches to avoid being seen. This charming youth was ashamed of his ardor and also horribly afraid of being teased: Félicité and Claude Vignon were so observant. In such matters, young people always think their foreheads are transparent. He followed the meanderings of the path across the maze of salt marshes, reached the sands and crossed them as though in one leap, in spite of the burning sun that shimmered there. He came to the beach, protected by a breakwater, beside which stands a house where travelers find shelter against storms, winds, rain and hurricanes. It is not always possible to cross the little strait since there are not always boats available. But even when there are, it is convenient, while waiting for them to arrive from the docks, to keep the horses, donkeys, cargo, and baggage under cover. From there, one can see the open sea and the town of Le Croisic. From there,

Calyste soon saw two rowboats arrive filled to the brim with cases, trunks, hand baggage, and boxes whose shape and size indicated to the natives that these were extraordinary things and could only belong to travelers of distinction. In one of the boats was a young woman wearing a straw hat with a green veil, in the company of a man. Their boat landed first. Calyste trembled. On seeing them he realized they were servants and dared not question them.

"Are you going to Le Croisic, Monsieur Calyste?" asked the sailors who knew him and whom he answered with a negative movement of the head, embarrassed at having his name mentioned.

Calyste was charmed by the sight of a case covered with a waterproof canvas reading MADAME DE ROCHEFIDE. The name glimmered before his eyes like a talisman. There was something fatidic about it. He knew without any doubt that he would love this woman. The minutest details regarding her already concerned him, interested him, excited his curiosity. Why? In the burning desert of its endless and objectless desires, does not youth concentrate all its energies on the first woman to appear within range? Béatrix fell heiress to the love that Camille rejected. Calyste watched the unloading, all the while looking out toward Le Croisic in the hope of seeing a boat come out of the port, approach that little promontory where the sea roared, and reveal to him that Béatrix who, in his imagination, had already become what Beatrice was for Dante—an eternal marble statue on whose hands he would hang his flowers and wreaths. He remained there, his arms crossed, lost in his meditative anticipation. One point deserving of notice, and that in fact has not been noticed, is how we subject our sentiments to our will, how we take on a commitment toward ourselves, and how we create our fate: chance certainly plays a much smaller role than we think.

"I see no horses," said the maid, sitting on a trunk.

"And I see no road here," said the manservant.

"Yet horses have been here," said the chambermaid, indicating the proof of their passage. "Monsieur," she said speaking to Calyste, "is this the road that leads to Guérande?"

"Yes," he replied. "Whom are you expecting?"

"We were told that someone would come for us from Les Touches. If they don't come soon, I don't know how madame is going to get dressed," she said to the manservant. "You ought to go on to Mademoiselle des Touches. What a barbarous place!"

Calyste had a vague feeling of the awkwardness of his position.

"Is your mistress going to Les Touches?" he asked.

"Mademoiselle des Touches came after her this morning at seven," she replied. "Ah, here are the horses . . . ."

Calyste raced off to Guérande with the speed and agility of an antelope, swerving widely to avoid being recognized by the servants from Les Touches; yet he passed two of them along the narrow path of the marshes. "Shall I go in or not?" he wondered as he saw the first pines of Les Touches. He was suddenly afraid. He went back to Guérande all meek and contrite, and walked along the mall where he continued his deliberations. He trembled as he caught sight of Les Touches; he stood staring at its weathervanes. "She has not the slightest idea of my excitement," he thought to himself. His capricious thoughts were like so many hooks digging into his heart and fastening the marquise to it. With Camille, he had had none of this terror, none of this joyful anticipation. He had met her on horseback and his desire was born as spontaneously as the desire to pick a pretty flower along a path. In timid souls, such uncertainties can, as it were, compose poems. Heated by the first flames of their imagination, such temperaments flare up, become enraged, calmed, and revived each in turn, and reach in silence and solitude the highest level of love even before coming in contact with the object of so much turmoil.

Further down the mall, Calyste noticed the Chevalier du

Halga who was strolling with Mademoiselle de Pen-Hoël. He heard his own name and hid. The chevalier and the old maid, thinking themselve alone, were speaking loudly.

"Since Charlotte de Kergarouët is coming," the chevalier was saying, "keep her here three or four months. How can you expect her to flirt with Calyste? She never stays long enough to attempt it, while by seeing each other daily, these two children will eventually develop a real passion for one another and you will see them married by next winter. If you say so much as two words to Charlotte, she will soon say four to Calyste, and a girl of sixteen will surely get the better of a woman of forty some."

The two old people turned to retrace their steps. Calyste heard nothing more but fully understood Mademoiselle de Pen-Hoël's intention. In his present state of mind, nothing could have been more fatal. Is it in the midst of a preconceived passion that a young man would accept to marry any girl imposed on him? Calyste, who was indifferent to Charlotte de Kergarouët, was tempted to discourage her. He was unconcerned with building a fortune, he had accustomed himself since childhood to the mediocrity of his family's existence, and he furthermore was unimpressed by Mademoiselle de Pen-Hoël's wealth seeing that her style of living was as impoverished as the du Géunic's. And in addition, a young man raised as Calyste had been would never pay heed to anything but his feelings, and all of them belonged to the marquise. Compared to the portrait drawn by Camille, what was Charlotte? His childhood playmate, whom he considered a sister. He did not return home until five o'clock. When he came into the room, his mother with a sad smile handed him a letter from Mademoiselle des Touches.

My dear Calyste, The lovely Marquise de Rochefide has arrived; we count on you to help celebrate her coming. Claude, always sardonic, insists that you

> *will be* Bice *and she* Dante. *It is the duty of Brittany*
> *and of the du Guénics to make a Casteran welcome.*
> *And so, until very soon, your friend*

> *Camille Maupin*

> *Come as you are, without ceremony, or we shall*
> *look ridiculous.*

Calyste showed the letter to his mother and left.

"Who are the Casterans?" she asked the baron.

"A very old Norman family, related to William the Conqueror," he replied. "They bear arms *in tierce per fess azure, gules and or, a horse rearing argent hoofed or.* The gorgeous creature Le Gars got himself killed for in 1800 at Fougères was the daughter of a Casteran who became a nun at Séez and later an abbess, after the Duc de Verneuil left her."

"And the Rochefides?"

"I don't know the name; one would have to look at their shield," he said.

The baroness was somewhat less disturbed on learning that the Marquise Béatrix de Rochefide was of ancient lineage; still, she was frightened by the thought of her son exposed to new seductions.

As he walked, Calyste felt the most violent yet agreeable sensations: his throat was tight, his heart was bursting, his brain confused, and fever raged within him. He would have liked to slacken his pace but some superior force urged him on. All young men have known this surging of the senses, excited by a vague hope. A delicate flame leaps within radiating a halo about them, like the sacred figures in religious paintings, through which they view nature ablaze and women glowing. Are they not then like the saints themselves, filled with faith, hope, ardor and purity?

The young Breton found the group in Camille's little sittting room. It was then about six o'clock. The setting sun cast its flaming rays, broken by the trees, through the windows. The air was still. The half-light so loved by women bathed the room.

"Here is the deputy from Brittany," Camille said smiling to her friend and pointing to Calyste as he raised the tapestry portiere. "He is as punctual as a king."

"You recognized his step," said Claude Vignon to Mademoiselle des Touches.

Calyste bowed to the marquise who greeted him with a nod; he had not looked at her. He shook Claude Vignon's extended hand.

"Here is the great man we have spoken so much about, Gennaro Conti," Camille said without answering Vignon.

She introduced Calyste to a slender man of medium height, with chestnut hair, eyes almost red, pale freckled skin, and bearing so marked a resemblance to Lord Byron that description would be superfluous, except that Conti held his head better. Conti was quite proud of the resemblance.

"I am enchanted for the one day that I am spending at Les Touches to meet monsieur," said Gennaro.

"It was for me to say that to you," replied Calyste with considerable aplomb.

"He is as beautiful as an angel," said the marquise to Félicité.

Standing between the divan and the two women, Calyste overheard these words with embarrassment, though they had been whispered. He sat down in an armchair and cast a few stolen glances at the marquise. In the soft light of the setting sun he noticed a pale, sinuous figure, placed on the divan as though by a sculptor, that made him dizzy. Without knowing it, Félicité's description was to her friend's advantage. Béatrix was superior to the unflattering portrait drawn by Camille the day before. Was it not in part for their guest that Béatrix had placed in her regal hair clusters of cornflowers that made the fairness of her curls stand out, curls arranged to frame her face and fall along her cheeks? The skin beneath her eyes, though ringed with fatigue, had the gleaming iridescence of mother-of-pearl, and her complexion was as bright as her eyes. Under the whiteness of her skin, as delicate as the lining of an egg, blue veins throbbed with vitality. The features were unbelievably fine. Her forehead seemed diaphanous. Her soft, gentle face, beautifully held by a long graceful neck, was capable of a wide range of expression. Her waist, slim enough to span between one's hands, had a ravishingly yielding quality. Her bare shoulders shimmered in the twilight like a camellia against black hair. Her bosom, artfully revealed though veiled by a light fichu, disclosed two curves of exquisite daintiness. Her gown of white organdy embroidered with blue flowers, with full sleeves, and a pointed unbelted bodice, her shoes with bands crossing over fine woven stockings, all indicated a deep understanding of the art of dressing. A pair of silver filigree earrings, a marvel of Genoese craftsmanship that would doubtless become fashionable, was perfectly suited to the delicious softness of that blond hair strewn with cornflowers. In one avid glance, Calyste took in all this beauty and engraved it in his soul. The blond Béatrix and dark Félicité reminded one of the keepsake contrasts so sought after by English engravers and designers. It was an example of Strength and Weakness in woman, in all its expression—a perfect antithesis. These women could never be rivals; each had her own empire. It was like a delicate myrtle or a lily beside a brilliant red poppy, or a turquoise next to a ruby. In an instant, Calyste was seized with a passion that was the final touch to the secret workings of his hopes, his fears and his doubts. Mademoiselle des Touches had awakened his senses, Béatrix inflamed his heart and his imagination. The young Breton felt growing within him an all-conquering power that would respect nothing. And so he looked at Conti with an envy, a hatefulness, a somberness, and a fear of rivalry that he had never felt toward Claude Vignon. Calyste employed all his strength to control himself, all the while thinking that the Turks were right in cloistering women, and that beautiful creatures should be prohibited from flaunting their disturbing enchantments to young men burning with desire. This tempestuous storm abated when Béatrix lowered her gaze to him and spoke in her sweet voice. Already then, the poor boy feared her as God's equal. The dinner bell was rung.

"Calyste, give the marquise your arm," said Mademoiselle des Touches taking Conti to her right and Vignon to her left, as she stood aside to let the young couple pass.

To descend the old staircase this way was for Calyste like a first battle: his heart failed him, his speech as well, and a cold sweat pearled his forehead and dampened his back. His arm trembled so noticeably that on the last stair the marquise asked him, "What is wrong with you?"

"Never," he said in a broken voice, "never in my entire life have I seen a woman as beautiful as you, except for my mother, and I am not in control of my emotions."

"But you have Camille Maupin here."

"Ah, what a difference!" Calyste naively replied.

"You see, Calyste," Félicité whispered into his ear, "didn't I tell you you would forget me as though I had never existed? Sit here, next to her on her right, and Vignon on her left. And you, Gennaro, I shall keep for myself," she added laughing. "We can keep an eye on her flirtations."

The particular stress Camille gave to those words struck Claude, who gave her that sidelong and almost distracted glance that betrayed how observant he was. During the whole of dinner he did not stop looking at Mademoiselle des Touches.

"Flirtation, indeed," replied the marquise taking off her gloves and revealing her magnificent hands, "I have every reason. On one side I have a poet, and on the other poetry."

Gennaro Conti gave Calyste a look filled with admiration. By candlelight, Béatrix appeared even more beautiful than before. The pale gleam of the candles cast a satiny shimmer on her forehead, lit sparks in her gazelle-like eyes, passing through her silken curls and making them shine like threads of gold.

She threw back her sheer scarf with a graceful movement and uncovered her shoulders. Calyste was then able to see the delicate milk-white chest furrowed by a deep cleavage parting into two curves that melted into each shoulder with gentle deceptive symmetry. These disclosures that women permit themselves have little effect on the jaded eyes of worldly people, but on unsophisticated people like Calyste they wreak untold havoc. This neckline, so different from Camille's, proclaimed a totally dissimilar character. It was there that one could recognize the pride of race, the special tenacity of nobility, a certain unyielding quality in that twinned appendage, that may well be the last vestige of the strength of ancient warriors.

Calyste went to great pains to appear to be eating, but his nervousness deprived him of any appetite. As in all young men, nature was writhing in the convulsions that precede a first love and engrave it so deeply in the soul. At that age, the ardor of the heart, hemmed in by moral ardor, produces an inner conflict that explains the long respectful hesitation, the profoundly meditative tenderness, the absence of any scheming—all those attributes unique to young people whose hearts and lives are pure. Though examining her stealthily to avoid arousing Gennaro's jealousy, Calyste perceived the details that made the Marquise de Rochefide so divinely beautiful, and was soon disheartened by the majesty of the woman he loved. He felt dwarfed by the arrogance of some of her expressions, by the imposing aspect of that face that exuded aristocratic sentiments, by a particular pride that women can express through the slightest movements, positions of the head, gestures of admirable languor, all of them effects of less artfulness and less affectation than one would suspect. These minute details of their ever-changing appearance correspond to the subtleties, to the many agitations of their souls, and in all of this there is a wealth of sentiment. The awkward situation in which Béatrix found herself obliged her to keep herself in check, to appear imposing without appearing ridiculous, something women of breeding know how to achieve and vulgar women are defeated by. From Félicité's expressions Béatrix guessed at the adoration she was inspiring in her dinner partner, and how unworthy of her to encourage it, and so from time to time she gave Calyste a repressive glance that fell on him like an avalanche. The unlucky lover appealed to Mademoiselle des Touches with a look that betrayed the tears held back by superhuman effort, and Félicité asked him amicably why he was not eating. Calyste stuffed himself as ordered and pretended to join in the conversation. The thought of being unwanted rather than desirable hammered at his brain. He became all the more embarrassed on seeing behind the marquise's chair the very servant he had seen that morning on the pier and who would doubtless tell her of his curiosity. Whether he was contrite or cheerful, Madame de Rochefide paid no attention to her neighbor. Having been led by Mademoiselle des Touches to the subject of her voyage in Italy, she managed to recount most wittily the mad passion with which a Russian diplomat in Florence had honored her, at the same time ridiculing the little young men who threw themselves at women like locusts on fields of grain. She made Claude Vignon, Gennaro, even Félicité, laugh although these mocking darts pierced Calyste who only heard words through the buzzing in his ears and brain. The poor boy did not swear to himself, as some headstrong people do, that he would have that woman at any price; no, he was not raging, he was suffering. When he realized Béatrix's intention to immolate him at Gennaro's feet, he said to himself, "At least I am of some use to her!" and with the docility of a lamb allowed himself to be mistreated.

"You who are such a lover of poetry," said Claude Vignon to the marquise, "how can you treat him so shabbily? This naive admiration, so charmingly expressed, so devoted and uncalculating, is this not the poetry of the heart? Admit it, does this not give you a feeling of pleasure and well-being?"

"Certainly," she said, "but we would be most unhappy and

above all unworthy, if we gave in to every passion we inspire."

"If you did not make a choice," said Conti, "we would not be so proud of being loved."

"When will I be chosen and singled out by a woman?" Calyste wondered, straining to repress his anguish. He reddened like someone whose open wound has accidentally been touched. Mademoiselle des Touches was struck by the expression that came over Calyste's face and tried to console him with a glance full of sympathy. That glance was intercepted by Claude Vignon who at once became irrespressibly gay and sarcastic. He asserted to Béatrix that love existed only through desire, that most women were deluding themselves when in love, that they loved for reasons often unknown to men or to themselves, that they frequently wished to delude themselves, that even the noblest among them was insincere.

"You restrict yourself to books and don't criticize our sentiments," said Camille imperiously.

The dinner ceased being gay. Claude Vignon's sarcasms had made both women pensive. Calyste in the midst of the happiness afforded him by the sight of Béatrix was suffering horribly. Conti was studying the marquise's eyes to guess her thoughts. When dinner was over, Mademoiselle des Touches took Calyste's arm sending the two other men ahead with the marquise in order to say to the young Breton: "My dear boy, if the marquise falls in love with you she will send Conti packing. But at the moment, you are behaving in a manner that will only strengthen their ties. Even if she were overwhelmed by your adoration, could she show it? Take hold of yourself."

"She has been unkind to me, she will never love me," said Calyste, "and if she doesn't love me I'll die."

"Die? You? My dear Calyste," said Camille, "you're a child! You would not have died for me?"

"You became my friend," he replied.

XII THE TWO LOVES After the chitchat that usually goes with coffee, Vignon asked Conti to sing something. Mademoiselle des Touches sat down at the piano and she and Gennaro sang the final duet of Zingarelli's *Romeo and Juliet,* "Dunque il mio bene tu mia sarai"—one of the most pathetic pages in modern music. The passage "Di tanti palpiti" expresses love in all its grandeur. Calyste, seated in the same armchair he had occupied when Félicité told him about the marquise, listened religiously. Béatrix and Vignon were at either side of the piano. Conti's sublime voice blended perfectly with Félicité's. Both of them had often sung this aria, knew all its possibilities and how best to bring them out. Their rendition was precisely what the composer had intended—the swan song of two lovers. When the duet was over, they were all gripped by emotions that vulgar applause cannot express.

"Ah, music is the first among the arts," exclaimed the marquise.

"Camille puts youth and beauty ahead of it, in first place among all artistic creations," said Claude Vignon.

Mademoiselle des Touches looked at Claude trying to hide a vague uneasiness. Béatrix, unable to see Calyste, turned her head to see what effect the music had on him, though less out of concern for him than for Conti's satisfaction. What she saw in the embrasure was a blanched face covered with tears. She hastily turned away from the sight, as though stricken with intense pain, and looked at Gennaro. Not only had the Genius of Music appeared before Calyste, touched him with her magic wand, flung him into Creation denuding it of its veils, but in addition he was overwhelmed by Conti's genius. In spite of what Camille Maupin had told him about his character, he was convinced of the man's beautiful soul and love-filled heart. How could one rival such an artist? How could a woman ever cease adoring him? That voice entered one's soul like a second soul. The poor boy was as overcome by the poetry as by the despair of it all. He saw himself as utterly insignificant. This ingenuous awareness of his nothingness was visible on his face along with his admiration. He did not notice Béatrix who, drawn to him by the contagion of authentic emotion, pointed him out to Mademoiselle des Touches with a gesture.

"What exquisite sensitivity!" said Félicité. "Conti, you will never receive any applause that equals the hommage of that boy. Let us sing a trio. Béatrix, my dear, will you come?"

When the marquise, Camille, and Conti grouped themselves around the piano, Calyste, unperceived by them, stole through the open door of the adjoining bedroom, flung himself on the sofa, and remained there plunged in despair.

"What is it, my boy?" asked Claude who had silently crept up to Calyste and taken his hand. "You are in love and you feel rejected, but that is not the case. In a few days, you will have the field to yourself, you will reign supreme, you will even be loved by more than one. If you know how to handle things, you will be like a sultan here."

"What are you saying?" exclaimed Calyste, rising and dragging Claude off into the library. "Who loves me here?"

"Camille," Claude replied.

"Camille loves me?" asked Calyste. "And what about you?"

"I," Claude started to say, "I . . . ." He stopped. He sat down and leaned his head with heavy melancholy against a pillow. "I am bored with life and lack the courage to leave it," he said after a moment's silence. "I wish I were mistaken in what I just told you, but for the last few days, more than one bright light has illumined my thoughts. I did not go hiking on the rocks of Le Croisic for my pleasure. The bitterness of my words on my return, when I found you talking with Camille, had its origin in the depth of my wounded pride. I will soon have a talk with Camille. Two farseeing minds like ours cannot be fooled. Between two professional duelists, the skirmish is brief. And so I can already announce to you my departure. Yes, I shall leave Les Touches with Conti, perhaps even tomorrow. Of course once we are no longer here, strange things will happen, terrible things perhaps, and I shall be sorry to miss these contests of passion that are so dramatic and so rare in France. You are very young for so dangerous a struggle; you interest me. Without the profound disgust that women inspire in me I would stay to help you play this match. It's a difficult one and you may lose. You are dealing with two extraordinary women and you are already too much in love with one to make use of the other. Béatrix is probably obdurate in character, and Camille is magnanimous. Perhaps like some frail, delicate thing you will be shattered between these two reefs and swept away by the currents of passion. Beware."

Calyste's stupefaction on hearing these words made it possible for Claude Vignon to say them and then leave the young Breton, who remained gaping like the Alpine tourist to whom a guide has demonstrated the depth of an abyss by throwing a stone into it. To learn from Claude's own mouth that he, Calyste, was loved by Camille, at the very moment he felt his love for Béatrix would last his lifetime—this was too much for such an unworldly young mind. Crushed by immense regret over the past, destroyed in the present by the difficulty of his position between Béatrix whom he loved, and Camille whom he no longer loved but who, according to Claude, loved him, the poor boy was in despair; he remained undecided and lost in thought. He tried vainly to understand why Félicité rejected his love and dashed off to Paris in search of Claude Vignon. At times Béatrix's pure fresh voice reached his ears causing him the violent emotions he had sought to avoid by leaving the drawing room. On a number of occasions he felt himself unable to control a fierce desire to take hold of her and carry her off. What would become of him? Could he return to Les Touches? And knowing that Camille loved him, how could he come there to worship Béatrix? He found no solution to his problems. Gradually, a hush fell over the house. Without paying it any attention, he heard the sound of doors closing. Then suddenly, he counted the twelve strokes of midnight from the clock in the neighboring room from which the voices of Camille and Claude awakened him out of the paralyzing contemplation of his future, and from which a light glowed out of the darkness. Before he could make his presence known, he heard Vignon's frightful words.

"You arrived in Paris hopelessly in love with Calyste," he was saying to Félicité, "but you were terrified by the consequences of such a love at your age; it could lead you to a precipice, to a living hell, to suicide perhaps! Love can subsist only by believing itself eternal, and you already perceived the dreadful separation ahead: disenchantment and old age would soon put an end to this sublime poetry. You thought of *Adolphe,* and the dreadful end to the love between Madame de Staël and Benjamin Constant, who were considerably closer in age than you and Calyste. You then took me, as one takes wooden stakes to raise barricades between one's enemies and oneself. But your desire to make me love Les Touches, was it not to spend your days in the secret adoration of your God? In order to achieve your project, which was both ignoble and sublime, you had to find a man either so unimaginative or so preoccupied with his own lofty thoughts as to be easily fooled. You thought I was simple, and as easily deceived as a genius. It would seem that I am no more than intelligent: I found you out. And yesterday, when I sang the praises of women of your age, did you believe I took those ecstatic, beaming, enchanted glances for myself? Had I not already seen into your soul? Your eyes were fixed on me, but your heart was beating for Calyste. You have never been loved, my poor Maupin, and never will be now that you have denied yourself the beautiful fruit chance offered you at the gates of a woman's hell—gates made to close on their hinges by the number 50."

"Why has love shunned me?" she asked in a broken voice. "Tell me, you who know everything."

"Because you are not lovable, you do not yield to love, you want love to yield to you. You may be capable of the pranks and playfulness of a schoolboy, but you are not young in heart; your mind runs too deep. You have never been naive and you cannot begin now. Your charm lies in your mystery; it is abstract rather than active. Your strength keeps strong people at a distance; they foresee a struggle. Your power may attract young men who, like Calyste, enjoy being protected, but in the long run, it is palling. You are grandiose and sublime. Endure the discomfort of these two qualities: they are tiresome."

"What a condemnation!" exclaimed Camille. "Can I never be a woman, am I such a monstrosity?"

"Perhaps," answered Claude.

"We shall see!" cried the woman in her, hurt to the quick.

"Adieu, my dear, I am leaving tomorrow. I hold nothing against you, Camille, I find you the most extraordinary of women. But if I continued to serve you as a screen or a shield," said Claude in two well chosen inflexions of his voice, "you would hold me in complete contempt. We can take leave of each other without chagrin or remorse; we have no happiness to regret, no hopes unfulfilled. For you, as for some infinitely rare men of genius, love is not what Nature made it—an imperious need, whose satisfaction is accompanied by intense though passing pleasures, that ultimately dies. You see it as Christianity has created it—an idealized realm composed of noble sentiments, grandiose trivialities, poetry, spiritual sensations, devotion, flowers of morality, enchanting harmonies, situated far above gross vulgarities and to which two beings reunited in one angel are transported on the wings of pleasure. That is what I hoped for. I thought I had found one of the keys to open the door that is closed to so many and through which one soars into infinity. But you were already there! And so you deceived me. I am returning to misery in the vastness of my Parisian prison. A deception like this at the outset of my career would have been enough to make me flee all women. Today, it fills my soul with a disenchantment that plunges me forever more into a dreadful solitude where I shall be without the faith that enabled the Church Fathers to people it with holy figures. So there, my dear Camille, is where superior intellect leads us. We can both intone the horrible hymn that Vigny placed in the mouth of Moses speaking to God:

O Lord, you have made me powerful and lonely!

At that moment, Calyste appeared.

"I must inform you of my presence," he said.

Camille's reaction betrayed intense fright. A sudden flush colored her impassive face a flaming red. All through this scene, she remained more beautiful than ever before in her life.

"We thought you had left, Calyste," said Claude, "but this involuntary indiscretion on either side is harmless. Perhaps you will even feel more at ease at Les Touches by knowing all about Félicité. Her silence proves I was not mistaken about the role she intended me to play. She loves you, as I told you, but she loves you for yourself, not for herself, a sentiment few women are capable of imagining or understanding. Few women know the sensuality of pain sustained by desire. It is one of the magnificent passions reserved for men, but she is part man!" he said with a wry smile. "Your passion for Béatrix will make her suffer and make her happy simultaneously."

Tears came to Camille's eyes; she dared not look either at the merciless Claude or the ingenuous Calyste. She was terrified to have been understood. She did not think it possible for any man, whatever his comprehension, to ferret out so painful a delicacy, so exalted a heroism as hers. Seeing her so humiliated by the discovery of her magnanimity unveiled, Calyste shared the emotions of this woman he had placed so high and now saw so downtrodden. Calyste flung himself with an irresistible impulse at Camille's feet, kissing her hands and burying his tear-streaked face in them.

"Claude," she said, "don't leave me. What will become of me?"

"What are you afraid of?" replied the critic. "Calyste already loves the marquise like a madman. You could not possibly find a stronger barrier between you and him than this passion that you yourself excited. It is more than my equal. Yesterday there was a risk for you and for him, but today, everything will turn out to provide you with maternal pleasure," he said with a mocking glance. "You will be proud of his triumphs."

Mademoiselle des Touches looked at Calyste who, at those words, suddenly raised his head. Claude Vignon, by way of vengeance, took delight in seeing their embarrassment.

"You pushed him toward Madame de Rochefide," he continued, "now he is under the spell. You dug your own grave. Had you entrusted yourself to me, you would have avoided the disasters that await you."

"Disasters?" cried Camille Maupin, raising Calyste's head to hers and kissing his hair as her tears fell on it. "No Calyste, you will forget everything you have just heard, you will mean nothing more to me!"

She stood up before the two men and hurled lightning bolts from those eyes that flashed out all of her soul.

"While Claude was speaking," she continued, "I imagined the beauty, the greatness of a love without hope—isn't that the only sentiment that brings us close to God? Do not love me Calyste; but I will love you as no woman ever loved!"

It was a cry more piercing than a wounded eagle ever shrieked from his aerie. Claude kneeled down, took Félicité's hand and kissed it.

"Leave us, my dear," said Mademoiselle des Touches to the young man, "your mother may be worried."

Calyste returned to Guérande with heavy steps, constantly turning back to see the light that burned from Béatrix's windows. He was surprised to feel so little compassion for Camille, he was almost annoyed with her for having deprived him of fifteen months of happiness. Then at times he felt the thrilling sensations that Camille had just provoked in him, he felt the tears she had left in his hair, he suffered her suffering, he thought he heard the sighs of this magnificent woman, so deeply desired only a few days ago. Upon opening the door of the manor where all was still, he saw his mother through the window, working by the light of that strange lamp as she waited for him. Tears came to his eyes at the sight of her.

"What happened to you now?" asked Fanny whose face expressed terrible anxiety.

His only reply was to take his mother in his arms, kiss her cheeks, her brow, her hair, with one of those passionate outbursts that overwhelm mothers and infuse them with gentle flames of the life they gave.

"It is you I love," said Calyste to his mother who was somewhat embarrassed and blushing, "you who live only for me, you whom I want to make happy."

"But what's come over you, my child," asked the baroness looking at her son. "What happened to you?"

"Camille loves me and I no longer love her," he said.

The baroness drew Calyste to her and kissed his forehead. In the heavy silence of the somber old room, further muted with tapestries, he could hear the rapid beating of a mother's heart. The Irishwoman was jealous of Camille and foresaw the truth. This mother, while waiting night after night for her son, had fathomed the passion of that woman; led by the flickering light of stubborn concentration, she had penetrated Camille's heart, and without being able to explain it, had envisioned in that barren female a fantasy of motherhood. Calyste's account terrified this simple, naive mother.

"Well then, go ahead and love Madame de Rochefide," she said after a pause, "she will cause me no pain."

Béatrix was not free, she would upset none of the projects formulated for Calyste's future, at least so Fanny thought. She saw in her a kind of daughter-in-law to love and not a rival mother to combat.

"But Béatrix will never love me!" Calyste cried out.

"Perhaps," replied the baroness slyly. "Didn't you say she would be alone tomorrow?"

"Yes."

"Well then, my beloved," she said blushing, "jealousy lies at the bottom of all our hearts, and I had no idea I would one day find it at the bottom of mine, for I did not think anyone could deprive me of my Calyste's affection." She sighed. "I thought marriage would be for you what it has been for me. What illuminations you have thrown into my soul these past two months, and what reflections shade your oh so natural love, my poor angel! Well then, continue to appear in love with your Mademoiselle des Touches; the marquise will be jealous and she will be yours."

"Oh mother darling, Camille would not have told me that!" Calyste exclaimed, taking his mother by the waist and kissing her neck.

"You make me highly perverse, you naughty child," she said, overjoyed by the radiance that hope brought to her son's face as he gaily climbed the turret stairs.

PART THREE

THE
RIVALRY

I Three Women for One   The following morning, Calyste told Gasselin to station himself on the road from Guérande to Saint-Nazaire, to watch for Mademoiselle des Touches' carriage and to count the number of people inside. Gasselin returned when the whole family was assembled and having breakfast.

"What is going on?" asked Mademoiselle du Guénic, "Gasselin is running as though Guérande were on fire."

"He must have caught the field mouse," said Mariotte who was bringing in the coffee, the milk, and the toast.

"But he is coming from town, not from the garden," replied Mademoiselle du Guénic.

"Yes, but the mouse's hole is behind the wall on the side of the square," said Mariotte.

"Monsieur le chevalier, there were five; four inside and the coachman."

"Two ladies in back?" asked Calyste.

"And two gentlemen in front," Gasselin continued.

"Saddle my father's horse, follow them, get to Saint-Nazaire when the boat leaves for Paimboeuf, and if the two men go aboard come back at full gallop to tell me."

Gasselin went out.

"My nephew, you are full of the devil this morning," said old Zéphirine.

"Let him amuse himself, sister," exclaimed the baron. "He was as gloomy as an owl, now he is as gay as a lark."

"Did you tell him perhaps that our dear Charlotte is coming?" asked the old maid turning to her sister-in-law.

"No," replied the baroness.

"I thought he wanted to be there when she arrived," Mademoiselle du Guénic archly said.

"If Charlotte is staying for three months at her aunt's, he surely has enough time to see her," the baroness replied.

"Oh my sister, what has happened since yesterday?" asked

the old maid. "You were so happy to know that Mademoiselle de Pen-Hoël was going to fetch her niece this morning."

"Jacqueline wants me to marry Charlotte to save me from damnation," said Calyste laughingly to his aunt, while eying his mother slyly. "I was on the mall when Mademoiselle de Pen-Hoël was talking to Monsieur du Halga. It never occurred to her that marriage at my age might be a greater damnation."

"It has been written in heaven that I shall die without knowing peace or happiness," said the old maid interrupting him. "I would have liked to see our family continued, and some of our lands redeemed, but nothing will come of it. Have you, my fine nephew, anything to weigh against such duties?"

"Why," said the baron, "will Mademoiselle des Touches prevent Calyste from marrying when he is ready? I must go to see her."

"I can assure you, father, Félicité will never be an obstacle to my marriage."

"I don't understand a thing!" said the old blind woman, who knew nothing of her nephew's sudden passion for the Marquise de Rochefide.

The mother kept her son's secret; in such matters, silence comes instinctively to all women. The old maid fell into deep meditation, listening with all her might to every voice, every sound to see if she could guess the mystery they were keeping from her.

Gasselin arrived shortly after and told his young master that it had not been necessary for him to go to Saint-Nazaire to know that Mademoiselle des Touches and her friend were returning alone; he had heard about it in town from Bernus, the driver who was carrying the baggage of the two gentlemen.

"They will be alone on the return trip!" Calyste exclaimed. "Saddle my horse."

From the sound of his young master's voice, Gasselin thought that something was seriously wrong. He saddled both horses, loaded the pistols without a word to anyone, and got dressed to accompany Calyste. Calyste was so pleased to know that Claude and Gennaro had left that he did not think of the meeting which would take place in Saint-Nazaire, he only imagined the pleasure of escorting the marquise. He took his father's hands and held them tenderly, he kissed his mother, and put his arm around his aunt's waist.

"I really do prefer him this way than sad," said Zéphirine.

"Where are you going, chevalier?" asked his father.

"To Saint-Nazaire."

"Well, I'll be hanged! . . . and when is the wedding?" asked the baron, thinking his son was racing off to see Charlotte de Kergarouët. "It's about time I became a grandfather."

When Gasselin indicated his evident intention of riding with Calyste, the young man realized he might ride back in Camille's carriage with Béatrix leaving his horse to Gasselin, and clapped him on the shoulder saying, "That was a bright idea."

"I should say so," Gasselin replied.

"My boy," called out his father coming out to the balcony with Fanny, "spare the horses, they have twelve leagues ahead of them."

Calyste left after exchanging a most significant look with his mother.

"Dearest love," she said, seeing him lower his head beneath the arch of the entrance way.

"May God protect him!" replied the baron, "for we cannot make another like him."

These words, somewhat in the ribald taste of country gentlemen, made the baroness shudder.

"My nephew hardly likes Charlotte well enough to go and meet her," said the old maid to Mariotte, who was clearing the table.

"Something exciting has happened at Les Touches, a marquise has arrived and he is running after her! Oh well, that's youth for you," said Mariotte.

"They will kill him, those women!" said Mademoiselle du Guénic.

"That won't kill him, mademoiselle, quite the opposite," replied Mariotte who seemed delighted by Calyste's enthusiasm.

Calyste was driving his horse at a killing pace when Gasselin fortunately asked him if he wanted to get there before the boat left, which was not at all his intention: he had no desire to be seen by Conti or by Claude. The young man slowed down his horse, and began looking complacently at the twin tracks of the carriage wheels left in the sandy part of the road. He was wildly gay at the mere thought: she came this way, she will return this way: her glance rested on these woods, on these trees! "What a charming path," he said to Gasselin.

"Ah monsieur, Brittany is the most beautiful place in the world," replied the servant. "Is there anywhere else where the bushes flower and the shaded roads wind like this?"

"Nowhere, Gasselin."

"There is Bernus' wagon," said Gasselin.

"Mademoiselle de Pen-Hoël and her niece are bound to be on it. Let's hide," said Calyste.

"Here sir? Are you mad? Hide in these sands?"

The wagon, which was in fact climbing a rather sandy hill above Saint-Nazaire, appeared before Calyste's eyes in all the rude simplicity of its Breton construction. To Calyste's great surprise, it was full.

"We had to leave Mademoiselle de Pen-Hoël, her sister and her niece behind, absolutely fuming, because all the space was taken by the Customs people," said the driver to Gasselin.

"That's the end!" Calyste exclaimed to himself.

The wagon was in fact filled with customs officials probably on their way to relieve the ones at the salt marshes. When Calyste arrived at the little esplanade around the church of Saint-Nazaire from which one sees Paimboeuf and the majestic estuary of the Loire struggling with the sea, he found Camille and the marquise waving their handkerchiefs in a last farewell to the two passengers being carried off by the steamboat. Béatrix was ravishing: her face softened by the shade of a straw hat trimmed with poppies and tied with a scarlet ribbon, a dress of flowered muslin, her graceful little foot advancing in its green gaiter, leaning on her slender parasol with her beautiful gloved hand. Nothing is more striking than a woman standing on a rock like a statue on its pedestal. Conti was able to see Calyste come up to Camille.

"I thought," said the young man to Mademoiselle des Touches, "that you would be going back without an escort."

"That was kind of you, Calyste," she said pressing his hand.

Béatrix turned around, looked at her young lover and threw him the most imperious glance in her repertory. The smile she caught sight of on Camille's eloquent lips made her sense the vulgarity of her own behavior, worthy of a *bourgeoise*. Madame de Rochefide then said to Calyste with a smile, "Was it not somewhat impertinent to think I could bore Camille along the way?"

"My dear, one man for two widows is hardly superfluous," said Mademoiselle des Touches, taking Calyste's arm and leaving Béatrix to watch the boat.

At that moment, Calyste heard, coming from the street that goes down to what can be called the port of Saint-Nazaire, the voices of Mademoiselle de Pen-Hoël, Charlotte, and Gasselin, all three chattering like magpies. The old maid was interrogating Gasselin and wanted to know why he and his master were in Saint-Nazaire where Mademoiselle des Touches' carriage had made a sensation. Before the young man could retreat, he was seen by Charlotte.

"There is Calyste," the little Breton lass called out.

"Go offer them my carriage; their maid can sit with my coachman," said Camille, who knew that Madame de Kergarouët, her daughter and Mademoiselle de Pen-Hoël had not found transportation.

Calyste, who was incapable of disobeying Camille, went to

deliver the message. As soon as she learned that she would be riding with the Marquise de Rochefide and the celebrated Camille Maupin, Madame de Kergarouët refused to understand her elder sister's reluctance to take advantage of what she called the devil's own carriage. In Nantes, one was in a somewhat more civilized latitude than in Guérande; there one admired Camille. She was considered the muse of Brittany and the pride of the region. She inspired as much curiosity as jealousy. The absolution granted in Paris by the world of society and fashion was consecrated by Mademoiselle des Touches' great personal fortune, and perhaps by her earlier success in Nantes which flattered itself on having been Camille Maupin's birthplace. Consequently, the vicomtesse, wildly curious, dragged her sister along without listening to her jeremiads.

"Hello, Calyste," said the little Kergarouët girl.

"Hello, Charlotte," replied Calyste, without offering her his arm.

Both taken aback, she by his coolness, he by his cruelty, climbed the hollow ravine that passed for a street in Saint-Nazaire and followed the two sisters without speaking. In that very instant, this girl of sixteen saw all her castles in Spain—constructed and furnished by her romantic longings—collapse. She and Calyste had so often played together when they were children, she was so deeply attached to him, she thought her future unassailable. She had arrived on the wings of dizzying happiness, like a bird plummeting toward a wheat field; she had been stopped in midflight without understanding what the obstacle was.

"What's the matter with you, Calyste?" she asked him, taking his hand.

"Nothing," replied the young man, freeing his hand hastily as he remembered the project concocted by his aunt and Mademoiselle de Pen-Hoël.

Tears came to Charlotte's eyes. She looked at Calyste, handsome Calyste, without hatred; but she was about to experience her first twinge of jealousy and feel the unspeakable rage of rivalry at the sight of those two beautiful Parisians, as she suspected the reason for Calyste's coolness.

Charlotte de Kergarouët was of medium height; she had an unrefined freshness, a little round face enlivened by seemingly intelligent black eyes, a full waist, a flat back, skinny arms and the curt, crisp speech of country girls who do not wish to be taken for bumpkins. She was very much the spoiled child of the family because of her aunt's predilection for her. At that moment, she was still wearing the plaid merino coat lined with green silk that she had worn on the boat. Her traveling dress, of cheap worsted with a chaste jumper bodice and a pleated collar, was bound to look horrible to her compared with the delicate gowns of Béatrix and Camille. She was painfully embarrassed by her white stockings, soiled by the rocks and by the boats she had jumped into, and by her ugly leather shoes, expressly selected to avoid spoiling anything good on the trip, following provincial customs. As to the Vicomtesse de Kergarouët, she was the prototype of a provincial. Tall, bony, faded; filled with pretensions that remained hidden until wounded; always talking and as a result able to catch hold of a few ideas, like a carom in billiards, which gave her the reputation of intelligence; always trying to humiliate Parisians with the fake good humor of provincial wisdom and a fake contentment on perpetual display; lowering herself expecting to be raised up and furious to be left on her knees; always fishing for compliments and rarely catching any; overdressed and undergroomed; mistaking a lack of affability for impertinence and thinking she could nonplus people by paying them no attention; refusing what she wanted in order to be begged beyond her ability to refuse; interested in what is no longer fashionable and then surprised not to be up to date; unable to hold out more than an hour without bringing in Nantes, the social lions of Nantes, the gossip of Nantes' high society, complaining about Nantes, criticizing Nantes, and taking as a personal of-

fense the words extorted from those who out of politeness
distractedly agreed with her. Her manners, her language, her
ideas had more or less rubbed off on her four daughters. To
meet Camille Maupin and Madame de Rochefide would open
up for her an entire future and provide the material for a hundred conversations! And so, she marched toward the church as
though she were about to take it by storm, waving her handkerchief which she unfolded to display the corners heavy with
domestic embroidery and worn lace. She had a loose-legged
walk that in a woman of forty-seven was of no further interest.

"Monsieur le chevalier," she said to Camille and Béatrix
indicating Calyste who approached pitifully with Charlotte,
"has communicated your kind offer, but my sister and I are
afraid to inconvenience you."

"It is not I, my sister, who will inconvenience these ladies,"
said the old maid haughtily, "for somewhere in Saint-Nazaire
I can surely find a horse to ride back."

Camille and Béatrix exchanged a sideways glance that
Calyste caught, and that one glance was enough to obliterate
all his childhood memories, his faith in the Kergarouët-Pen-
Hoëls, and undo forever the projects of the two families.

"We can perfectly well hold five in the carriage," replied
Mademoiselle des Touches, to whom Jacqueline had turned
her back. "Even if we were dreadfully uncomfortable, which
is not possible given the slenderness of your waists, it would be
well worth it for the pleasure of helping Calyste's friends. Your
maid, madame, will have a seat, and your baggage can go in
the back since I did not bring along a servant."

The vicomtesse was beside herself with thanks and chastised
her sister Jacqueline for having wanted her niece to arrive so
quickly that she had not been given the time to come by land
in her carriage; however, it was true that the post road was not
only longer but more costly, and she had to return promptly to
Nantes where she left three other little kittens who awaited
her impatiently, she said stroking her daughter's neck. Char-

lotte, looking up at her mother like a victim, led one to suppose that the vicomtesse thoroughly annoyed her daughters by showing them off as often as Corporal Trim, in *Tristram Shandy,* dons his cap.

"You are a fortunate mother, and you must be . . ." said Camille interrupting herself at the thought of the marquise deprived of her son when she left with Conti.

"Oh!" answered the vicomtesse, "if I have the misfortune to live my life in the country and in Nantes, I have the consolation of being adored by my children. Do you have children?" she asked of Camille.

"I am Mademoiselle des Touches," replied Camille. "Madame is the Marquise de Rochefide."

"Then you must be pitied for not knowing the greatest joy there is for most of us poor women. Isn't that so, madame," said the vicomtesse to make up for her blunder. "But you have so many compensations!"

Hot tears came to Béatrix's eyes. She quickly turned and walked over to the parapet with Calyste following her.

"Madame," Camille whispered to the vicomtesse, "didn't you know that the marquise is separated from her husband and hasn't seen her son in two years, nor does she know when she will see him again?"

"Good heavens!" said Madame de Kergarouët, "That poor woman! Is it a legal separation?"

"No, it is by choice," Camille answered.

"Oh indeed, I understand," the vicomtesse intrepidly replied.

Old Mademoiselle de Pen-Hoël, in despair at finding herself in the enemy camp, took up her position a few paces away with her beloved Charlotte. Calyste, after verifying that no one could see them, took the marquise's hand and kissed it leaving his tears on it. Béatrix whirled around, her eyes suddenly dried with rage. She was about to hurl some insult at him but could find nothing to say when she saw her own tears reflected in the face of that beautiful angel as deeply moved as she herself.

"My God, Calyste," Camille whispered in his ear when he returned with Madame de Rochefide, "you're going to have *that* for a mother-in-law and that little goose for a wife!"

"Because her aunt is rich," Calyste said ironically.

The whole group started off toward the inn, and the vicomtesse felt obliged to provide Camille with a satire on the savages of Saint-Nazaire.

"I love Brittany, madame," Félicité replied gravely. "I was born in Guérande."

Calyste could not refrain from admiring Mademoiselle des Touches who, by the sound of her voice, the steadiness of her gaze and the stability of her manners, put him at ease despite the horrible revelations that had been made during last night's scene. She nonetheless seemed a bit tired. Her features betrayed insomnia, they were almost swollen, but her forehead dominated the internal storm with cruel passivity.

"What queens!" he said to Charlotte pointing to the marquise and to Camille, as he gave his arm to the young girl, to Mademoiselle de Pen-Hoël's great pleasure.

"What an idea your mother had," said the old maid giving her bony arm to her niece, "to place herself in the company of that reprobate."

"Oh aunt! that woman is the pride of Brittany."

"The shame, little one. Are you also going to shine up to her?"

"Mademoiselle Charlotte is right; you are unfair," said Calyste.

"Oh you!" replied Mademoiselle de Pen-Hoël, "You have been bewitched by her."

"I bear the same friendship toward her as toward you," said Calyste.

"Since when do du Guénics tell lies?" said the old maid.

"Since the Pen-Hoëls have become deaf," retorted Calyste.

"You are not in love with her?" asked the old maid, overjoyed.

"I was, but no longer am," he replied.

"Naughty child! Why did you worry us so? I always knew that love is nonsense. The only thing that is solid is marriage," she said looking at Charlotte.

Charlotte, somewhat reassured and hoping to regain her advantage by reawakening all their childhood memories, squeezed Calyste's arm. Calyste, however, promised himself to come to a complete understanding with the little heiress.

"Ah, what delightful games of Mouche we'll have, Calyste, and how we'll laugh!"

The horses were ready. Camille led the vicomtesse and Charlotte to the back of the carriage, while she and the marquise took the forward seats; Jacqueline had disappeared. Calyste, deprived of the anticipated pleasure, accompanied the coach on horseback; the tired horses trotted along slowly enough for him to look at Béatrix. History has lost any record of the bizarre conversations between these four people whom chance so remarkably assembled in the same coach, for it is impossible to accept the thousand and one versions that made the rounds of Nantes of the anecdotes, the replies, the witticisms that the vicomtesse had from Camille Maupin *in person*. She took good care not to repeat, or even understand, Camille's replies to the idiotic questions that authors so often are asked and that serve as a cruel expiation for their few pleasures.

"How do you write your books?" asked the vicomtesse.

"Why in the same way that you do your tatting or needlepoint," replied Camille.

"And where did you find those deep observations and enchanting descriptions?"

"Where you find the clever things that you say, madame. There is nothing easier than writing, and if you wanted to . . ."

"Oh indeed, it's all in the wanting. I would never have guessed! And which is your favorite book?"

"It is so hard to choose among the little kittens."

"It is so hard to pay you any new compliments, you hear so many."

"Believe me, madame, I am very sensitive to the way you pay yours."

The vicomtesse did not wish to seem neglectful of the marquise and said to her, shrewdly, "I shall never forget this trip with Wit on one side and Beauty on the other."

"You flatter me, madame," said the marquise laughing. "It is hardly natural that wit should be noticed in the company of genius, and as yet I have said nothing really."

Charlotte, who was keenly aware of her mother's ridiculous behavior, looked at her in the hope of stopping her, but the vicomtesse fearlessly continued her skirmish with the mocking Parisian ladies. The young man who trotted alongside the carriage slowly and distractedly, could only see the two ladies on the forward seat, and his glance caressed them alternately while at the same time betraying the sadness of his thoughts. Obliged to remain exposed to his view, Béatrix constantly avoided looking at him by a subterfuge that exasperates suitors—she kept her shawl crossed over her crossed hands, giving the impression of deep meditation. At a spot where the road lies under fresh green shade like some delicious woodland grove, where the sound of the carriage wheels could barely be heard, where leaves brushed against the roof and a breeze carried the scent of balsam, Camille pointed out the loveliness of the place, and touching Béatrix's knee gestured toward Calyste, "Doesn't he ride well?"

"Calyste?" replied the vicomtesse. "He is a splendid horseman."

"Oh, Calyste is so nice," said Charlotte.

"There are so many Englishmen who look like him . . ." answered the marquise sluggishly, without finishing her sentence.

"His mother is Irish, an O'Brien," countered Charlotte, feeling personally attacked.

Camille and the marquise drove into Guérande with the Vicomtesse de Kergouët and her daughter to the great surprise of the whole gaping town. They left their traveling companions at the passageway to the du Guénic manor where within moments a crowd would have assembled. Calyste spurred his horse to inform his mother and aunt of the arrival of their dinner guests. The meal had been graciously postponed until four o'clock. The chevalier returned to escort the ladies. He then kissed Camille's hand and hoped to take Béatrix's as well, but she resolutely kept her arms folded; he looked at her beseechingly with an expression of wasted tenderness.

"Little fool," Camille said to him as she brushed his ear with a chaste kiss of friendship.

"It's true," he thought to himself, as the carriage drove off. "I keep forgetting my mother's advice, but I fear I will always forget it."

II FEMININE DIPLOMACY Mademoiselle de Pen-Hoël, who courageously arrived on a hired mount, the vicomtesse, and Charlotte found the table already laid and a cordial if not luxurious reception awaiting them. Old Zéphirine had a few bottles of good wine sent up from the depths of the cellar, and Mariotte surpassed herself with her Breton dishes. The vicomtesse, delighted by her trip with the illustrious Camille Maupin, tried to expound on modern literature and Camille's place in it; it was the same with modern literature as it had been with whist—neither the du Guénics, nor the priest who came later, nor the Chevalier du Halga, understood a thing. The Abbé Grimont and the old sailor partook of the dessert wine. As soon as Mariotte with Gasselin's help cleared the table, an enthusiastic cry for mouche went up. Joy spread through the house. Everyone thought Calyste was liberated and saw him married to Charlotte in no time at all. Calyste remained silent. For the first time in his life, he was making comparisons between the Kergarouëts and those two elegant, witty women of great taste who at that very moment were probably ridiculing the two provincials, to judge by that first look they exchanged. Fanny, who knew Calyste's secret, observed her son's sadness; all of Charlotte's flirtatiousness and all of the vicomtesse's barbs had no effect on him. Her dear boy was bored; his body was in that room where once the pleasantries of mouche amused him, but his mind was wandering around Les Touches. How could she send him to Camille, she wondered, sympathizing with her son, loving him and sharing his boredom. Her awakened tenderness inspired her thinking.

"You are aching to go to Les Touches to see *her*," said Fanny in Calyste's ear. He replied with a smile and a blush that made this adorable mother quiver to the depths of her heart.

"Madame," she said to the vicomtesse, "you will be most uncomfortable in the wagon tomorrow, and above all forced to leave very early. Would it not be better to take Mademoiselle des Touches' carriage? Go Calyste," she said looking at her son, "and arrange it at Les Touches, but come back to us quickly."

"It won't take ten minutes," Calyste exclaimed, frantically kissing his mother who followed him out to the perron.

Calyste ran like a gazelle and arrived in the hall of Les Touches just as Camille and Béatrix were coming out of the dining room. He had the presence of mind to offer his arm to Félicité.

"You have abandoned the vicomtesse and her daughter for us?" she said pressing his arm. "We are fully cognizant of the extent of this sacrifice."

"Are these Kergarouëts related to the Portenduères and old Admiral Kergarouët, whose widow married Charles de Vandenesse?" Madame de Rochefide asked Camille.

"The admiral was Charlotte's great-uncle," Camille replied.

"She is a sweet girl," said Béatrix, sitting down on a Gothic chair, "she will be just right for Monsieur du Guénic."

"Such a marriage will never take place," Camille retorted.

Taken aback by the marquise's cool indifference, and by her indication that the little Breton girl was the only possible match for him, Calyste remained speechless and mindless.

"Why do you say that, Camille?" asked Madame de Roche-fide.

"My dear," answered Camille, seeing Calyste's despair, "I did not advise Conti to get married, and I think I behaved charmingly toward him. You are not generous."

Béatrix looked at her friend with surprise mixed with vague suspicion. Calyste more or less understood Camille's devotion when seeing that pale blush on her cheeks that announced her more intense emotions. He approached her rather awkwardly, took her hand and kissed it. Camille nonchalantly sat down at the piano, turning her back to them and leaving them almost alone, like a woman equally sure of her friend and of the admirer she claims as her own. She improvised variations on themes unconsciously provided by her mood, for they were extremely sad. The marquise pretended to be listening but she was observing Calyste who, too young and too naive to play the part assigned by Camille, was in ecstasy before his true idol. After an hour, during which time Mademoiselle des Touches naturally fell prey to jealousy, Béatrix went to her own rooms. Camille immediately led Calyste into her room so as not to be overheard, for women have a remarkable instinct for mistrust.

"My dear boy," she said, "you must appear to be in love with me or you are lost. You are a child, you know nothing about women, you only know how to love. To love and to be loved are two very different things. You are running the risk of great suffering, and I want you to be happy. If you irritate not her pride but her obstinacy, she is capable of racing away to be near Conti, outside of Paris. What would become of you then?"

"I would still love her," replied Calyste.

"You would no longer see her."

"Oh yes," he said.

"How?"

"I would follow her."

"But you are as poor as Job, my child."

"My father, Gasselin, and I managed for three months in Vendée with one hundred fifty francs, walking day and night."

"Calyste," said Mademoiselle des Touches, "listen to me carefully. I see that you are too honest to pretend. Since I do not wish to corrupt so fine a nature as yours, I shall take the whole thing upon myself. You will be loved by Béatrix."

"Is it possible?" Calyste asked joining his hands.

"Yes," Camille replied, "but it will be necessary to loosen the bonds she has placed on herself. I will lie for you; however, you must not disturb anything in the complex arrangements I am about to undertake. The marquise has an aristocratic shrewdness and an innate lack of trust. Never was a hunter after more difficult game. In this case, my poor child, the hunter must be advised by his hound. Can you promise me blind obedience? I shall be your Fox," she said giving herself the name of Calyste's prize hound.

"What must I do?" replied the young man.

"Very little," Camille answered. "You will come here every day at noon. Like an impatient mistress, I shall be waiting at one of the corridor windows that looks out on the road to Guérande, watching your arrival. I shall escape to my room in order not to be seen, and not to make you feel the weight of a passion that is burdensome to you. But from time to time you will see me and wave to me with your handkerchief. In the courtyard and coming up the stairs, you will look somewhat annoyed. That should cost you no effort, my dear, should it?" she asked, leaning her head on his chest. "You will not rush; you will look through the staircase window that overlooks the garden in search of Béatrix. When she is there (she will surely be strolling there, I promise you!), if she notices you, you will go directly but slowly into the little salon and from there to my room. If you see me at the window spying on your treachery, you will step back quickly so that I do not catch you begging for a glance from Béatrix. Once in my room you are my prisoner, and we shall remain there together until four o'clock, you reading, I smoking. You will be thoroughly annoyed not to see her, but I'll find you some engrossing books. You have read nothing of George Sand. I am sending one of my servants to Nantes this very evening to buy her books and also some others by authors you don't know. I shall go out first, but you will not leave your book or come into my little sitting room until you hear Béatrix talking with me. Whenever you see a volume of music open on the piano you may ask to remain. I give you permission to be as openly intimate with me as you can, and all will go well."

"I know Camille that you have for me the rarest affection; it makes me regret that I ever saw Béatrix," he said with charming candor, "but what are you hoping for?"

"In a week, Béatrix will be madly in love with you."

"O my God! Could it be?" he said falling at Camille's knees with hands clasped as though in prayer, while she looked at him, moved and happy to give him pleasure at her own expense.

"Listen to me carefully," she said. "If you have, I don't mean an extensive conversation with the marquise, but even an exchange of a few words, if you allow her to ask you anything, if you fail in your role of mute, which is easy enough to play, then understand this," she said gravely, "you will lose her forever."

"I really don't understand a thing you're saying, Camille," Calyste exclaimed looking at her with adorable innocence.

"If you understood, you would not be the sublime child, the noble, beautiful Calyste that you are," she said, taking his hand and kissing it.

Calyste then did something he had never done before. He took Camille by the waist and kissed her neck gently, without passion, but with tenderness, the way he kissed his mother. Mademoiselle des Touches could not hold back a flood of tears.

"Go my child, and tell your vicomtesse that my carriage is at her disposal."

Calyste would have liked to stay, but he was obliged to obey her imperative and imperious gesture. He came back to Guérande full of joy, convinced he would be loved by the beauteous Rochefide within eight days. The mouche players rediscovered in him the Calyste who had been missing for the last two months. Charlotte thought herself responsible for the change. Mademoiselle de Pen-Hoël was charming in the way she teased Calyste. The Abbé Grimont tried to read in the baroness' eyes the reason for the tranquillity he saw in them. Chevalier du Halga rubbed his hands with glee. The two old maids were as full of life as lizards. The vicomtesse owed one hundred sous in penalties. Zéphirine's cupidity was so aroused that she deeply regretted not seeing the cards, and spoke sharply to her sister-in-law who was distracted by Calyste's good humor and from time to time asked him questions without understanding the answers. The game lasted until eleven. There were two defections; the baron and the chevalier fell asleep in their respective chairs. Mariotte made some crêpes, the baroness brought out her special tea. The illustrious house of du Guénic served to the Kergarouëts and Mademoiselle de Pen-Hoël a supper of fresh butter, fruit, and cream, for which the silver teapot was taken out of the cabinet along with the English china sent to the baroness by one of her aunts. This appearance of modern splendor in the ancient hall, the exquisite grace of the baroness, raised like a proper Irishwoman to brew and serve tea, that great English ceremony, created a scene of great charm. The most unbridled luxury could not have achieved the simple, modest, noble effect produced by this joyful hospitality. When there was no one left in the room but the baroness and her son, she looked at Calyste curiously.

"What happened at Les Touches this evening?" she asked.

Calyste related the bizarre instructions Camille had given him and the hope she had kindled.

"Poor woman!" she cried, clasping her hands and pitying Mademoiselle des Touches for the first time.

A few moments after Calyste's departure, Béatrix, on hearing him leave Les Touches, came back to her friend whom she found crying on a sofa.

"What is it, Félicité?" the marquise asked.

"I am forty years old and in love, my dear!" said Mademoiselle des Touches in a voice raging with fury that made her eyes suddenly dry and bright. "If you only knew, Béatrix, how many tears I shed over the lost days of my youth! To be loved out of pity, to know that one's happiness is merely the result of hard work, feline cunning, and snares laid out for the innocence and virtue of a child—isn't that infamous? Fortunately, it is possible to achieve a kind of absolution in the infinitude of love, the energy of happiness and the certainty of forever being superior to all other women by engraving in a young heart one's memory through unforgettable pleasures and unparalleled devotion. Indeed, if he asked me to, I would throw myself into the sea at his first request. At times, I am surprised to discover that I wish he would; it would be a sacrifice, not a suicide . . . . Ah, Béatrix, you have imposed a terrible task on me by coming here. I know it is hard to win out over you, but you love Conti, you are noble and generous, and you will not deceive me. You will, on the contrary, help me hold on to my Calyste. I was prepared for the impression you have made on him, but I have not committed the mistake of seeming to be jealous; that would only mean honing the edge. Quite the opposite, I announced your arrival by painting you in such brilliant colors that you could never measure up to my portrait, and to my misfortune, you are even more beautiful."

This violent elegy, in which truth mingled with deceit, completely misled Madame de Rochefide. Claude Vignon had told Conti of the reasons for his departure, and Béatrix was naturally informed. She therefore gave proof of generosity in appearing cold to Calyste. But at that moment, there arose in her heart a sensation of joy that thrills any woman on learning she is loved. The love she inspires in a man produces unhypocritical admiration which she cannot refrain from enjoying, and when that man belongs to a friend, his admiration causes more than enjoyment; it becomes heavenly bliss. Béatrix sat down beside her friend and paid her all manner of little compliments.

"You don't have a single white hair," she said, "you don't have a wrinkle, your temples are still fresh looking, while I know more than one thirty-year-old woman obliged to hide hers. Look here my dear," she said raising her curls, "do you see what this trip cost me?"

The marquise showed her the barely noticeable puffiness that spoiled the delicacy of her skin. She raised her sleeves and displayed a similar puckering at the wrists where the transparency of the already wrinkled skin revealed the network of enlarged veins and three deep lines made a bracelet of creases.

"Aren't these, in the words of a writer who analyzed our misfortunes, the two spots in women that never lie? One must have suffered considerably to recognize the truth of his cruel observation. Fortunately for us, most men understand nothing of these things and do not read that vile author."

"Your letter told me everything," replied Camille. "Happiness is never conceited, and you boasted too much about being happy. In love, isn't truth deaf, dumb, and blind? And so, knowing you had reasons for leaving Conti, I dreaded your visit here. My dear, Calyste is an angel, he is as good as he is beautiful; the poor boy could not resist a single one of your glances; he admires you too much already to avoid falling in love with you at the slightest encouragement. Your disdain will prevent my losing him. I confess with the shamelessness of true passion: to take him from me would kill me. *Adolphe,* that dreadful book by Benjamin Constant, has told us only of Adolphe's sufferings; but what about the woman's? He did not observe them closely enough to portray them for us, and what woman would dare reveal them? They would discredit our sex, humiliate our virtues, aggrandize our vices. Ah, if I judge them by my fears, those sufferings must be the sufferings of hell. However, if he leaves me, my decision is made."

"What have you decided?" asked Béatrix with an intensity that made Camille shudder.

The two friends looked at each other with the penetrating glance of two Venetian inquisitors, a swift glance in which their souls collided and sparked like two flints. The marquise lowered her eyes.

"After man, there is only God," the famous lady replied. "God is the unknown. I would fling myself into this as though into an abyss. Calyste just swore to me that he only admired you as one admires a painting, but at twenty-eight, you are at the peak of your beauty. The struggle between him and me has therefore begun with a lie. Fortunately, I know what to do to win."

"What is that?"

"That is my secret, my dear. Allow me the benefits of my age. If Claude Vignon has brutally hurled me into the depths, I who had raised myself to a level I thought inaccessible, then at least I will gather all the pale, drooping, but enchanting little flowers that grow at the foot of the precipice."

The marquise was being molded like a piece of wax by Mademoiselle des Touches who took savage delight in enmeshing her in ruses. Camille sent her friend to bed tingling with curiosity, floating between jealousy and generosity, but certainly much concerned with the handsome Calyste.

"She will be delighted to deceive me," she thought as she gave her a goodnight kiss.

Then, when she was alone, the author gave way to the woman. She collapsed in tears. She filled the bowl of her hookah with tobacco macerated in opium and spent the better part of the night smoking, thus anesthetizing the pain of her love and envisioning across the clouds of smoke Calyste's exquisite head.

"What a marvelous book to write—the story of my own suffering," she said to herself. "But it has already been done. Sappho lived before me, and Sappho was young! What a heart-rending heroine, a woman of forty! Smoke your hookah, my poor Camille, you don't even have what it takes to make a poem of your unhappiness, and that is the final blow!"

She finally went to bed at dawn, having intermingled tears, outbursts of rage, and sublime decisions in her lengthy meditation, during which she considered the mysteries of the Catholic religion, something she never even dreamed about in her unfettered, unbelieving life as an artist.

The next day, Calyste, whose mother had told him to follow Camille's instructions to the letter, arrived at noon and mysteriously crept up to Camille's room where he found the books. Félicité stayed in an armchair, busying herself with her pipe while contemplating the savage landscape of the marshes, the sea, and Calyste, with whom she exchanged a few words about Béatrix. At a given moment, seeing the marquise walking in the garden, she went to the window, where she let her friend see her, and drew the curtains to keep the light out leaving only a narrow band that fell on Calyste's book.

"Today, my dear, I shall ask you to stay for dinner," she said ruffling his hair, "and you will refuse while looking at the marquise; you should have no difficulty making her understand how much you regret not being able to stay."

Around four o'clock, Camille left the room and went to play the atrocious comedy of her fake happiness for the marquise, whom she brought to her sitting room. Calyste came out of the bedroom and at once understood the awkwardness of his position. The look he gave Béatrix, though anticipated by Félicité, was even more expressive than she expected. Béatrix was wearing a charming outfit.

"How fetching you look, my sweet," said Camille when Calyste left.

This stratagem went on for six days. It was accompanied, to Calyste's unknowing, by the most skillful conversations between Camille and her friend. A relentless duel ensued between these two women during which they made use of ruses, feints, fake generosity, false confessions, calculated admissions, with one concealing and the other exposing her love, and all the while the steel, sharpened and heated by Camille's treacherous words, reached the core of her friend's heart pricking a few of those wicked impulses that honest women have such trouble suppressing. Béatrix was finally offended by Camille's suspicions; she found them unflattering to both of them. She was enchanted to discover in this great writer the same weaknesses shared by the rest of her sex; she wanted to have the pleasure of showing her where her superiority ended and her humiliation began.

"My dearest, what are you going to find to say to him today?" Béatrix asked, looking maliciously at her friend when the so-called lover asked to stay on. "On Monday we had things to talk about alone, on Tuesday the dinner wasn't worth staying for, on Wednesday you didn't want to anger the baroness, on Thursday you wanted to go for a long walk with me, yesterday you said good-bye to him as soon as he opened his mouth. Well then, today I want him to stay, poor boy!"

"So soon, my pet?" said Camille with biting irony. The marquise blushed. "You may remain, Monsieur du Guénic," she said with the combined airs of a queen and a woman slighted.

Béatrix became hard and icy; she was cutting, sarcastic, and thoroughly unpleasant to Calyste who was finally sent off by Félicité to play mouche with Mademoiselle de Kergarouët.

"She's not dangerous, that one isn't," said Béatrix smiling.

Young people in love are like people dying of starvation; the preparations of the cook cannot satisfy them, they are too concerned with the end to understand the means. Returning to

Guérande from Les Touches, Calyste was obsessed with Béatrix. He was unaware of the consummate feminine skill Félicité was employing—to use a cliché—to further his interests. During that entire week, the marquise had written only one letter to Conti, a symptom of indifference that had not escaped Camille's notice. The whole of Calyste's life was now concentrated in that brief instant when he saw Béatrix. That drop of water, instead of quenching his thirst, only intensified it. The magic words "You will be loved!" said to him by Camille and seconded by his mother, were the talisman that kept his passion under control. He consumed time; he no longer slept, he cheated his insomnia by reading; each evening he brought back what Mariotte called wagonloads of books. His aunt cursed Mademoiselle des Touches, but his mother, who had often gone to his room when seeing his light on, knew the secret of these vigils. Although she had never gone beyond the timidities of an innocent young girl to whom the secrets of love had never been disclosed, she managed by virtue of her maternal tenderness to acquire certain insight. Nevertheless, the depths of this emotion remained clouded over and obscure to her, and she was considerably alarmed by her son's state. She was frightened by this sole, incomprehensible desire that devoured him. Calyste no longer thought about anything else; he seemed always to have Béatrix before his eyes. In the evening during the game, his absentmindedness resembled his father's lapses into sleep. On finding him so different from what he had been when he thought himself in love with Camille, the baroness recognized with near terror the symptoms that indicated true passion— something utterly unknown in that ancient manor. Feverish irritability and constant distraction had reduced him to a state of dullness. He often remained for hours staring at a figure in the tapestry. One morning, his mother advised him not to go to Les Touches any more and to give up those two women.

"Not go again to Les Touches!" Calyste exclaimed.

"No my love, go, go, don't get angry," she replied, kissing the eyes that had flamed at her.

In a condition such as this, Calyste risked losing the fruits of Camille's brilliant strategy through the Breton fury of his passion, over which he was no longer master. He swore to himself, in spite of his promises to Félicité, that he would see Béatrix and talk to her. He wanted to gaze into her eyes, plunge into their depths, study the smallest details of her clothing, inhale its fragrance, listen to the music of her voice, follow the graceful flow of her movements, take in at a glance all of her body, survey it, like a great general surveying the field on which a decisive battle will be fought; all this he wanted with the fervor of a lover. He had become prey to a desire that deafened his hearing, obscured his intelligence, weakened him to the point where he no longer recognized obstacles or distances and was no longer even aware of his own body. He then began thinking of going to Les Touches before the decided hour in the hope of finding Béatrix in the garden. He knew she usually strolled there before lunch. One morning, Mademoiselle des Touches and the marquise went to the salt marshes and the lagoon edged with silken sand where the sea penetrates, suggesting a lake in the midst of the dunes. They came back chatting as they turned into the yellow paths around the lawn.

"If this landscape interests you," Camille was saying, "you must go with Calyste to visit Le Croisic. There are marvelous rocks there, and cascades of granite, and little bays with natural pools, remarkable things filled with surprises, and then there is the sea with its thousands of marble fragments, a world of entertainments. You will see women making fuel, so to speak. They slap clods of manure on the walls to dry, then they pile them up like squares of peat in Paris and in the winter burn them for fuel."

"You would trust Calyste?" said the marquise laughing, which proved that Camille's sulking the day before had forced her into thinking about Calyste.

"Oh my dear, when you get to know the angelic nature of such a creature, you will understand me. Beauty in him is the least of it; one must delve into the purity of that heart, into that innocence which marvels at every step it takes into the realm of love. What fealty, what candor, what grace! How right the ancients were to make a cult of beauty. I forget which traveler tells us that wild horses choose the most beautiful among them as their leader. Beauty, my dear, is the essence of things. It is Nature's hallmark for her most perfect creations; it is the truest of symbols as it is the greatest of accidents. Has anyone ever imagined a deformed angel? Isn't an angel the combination of grace and strength? What is it that makes us stand for hours on end before certain Italian paintings in which genius has sought for years to accomplish one of those accidents of nature? Let us be honest, wasn't it the ideal of beauty that we combined with moral greatness? Well then, Calyste is one of those dreams brought to fulfillment. He has the courage of a lion, who remains peaceful without suspecting his kingliness. When he feels at ease he is heavenly; I enjoy his girlish timidity. Within his heart, I find myself freed of all the corruptions, all the ideas of science, literature, worldliness, politics—all the useless accessories that stifle our happiness. I become what I have never been, a child! I am certain of him, but I like to pretend jealousy; it pleases him. Furthermore, that is part of my secret."

Béatrix walked along, silent and pensive. Camille was going through indescribable martyrdom and threw sideways glances at her that were like darting flames.

"Oh my dear, you are a lucky woman!" said Béatrix leaning on Camille's arm with a heaviness that implied the fatigue of a long and secret struggle.

"Oh yes, very lucky!" replied the pathetic Félicité with savage bitterness.

The two women sank down on a bench, exhausted. Never had any creature of her sex been subjected to more ingenious seductions or to more penetrating Machiavellianism than the marquise for the preceding week.

"While I . . . I have to look at Conti's infidelities, swallow them . . ."

"Then why don't you leave him?" said Camille, spotting a propitious moment for striking a decisive blow.

"Could I?"

"Oh! My poor darling."

They remained there staring fixedly at a clump of trees.

"I am going in to hurry lunch," said Camille, "this walk has given me an appetite."

"Our conversation has taken mine away," said Béatrix.

Béatrix in her morning attire stood out against the masses of green foliage as a white form. Calyste, who had stolen into the garden through the drawing room, walked slowly along the path as though to meet the marquise by chance. Béatrix could not withhold a shudder of surprise on seeing him.

"In what way did I displease you yesterday?" Calyste asked, after a brief exchange of banalities.

"But you neither please me nor displease me," she answered gently.

Her tone, her manner, her exquisite grace encouraged Calyste.

"I am indifferent to you," he said in a voice made hoarse by the tears gathering in his eyes.

"Shouldn't we be indifferent to one another?" replied the marquise. "We each have a serious attachment . . . ."

"Oh," said Calyste impetuously, "I did love Camille, but I no longer do."

"What then do you do all afternoon every day?" she asked with a perfidious smile. "I can hardly imagine that in spite of Camille's passion for tobacco she prefers a cigar to you, or that despite your admiration for lady writers, you spend four hours reading novels by women."

"You know then . . ." said the naive Breton ingenuously, his face alight with the happiness of seeing his idol.

"Calyste!" Camille cried out violently, coming up and interrupting him. She took him by the arm, leading him off a few steps. "Is that what you promised me?"

The marquise was able to overhear this reproach as Mademoiselle des Touches went off scolding Calyste. She was stupefied by Calyste's confession, though she understood nothing. Madame de Rochefide was not as shrewd as Claude Vignon. The truth of the horrible and sublime role played by Camille lay in the infamous greatness that women only resort to in extremes. At that point, their hearts are shattered, their emotions as women have ended, and what begins is an abnegation that flings them into hell or leads them into heaven.

<hr />

III Correspondence During lunch, to which Calyste had been invited, the marquise, whose sentiments were proud and noble and who had already done an about-face stifling the love that was burgeoning in her heart, was neither cold nor unpleasant to Calyste; but her kind indifference pained him. Félicité proposed that they make an excursion the day after next to the singular countryside that lay between Les Touches, Le Croisic and Le Bourg de Batz. She asked Calyste to make arrangements the following day for a boat and sailors in case they wished to be out on the sea. She would take care of the food, the horses, and everything needed to avoid fatigue. Béatrix put an end to the whole idea by saying she would not run the risk of being seen dashing around the countryside. Calyste's face, until then radiant with joy, suddenly darkened.

"And what are you afraid of, my dear?" asked Camille.

"My position is too delicate for me to compromise, if not my reputation, then my happiness," she said emphatically while looking at the young Breton. "You know how jealous Conti is, and if he knew ...."

"Who would tell him?"

"Isn't he coming back for me?"

These words made Calyste grow pale. Despite Félicité's urging, and the young Breton's entreaties, Madame de Rochefide was unbending and gave proof of what Camille had termed her obstinacy. Calyste, in spite of Félicité's reassurances, left Les Touches stricken with one of those lover's agonies whose intensity can reach madness. Once back at the du Guénic manor, he did not leave his room except for dinner, and returned to it immediately after. At ten o'clock, his anxious mother came to see him and found him in the midst of a pile of crossed-out, crumpled papers. He was writing to Béatrix for he distrusted Camille; the marquise's manner had singularly encouraged him during their meeting in the garden. Contrary to what one might think, a first love letter was never a geyser bubbling out of the heart. For any young man still untainted by corruption, a letter like this is accompanied by outbursts too overflowing, too repetitive to avoid being the elixir of several letters attempted, rejected, rewritten. Here is the one Calyste finally ended with, and that he read to his gaping mother. To her, the ancient manor seemed to be burning; her son's passion flamed through it like tongues of fire.

CALYSTE TO BÉATRIX *Madame, I loved you when you were as yet only a dream for me; you can imagine the fervor of my love now that I have seen you. The dream has been surpassed by the reality. My regret is that I am telling you nothing you do not already know when I tell you how beautiful you are. However, your manifold beauty has perhaps never awakened in anyone as many responses as it has in me. You are beautiful in more ways than one, and I have studied you so carefully during the days and nights I have devoted to you that I have penetrated the mysteries of your being, the secrets of your heart, and your unappreciated delicacy. Have you ever*

*been understood and adored as you deserve to be?
Let me tell you, there is not a single trait in you that
has gone unnoticed by me: your pride echoes my
own, the nobility of your expressions, the grace of
your carriage, the distinctiveness of your movements,
everything about you is harmonious with the
thoughts, the desires hidden in the depths of your
soul. It is in divining these things that I have come
to believe myself worthy of you. If in these last days
I had not become an extension of you, another you,
would I speak to you about myself? To read about
me would be egotism! This letter is much more concerned with you than with Calyste. In order to write
to you, Béatrix, I have silenced my twenty years, I
have taken myself in hand, I have aged my mind, or
perhaps you have aged it by causing a week of the
most dreadful suffering, certainly caused unwittingly
by you. Do not think me one of those vulgar lovers
of whom you so rightfully made fun. Oh, the great
merit of loving a young, beautiful, intelligent, noble
woman! Alas, I do not even believe I merit you!
What am I for you? A child attracted by sublime
beauty and moral integrity as an insect is by light.
You can do nothing else but trample the flowers of
my soul, yet my entire happiness would be to see
you trample them. Total devotion, limitless faith, unbridled love, all these treasures of a sincere and loving heart are meaningless; they make it possible to
love but not to be loved. At times, I cannot understand how such wild fanaticism does not succeed in
arousing the idol; when I see your cold severity, I
feel frozen. It is your disdain that has the upper
hand, not my adoration. Why? You cannot possibly
despise me as much as I love you; should the weaker
emotion then win out over the stronger? I loved*

Félicité with all the power of my heart; I forgot her in one day, in the one moment I saw you. She was my error, you are my truth. You have, without knowing it, destroyed my happiness, yet you owe me nothing in return. I loved Camille without hope, you give me no hope; nothing but the divinity has changed. I was a pagan, now I am a Christian, that is all there is to it. However, you have taught me that to love is the prime happiness, to be loved is secondary. According to Camille, to love briefly is not to love at all; love that does not grow from day to day is a miserable passion; and in order to grow, love must not be able to foresee its end. She could see the setting of our sun. On seeing you, I understood these arguments that I had been combatting with all of my youth, all the fire of my desires, and all the tyrannous asceticism of my twenty years. That sublime, magnificent Camille mingled her tears with mine. I can, therefore, love you on earth and in heaven as one loves God. If you loved me, you would not have available Camille's reasons for undermining my efforts. We are both young, we can fly with the same wings, under the same sky, without fearing the storm anticipated by that eagle. But what am I saying? I am carried far beyond the modesty of my hopes. You no longer believe in the submission, the patience, the mute adoration that I have just begged you not to injure carelessly. I know, Béatrix, that you cannot love me without losing your self-respect. And so I ask for no return. Camille once said, when speaking of herself, that there was a certain fatality inherent in names. This fatality I foresaw for myself in your name when, standing on the dock in Guérande looking out over the edge of the ocean, I was struck by the thought that you will pass through my life as

*Beatrice passed through Dante's. My heart will pro-
vide the pedestal for a white, vindictive, jealous, op-
pressive statue. You are prohibited from loving me;
you will suffer a thousand deaths, you will be betrayed, humiliated, unhappy. There is in you a demonic pride that binds you to your column; you
will perish bringing down the temple with you, like
Samson. These things I do not foresee clairvoyantly;
my love is too blind. Camille has told me these
things. It is not my mind that speaks to you now,
it is hers. I no longer have a mind when it comes to
you. A tide of blood surges from my heart, its waves
obscuring my reason, depriving me of my strength,
paralyzing my tongue, breaking my knees and making them bend. All I can do is adore you, no matter
what you do. Camille calls your resoluteness obstinacy; I defend you believing it is dictated by virtue.
You are only more beautiful in my eyes. I know my
destiny: Breton pride is on a par with the woman
who has made a virtue of her own. And so dear
Béatrix, be kind and consoling to me. When victims
were selected for immolation they were crowned
with flowers. You owe me the garlands of pity, the
music of sacrifice. Am I not the proof of your greatness, and will you not be elevated by the exaltation of
my love—rejected despite its sincerity, its undying
ardor? Ask Camille how I behaved once she told me
that she loved Claude Vignon. I remained mute, I
suffered in silence. For you, I will find even greater
strength if you do not torment me, if you appreciate
my heroism. One word of praise from you would
enable me to endure the agonies of martyrdom. If
you persist in this icy silence, in this deadly contempt, you will lead me to believe I am a threat. Oh,
be with me everything that you are—charming, gay,*

*witty, tender. Speak to me about Gennaro, as Ca-
mille spoke to me about Claude. Aside from love I
have no talent, there is nothing to fear in me, and I
will behave in your presence as though I did not love
you. Can you reject the entreaty of such a humble
love, of a poor child whose only request of his lamp
is that it give him light, of his sun that it give him
warmth? The one you love will continue to see you,
while poor Calyste has only a few days ahead and
then you will be done with him. And so, I shall return to Les Touches, and you will not refuse my arm
to escort you on a visit along the shores of Le Croisic
and Le Bourg de Batz, will you? If you do not
come, that will be an answer and Calyste will hear
it."*

There were four more pages of cramped writing in which
Calyste explained the terrible threat that lay in those last words
by relating his childhood and his life, but he proceeded by exclamations; there were many of those dots so favored by modern literature in dangerous passages, offered to the reader like
planks on which to cross the gulf. This naive portrayal would
be repetitive in our story. If it could not move Madame de
Rochefide, it would hardly interest the seeker of strong emotions. It did make his mother cry. "Have you really not been
happy?"

This wild poem of emotions that erupted in Calyste's heart
like a volcano, and would go on to wreak havoc in yet another,
frightened the baroness. This was the first time in her life she
had ever read a love letter. Calyste was in a terrible dilemma;
he did not know how to deliver his letter. The Chevalier du
Halga was still in the room where they were playing out the
last round of a very exciting mouche. Charlotte de Kergarouët,
in despair over Calyste's indifference, tried to charm the elders
in the hope of guaranteeing her marriage through them.

Calyste followed his mother and reappeared in the room, the letter in an inside pocket scorching his heart. He moved about nervously, coming and going like a bird that has mistakenly flown into a room. Finally, both mother and son maneuvered the Chevalier du Halga into the hall, sending away Mademoiselle de Pen-Hoël's little servant and Mariotte, who had been chatting there.

"What can they want of the chevalier?" asked the aged Zéphirine of the aged Pen-Hoël.

"Calyste behaves like a lunatic," she replied. "He pays no more attention to Charlotte than if she were a marsh worker."

"What is the best way to get a letter to one's mistress in secret?" Calyste whispered into the chevalier's ear.

"One puts the letter into the hand of her maid, along with a few louis, for sooner or later the maid is in on the secret and it is better that it be sooner," replied the chevalier, unable to suppress a smile. "However, it is wiser to do it oneself."

"A few louis!" exclaimed the baroness.

Calyste went for his hat, ran to Les Touches and appeared there like a ghost in the little sitting room where he heard Béatrix and Camille talking. Calyste, with the sudden ingenuity that love inspires, threw himself carelessly on the couch beside the marquise, taking her hand into which he put the letter without Félicité, observant as she was, being able to notice. Calyste's heart heaved with a sensation that was both painful and delicious as he felt his hand grasped by Béatrix who, without interrupting her sentence or appearing to be distracted, slipped the letter into her glove.

"You throw yourself on women as though they were couches," she said laughing.

"But he does not go as far as the Turks," retorted Félicité, who could not resist the epigram.

Calyste stood up, took Camille's hand and kissed it. He then went over to the piano sounding all the notes as he slid his finger in one long scale down the keyboard. This joyful enthusiasm perplexed Camille who called him over.

"What is it?" she asked in a whisper.

"Nothing," he replied.

"There is something going on between them," she said to herself.

The marquise was impenetrable. Camille tried to make Calyste talk in the hope he would give himself away. But he, pleading his mother's anxiety, left Les Touches at eleven o'clock having withstood the fire of Camille's piercing glances; it was the first time he had ever made such an excuse.

After an agitated night filled with thoughts of Béatrix, after twenty trips to Guérande during the morning in anticipation of a reply that did not come, the marquise's maid appeared at the Hôtel du Guénic bearing this reply which Calyste went to read at the far end of the garden under the arbor.

BÉATRIX TO CALYSTE *You are a noble child, yet a child. You owe yourself to Camille who adores you. You would find in me neither the perfections that distinguish her, nor the happiness that she lavishes on you. Contrary to what you think, it is she who is young and I who am old. Her heart is filled with treasures and mine is empty; she has for you a devotion that you do not appreciate enough. She is devoid of egotism and lives entirely for you, while I would be filled with doubts, I would drag you into a life of problems, of ignominy, a life ruined by my transgression. Camille is free, she can come and go as she pleases; I am enslaved. And finally, you forget that I love and am loved. The situation I am in ought to protect me from such attentions. To love me, or even tell me I am loved, is an insult to a man. Would another transgression not place me on the level of the wickedest creatures of my sex? You who are young and easily embarrassed, how can you oblige me to tell you these things which are only wrung from the heart by tearing it open? I preferred the scandal of an irreparable disaster to the shame of perpetual deceit, my own loss to the loss of probity. In the eyes of many people whom I esteem, I have remained honorable; by altering, I would fall considerably lower. The world is moderately indulgent toward people whose constancy cloaks the illegitimacy of their happiness, but it is pitiless toward the habit of vice. I am neither disdainful nor angry; I am answering you with frankness and simplicity. You are young and ignorant of the world, you are carried away by your imagination and are incapable, like all who are pure in heart, of calculating the wages of sin. I will go further. Were I the most despised woman on earth, were I to conceal the most dreadful anguish, were I betrayed, or ultimately abandoned— and thank heaven none of that is possible, but if out of some divine vengeance this were to happen—I would not be seen by anyone on earth again. I would then find the courage to kill any man who spoke to me of love, if in such a situation any man were still able to reach me. There you have the essence of my position. And so, perhaps I ought to thank you for having written to me. After your letter, and above all after my reply, I can be at ease with you at Les Touches, I can behave naturally, as you asked me to. I do not even mention the ridicule that would pursue me should my eyes ever cease to express the sentiments that you deplore. To rob Camille a second time would be a proof of her insufficiency, something to which no woman could twice resign herself. Were I madly in love with you, blind, oblivious of everything, I could never lose sight of Camille! Her love for you is one of those barriers too high to be surmounted by any power, not even by the wings of an angel; only a demon would not recoil from such infamous treachery. In such matters, my child, there is a world of reasons that noble, sensitive women keep to themselves and that you men know nothing about, not even when they are as much like us as you are now. And in addition, you have a mother who has shown you what a woman should be in this world. She is pure and untarnished. She has fulfilled her destiny with nobility. What little I know about her has brought tears to my eyes and envy to my heart. I could have been like that! And that is what your wife should be, Calyste. I shall no longer send you nastily, as I did, to that silly little Charlotte who would bore you immediately, but to some divine young woman worthy of you. If I were to become yours, I would deprive you of the life you deserve. There would either be a loss of faith, of fidelity, in you, or you would consecrate your entire existence to me. I am honest, I would accept it, and I would lead you God knows where—out of this world. I would make you very unhappy. I am jealous, I see monsters in a drop of water; I am in despair over irritations that most women adjust to. There are even inexorable thoughts that would arise in me, not stemming from you, which would wound me mortally. When a man in his tenth year of happiness is not as deferential and attentive as on the eve of the day he sought my favors, I see him as a villain and am degraded in my own eyes. Such a lover can no longer live up to the Amadises and Cyruses, the chivalric heroes of my dreams. Today, pure love is a fairytale, and in you I can only see the illusion of a desire that cannot*

*look ahead to its outcome. I am not forty, I have
not yet learned the love that makes one humble. I
am, in short, a woman whose character is still so
immature as to be detestable. I am not in control of
my moods, and my grace is merely superficial. Perhaps I have not yet suffered enough to have the
indulgent manners and all-embracing tenderness
that cruel deception teaches us. Happiness has its
impertinence, and I am very impertinent. Camille
will always be a devoted slave to you, while I would
be an irrational tyrant. Furthermore, was Camille
not placed at your side by your guardian angel to
permit you from the very outset to attain the life
you were destined, and must not fail, to lead? I know
Félicité; her tenderness is inexhaustible. She may be
lacking in the graces of our sex, but she embodies
that generative force, that genius of constancy, that
noble courage that make the acceptance of everything possible. She will marry you off, though en-
during endless suffering. She will know how to find
you an unattached Béatrix, if that is what corresponds to your ideal of a woman and to your dreams;
she will smooth out all the difficulties in your future.
The sale of one acre of her property in Paris will
redeem your lands in Brittany; she will make you
he heir. Has she not already made of you an adop-
tive son? Alas, what can I do for your happiness?
Nothing. Do not betray a love so infinite that it has
found fulfillment in motherly care. I consider her
very fortunate, that Camille! The admiration that
poor Béatrix inspires in you is one of those pecca-
dilloes that women of Camille's age view with indulgence. When they are sure of being loved, they grant
constancy an occasional infidelity, they even take a
certain pleasure in triumphing over the youth of*

their rivals. Camille is way above other women; this has no bearing on her, I merely tell you this to relieve your conscience. I have studied her carefully. In my opinion, she is one of the greatest figures of our time. She is intelligent and kind, two almost incompatible qualities in women; she is generous and sincere, two other marks of greatness rarely found together. I have seen in the depths of her heart unfailing treasures. It would seem that Dante, in his Paradiso, *wrote for her that beautiful stanza on eternal happiness that she was explaining to you the other evening and that ends with* Senza brama sicura richezza.* *She spoke to me of her destiny, she told me the story of her life, proving to me that love, the object of all our hopes and dreams, had always fled her. I replied that she seemed to me the proof of the difficulty in pairing sublime things, which accounts for many misfortunes. You are one of the angelic souls whose sister would seem impossible to find. This misfortune, my dear boy, Camille will spare you. She will find you, at the cost of her life, a creature with whom you will be able to live happily.*

I offer you my hand in friendship and count, not on your heart but on your intelligence to be as brother and sister from now on, and to end here this correspondence which from Les Touches to Guérande is, to say the least, bizarre.

Béatrix de Casteran

Deeply concerned over the details and progress of her son's relationship with the Marquise de Rochefide, the baroness was

* "Without desire, assured great wealth," *Paradiso*, XXVII, 9.

unable to sit quietly in the room where she had been embroidering, looking up at Calyste with every stitch. She left her chair and came up to him with a mixture of humility and boldness. At that moment, the mother had the insinuating grace of a courtesan seeking to obtain some favor.

"Well then," she said trembling, but without actually asking for the letter.

Calyste showed it to her and read it aloud. Those two beautiful souls, so pure, so naive, did not discern in that cunning, perfidious reply any of the pitfalls that the marquise had prepared.

"What a fine, noble woman!" said the baroness, her eyes glistening with tears. "I shall pray for her. I would not have believed that a woman capable of abandoning her husband and her child could still remain virtuous. She is worthy of forgiveness."

"Am I not right to adore her?" asked Calyste.

"But where will this love lead you?" exclaimed the baroness. "Oh my child, how dangerous are women of noble sentiments! The truly wicked ones are to be feared less. Marry Charlotte de Kergarouët and buy back two-thirds of the family's estates. Mademoiselle de Pen-Hoël can easily accomplish this by selling a few farms, and the dear woman will see to it that your holdings prosper. You will then be able to leave your children a fine name and a handsome fortune . . . ."

"Forget Béatrix?" asked Calyste in a hollow voice, his eyes glazed.

He left the baroness and went to his room to answer the marquise. Madame du Guénic had Madame de Rochefide's letter engraved in her heart; she was eager to find out on what Calyste could base his hopes. At about that hour, the Chevalier du Halga usually walked his dog on the mall; the baroness, certain of finding him there, put on her hat and shawl and went out. The sight of the baroness outside of church, or along either of the paths favored for holiday strolls when she accompanied her husband and Mademoiselle de Pen-Hoël, was so remarkable an event that within two hours the entire town was asking the same question: "Madame du Guénic went out today, did you see her?"

Soon the news reached Mademoiselle de Pen-Hoël as well, who said to her niece, "Something extraordinary is going on at the du Guénics."

"Calyste is madly in love with that gorgeous Marquise de Rochefide," said Charlotte. "I ought to leave Guérande and go back to Nantes."

At that moment, the Chevailer du Halga, surprised that the baroness was looking for him, unleashed Thisbé realizing the impossibility of dividing his attention.

"Chevalier, you have some experience in matters of gallantry," said the baroness.

Captain du Halga threw his shoulders back with considerable aplomb. Without mentioning her son or the marquise, Madame du Guénic described the love letter and asked what the meaning of such a reply could be. The chevalier stood with his nose in the air and stroked his chin; he listened, made little grimaces, then looked straight at the baroness with a sly expression.

"When thoroughbred horses have to jump hurdles, they first sniff them to become familiar with them," he said. "Calyste will be the happiest rascal in the world."

"Shhh!" said the baroness.

"I am a tomb. In the past, that was my only virtue," said the old chevalier. "The weather is fine," he continued after a pause, "the wind is north-east. By Jove, how the *Belle-Poule* nipped a wind like that on the day ... But," he said, interrupting himself, "my ears are ringing and my floating ribs are aching, there will be a change in the weather. You know, the battle of the *Belle-Poule* became so famous that ladies wore bonnets *à la Belle-Poule*. Madame de Kergarouët was the first to come to the opera with a bonnet like that. 'You are in battle dress,' I said to her. My words were repeated in every box."

The baroness listened politely to the old man who, faithful to the laws of gallantry, escorted her all the way home neglecting Thisbé. He let the secret of Thisbé's background slip out. Thisbé was the granddaughter of the delightful Thisbé who had belonged to Madame L'Amirale de Kergarouët, first wife of the Comte de Kergarouët. This Thisbé III was now eighteen years old. The baroness went up to Calyste's room with a sprightly step, as joyously lighthearted as though it were she who was in love. Calyste was not in his room, but Fanny spotted a letter on the table, folded though not sealed, and addressed to Madame de Rochefide. An irresistible curiosity prodded this troubled mother to read her son's reply. Her indiscretion was cruelly punished. She suffered horribly on discovering how close to disaster love was urging Calyste.

CALYSTE TO BÉATRIX *"What do I care about the future of the du Guénics at a time like this, dear Béatrix! My name is now Béatrix, the happiness of Béatrix is my happiness, her life is my life, and my entire fortune lies in her heart. Our lands have been mortgaged for two hundred years; they can stay that way for another two hundred years. Our farmers will look after them, and no one can take them away. To see you, to love you, this is my religion. Me, marry? I will marry no one but you, even if I have to wait twenty years. I am young and you will always be beautiful. My mother is a saint, I have no right to judge her. But she has not loved! I know how much she has been deprived of and what sacrifices she has made. You have taught me, Béatrix, to love my mother even more. She is the only one to share my heart with you, and no one else ever will. She is your only rival. Does this not amount to saying that you reign alone? And so your reasoning has no effect on my thinking. As to Camille, you have only*

*to give me the signal, and I shall ask her to tell you
herself that I do not love her. She is the mother of
my intellect—nothing more, nothing less. As soon
as I saw you, she became my sister, my confidante,
my comrade—whichever you like. The only rights
we have over one another are those of friendship. I
had taken her for a woman until I saw you; but you
showed me that Camille is a boy. She swims, she
hunts, she rides, she smokes, she drinks, she writes,
she analyzes hearts or books, she has no weaknesses,
she strides through life on her own strength. She
has neither your agile movements, nor your step
like a bird in flight, nor your amorous voice, nor
your subtle glances, nor your graceful carriage. She
is Camille Maupin and nothing else. She has nothing of the woman in her, and you have everything
I love in a woman. It seemed to me, as of the first
day I saw you, that you were mine. You will laugh
at this feeling, but it has only grown since then, and
now it would seem monstrous if we were separated.
You are my soul, my life, I could not live where you
are not. Let me love you! We will fly away, far from
the world, to some land where you will meet no one
you know, where you will have only me and God
for companions. My mother, who loves you, will
come one day to stay with us. Ireland has many
castles, and my mother's family will surely lend me
one. Good God, let us go! A boat and some sailors
and we will have arrived before anyone knows we
have left this world you fear so much. You have
never been loved; I sense this on re-reading your
letter, and I also find that if none of the reasons you
speak of existed, you would let yourself be loved by
me. Béatrix, a holy love erases the past. Can one
think of anyone else after seeing you? I love you so*

> *much I would have you a thousand times more sin-*
> *ful in order to prove the power of my love by ador-*
> *ing you as the saintliest of creatures. You call my*
> *love an insult. Oh Béatrix, you do not mean it! The*
> *love of a noble child—did you not call me that?—*
> *would do honor to a queen. And so tomorrow we*
> *will walk along the rocks and the sea like lovers,*
> *and you will walk on the sands of ancient Brittany*
> *to consecrate them once again, for me. Give me this*
> *day of happiness; and this moment of charity—*
> *perhaps, alas, without future memory for you—will*
> *mean eternal wealth for Calyste . . . ."*

The baroness let the letter fall without finishing it. She knelt at a chair and silently begged God to protect her son's reason, to keep him from madness, from error, and to remove him from the path he was taking.

"What are you doing, mother?" Calyste asked.

"I am praying to God for you," she said turning her tear-filled eyes to him. "I have just committed the indiscretion of reading that letter. My Calyste has gone mad!"

"The sweetest of madnesses," said the young man, kissing his mother.

"I should like to see this woman, my child."

"All right, mother," said Calyste, "we are setting out tomorrow for Le Croisic, be on the pier."

He sealed his letter and took off for Les Touches. What the baroness found most staggering was to see how emotions, by sheer force of instinct, could achieve the foresight of consummate experience. Calyste had just written to Béatrix as though guided by the Chevalier du Halga.

IV A FEMININE DUEL   Perhaps one of the greatest delights that small minds or inferior beings can experience is that of tricking great souls and catching them in some kind of trap. Béatrix knew she was far inferior to Camille Maupin. Her inferiority lay not only in that totality of moral attributes known as *talent,* but also in those attributes of the heart known as *passion.* From the moment Calyste arrived at Les Touches with the impetuousness of first love borne on the wings of hope, the marquise experienced an intense joy in knowing she was loved by that adorable young man. She did not go quite so far as to desire any complicity in this feeling. She employed her heroism to contain this *capriccio,* as the Italians call it, and thus considered herself her friend's equal. She was pleased to offer her this sacrifice. In short, the particular vanity of French-women, which constitutes the famous coquettry that grants them their superiority, was flattered and fully satisfied in her. Exposed to endless seductions, she resisted, and her virtues filled her ears with their chorus of sweet praise. These two women, giving an impression of indolence, were reclining on the couch in the little sitting room, that world of harmony and flowers, with the window open since the north wind had stopped blowing. A melting southerly breeze rippled the salt water lake that could be seen from the window, and the sun gilded the sands. Their souls were as profoundly agitated as the scene was calm, and equally ardent. Caught up in the wheels of the machine she had set in motion, Camille was obliged to keep an eye on herself, given the prodigious cunning of the friendly enemy she had led into her cage. In order not to reveal her secret, she abandoned herself to the contemplation of nature's secrets. She distracted herself from her anguish by seeking a meaning to the movement of the universe, and discovered God in the sublime desert of the heavens. Once an unbeliever has recognized God, he throws himself into orthodox Catholicism which, viewed as a system, is complete. That morning, Camille had shown the marquise a face still illumined by the radiance of her quest during a night of moaning. Calyste stood before her, like a celestial image. That handsome young man to whom she was devoting herself appeared to her as a guardian angel. Was it not he who was guiding her to the lofty regions where suffering ceased under the force of an incomprehensible immensity? However, Béatrix's triumphant look disturbed Camille. A woman does not gain an advantage like that over another without letting it be guessed, all the while justifying herself for having taken it. Nothing could have been more bizarre than this silent moral struggle between two friends, each hiding a secret from the other, and each believing herself the creditor of unknown sacrifices. Calyste arrived holding his letter between his hand and his glove, ready to slide it into Béatrix's hand. Camille, who was not unaware of her friend's altered mood, pretended not to look at her, watching her instead in a mirror at the moment when Calyste came into the room. This is a woman's greatest pitfall. The brightest and the dullest, the most candid and most cunning, are no longer mistress of their secret; at that moment, it explodes before the eyes of the other woman. Too much reserve or too little restraint, a direct glowing glance or a mysterious lowering of the eyelids—anything can betray the sentiment most difficult to hide, for indifference has a quality of such utter coldness that it can never be simulated. Women have the gift of nuances; they use them too often not to recognize all of them. On occasions like this, their glance can take in a rival from head to toe; they perceive the slightest movement of a foot underneath a dress, the most imperceptible contraction in the body, and understand the significance of what seems insignificant to a man. Two women in the process of examining each other play one of the best comic scenes there are.

"Calyste has done something foolish," Camille thought as she observed in each of them that indefinable quality in people who share some understanding.

The marquise was no longer either standoffish or indifferent; she looked at Calyste with a proprietary air. Calyste's face provided an explicit avowal; he blushed, out of guilt and happiness. He had come to settle arrangements for the next day.

"Have you decided to come then, my dear?" asked Camille.

"Yes," answered Béatrix.

"How did you know?" Mademoiselle des Touches asked Calyste.

"I came to find out," he replied after the look Madame de Rochefide threw him; she did not want any glimmer of their correspondence to reach her friend.

"They already understand each other," thought Camille, who caught that glance from the side of her eye. "It is all over now; I may as well disappear."

The weight of this thought produced a collapse in her face that made Béatrix tremble.

"What is it, my dear?" she asked.

"Nothing. And so, Calyste, you will send my horses and yours ahead so that we find them outside of Le Croisic and can ride back through Batz. We will have lunch in Le Croisic and dinner at Les Touches. You take care of the boatmen. We shall leave at 8:30. What marvelous sights!" she said to Béatrix. "You will see Cambremer, a man doing penance on a rock for having willfully murdered his son. Here you are in a primitive land where emotions are not run-of-the-mill. Calyste will tell you that story."

She went to her room, choking. Calyste delivered his letter and followed Camille.

"Calyste, you are loved, I do believe, but you are hiding some escapade from me, and you have certainly disobeyed my orders."

"I, loved!" he said collapsing into a chair.

Camille looked outside the door; Béatrix had disappeared. That was strange. A woman does not leave the room where her lover had been and to which he will return unless she has something better to do. "Could she have a letter from Calyste?" Mademoiselle des Touches wondered, but she considered the innocent young Breton incapable of such daring.

"If you have disobeyed me, all will be lost because of you," she said gravely. "Go prepare your pleasures for tomorrow."

She sent Calyste away with a gesture that precluded any discussion; unexpressed sorrow can be despotically eloquent. On his way to Le Croisic to see the boatmen, crossing the sands and the marshes, Calyste became apprehensive. Camille's words carried a certain fatality that suggested maternal foresight. When he returned four hours later, exhausted, expecting to dine at Les Touches, he was greeted by Camille's maid on the doorstep, who told him that her mistress and the marquise would be unable to see him that evening. And when, mystified, he tried to question her, she closed the door and disappeared into the house. The bell tower of Guérande struck six. Calyste returned home, requested dinner, and played mouche in a state of somber depression. These alternatives of happiness and unhappiness, the annulment of all hope giving way to the near certainty of being loved, clipped the wings of this young soul whose flight had soared so high into the sky that the fall would be horrible.

"What is it, Calyste dear?" his mother asked whispering.

"Nothing," he replied, revealing eyes in which the light of the soul and the fire of love had been extinguished.

It is not hope but despair that provides the measure of our aspirations. We indulge secretly in the beautiful poetry of hope, while sorrow is seen unmasked.

"Calyste, you are not nice," said Charlotte after having tried vainly to attract his attention with her provincial flirting that always degenerated into bantering reproaches.

"I am tired," he said getting up and bidding everyone good night.

"Calyste has certainly changed," said Mademoiselle de Pen-Hoël.

"We don't have lovely dresses edged with lace, we don't wave our sleeves around like this, we don't pose like that, we don't know how to look sideways and turn our heads," said Charlotte mimicking the airs, the poses and the glances of the marquise. "We don't talk through our noses, or cough that interesting little *heu! heu!* that sounds like the sigh of a spectre. We have the misfortune to be robustly healthy and to love our friends without affectations; when we look at them we don't throw daggers at them or examine them with a hypocritical eye. We don't know how to hang our heads like weeping willows or appear amiable just by raising our heads!"

Mademoiselle de Pen-Hoël could not keep back her laughter at her niece's imitations. But neither the chevalier nor the baron understood this satire on the provinces versus Paris.

"The Marquise de Rochefide is nevertheless very beautiful," said the old maid.

"My dear," said the baroness to her husband, "I know she is going to Le Croisic tomorrow. Why don't we go there for a stroll? I should so much like to meet her."

While Calyste was dredging his brains to find out what could have barred the doors of Les Touches to him, a scene between the two ladies was taking place that was to affect the next day's events. Calyste's letter had awakened unknown emotions in Madame de Rochefide. Women are not always the object of a love as young, as naive, as sincere, as total as was Calyste's for her. Béatrix had given more love than she had received. Having been the slave, she experienced an unavowable desire to be the tyrant. In the midst of her pleasure, while reading and rereading Calyste's letter, she was struck by a cruel thought. What had Calyste and Camille been doing during all those hours together since Claude Vignon left? If Calyste was not in love with Camille and Camille knew it, how then were they spending those mornings? Alongside this thought, she aligned everything she remembered of Camille's remarks. Suddenly it was as though a grinning devil had held up a magic mirror revealing this heroic woman with the gestures and expressions that completed Béatrix's enlightenment. Instead of being her equal, she was crushed by Félicité; far from deceiving her, it was she who was being deceived. She was no more than an amusement that Camille wanted to give the child she loved with so unique, so lofty a passion. For a woman like Béatrix, this discovery was a lightning bolt. She reviewed each minute detail of the preceding week. At once, Camille's role and her own unfolded in all their development; she felt singularly demeaned. In the throes of her jealous loathing, she thought she perceived in Camille a desire for vengeance against Conti. These last two weeks had perhaps been determined by everything that had happened in the past two years. Once on the down grade to distrust, suspicion, and anger, Béatrix no longer stopped. She paced up and down her room propelled by her impetuous reactions, and sat down from time to time while trying to come to a decision. She remained in this state of indecision until dinner time, and then went down without changing. As soon as she saw her rival appear, Camille guessed everything. Béatrix, negligently attired, had that taciturn coldness that to an observer as perceptive as Maupin denoted the hostility of an embittered heart. Camille went out and immediately gave the order that so surprised Calyste; she realized that if the naive Breton appeared with his uncontrolled passion in the midst of the quarrel, he would probably never see Béatrix again by compromising the future of this passion through some foolish confession. She preferred to be without witnesses to this duel of deceits. Béatrix with no one to second her would have to lose. Camille knew only too well the aridity of that soul, the pettiness of that overbearing pride that she so rightfully called obstinacy. Dinner was cheerless. Both of these women had too much intelligence and too much taste to have it out before the servants, or be overheard by them. Camille was sweet and good-natured; she felt so superior. The marquise was hard and cutting; she knew she was being taken in like a child. During dinner, there was a battle of glances, gestures, double-edged remarks, that the servants could not possibly understand but that heralded a violent outbreak. When it was time to go up again, Camille craftily offered her arm to Béatrix who pretended not to notice and dashed up the staircase alone. When coffee was served, Mademoiselle des Touches told her valet "Leave us now!" which was the signal for the combat to begin.

"The novels you act out are more dangerous than the novels you write, my dear," said the marquise.

"They have one great advantage, however," said Camille taking a cigarette.

"What is that?" asked Béatrix.

"They are unpublished, my love."

"Will the one in which you have placed me become a book?"

"I do not share Oedipus' talent, though you have the beauty and wit of the Sphinx. Don't ask me riddles, dear Béatrix, speak out clearly."

"When we enlist the aid of the devil in order to make our men happy, to entertain them, please them and relieve their cares...."

"They later blame us, believing our efforts to have been dictated by some evil genius," said Camille putting out her cigarette as she interrupted her friend.

"They forget the love that carried us away and that justified our excesses, for to what lengths would we not have gone! ... But they are only fulfilling their masculine nature, they are ungrateful and unjust," Béatrix continued. "Women understand each other; they know how proud they can be in all circumstances, how noble, and even how virtuous. However, Camille, I have come to recognize the truth in criticisms you have often complained of. Yes, my dear, you do have something of a man in you, you behave like them, nothing stops you, and even if you do not share all their advantages, you have their way of thinking, and you share their contempt for us. I have had reason to be displeased with you, my dear, and I am too frank to conceal it. No one will probably ever hurt me as deeply as I have been hurt of late. If you are not always womanly in love, you become so in revenge. One must be a woman of genius to discover the most sensitive spot in our weaknesses. I am speaking of Calyste and of the ruses, my dear, for that is what they are, that you have used against me. How low will you sink, Camille Maupin, and for what purpose?"

"Still more and more the Sphinx!" said Camille smiling.

"You wanted me to throw myself at Calyste; I am still too young for such behavior. For me, love is love with all its atrocious jealousy and all its imperious demands. I am not a writer. It is impossible for me to see ideas in emotions . . . ."

"Do you think yourself capable of loving stupidly?" asked Camille. "Be reassured, you still have all your wits about you. You underrate yourself, my dear; you are quite cold enough to make your head the final judge of your heart's grand exploits."

This epigram made the marquise blush. She threw Camille a glance filled with hate, with venom, and without looking for them found the sharpest arrows in her quiver. Smoking her cigarettes, Camille listened placidly to this fuming tirade that bubbled with insults so piercing that it is impossible to repeat them. Béatrix, irritated by her adversary's unruffled calm, brought up horrible examples of women who had reached the age of Mademoiselle des Touches.

"Have you finished?" asked Camille, blowing out a cloud of smoke. "Do you love Calyste?"

"Certainly not."

"So much the better," Camille replied. "For I do, and much too much for my own peace of mind. He is probably infatuated with you. You are the most delicious blond in the world, while I am dark as a mole. You are slender and willowy; I am imposing around the waist. And finally, you are young! There is the key word, and you have not spared me from hearing it.

You have abused your advantages over me as a woman, just as a second-rate newspaper abuses irony. I did everything to avoid what is happening," she said, raising her eyes to the ceiling. "However little of the woman there may be in me, there is still enough, my dear, so that a rival needs my help to triumph over me." (The marquise was wounded to the quick by these cruel words spoken with feigned innocence.) "You must take me for quite a fool if you believe what Calyste would like you to believe about me. I am neither so great nor so small. I am merely a woman, and very much so. Leave off your grand airs, and give me your hand," said Camille, taking hold of Béatrix's hand. "You do not love Calyste, that is the truth, isn't it? In that case, there is no need for such excitement. Be cold and severe with him tomorrow. He will eventually calm down after the quarrel I shall pick with him tomorrow, and especially after the reconciliation, for I have not yet exhausted all the weapons in a woman's arsenal. Furthermore, pleasure is always stronger than desire. But Calyste is a Breton, and consequently obdurate. If he persists in courting you, tell me so, and you can go to a little country house I own just six leagues outside of Paris, where you will find every comfort and where Conti can come to see you. Let Calyste slander me! Good Lord, even the purest love is full of deceptions; its frauds only attest to its strength."

There was in Camille's face a cold arrogance that made the marquise nervous and fearful. She did not know what to say. Camille struck the final blow.

"I am more trusting and less bitter than you," Camille continued. "I do not suspect you of trying to camouflage behind recriminations an attack that would compromise my life. You know me. I would not survive the loss of Calyste, yet sooner or later I must lose him. However, Calyste loves me, that much I know."

"Here is his reply to a letter in which I spoke only of you," said Béatrix, handing Calyste's letter to her.

Camille took it and read it, but while reading, her eyes filled with tears. She cried as all women cry when their pain is acute.

"My God!" she exclaimed. "He does love her. Then I shall die without ever having been loved or understood!"

She remained for a few moments with her head against Béatrix's shoulder. Her suffering was authentic. She felt deep within her the same terrible shock that the baroness had experienced when reading this same letter.

"Do you love him?" she asked, straightening up and looking at Béatrix. "Do you have for him that infinite adoration that can endure all suffering and even survive contempt, betrayal and the certainty of no longer being loved? Can you love him for himself and for the very pleasure of loving him?"

"Dearest friend," said the marquise, deeply moved. "Be assured, I shall leave tomorrow."

"Don't leave, he loves you, I see it! And I love him so much I could not bear to see him suffer or be unhappy. I had made many plans for him, but if he loves you, then it is all finished."

"I love him, Camille," the marquise then said with disarming simplicity, and blushing.

"You love him and you can resist him?" Camille exclaimed. "Ah, you do not love him!"

"I do not know what fresh virtues he has awakened in me, but what is certain is that he has made me ashamed of myself," said Béatrix. "I would like to be free and virtuous in order to make him the sacrifice of something more than the remnants of my heart and my disgraceful chains. I do not want an incomplete future for him or for me."

"Cold creature! How can you love and still calculate!" cried Camille with horror.

"Say what you will. I will not ruin his life, be a weight around his neck, or become an eternal regret. Since I cannot be his wife, I will not be his mistress. I have been . . . You won't make fun of me? No? Well then, I have been purified by his exquisite love."

Camille threw Béatrix the most savage, most ferocious look any jealous woman ever gave her rival.

"In that domain," she said, "I thought I was alone. Béatrix, those words have separated us forever. We are no longer friends. We are beginning a dreadful struggle. Now let me tell you, you will give in or you will flee . . . ."

Félicité dashed into her room after astounding Béatrix with her expression of a raging lioness.

"Are you coming to Le Croisic tomorrow?" asked Camille raising the portiere.

"Of course," the marquise proudly replied. "I will not flee and I will not give in."

"I will not hide my hand—I am going to write to Conti," replied Camille. Béatrix turned as white as her scarf.

"We are both playing for our lives," Béatrix answered, no longer knowing what to do.

The violent emotions provoked by this scene between the two women were calmed during the night. Both of them tried to be reasonable and fell back on the perfidious tendency toward postponement which most women are prey to—an excellent system between them and men, but very bad between themselves. It was in the middle of this last storm that Mademoiselle des Touches heard the great voice that overpowers even the most fearless. Béatrix listened to the counsel of worldly jurisprudence; she was afraid of society's contempt. Félicité's final deceit, accompanied by the most atrocious jealousy, was therefore a total success. Calyste's mistake was repaired, but any further indiscretion could put an end to his hopes.

V EXCURSION TO LE CROISIC The month of August was coming to its end, the sky was magnificently clear. The ocean at the horizon, like southern seas, was the color of molten silver, and tiny waves rippled toward the shore. A kind of glowing vapor, caused by the rays of the sun falling directly on the sand, produced an almost tropical atmosphere. The salt formed tiny white flowers on the surface of the pools. The hard-working marshmen dressed in white, precisely to withstand the sun's rays, were at work by dawn with their long rakes; some stood leaning against the mud walls that separated each property, watching the natural chemistry that they had known from childhood; others were playing with their children beside their wives. The green dragons, otherwise known as customs inspectors, placidly smoked their pipes. There was something almost oriental about the scene, for certainly a Parisian, suddenly transported there, would never have believed himself in France. The baron and baroness, who had come on the pretext of watching the gathering of the salt, were on the jetty admiring the silent landscape in which no sound intruded except the sea's rhythmic groan, and boats sliced through the water, and the green belt of cultivated land seemed all the lovelier for its rarity along the desolate shores of the ocean.

"So then my friends, I shall have seen Guérande's salt marshes once more before dying," said the baron to the marshmen who had formed a circle to greet him.

"The du Guénics don't die!" said a marshman.

At that moment, the caravan that had left Les Touches reached the little road. The marquise rode ahead alone, Calyste and Camille followed her holding hands. Gasselin held up the rear twenty paces behind.

"There are my parents," said the young man to Camille.

The marquise halted. Madame du Guénic experienced the most violent revulsion on seeing Béatrix who was, however, most flatteringly attired: a broad-brimmed straw hat trimmed with cornflowers, her hair curled beneath it, a gray dress of raw silk with a flowing blue sash—in other words, a princess disguised as a shepherdess.

"That woman has no heart," the baroness said to herself.

"Mademoiselle," said Calyste to Camille, "this is Madame du

Guénic and my father." Then turning to the baron and the baroness, "Mademoiselle des Touches and Madame la Marquise de Rochefide, née Casteran, my father."

The baron bent over the hand of Mademoiselle des Touches, who gave the baroness a greeting filled with humility and gratitude.

"Now that one," thought Fanny, "really loves my son. She looks at me as though she were thanking me for having given birth to him."

"You have come, as I have, to see if there is a good harvest, but you have better reasons than I for being curious," the baron said to Camille, "for you have a major interest here."

"Mademoiselle is the richest proprietor around here," said one of the marshmen, "and may God protect her, for she is a fine lady."

The two parties bowed to each other and left.

"One would not take Mademoiselle des Touches for more than thirty," said the old baron to his wife. "She certainly is beautiful. And Calyste prefers that wench of a Parisian marquise to this fine Breton girl?"

"Alas!" said the baroness.

A boat was waiting at the pier where they cheerlessly embarked. The marquise was cold and dignified. Camille had scolded Calyste for his disobedience, explaining to him the state of his amorous affairs. Calyste, grim with despair, threw glances at Béatrix that alternated from love to hate. Not a word was said during the short ride from the pier at Guérande to the far end of the port of Le Croisic where the salt is loaded, and carried by the women in large jugs on their heads, making them look like caryatids. These women go barefoot and wear short skirts. Many of them carelessly let the kerchiefs covering their chests fly loose; many wear only their shifts and are all the more dignified, for the less clothing a woman wears, the more she evidences dignified modesty. The little Danish vessel had finished loading its cargo. The landing of these beautiful ladies aroused the curiosity of the salt carriers. As much to get away as to be helpful to Calyste, Camille slipped away quickly toward the rocks, leaving Béatrix with him. Gasselin left a distance of a good two hundred paces between him and his master. The seaward side of the peninsula of Le Croisic is bordered by granite rocks of such extraordinary shapes that only the traveler with some experience of natural spectacles can appreciate them. It may be that the rocks of Le Croisic are as superior in their category as the road to the Grande Chartreuse compared with other narrow valleys. Neither the coast of Corsica where the granite has formed very strange reefs, nor the Sardinian coast where nature has allowed itself the most grandiose and frightening effects, nor the basalt rocks of the North Sea, provided a sight so unique. Every possible shape can be seen there. Fantasy ran wild there, creating endless arabesques in which the most fanciful figures weave in and out. The imagination may well be exhausted by this immense gallery of monstrosities where the sea, in stormy weather, rushes in and has succeeded in polishing down all the rough edges. Under a natural arch—whose daring curve was only feebly imitated by Brunelleschi, for the greatest artistic endeavors are never more than a timid facsimile of nature's achievements— one comes upon a polished basin, as smooth as a marble tub, surrounded by fine white sand where one can bathe in perfect safety in four feet of tepid water. One walks along admiring the fresh little coves protected by roughhewn but majestic porticoes, somewhat in the style of the Pitti Palace, another imitation of nature's caprices. Such accidents are innumerable; nothing is lacking in nature that the wildest imagination could invent or desire. There is even something so rare along the shores of the Atlantic that this may be the only example: a large bush of the species that gave rise to word *buisson*.* This box tree, one of the greatest curiosities in Le Croisic where

* *Buis* is the French word for box tree; *buisson*, the word for shrub or bush.

trees cannot survive, is about one league from the port on the outermost cape along the coast. On one of the granite promontories facing south and rising so high above the sea that even in the most violent storms the waves cannot reach it, a shallow shelf, projecting about four feet, has been created by wind and water. Into this cleft, chance or man left enough soil to allow a box tree, seeded by birds, to grow short and thick. The roots would seem to indicate an age of at least three hundred years. Underneath, the rock falls away in a sheer drop. Some manner of trauma, whose traces are indelibly marked along the coast, has carried away chunks of granite. The sea, more than five hundred feet deep at this point, sweeps up to this cliff without any reefs to break its impetus. All around, the rocks at water level, noticeable from the foam that bubbles around them, form a kind of large circle. It takes courage and resolution to go as far as the summit of this miniature Gibraltar, with its rounded head, where a gust of wind can blow the tourist into the sea, or even worse, onto to the rocks below. This gigantic sentinel resembles the lookout towers of ancient castles from which one could survey the entire countryside, thereby anticipating any attack. From this spot one can see the bell tower and the meager lands of Le Croisic, the sand dunes that threaten the arable land and that have already invaded the region of Batz. A few old denizens claim that there was once a castle on that spot. The sardine fishermen have given this rock, which can be seen far out at sea, a name, but I will have to be excused for forgetting that Breton word, as hard to pronounce as to remember. Calyste led Béatrix toward this point from which the view is superb and the granite arabesques surpass anything that one has seen earlier along the sandy road that borders the sea. It is unnecessary to explain why Camille ran on ahead. Like a wounded animal, she needed solitude. She wandered into grottoes, reappeared on top of rocks, snatched crabs out of their holes or watched their strange behavior. To avoid being hampered by skirts, she had put on

Turkish trousers with embroidered cuffs, a short blouse, a beaver hat, and for a walking stick carried a riding crop, for she was always proud of her strength and agility. In this attire, she was a hundred times more beautiful than Béatrix. She wore a little Chinese shawl of red silk crossed around her chest as one wraps children. For some time, Béatrix and Calyste could see her flit across the rocks like a will-o'-the-wisp, trying to divert her suffering by risking her safety. She was the first to reach the promontory where the box tree grew, and sat down in one of the shaded rifts to meditate. What could a woman like her do in her old age having drunk from the cup of fame that all great talents, too avid to sip the heady brew of vanity, empty at one gulp? She has since admitted that while there, one of those ideas inspired by a triviality, one of those accidents that seems like foolishness to mediocre minds but provokes great minds to endless contemplation, convinced her to make the startling decision by which she was to finish off her life in society. She had pulled out of her pocket a little box containing strawberry candies, taken along in case of thirst. She had taken a few and while tasting them, began thinking that although the strawberries no longer existed, they survived through their flavor, their particular quality. And from that, she went on to conclude it could be the same with people. The sea at that moment was offering her an image of infinity. No great mind can come to terms with infinity, having accepted the immortality of the soul, without acknowledging some religious future. This idea was further confirmed when she sniffed her flacon of Eau de Portugal.* Her conniving to make Béatrix succumb to Calyste suddenly struck her as unworthy. She felt the woman in her expire and the noble angelic creature, until then hidden beneath the flesh, emerge. What had her immense

---

* Eau de Portugal was a toilet water made of orange and lemon essences. Camille's experience of an after-taste, followed by an after scent of things that had ceased to exist, brought her to the conclusion that the soul was immortal.

intellect, her knowledge, her comprehension, her erroneous loves, brought her face to face with?—and who could have predicted it to her?—with the fecund mother, the consolation of the afflicted: the Catholic Church, so loving to repenters, so poetic to poets, so childlike to children, so deep and full of mystery that wild troubled minds can continually search and continually satisfy in her their insatiable curiosity. She thought back to the detours she had followed because of Calyste and compared them to the twisting paths among those rocks. Calyste had always been in her eyes the beautiful messenger from heaven, the divine guide. She smothered her earthly love in heavenly love.

After walking for some time in silence, Calyste, in response to an exclamation by Béatrix on the beauty of the Atlantic which is so unlike the Mediterranean, could not refrain from comparing the vastness, the agitation, the depth, the purity, the eternity of this ocean with his love.

"It is bounded by rock," Béatrix answered laughing.

"When you talk to me this way," he replied looking at her adoringly, "I can see you, I can hear you, and can summon up the patience of an angel. But when I am alone . . . you would pity me if you saw me. Even my mother weeps at my sorrow."

"Listen Calyste, this has to end," said the marquise returning to the sandy path. "We may well have come to the most propitious spot to discuss these things, for never in my life have I seen nature more in harmony with my thoughts. I have seen Italy where everything speaks of love; I have seen Switzerland where everything is fresh and expresses true happiness, hard-earned happiness, where the meadows, the peaceful streams, the most exhilarating of landscapes is oppressed by the snow-crowned Alps. But I have seen nothing that better expresses the burning barrenness of my life than this little plain dessicated by the sea's gales, corroded by the salty mists, where a pitiful agriculture struggles before this enormous ocean, amid the bouquets of Brittany, out of which rise the towers of your

Guérande. Well then Calyste, this is Béatrix. Do not become attached to that. I love you, but I will never, under any circumstances, be yours for I am fully aware of my inner desolation. Ah, you have no idea how hard it is for me to say these things, how unkind to myself. But no, you will never see your idol, if I am one, debased; she will not fall from your pedestal. I now view with horror a passion that is repudiated by society and religion alike. I do not wish to be humiliated any further or to hide my happiness. I shall remain as I am and become the sandy, barren desert, bereft of fruits or flowers, that you see before you."

"And if you were abandoned?" said Calyste.

"Then I would go to plead for mercy, I would humble myself before the man I offended, but I would never run the risk of throwing myself into a happiness that I know must end."

"End!" cried Calyste.

The marquise interrupted the dithyramb that her lover was about to begin by repeating "End!" in a tone that silenced him.

This denial provoked in the young man one of those mute furies that are only known by those who have loved without hope. Béatrix and he walked on for another three hundred paces in total silence, no longer looking at the sea, or the rocks or the fields of Le Croisic.

"I could make you so happy!" said Calyste.

"All men begin by promising us happiness, and then bequeath us deprecation, desertion, and disgust. I have no reproach to make the man to whom I must remain faithful: he promised me nothing, it was I who went to him. But the only means I have to attenuate my transgression is to make it eternal."

"Why not say that you do not love me! I who do love you, I know through myself that love does not discuss, it only sees itself; there is no sacrifice I would not make. Command, and I will attempt the impossible. He who long ago spurned his mistress for having thrown her glove to the lions, commanding him to retrieve it, did not love! He underestimated your right to test us in order to test our love, and never to lay down your weapons except for superhuman feats. I would sacrifice to you my family, my name, my future."

"How insulting, that word sacrifice!" she said in a tone of reproach that made Calyste realize the ineptness of his choice of words.

Only women deeply in love or seasoned coquettes know how to use a word as a springboard and soar up to prodigious heights; wit and feeling proceed in the same manner, only the woman in love is sorrowful while the coquette is contemptuous.

"You are right," said Calyste, letting fall two tears, "this word can only be used for the demands you would make of me."

"Be quiet," said Beatrix, struck by this reply which for the first time clearly expressed Calyste's love, "I have committed enough wrongs, do not tempt me."

At that moment they reached the foot of the rock with the box tree. Calyste experienced the most intoxicating pleasures in helping the marquise climb up the rock; she wanted to go all the way to the top. For the poor boy it was the most exquisite favor to hold her by the waist, to feel this somewhat frightened woman who needed him! This unhoped for joy made him dizzy. He no longer saw clearly and seized Béatrix by the belt.

"Well?" she asked imperiously.

"You will never be mine?" he asked in a voice choked by his raging blood.

"Never, my friend," she replied. "I can be no more than Beatrice for you—a dream. Isn't that a beautiful thing? We will never suffer bitterness, or resentment, or remorse."

"And you will go back to Conti?"

"I have to."

"Then you will never belong to anyone," said Calyste pushing the marquise with frenetic violence.

He had wanted to hear her fall before throwing himself after her, but all he heard was a dull sound, the strident tearing of cloth and the quiet thud of a body falling on earth. Instead of plunging head down, Béatrix veered and fell over in the box tree. She would nonetheless have rolled into the sea had her dress not caught on an edge and slackened her fall against the bush. Mademoiselle des Touches, who witnessed the scene, was unable to cry out; she was so panic-stricken she could only signal for Gasselin to run over. Calyste leaned over through vicious curiosity, saw what had happened to Béatrix and shuddered. She seemed to be praying, convinced of her death, for she felt the box tree giving way. With the sudden competence that love inspires and the supernatural agility that youth discovers in danger, he let himself drop nine feet, then clinging to a few crags, made his way to the edge of the rock and managed to catch hold of the marquise taking her in his arms at the risk of both of them falling into the sea. When he lifted Béatrix she was unconscious, but he could imagine she was wholly his in this aerial bed where they would remain alone for some time. His first impulse was one of pleasure.

"Open your eyes, forgive me," Calyste said, "or we will die together."

"Die?" she asked opening her eyes and parting her pale lips.

Calyste greeted this word with a kiss and felt in the marquise a convulsive quiver that made him ecstatic. At that moment, Gasselin's hobnailed boots were audible above them. He was followed by Camille with whom he was considering the means of saving the lovers.

"There is only one way, mademoiselle," said Gasselin. "I will slide down, they will climb up my shoulders and you will hold out your hand."

"And you?" asked Camille.

The servant was surprised to be of any concern in the midst of his master's danger.

"It would be wiser to get a ladder in Le Croisic," Camille said.

"She's a clever one all right," Gasselin said to himself, going down.

Béatrix asked feebly to lie down, she felt faint. Calyste laid her down on the cool earth between the granite and the box tree.

"I saw you, Calyste," Camille said. "Whether Béatrix lives or dies, this must never be anything but an accident."

"She will despise me!" he said, his eyes brimming with tears.

"She will adore you," Camille replied. "We have come to the end of our excursion, she must be taken to Les Touches. What would you have done had she died?" she asked.

"I would have followed her."

"And your mother? . . ." Then after a pause, "And me?" she said feebly.

Calyste stood pale, silent, motionless, leaning against the rock. Gasselin returned immediately from one of those little farms that dotted the countryside, running with a ladder he had found there. Béatrix had made a slight recovery. When Gasselin put the ladder in place, the marquise, aided by Gasselin who asked Calyste to put Camille's red shawl under Béatrix's arms and hand him the ends, was able to climb up to the round platform where Gasselin took her in his arms like a child, and carried her to the shore.

"I would not have refused death, but suffering!" she said to Mademoiselle des Touches in a whisper.

Béatrix's weakness and shock obliged Camille to have her carried to the farm from which Gasselin had borrowed the ladder. Calyste, Gasselin, and Camille took off what clothes they could to make a mattress on the ladder, laid Béatrix on it and carried her as though on a stretcher. The farmers offered their bed. Gasselin ran to the spot where the horses were tethered, took one and went to find the doctor in Le Croisic after advising the boatmen to come to the cove nearest to the farm. Calyste, seated on a stool, by nods and occasional monosyllables answered Camille whose anxiety was alarmed both by Béatrix's condition and by Calyste's. After being bled, the patient was somewhat better; she was able to speak, and agreed to leave. At about five o'clock she was carried from the dock in Guérande to Les Touches, where the doctor was awaiting her. The news of the accident spread with inexplicable rapidity in this lonely countryside with almost no visible inhabitants.

Calyste spent the night at Les Touches, keeping vigil with Camille at the foot of Béatrix's bed. The doctor had promised that the next day the marquise would have no more than a few stiff joints. In the midst of his despair, Calyste experienced an intense joy: he was at the foot of Béatrix's bed, watching her doze off and wake up; he could examine her pale features and slightest movements. Camille smiled with bitterness as she recognized in Calyste the symptoms of one of those passions that permanently mark the soul and faculties of a man by entering into his life at a time when no thoughts, no cares interfere with this cruel inner process. Calyste would never see the true woman within Béatrix. How naively he allowed his most secret thoughts to be read! . . . he imagined this woman was truly his through his presence in her room, admiring her in the disarray of her bed. He examined with ecstatic concentration her every movement. His expression betrayed such charming curiosity, his happiness was so candidly revealed, that at one moment the two women looked at each other and smiled. When Calyste saw in the sea green eyes of the patient a mixture of embarrassment, affection and amusement, he blushed and looked away.

"Didn't I tell you, Calyste, that you men always promise us happiness and end up by throwing us over a cliff?"

On hearing this little joke, said in a delightful tone, that indicated some change in Béatrix's feelings, Calyste fell to his knees, took one of her damp hands which she allowed him to hold, and kissed it submissively.

"You have the right to reject my love forever, and I no longer have the right to say a word."

"Ah!" Camille exclaimed to herself, seeing the expression on Béatrix's face and comparing it to the one produced by her diplomatic plotting, "love left to itself will always outwit the whole world put together! Take your sedative, my dearest, and sleep."

That night, spent by Calyste beside Mademoiselle des Touches who read books on mystical theology while Calyste read *Indiana*—the first book by Camille's celebrated rival, which holds the captivating image of a young man idolatrously, devotedly, with mysterious calm and for the rest of his life in love with a woman in the same awkward position as Béatrix; a book that was a fatal example for him!—that night left indelible traces in the heart of this young man who was made to understand by Félicité that short of being a monster, a woman could only be happy and flattered in all her vanity to be the object of a crime.

"You would not have thrown me into the sea!" said the pitiable Camille, wiping away a tear.

✽⤳✿⤚✽⤳✿⤚✽⤳✿⤚✽⤳✿⤚✽⤳✿⤚✽⤳✿⤚✽⤳✿⤚✽⤳✿⤚✽⤳✿⤚

VI Conti Toward morning, Calyste, worn out, fell asleep in his chair. It was the marquise's turn to contemplate this enchanting young man, blanched by his emotions and his first vigil of love; she heard him murmur her name in his sleep.

"He loves even while sleeping," she said to Camille.

"He must be sent home to bed," said Félicité waking him.

No one was anxious at the Hôtel du Guénic since Mademoiselle des Touches had written a note to the baroness. Calyste returned to Les Touches for dinner and found Béatrix up, pale, weak, and languid; but there was not the slightest coolness in her words or expressions. From that evening on, filled with the music Camille provided at the piano to allow Calyste to hold Béatrix's hands without either being able to talk, there was no longer any disturbance at Les Touches. Cold, frail, hard, slender women, like Madame de Rochefide, whose bony necks confer on them a certain feline resemblance, whose souls have the pallor of their light gray or green eyes, require a lightning bolt to melt down their stoniness. For Béatrix, Calyste's raging passion and attempt on her life had been this lightning bolt that nothing withstands and that alters the most refractory natures. Béatrix felt her insides grow limp; true, pure love bathed her heart with its molten flowing warmth. She was living in the soothing atmosphere of unknown sensations in which she felt ennobled, elevated; she was entering the heavenly realm in which Brittany has always enshrined women. She savored the respectful adorations of this youth whose happiness cost her so little, for a gesture, a glance, a word were all Calyste required to be satisfied. The enormous value love places on such little things moved her deeply. The touch of her glove could mean more to this angel than her whole body to the one who should have adored her. What a difference! What woman could resist such constant veneration? She was certain of being obeyed and understood. Were she to ask Calyste to risk his life for her pettiest whim, he would not even have stopped to think. As a result, Béatrix took on a certain quality of imposing nobility. She saw love in all its greatness and sought in it some foothold in order to remain the most magnificent of all women in Calyste's eyes, for she wished to keep him her eternal subject. Her coquettish ploys became all the more persistent as she felt herself weakening. She played the invalid for an entire week with charming hypocrisy. How many times she crossed the lawn in front of garden side of Les Touches, leaning on Calyste's arm and paying back Camille for the torments she had endured during the first week of her stay.

"Ah, my dear, you are making him take the grand tour," said Mademoiselle des Touches to the marquise.

One evening before the excursion to Le Croisic, the two women had been talking about love and laughing about the different styles men had for making their declarations, admitting to each other that the most skillful and naturally the least loving did not waste time meandering through the labyrinth of sentimentality, and were perfectly justified. Which meant that those men who loved most sincerely were, at times, the most shabbily treated. "They go about it like La Fontaine seeking election to the Académie!" Camille said. Her remarks on the grand tour now reminded the marquise of this conversation and made her resentful of Camille's Machiavellism. Madame de Rochefide had the absolute power of keeping Calyste within the limits set by her; she had only to remind him by a word or gesture of his dreadful violence at the edge of the sea. The poor martyr's eyes would fill with tears, he would silence his entreaties, and stifle his hopes, his torments, with a heroism that would surely have moved any other woman. She led him with her diabolic coquetry to such abysmal despair that one day he threw himself into Camille's arms begging her advice. Béatrix, armed with Calyste's letter, had extracted the passage in which he wrote that to love is the prime happiness, to be loved came after; she made use of this axiom to limit his passion to the reverential idolatry that suited her. She was so delighted to have her soul caressed by the paeans of adoration that nature inspires in young men; there is so much effortless art, so much innocent seductiveness in their cries, their prayers, their exclamations, their appeals to themselves, their willingness to mortgage the future, that Béatrix was careful not to answer him. She merely said she was doubtful! It was not yet a question of gratifying his desire, but the permission to love that this boy kept asking, this child determined to take his stand on the stronger side, the moral side. The woman bravest in words is often the weakest in action. After seeing the progress made by pushing Béatrix into the sea, it seemed strange that Calyste did not continue to resort to violence to attain his happiness. But a young man's love is so ecstatic and religious that it seeks to obtain everything through moral conviction, and in that lies its sublimity.

Nonetheless, there came a day when the young Breton, exasperated by desire, complained bitterly to Camille about Béatrix's behavior.

"I had hoped to cure you by making you get to know her quickly," replied Mademoiselle des Touches. "But you spoiled everything with your impatience. Ten days ago you were her master; today, my poor child, you are her slave. It is clear you will never have the strength to carry out my orders."

"What must I do?"

"Pick a quarrel with her on the subject of her inflexibility. A woman is always carried away by discussions. Make her mistreat you and then don't return to Les Touches until she sends for you."

There is a moment in all serious diseases when the patient accepts the most frightful remedies and submits to the most horrible operations. Calyste had reached that point. He listened to Camille's advice and for two days remained at home; but the third, he was scratching at Béatrix's door to tell her that Camille and he were expecting her for lunch.

"Another opportunity lost," Camille told him when she saw his cowardly return.

Béatrix during those two days had often stopped before the window that looks out on the road to Guérande. When Camille caught her staring out, Béatrix said she was looking at the furzes along the path whose golden flowers were illuminated by the September sun. Camille therefore learned Béatrix's secret and had only to say a word to make Calyste happy, but she did not: she was still too feminine to push him to that act that young hearts fear, as though aware of all that their ideal will lose. Béatrix kept them waiting for some time. With anyone else, this delay might have been significant, for the marquise's appearance indicated the desire to fascinate Calyste and prevent any renewed separation. After lunch, she went for a walk in the garden and overwhelmed with joy the young man she overwhelmed with love, by expressing the desire to revisit with him the rock where she almost perished.

"Let us go alone," Calyste asked in tense voice.

"If I refuse," she replied, "I will give you the idea that you are dangerous. Alas, I have already told you a thousand times, I belong to someone else and can only be his. I chose him without any knowledge of love. The crime was twofold, the punishment is double."

When she spoke this way, her eyes slightly damp with the scant tears women like her shed, Calyste felt a compassion that assuaged his burning desire; at such times, he adored her as a madonna. It is as impossible to expect diverse characters to resemble each other in their expression of emotion as it is to expect the same fruits from diverse trees. Béatrix was at that moment anguishing over a horrible dilemma. She was hesitating between herself and Calyste, between the world she hoped to re-enter one day and complete happiness, between the eternal perdition of a second unpardonable passion and the pardon of society. She was beginning to listen to the language of blind love without even the pretense of irritation. She let herself be stroked by the gentle hands of Pity. Already more than once, she had been moved to tears when Calyste promised her a love that would compensate for everything she had lost in the eyes of the world, and pitied her for being attached to a man of such evil genius and insincerity as Conti. More than once she had not stopped Calyste, when telling him of the miseries and torments that had befallen her in Italy after she discovered she was not alone in Conti's affections. Camille had given Calyste more than one lesson on this subject and Calyste had profited from it.

"I would love you totally," he told her. "You would not find in me the triumphs of art, the excitement provided by an audience enthused by the marvels of talent; my one talent would be to love you, my only excitements would be yours, no other woman's admiration would warrant my notice; you would have no odious rivals to fear; you are not appreciated, and just as you are taken for granted, it is I who would wish to be taken for granted every moment of every day."

She listened to his words with her head lowered, allowing him to kiss her hands, silently but graciously admitting that perhaps she was an unrecognized angel.

"I am too humiliated," she replied, "my past divests the future of any security."

It was a glorious morning for Calyste when, on arriving at Les Touches at seven o'clock, he spotted Béatrix between two furze shrubs standing at a window wearing the same straw hat she had worn the day of their excursion. It made him dizzy for a moment. It is by such trivialities that love makes the world greater. It may be that only Frenchwomen know the secrets of such theatricality; they owe it to the subtlety of their intelligence, they know what touches to add without diminishing the power of sentiment. How lightly she weighed on Calyste's arm! They walked out together through the garden door that led to the dunes. Béatrix thought the sands were lovely; she noticed the tough little plants with pink flowers that grow there and gathered some to which she added the Carthusian pinks that also grow in the arid sands. She then divided the flowers with Calyste in a meaningful way; they would become for him an eternally sinister image.

"We must add some sprigs of box tree," she said smiling. While waiting for the boat, she stood for some time on the jetty listening to Calyste relate his foolish behavior the day of her arrival.

"Your escapade, which I learned about, was the reason for my severity that day," she said.

During their outing, Madame de Rochefide had that half-teasing tone of a woman in love, and the same tenderness and abandon. Calyste could easily believe he was loved. But later, wandering beside the rocks along the shore—they went down to one of those charming inlets where the waves deposit the most extraordinary mosaic of odd marble fragments, and played like children in search of the choicest pieces—when Calyste, drunk with joy candidly proposed that they run away to Ireland, she reassumed her air of mysterious dignity, took his arm and continued walking toward the rock that she named her "Tarpeian Rock."

"My dear," she said, slowly climbing the splendid granite mass that would serve as her pedestal, "I do not have the strength to conceal what you mean to me. In ten years I have not known any happiness comparable to what we have just experienced looking for shells among the rocks, exchanging them for these pebbles which I shall have made into a necklace that will be more precious to me than the most brilliant diamonds. I have just become a little girl, a child, as I was at fourteen or sixteen, when I was deserving of you. The love I have been fortunate enough to inspire in you has raised me up in my own eyes. You have made me the proudest, the happiest of women, and you will probably remain in my memory far longer than I in yours."

At that moment, she reached the shelf of the rock where one could see the immense ocean on one side, and Brittany, with its golden islands, its feudal towers and clumps of furze. Never was a woman on a grander stage to make so great an avowal.

"However," she said, "I am not my own, I am more bound by my will than I was by law. Consider yourself punished for my misfortune, and console yourself by knowing that we will suffer together. Dante never saw Beatrice again, Petrarch never possessed his Laura. Such disasters only befall the truly great. Ah, if I am abandoned, if I fall immeasurably lower in shame and infamy, if your Béatrix is cruelly misunderstood by the world that will be unbearable to her, if she becomes the lowest of women! . . . then, beloved boy," she said taking his hand, "you will know that she is first among women, that led by you, she could rise to the skies. But then, my dear, if you want to push her over a cliff, don't miss; after your love, death!"

Calyste was holding Béatrix by the waist; he pulled her close to him. To confirm her sweet words, Madame de Rochefide deposited the most chaste, most timid of kisses on Calyste's forehead. Then they climbed down and walked back slowly, chatting like people in perfect agreement, she convinced of her peace, he no longer doubting his happiness, and both mistaken. Calyste, judging from Camille's impressions, hoped that Conti would be delighted by this occasion to leave Béatrix. The marquise gave herself up to the vagueness of her situation, awaiting an accident of chance. But Calyste was too inexperienced, too loving to invent that accident. They had both reached the most delightful frame of mind and returned to Les Touches through the garden gate for which Calyste had taken the key. It was about six o'clock. The heady scents, the soft air, the golden rays of setting sunlight, everything was in keeping with the way they felt and with the tender words they had exchanged. They walked in the even pace of lovers whose movements express the harmony of their thoughts. There was so heavy a silence over Les Touches that the noise of the gate opening and closing must have clanged throughout the garden. Since Calyste and Béatrix had told each other everything they had wanted to say, and their emotion-filled excursion had tired them, they came in quietly without speaking. Suddenly, in the curve of a path, Béatrix contracted in horror, that contagious fright that is caused by the sight of a snake and that froze Calyste before he knew why. On a bench under a weeping willow, Conti sat talking with Camille. The marquise's convulsive trembling was more revealing than she would have wished. Calyste understood then how much he meant to this woman who had just set up a barrier between them, doubtless to allow herself a few more days of flirtation before crossing it. At that moment, a tragic drama in all its dimensions unfolded in their hearts.

"You were not expecting me quite so soon, were you?" said the singer, offering Béatrix his arm.

The marquise could not avoid relinquishing Calyste's arm and taking Conti's. This ignominious transition, so imperiously ordered, and so dishonoring to the new love, overwhelmed Calyste who flung himself down on the bench beside Camille after having exchanged the coolest of greetings with his rival. He experienced a host of contradictory sensations. After learning how much Béatrix loved him, he would have wanted to take hold of the singer and tell him that Béatrix was now his. But the inner convulsion of that poor woman, betraying everything she felt, for in that one moment she paid for all her sins, had moved him so deeply that he was struck dumb, cognizant, like her, of an implacable necessity. These contradictory impulses produced in him the most violent upheaval he had had to endure since falling in love with Béatrix. Madame de Rochefide and Conti walked past the bench where Calyste was sprawling beside Camille. The marquise looked at her rival and gave her one of those frightening looks with which women can manage to say everything; she avoided Calyste's eyes and appeared to be listening to Conti who seemed to be joking.

"What can they be saying to each other?" Calyste asked Camille.

"My dear child, you know nothing as yet of the dreadful rights that an extinguished passion bequeaths on a man. Béatrix could not refuse to take his arm. He is doubtless teasing her about her love affairs; he must have guessed from your manner and the way you appeared before him."

"He is teasing her? . . ." asked the impetuous young man.

"Calm yourself, or you will lose the few opportunities that still remain. If he offends Béatrix's vanity too much, she will crush him like a worm under her feet. But he is clever, he will know how to handle her with humor. He will hardly assume that the proud Madame de Rochefide could have deceived him. It would be too depraved to love a man merely for his beauty! He will probably depict you as a child possessed by the vanity of having a marquise and deciding the destinies of two women. And finally, he will fire a cunning barrage of the most offensive insinuations. Béatrix will then be obliged to counter with false denials which will grant him the upper hand."

"Ah!" said Calyste, "he does not love her. If it were I, I would set her free. Love implies a choice made at each moment and confirmed from day to day. Each new day validates the last and swells the treasury of our pleasures. A few more days and he would not have found us. What brought him back?"

"A journalist's cutting remark," said Camille. "The opera on whose success he had been counting was a flop, a total flop. The remark: 'It is hard to lose one's reputation and one's mistress at the same time!' said in the lobby perhaps by Claude Vignon, hit him squarely in his pride. Love based on petty emotions is pitiless. I tried to question him, but who can know a character as false and deceitful as his? He seemed fed up with his money problems and his love affair, disgusted with life. He regretted being so publicly allied with the marquise, and speaking of his former happiness, sang me an ode of melancholy too exalted to be sincere. He was probably hoping to extort from me the secret of your love assuming I would be transported by the raptures of his flattery."

"Well?" said Calyste, no longer listening as he watched Béatrix and Conti come back.

Camille had prudently kept her guard up; she had betrayed neither Calyste's nor Béatrix's secret. Conti was capable of taking in anybody, and Mademoiselle des Touches warned Calyste not to trust him.

"My dear boy, this is the most critical moment for you; one would need prudence and skill that you do not have, and you will be taken in by the craftiest conniver on earth, for now I can no longer help you."

The dinner bell was rung. Conti offered his arm to Camille; Béatrix took Calyste's. Camille allowed the marquise to precede her thereby permitting her to look at Calyste and counsel absolute discretion by placing her finger to her lips. Conti was exceedingly gay throughout dinner. It may have been his way of sounding out Madame de Rochefide who played her part badly. In the role of a flirt, she might have deceived Conti; but as a woman in love, he saw through her. The wily musician, in no way trying to embarrass her, pretended not to notice her embarrassment. At dessert, he began a conversation on women and praised the nobility of their feelings. "A woman on the point of abandoning us in prosperity will sacrifice everything to us in misfortune," he said. "Women have over men the advantage of constancy; they must have been deeply wounded to leave their first lover, they cling to him as to their honor. A second love is disgraceful . . ." and so on. He was sublimely moral; he wafted incense over the altar on which lay a bleeding heart, pierced by a thousand stabs. Only Camille and Béatrix understood the bitterness of the acrid epigrams fired off with every panegyric. At times, both of them blushed, but they were obliged to control themselves. Arm in arm on their way to Camille's room, they passed, by mutual understanding, through the darkened drawing room where they could be alone for a moment.

"I cannot allow Conti to walk all over me and let him think he is justified," said Béatrix under her breath. "The convict is always at the mercy of his comrade-in-chains. I am lost, I will have to return to my prison of love. And it is you who have thrown me back into it! Ah, it is you who made him come one day too early or one day too late. I recognize your diabolic literary talent. Now the revenge is complete and the ending perfect."

"I may have *said* I would write to Conti, but to do it . . . ! I am not capable of that!" exclaimed Camille. "You are suffering, I forgive you."

"What will become of Calyste?" asked the marquise with the disarming innocence of conceit.

"Is Conti really taking you away?" asked Camille.

"What, you think you will win out?" cried Béatrix.

It was with her beautiful face distorted with rage that the marquise hurled these terrible words at Camille who tried to conceal her pleasure beneath an expression of false distress. However, the brilliance of her eyes belied the grimace of her mask, and when it came to grimaces, Béatrix was a past master! And so, when they saw each other in the light and sat down on the couch where for the last three weeks so many comedies had been played, and where the intimate tragedy of so many frustrated passions had begun, these two women examined each other for the last time. They saw themselves separated by a gulf of hatred.

"Calyste remains yours," said Béatrix seeing her friend's eyes, "but I am entrenched in his heart and no woman can drive me out."

Camille retorted with inimitable irony, hitting the marquise squarely in the heart, by quoting the famous words of Mazarin's niece to Louis XIV: "You reign, you love and you leave!"

During this intense exchange neither of them had noticed the absence of Calyste and Conti. The singer had remained at the table with his rival urging him to keep him company and finish off a bottle of champagne.

"We have things to discuss," said the singer to ward off any refusal on Calyste's part.

Given the situation, the young Breton had no choice but to accede.

"My dear friend," said the musician in a wheedling voice at the moment when the poor boy had drunk two glasses of wine, "we are both decent chaps and can speak openly. I did not come here out of suspicion. Béatrix loves me," he said with an expression of total complacency, "but I no longer love her. I have not come to carry her off but rather to break with her and leave her the honors of this separation. You are young, you do not know how useful it is to appear to be the victim when one is in fact the executioner. Young men spit fire and flame, they leave a woman by storming out, they often hold her in contempt and make themselves despised. But the mature man has himself sent away, and puts on a pathetic air of humility that leaves a woman with regrets and with the sweet sentiment of her superiority. The divinity's disfavor is not irreparable, while abjuration is irremediable. You do not yet know, fortunately for you, how hampered we are by the wild promises that women are foolish enough to believe which gallantry obliges us to make into nooses to fill the idle hours of happiness. Each then swears eternal love to the other. When we have a passing adventure with a woman, we never fail to tell her politely that we would like to spend a lifetime with her. We pretend to desire the husband's death fervently, while really hoping he enjoys the most perfect health. When the husband dies, there are those women so provincial or so persistent, either dumb enough or daring enough, to run after you saying 'Here I am! I'm free!' None of us is free. This exploded shell fires again and falls into the midst of our greatest triumphs or most carefully planned pleasures. I saw that you could fall in love with Béatrix, and deliberately I left her in a situation where, without any loss to her sacred majesty, she could flirt with you, were it only to tease that angel of a Camille Maupin. Well then, dear chap, love her, you will be doing me a favor. I would like her to behave atrociously toward me. What I fear are her pride and her virtue. Perhaps in spite of my good will, we will need time for this partner-swapping. In such circumstances he who does not initiate is the victor. Just before, while walking around the lawn, I tried to tell her I knew everything and to congratulate her on her happiness. Well, she got angry. At the moment, I am madly in love with the loveliest, the youngest of our singers, Mademoiselle Falcon of the Opéra, and I want to marry her! Yes, I am at that stage. But then, when you come to Paris, you will see that I have traded a marquise for a queen!"

Happiness radiated its glow all over Calyste's candid face; he confessed his love, and that was all that Conti wanted to know. There is not a man in the world, however blasé or depraved he may be, whose passion is not re-ignited the moment he sees it threatened by a rival. One is perfectly willing to leave a woman, but not be left by her. When lovers reach that extreme, both men and women do their utmost to maintain their priority, for such is the gravity of the wound to self-pride. Perhaps it has to do with what society has invested in this sentiment which is less concerned with self-pride than with the whole future of life itself; one risks losing the capital, not just the interest. Questioned by the singer, Calyste recounted everything that had happened during those three weeks at Les Touches and was enchanted by Conti who dissembled his fury behind the most charming amiability.

"Let us go up," he said. "Women are suspicious, they cannot understand how we could be together without tearing out each other's hair and might try to overhear us. For your benefit, my dear boy, I will play a double role. I will be unbearable, gross, jealous with the marquise, I will relentlessly suspect her of trying to deceive me: there is nothing more effective to determine a woman to deceive one; you will be happy and I will be free. Tonight you play the part of the thwarted suitor and I will play the jealous suspicious lover. Pity that poor angel for belonging to a man so utterly lacking in delicacy, weep for her! You can weep, you are young; I, alas, no longer can. That is one great advantage lost to me."

Calyste and Conti went upstairs. The musician, urged by his young rival to sing something, selected the greatest musical masterwork there is for the voice, the famous *Pria che spunti l'aurora,* that even Rubini never attempted without trembling and that has often been Conti's triumph. Never was he more extraordinary than at that moment when a multitude of feelings seethed within him. Calyste was in ecstasy. With the first word of this cavatina, the singer threw the marquise a glance that bestowed a cruel meaning on the words and which was fully understood. Camille, who was accompanying him, was aware of this summons that made Béatrix lower her head; she looked at Calyste and thought the boy had fallen into some kind of trap despite her warning. She was certain of it when the happy young Breton came to bid Béatrix good night, kissing her hand and pressing it with a certain confident knowing air. By the time Calyste returned to Guérande, the servants had loaded Conti's carriage and before dawn, following with the words of the aria he had sung, he took off with Béatrix and Camille's horses to the post station. The shadowy light permitted Madame de Rochefide to look at Guérande, whose towers white by day gleamed in the half light, and to indulge in her deep melancholy. She was leaving behind one of the most precious moments of her life, a love such as the purest young girl might dream of. Human decency was destroying the only true love this woman could or would ever know in her entire life. The woman of the world was yielding to the laws of the world, she was sacrificing love to decorum, as it is sacrificed by some women to Religion or to Duty. Pride frequently attains the level of Virtue. In this light, hers is the same unhappy tale of many women. The following day, Calyste appeared at Les Touches around noon. When he reached that point in the road from which he had seen Béatrix at the window the day before, he spotted Camille who ran to meet him. At the foot of the stairs, she spoke the cruel word "Gone!"

"Béatrix?" Calyste replied, as though struck by lightning.

"You were duped by Conti and said nothing to me; there was nothing I could do."

She led the poor boy to her little sitting room; he threw himself down on the very couch where he had so often seen the marquise and collapsed in tears. Félicité said nothing. She sat smoking her hookah knowing there is nothing to alleviate that first attack of anguish which is always deaf and dumb. Calyste, unable to think clearly, spent the entire day in a state of near paralysis. Just before dinner, Camille tried to talk to him, having begged him to listen to her.

"My dear Calyste, you caused me even deeper grief, and unlike you I did not have the remedy of a splendid future ahead. For me, the earth has no more springtimes and the heart has no more love. And so to find some consolation, I must seek higher. Here, in this very room, the day before she arrived, I drew Béatrix's portrait for you; I did not want to tarnish her, for you would have thought me jealous. Today, let me tell you the truth. Madame de Rochefide is utterly unworthy of you. The scandal of her downfall is unimportant; without it she would have been a nobody. She did it calculatingly to make herself important. She is one of those women who prefers the noise of scandal to the tranquillity of happiness; they insult society in the hope of extorting the deadly alms of slander; they will pay any price to be talked about. She was devoured by vanity. Her wealth, her wit were unable to grant her the feminine royalty she sought to conquer by reigning over a salon; she hoped to achieve the celebrity of the Duchesse de Langeais and the Vicomtesse de Beauséant; but the world is just and only accords the honors of its notice to genuine feelings. Béatrix playing a comedy was judged to be a second-class actress. Her elopement was not justified by any interference. The sword of Damocles did not hang glistening over her pleasures, and furthermore, it is very easy in Paris to enjoy one's happiness covertly, if one loves deeply and sincerely. And finally, had she been all love and tenderness, she would never have followed Conti that night."

Camille spoke long and eloquently, but this final effort was useless. She stopped in midsentence following a gesture of Calyste that indicated his complete faith in Béatrix. She forced him to come down and be present at dinner even though he was unable to eat. It is only in very early youth that such spasms take place. Later on, the organs acquire their habits and become somewhat inured. The effect of morale on the body is not strong enough to induce a fatal disease unless the body has maintained its childhood vulnerability. A mature man can withstand a violent shock that might kill a young man, not out of weaker emotions but stronger organs. Consequently, Mademoiselle des Touches was immediately alarmed by the attitude of calm resignation into which Calyste lapsed after his first outburst of tears. Before leaving, he wanted to see Béatrix's room again, and buried his head in the pillow that had cradled hers.

"This is mad," he said, clasping Camille's hand and departing in a state of deep melancholy.

He returned home, found the usual company engaged in the usual card game, and spent the entire evening at his mother's side. The priest, the Chevalier du Halga, Mademoiselle de Pen-Hoël, all knew about Madame de Rochefide's departure and were delighted; Calyste would now return to them, and so they watched him surreptitiously when noticing how taciturn he was. No one in that ancient manor could possibly imagine the end of this first love in a heart as innocent, as righteous as Calyste's.

❋↣✪↣❋↣✪↣❋↣✪↣❋↣✪↣❋↣✪↣❋↣✪↣❋↣✪↣❋↣✪↣❋↣✪↣❋↣✪↣

VII THE YOUNG PATIENT For a number of days, Calyste continued to go regularly to Les Touches; he wandered around the lawn where he had walked with Béatrix's arm on his. Often, he went as far as Le Croisic, climbing to the rock where he had tried to throw her into the sea; he lay for hours on end beneath the box tree, for having studied the footholds along this rift, he had learned how to climb up and down. His solitary walks, his silence and his self-denial finally alarmed his mother. After two weeks of this behavior reminiscent of an animal in a cage—the cage of this desperate lover being, in La Fontaine's words, *les lieux honorés par les pas, éclairés par les yeux* * of Béatrix—Calyste gave up crossing the little inlet. He

* "Can one be bored in those places/Honored by the steps, illumined by the eyes/Of a gracious and charming princess [...]?"

no longer felt strong enough to drag himself as far as the point along the road from which he had seen Béatrix at the window. His family, overjoyed by the departure of the "Parisians," in the expression of the provinces, noticed nothing either baleful or unhealthy about Calyste. The two old maids and the priest, pursuing their project, had kept Charlotte de Kergarouët who in the evening tried out all her charms on Calyste and got nothing in return but his advice on how to play her hand. All during the evening, Calyste would remain between his mother and his Breton fiancée, observed by the priest and Mademoiselle de Pen-Hoël who, on their way home, compared notes as to the degree of his depression. They mistook the apathy of this unhappy boy for submissiveness to their projects. One evening when Calyste, pleading fatigue, went to bed early, they all lay down their cards and looked at each other as they heard him close his door. They had been listening to his footsteps with anxiety.

"There is something wrong with Calyste," said the baroness wiping her eyes.

"There is nothing wrong with him," replied Mademoiselle de Pen-Hoël. "We must marry him off at once."

"Do you really think that would amuse him?" asked the chevalier.

Charlotte looked sternly at the Chevalier du Halga whom that evening she found in extremely bad taste, immoral, depraved, irreligious, and ridiculous with his dog, despite her aunt's active defense of the old salt.

"Tomorrow morning, I'll give him a talking-to," said the baron whom everyone assumed to be asleep. "I have no desire to leave this world without having seen my grandchild, a pink and white Guénic wearing a Breton bonnet in his cradle."

"He doesn't say a word," commented Zéphirine, "one doesn't know what's the matter with him. Never has he eaten less; what does he live on? If he eats at Les Touches, that infernal cooking is hardly doing him any good."

222

"He is in love," said the chevalier, venturing this opinion with considerable timidity.

"Come now, you old rogue! You have forgotten to put your chip in the basket," said Mademoiselle de Pen-Hoël. "When you start remembering your gay youth you forget everything."

"Come have lunch with us tomorrow," said old Zéphirine to Charlotte and Jacqueline, "my brother will reason with his son and we will settle everything. One nail drives another."

"Not in Bretons," said the chevalier.

The next morning, Calyste saw Charlotte arrive, already dressed to the teeth, at the moment when the baron had just ended his lecture on matrimony to which he had no reply. He fully understood the ignorance of his aunt, his father, his mother, and all their friends; he had been gathering the fruits of knowledge, and now found himself isolated and no longer conversant with domestic jargon. He consequently asked his father to give him a few more days. The baron, rubbing his hands with glee, restored the baroness' cheer by whispering the good news to her. Lunch was very gay. Charlotte, who had received the baron's signal, was effervescent. Throughout the town, Gasselin spread the news of an agreement between the Guénics and the Kergarouëts. After lunch, Calyste walked out on the balcony and went down to the garden where Charlotte followed him. He took her arm and led her to the arbor at the back. The family watched from the window with emotion. Charlotte looked back at the lovely façade, rather concerned over the silence of her betrothed, and took advantage of what she saw to begin a conversation with Calyste: "They are watching us!"

"But they can't hear us," he replied.

"Yes, but they can see us."

"Let's sit down, Charlotte," Calyste gently answered, taking her by the hand.

"Is it true that your pennant used to fly from that twisted column?" asked Charlotte, surveying the house as though it were hers. "How nice it would look! And how happy one could be here! You will make some changes in the house, won't you, Calyste?"

"I won't have time for that, my dear Charlotte," said the young man raising her hands and kissing them. "I will confide to you my secret. I am too much in love with someone you have seen and who loves me to be able to make any other woman happy. I know that since our childhood we have been intended for each other."

"But she is married, Calyste," said Charlotte.

"I can wait," he replied.

"And so can I," said Charlotte, her eyes filled with tears. "You can't love that woman for very long; they say she's gone off with a singer . . . ."

"Get married, my dear Charlotte," Calyste continued. "With the fortune your aunt has promised you, which is enormous for Brittany, you can find a better husband than me . . . You might find someone with a title. I did not take you aside to tell you what you already know, but to implore you, in the name of our childhood friendship, to take upon yourself our rupture and refuse me. You can say that you wanted no part of a man whose heart is mortgaged, and at least this way, my passion will have served to spare you any unfairness. You have no idea how heavily life weighs on me! I cannot face any struggle, I am as weak as a body without a soul, lacking in the very essence of life. If it were not for the grief it would cause my mother and my aunt, I would already have thrown myself into the sea. I have not been back to the cliffs of Le Croisic since the day that temptation became irresistible. Please do not mention this. Good-bye, Charlotte."

He took her face between his hands, kissed her hair, left by the path beneath the gable and ran off to Camille's where he stayed half the night. When he returned home at one in the morning, he found his mother at her needlework, waiting for him. He came in softly, took her hand and asked, "Has Charlotte left?"

"She is leaving tomorrow with her aunt, both of them in despair. Come to Ireland, my darling," she said.

"How often I have thought of running away!" he said.

"Ah!" exclaimed the baroness.

"With Béatrix," he added.

A few days after Charlotte's departure, Calyste accompanied the Chevalier du Halga on his customary stroll along the mall. He sat down on a bench in the sun from which his view took in the entire countryside, from the weathervanes of Les Touches to the reefs sketched out by the fingers of foam that played above the shoals at high tide. Calyste by then was thin and pale, his strength was ebbing, and he had begun to feel the first recurrent chills that denote fever. His sunken eyes had the bright glaze seen in lonely people possessed by a single idea, or communicated by the ardent courage of the daring fighters of our contemporary society. The chevalier was the only person with whom he could have any exchange. He sensed in this old man an apostle of his own religion, and recognized in him the vestiges of an undying love.

"Have you loved many women in your lifetime?" Calyste asked him the second time they were *in convoy,* in the words of the old sailor.

"Only one," answered the captain.

"Was she free?"

"No," answered the chevalier. "Oh, how I suffered! She was the wife of my best friend, my protector, my chief, and how we loved each other."

"She loved you too?" asked Calyste.

"Passionately," replied the chevalier with unusual verve.

"Were you happy?"

"Up until her death. She died at the age of forty-nine, emigrating to Saint Petersburg where the climate killed her. She must be terribly cold in her coffin. I have often thought of getting her and laying her to rest in our beloved Breton earth, close to me! However, she is buried in my heart."

The chevalier wiped his eyes. Calyste took his hands and clasped them.

"This dog means more to me than my life," he said pointing to Thisbé. "This little thing is exactly like the one she used to stroke with her beautiful hands and take on her lap. I can never look at Thisbé without seeing the hands of Madame de Kergarouët."

"Have you seen Madame de Rochefide?" Calyste asked.

"No," the chevalier replied. "It is now fifty-eight years since I took notice of any woman, except your mother who has something of Madame de Kergarouët's coloring."

Three days later, the chevalier told Calyste, while walking on the mall: "My boy, my entire fortune consists of one hundred forty louis. When you know where Madame de Rochefide is, come to me for the money and go see her."

Calyste thanked the old man, whose way of life he envied. But from day to day, he became more morose. He seemed to care for no one. He behaved as though the whole world offended him. He was gentle and kind only to his mother. The baroness followed the progress of this mania with growing concern. She alone, by begging him, managed to get him to take some nourishment. Toward the beginning of October, the young invalid ceased going to the mall with the chevalier, who, in vain tried to persuade him with the cajoleries of an old man: "Come, we will talk about Madame de Rochefide, I will tell you about my first adventure."

"Your son is very ill," he said to the baroness the day his urging proved useless.

To all questions about his health, Calyste replied that he felt perfectly well, and like all young melancholics, he took pleasure in savoring death. He no longer left the house, he remained in the garden, warming himself in the pale autumn sun on a bench, alone with his thoughts, avoiding all company.

When Calyste stopped coming to see her, Félicité asked the Abbé Grimont to come to Les Touches. The frequency of the priest's visits to Les Touches where he spent almost every morning and often dined, became a great piece of news. It was talked about throughout the countryside and even as far as Nantes. He nonetheless never missed an evening at the Guénics where despair reigned. Masters and servants alike were suffering over Calyste's intractability, without however thinking him in danger. It never occurred to any of these people that the poor young man could die of love. The chevalier, in all his travels and memories, knew of no examples of such a death. Everyone attributed Calyste's gauntness to lack of adequate food. His mother went down on her knees to beg him to eat. Calyste tried to overcome his repugnance to please his mother, but the food eaten against his will only accelerated the slow fever that was consuming this handsome young man.

Toward the end of October, the beloved child no longer went up to bed in his own room on the second floor. He had a bed in the sitting room downstairs and spent most of the day in it surrounded by his family, who finally called in the doctor of Guérande. The doctor tried to lower the fever with quinine, and for a few days the fever dropped. The doctor had ordered exercise and diversion for Calyste. The baron regained some of his strength and came out of his apathy; he became young as his son grew old. He went out with Calyste, Gasselin, and his two fine hunting dogs. Calyste obeyed his father, and for a few days, all three of them went hunting. They hunted in the forest, they visited their friends in neighboring castles, but Calyste bore no trace of gaiety; no one could raise a smile in him; his face, a livid contracted mask, betrayed total passivity. The baron, overcome with fatigue, fell into a dreadful prostration that obliged him to return home, bringing back Calyste in the same condition. Shortly after their return, father and son were so dangerously ill that on the request of the doctor himself they had to send for the two most famous doctors in Nantes.

It was as though the baron had been struck down by the visible change in Calyste. With the terrifying lucidity that nature bestows on the dying, he saw the extinction of his race and trembled like a frightened child; saying nothing, he merely clasped his hands and prayed from the armchair to which his weakness bound him. He sat facing Calyste's bed and watched him ceaselessly. His son's slightest movement produced in him an intense agitation, as though the flame of his life were wavering. The baroness no longer left the room, and old Zéphirine sat knitting by the fireplace in horrible anxiety. She was constantly being asked for more wood, for both father and son were cold; her provisions were being attacked, and so she decided to hand over her keys, no longer agile enough to run after Mariotte. However, she wanted to know exactly what was going on, and every moment whispered questions to Mariotte and her sister-in-law. She took them aside to find out the condition of her brother and nephew. One evening, as Calyste and his father were dozing, the old spinster Pen-Hoël told her that they would probably have to resign themselves to the death of the baron whose face had turned white and waxen. She dropped her knitting, fished out of her pocket an old rosary of black beads, and started to recite it with such fervor, restoring to her parched and ancient face such a glow of vigor, that the other old maid at once began imitating her. Then, at a signal from the priest, they all joined in Mademoiselle du Guénic's spiritual exaltation.

"I was the first to implore God," said the baroness remembering the fatal letter written by Calyste, "but he did not hear my prayers!"

"It might be a good idea," said the priest, "to ask Mademoiselle des Touches to come and see Calyste."

"That one!" exclaimed Zéphirine, "the cause of all our troubles. It was she who lured him away from his family, she who took him away from us, who gave him impious books to read, taught him the language of heresy. May she be damned, and

my God never forgive her! It is she who has destroyed the du
Guénics."

"And it is she who may restore them," said the priest gently.
"She is a saintly, virtuous person. I can vouch for her. She has
only the best of intentions toward Calyste. May she be able to
realize them!"

"Let me know the day she sets foot in this house, and I will
leave!" cried the old maid. "She has killed the father and the
son. Don't you think I can hear how weak Calyste's voice is?
He has hardly enough strength to talk."

It was at that moment that the three doctors came in. They
exhausted Calyste with their questions, but as for the father, the
examination was brief. Their diagnosis was made in an instant;
they were surprised he was still alive. The doctor from Guérande calmly announced that it would probably be necessary to
take Calyste to Paris for consultation with the most eminent
specialists, for it would cost more than a hundred louis if they
were summoned to Guérande.

"One dies of a disease, but not of love; that is nothing," said
Mademoiselle de Pen-Hoël.

"Alas, whatever the cause, Calyste is dying," said the baroness.
"I recognize in him all the symptoms of consumption—the
most horrible disease in my country."

"Calyste is dying?" asked the baron opening his eyes, from
which two big tears slowly rolled down the innumerable folds
of his face and landed on his cheeks—the only two tears he had
probably ever shed in his life. He got to his feet, took a few steps
to his son's bed, took hold of his hands and looked at him.

"What do you want, father," Calyste asked.

"I want you to live!" cried the baron.

"I cannot live without Béatrix," replied Calyste as the old
man fell back into his chair.

"Where can we find a hundred louis to send for the doctors
in Paris? There is still time," said the baroness.

"A hundred louis!" exclaimed Zéphirine. "Can they save him?"

Without waiting for her sister-in-law's reply, the old maid put her hands through the opening in her pockets and undid her underskirt which fell heavily to the floor. She knew the places where she had sewn her louis so well that she ripped them open with a speed that bordered on magic. The gold coins clanged as they fell one by one onto her underskirt. Old Pen-Hoël watched her with an expression of dumb amazement.

"But they can all see you!" she whispered into Zéphirine's ear.

"Thirty-seven," replied Zéphirine continuing her count.

"Everyone will know how much you have!"

"Forty-two."

"Double louis all new! Where did you get them, you who cannot even see clearly?"

"I felt them. Here are one hundred and four louis," announced Zéphirine. "Is that enough?"

"What's going on?" asked the Chevalier du Halga, arriving just then and unable to account for the pose of his old friend holding out her petticoat filled with louis.

In two words Mademoiselle de Pen-Hoël explained it to him.

"I heard about it," he said, "and came to offer the hundred and forty louis I had been keeping for Calyste, as he knows."

The chevalier pulled two rolls out of his pocket and held them out. Mariotte, seeing all this wealth, told Gasselin to close the door.

"Gold will not restore his health," said the baroness in tears.

"But it may allow him to run after his marquise," replied the chevalier. "Come on, Calyste!"

Calyste sat up and cried out joyfully, "Let's go!"

"Then he will live," said the baron in a mournful voice. "Now I can die. Go send for the priest."

These words spread terror. Calyste, seeing his father turn ashen from the painful emotions of this scene, could not hold back his tears. The priest, knowing the doctors' verdict, had gone to get Mademoiselle des Touches, for just as he had formerly found her repulsive, so he now found her admirable, and defended her as a shepherd defends his favorite lamb.

***

VIII DEATH AND MARRIAGE As soon as the news of the baron's desperate condition spread through the town, a crowd gathered outside the house. Farmers, marsh workers, and townspeople knelt in the courtyard while the priest administered extreme unction to the old Breton warrior. The entire town was grieved by the news of the father dying beside his ailing son. The extinction of this ancient Breton race was considered a public calamity. Calyste was deeply moved by this ceremony. For a while, his grief silenced his passion. During the death agony of this heroic defender of the monarchy, he remained kneeling as he watched the advance of death, and wept. The old man expired in his armchair in the presence of the assembled family.

"I die faithful to the King and to the Church. My God, as a reward for my endeavors, grant that Calyste live!" he said.

"I will live, father, and I will obey you," replied the young man.

"If you wish to make my death as sweet as Fanny made my life, promise me you will marry."

"I promise, father."

It was touching to see Calyste, or rather his ghost, leaning on old Chevalier du Halga, a specter leading a shade, as he followed the baron's coffin in his role of chief mourner. The church and the little square in front were filled with people who came from ten leagues around.

The baroness and Zéphirine were plunged into despair on seeing that despite his attempts to obey his father, Calyste remained in an ominous stupor. The day the family went into mourning, the baroness took Calyste out to a bench in the garden and questioned him. Calyste replied sweetly and submissively, but his answers were totally disheartening.

"Mother," he said. "There is no life left in me. The food I eat does not nourish me, the air I take into my lungs does not refresh my blood; the sun seems cold to me. And when, as at this moment, it illumines the façade of the house for you, there where you can see the sculptures bathed in light, I only see indistinct forms shrouded in fog. If Béatrix were here, everything would become bright again. There is only one thing in this world that has its proper color and shape, and it is this flower and these leaves," he said, showing her the withered bouquet that the marquise had given him.

The baroness did not dare ask him any more. Her son's replies betrayed even greater madness than his silence betrayed his sorrow. However, on seeing Mademoiselle des Touches through the windows opposite the garden, Calyste thrilled with joy—Félicité reminded him of Béatrix. It was thus to Camille that the two disconsolate women owed the only ray of joy that broke through their mourning.

"So Calyste," said Mademoiselle des Touches on seeing him, "the carriage is waiting. We will go together to find Béatrix. Are you coming?"

The pale, haggard face of this young man in mourning suddenly flushed with excitement and a smile brightened his features.

"We will save him," said Mademoiselle des Touches to his mother who gripped her hand as tears of joy fell from her eyes.

Mademoiselle des Touches, the Baroness du Guénic, and Calyste left for Paris a week after the baron's death, leaving the household in the care of old Zéphirine.

Félicité, in her loving concern for Calyste, had arranged a brilliant future for the poor boy. Related to the Grandlieu family whose ducal branch ended in five daughters, she had written to the Duchesse de Grandlieu about Calyste and informed her that she was selling her house on the rue du Mont-Blanc, for which a number of speculators were offering two million, five hundred thousand francs. Her lawyer had just arranged for her to purchase in its place one of the most beautiful houses on the rue de Bourbon, at a cost of seven hundred thousand francs. With the difference in the sale price of the house on the rue de Mont-Blanc and the purchase price of the new house, she was setting aside one million francs for the reacquisition of the du Guénic lands, and was leaving her entire fortune to Sabine de Grandlieu whose task it would be to cure Calyste of his passion for Madame de Rochefide. Félicité knew the plans of the duke and duchess who had betrothed the last of their five daughters to the Vicomte de Grandlieu, the heir to all their titles; she knew that Clotilde-Frédérique, the second, wanted to remain unmarried without, however, becoming a nun as the eldest had done. Consequently, the only one left to marry off was the next to the last, the lovely Sabine, then twenty years old.

During the trip, Félicité informed the baroness of these arrangements. The house on the rue de Bourbon, which she intended for Calyste in the event her projects worked out, was in the process of being furnished. The three of them stayed at the hôtel de Grandlieu where the baroness was received with all the distinction to which her maiden and married names entitled her. Mademoiselle des Touches naturally advised Calyste to visit Paris while she tried to locate Béatrix, and she exposed him to all the pleasures the city had to offer. The duchess, her two daughters and their friends introduced Calyste to Paris at just the season when all the festivities were beginning. The excitement of Paris proved to be a major distraction for the young Breton. He found a certain similarity of spirit between Madame de Rochefide and Sabine de Grandlieu, who was at the time one of the loveliest and most charming young ladies in Parisian society, and from then on became receptive to her advances, something no other woman could have obtained from him. Sabine played her part all the better since she was attracted to Calyste. Things went so well that during the winter of 1837, the young baron, who had regained his color and bloom of youth, listened without revulsion as his mother reminded him of the promise made to his dying father and spoke of his marrying Sabine de Grandlieu. Still, while holding to his promise, he hid a secret apathy that the baroness was aware of and hoped would dissolve in the pleasures of a happy marriage. The day when the Grandlieu family and the baroness, joined for the occasion by her relatives from England, were assembled in the drawing room of the hôtel de Grandlieu to hear the family notary, Léopold Hannequin, explain the marriage contract before reading it, Calyste, visibly disturbed, categorically refused to accept the settlement Mademoiselle des Touches had made in his behalf. He still counted on her devotion to locate Béatrix. At that moment, to the surprise of both families, Sabine came in, dressed in a manner to recall Madame de Rochefide, despite her dark hair, and handed the following letter to Calyste.

CAMILLE TO CALYSTE   *Calyste, before entering my novice's cell, I am permitted one last glance at the world I am about to leave in order that I may soar up to the world of prayer. That glance is solely at you who, until now, have been the whole world for me. My voice, if my calculations are correct, will reach you in the midst of a ceremony at which I could not possibly be present. The day you are at the altar, giving your hand to a charming young girl who will be able to love you before heaven and earth, I shall be in a convent in Nantes. I too at an altar, but forever betrothed to Him who never deceives or betrays. I do not mean to sadden you, but to beg you not to undo by any false delicacy the good I have wished to do for you since I first saw*

you. Do not dispute these rights I have so dearly ac-
quired. If love is suffering, then Calyste, I have loved
you well! But have no regrets. The only pleasures I
have tasted in my life I owe to you; the pains were
my own doing. Repay me for all those past pains by
granting me eternal joy. Allow poor Camille, who
is no more, to participate at least in the material hap-
piness that you will be able to enjoy daily. Allow me,
my dear, to be as it were the perfume in the flowers
of your life, to be eternally present without ever be-
ing in the way. I probably owe to you the happiness
of eternal life; would you not have me reciprocate by
my gift of a few worldly goods? Would you be un-
generous? Could you fail to see in this the ultimate
subterfuge of a repressed love? Calyste, the world
without you held no further meaning for me, you
made it a desolate emptiness for me, and you led the
unbelieving Camille Maupin, author of books and
plays that I now solemnly disclaim, you threw that
insolent perverse woman, bound hand and foot, be-
fore God. Today, I am what I should have been, a
child full of innocence. Yes, I have bathed in the
tears of repentance, and may now be presented at the
altar by an angel, my beloved Calyste! How sweet to
call you by this name that has been sanctified by my
decision! I love you unselfishly, as a mother loves her
son, as the Church loves a child. I can pray for you
and yours without intermingling any other desire
beside your happiness. If you only knew what sub-
lime tranquillity I live in now, having raised my
mind above petty mundane concerns, and how sweet
is the knowledge of having done one's duty, in the
words of your noble motto, you would stride into
your beautiful life with an unhesitating step, with-
out looking backward or sideways. I am therefore

*writing to you to ask you above all to be true to
yourself and to your loved ones. My dearest, the
world in which you must live cannot subsist without the faith of duty, and you would be abusing it,
as I did, by giving yourself up to passion and fantasy, which is what I did. A woman is a man's equal
only by making of her life a continual offering,
just as man's life is a perpetual action. Now then,
my life was like a long siege of egotism. Perhaps for
that reason, God placed you on the doorstep of my
house, in the twilight of my life, as the messenger responsible for my punishment and my pardon. Listen
to this confession of a woman for whom fame was
the beacon leading her to the right path. Be noble,
sacrifice your fantasies to your duties as head of family, husband, father! Raise up the fallen banner of
the ancient du Guénics, show this age without religion or principle what a gentleman in all his glory
and splendor can be. Dearest child of my heart, let
me play just a bit at being a mother; adorable Fanny
can no longer be jealous of woman who is deaf as
far as the world is concerned, and of whom you
will no longer perceive anything but her hands forever raised to heaven. Today more than ever, the
nobility requires a fortune, and so accept part of
mine, Calyste, and use it well. It is not a gift but a
trust fund. I was more concerned for your children
and your ancient Breton estates than for you in offering you the profit that the years have amassed on
my property in Paris.*

"Let us sign the contract," said the young baron to the great
satisfaction of all.

THE
HONEYMOON

PART ONE

SHADY
ENTANGLEMENTS

I ABOUT TRAVEL AND ITS RELATIONSHIP TO MARRIAGE The following week, after the nuptial mass held at seven in the morning at the church of Saint Thomas Aquinas, as was the custom of some of the families of the Faubourg Saint-Germain, Calyste and Sabine climbed into a handsome coach amid the embraces, congratulations and tears of some twenty people herded under the awning of the hôtel de Grandlieu. The congratulations came from the four witnesses and from the male guests, while the tears were to be seen in the eyes of the duchess and her daughter Clotilde, both of whom trembled with the same fearful thought: "Here she is starting out in life. Poor Sabine! She is at the mercy of a man who did not exactly marry out of his own volition."

Marriage consists not only of pleasures, as fleeting in this state as in any other; it also involves harmony of moods, physical compatibility, agreement of character, which render this social necessity an eternal problem. Marriageable daughters understand as well as their mothers the terms and hazards of this lottery. That is why women cry at weddings while men smile. Men feel they have nothing to lose; women have a fair idea of the risks they run.

In another carriage ahead of the newlyweds sat the Baroness du Guénic, to whom the duchess said, "You are a mother, even though you have had an only son. Try to take my place for my dear Sabine."

Seated in front of the carriage was a page boy who served as courier, and behind were two chambermaids. The four postilions dressed in their finest livery, for each carriage was harnessed to four horses, all wore flowers in their buttonholes and ribbons on their hats which the Duc de Grandlieu had tried desperately to make them remove, even bribing them with money. The French postilion is eminently intelligent, but he is attached to his pranks; so they took the money and once at the gates of the city put the ribbons back.

"So then, good-bye, Sabine," said the duchess, "remember

your promise, write me often. Calyste, I need say no more to you, you understand me!"

Clotilde, leaning against her youngster sister Athenaïs at whom the Vicomte Juste de Grandlieu was smiling, gave the bride a knowing glance through her tears, and watched the coach disappear with the accompanying volleys of four whips that cracked louder than rifles. In a few seconds, the merry convoy reached the esplanade of the Invalides, crossed over the Pont d'Iéna, and reached the limits of Passy, then on to the road to Versailles and at last the highway to Brittany.

Is it not remarkable, to say the least, that from the artisans of Switzerland and Germany to the great families of France and England, all observe the same custom of taking off on a trip after the wedding ceremony? The great pile into a rolling box, while the simple wander gaily off into the woods, banqueting at all the inns so long as their merriment, or rather their money, lasts. A moralist would be hard put to decide where the greater modesty lies—in the one that hides from the public while inaugurating the home and the conjugal bed as good bourgeois do, or the one that hides from the family while exhibiting itself in broad daylight to total strangers. Sensitive souls doubtless prefer solitude and would shun the world and the family alike. The sudden love that begins a marriage is a diamond, a pearl, a jewel fashioned by the greatest of all arts, a treasure to be buried deep within the heart.

Who can describe a honeymoon better than the bride? And how many women will acknowledge that this season of uncertain duration (for some it lasts only one night!) is the preface to married life! Sabine's first three letters to her mother indicate a situation that, alas, is hardly new for some young brides and many older women. Not all women who found they were nurses for a broken heart, so to speak, realized it as quickly as Sabine. However, young girls from the Faubourg Saint-Germaine, when they are clever, are already mature women mentally. Before their marriage they received from society and from their mothers the baptism of good manners. Duchesses eager to have their traditions carried on are often unaware of the extent of their teaching when they say to their daughters: "One does not gesture like that."—"One does not laugh at such things."—"One does not throw oneself on a couch, one sits down on it."—"Stop those dreadful manner-isms!"—"Such things are simply not done, my dear!", and so on. Consequently, middle-class critics have unjustly discredited the innocence and virtue of these young girls who, like Sabine, are virgins exclusively perfected by the mind, by the habit of grand airs, good taste, and who from the age of sixteen know how to use their opera glasses. For Sabine to have lent herself to the matchmaking of Mademoiselle des Touches, she must have come from the same school as Mademoiselle de Chaulieu.* Her innate finesse, her marks of good breeding will perhaps make this young lady as interesting as the heroine of *Les Mémoires de deux jeunes mariées,* when one sees the useless-ness of such social advantages at the critical moments of mar-ried life, when they are often annulled by the combined weight of passion and misery.

* The Duchesse de Chaulieu, whose daughter (Louise, the heroine) intended to make "a husband out of her lover," warned her of the difficulty of making "a lover out of her husband," which is "an equally difficult operation." Unlike the Duchesse de Grandlieu, she advised Louise to "sacrifice everything to her husband." (Balzac, *Mémoires de deux jeunes mariées*)

To Madame la Duchesse de Grandlieu

Guérande, April 1838

Dear Mother,

*You will surely understand why I have not writ-
ten to you during the trip; our thoughts at such
times are in constant motion like the coach wheels.
Here I am, as of two days ago, in the depths of Brittany, at the hôtel du Guénic, a house decorated all
over like a coconut shell box. Despite the affection
of Calyste's family, I feel the need to be near you, to
tell you the many things that I know can only be
confided in a mother. Mama dear, Calyste got married while suffering from a deep depression, which
all of us knew; but though you did not hide from
me the difficulties of my position, alas, they are
greater than you thought! Oh dear mama, what a
wealth of experience we acquire in a few days and,
why should I not tell you, even in a few hours! All
your advice has become pointless, and you will guess
why by just these words: I love Calyste as though he
were not my husband. Which is to say that if I were
married to someone else and were traveling with
Calyste, I would love him and hate my husband.
And so, imagine a man loved so completely, so in-
voluntarily, so absolutely (without supplying any
other adverbs you might wish to add) that I have
entered into slavery despite your sound warnings!
You advised me to remain lofty, noble, dignified and
proud in order to obtain from Calyste those feelings
that are subject to no alteration in life—the esteem
and consideration that should sanctify a woman
within her home. You were doubtless justified in*

your opposition to the young women of today who, under the pretext of a close relationship with their husbands, begin by being docile, compliant, good-natured, familiar, by indulging in an abandon that you consider sluttish (something I admit I do not yet understand, but we shall see later on) and which, if I am to believe you, are like steps toward the rapid descent to indifference and even perhaps contempt. "Remember you are a Grandlieu!" you whispered. These counsels, full of the maternal eloquence of a Dedalus, shared the destiny of all mythological things. Dearest beloved mother, would you have guessed that I would begin with the catastrophe that according to you ends the honeymoon of present-day brides?

When Calyste and I found ourselves alone in the coach, we were each so dull-witted, sensing the importance of the first word, the first glance, that both of us, overwhelmed by the responsibility, stared out the window. It was so ridiculous that near the gates of the city, monsieur in a shaking voice began a speech, doubtless prepared in advance like all improvisations, which I listened to with a quaking heart and take the liberty of abridging for you. "My dear Sabine, I want you to be happy and above all to be happy in the way you would like to be. And so, given our situation, instead of deceiving each other with noble subterfuges about our characters and our feelings, let us both be what we will become in a few years. Consider that you have a brother in me as I should like to have a sister in you." Though phrased with great tact, I found nothing in this first statement of conjugal love that corresponded to the throbbing of my soul, and after replying that I felt the same way remained silent. Following this decla-

ration of our rights to mutual frigidity, we talked about the weather, the dust, the stops along the way, the landscape, with the most exquisite politeness, I laughing a forced little laugh, he very pensive.

Finally, on leaving Versailles, I asked Calyste right out, calling him "my dear Calyste," as he had been calling me "my dear Sabine," to tell me what it was that had brought him so close to death and to which I owed the pleasure of being his bride. For some moments he hesitated, and for the length of three posting stops it became a contest of wills between us—I trying to appear headstrong and determined to sulk, he weighing the fatal question like Charles X faced with the challenge of the newspapers: "Will the King concede?" * *Finally, after the stop in Verneuil and after swearing enough oaths to satisfy three dynasties—never to reproach him for this madness, not to treat him scornfully, etc.—he described his love for Madame de Rochefide. "I do not want any secrets between us," he said in conclusion! Poor sweet Calyste! He evidently did not know that his friend, Mademoiselle des Touches, and you had been obliged to tell me everything, for one does not costume a girl the way I was costumed when we signed the contract without preparing her for the part. To a mother as loving as you everything can be confessed. Well then, I was deeply hurt to discover that he had complied much less with my desire to hear about it than with his own to talk about this secret passion. Can you blame me, mother dear, for wanting to evaluate the extent of this grief, this open wound that you had already pointed out to me? So, eight hours after being blessed by the priest of Saint*

* This was the question posed by the liberal press at the time of the general elections in 1830.

Thomas Aquinas, your Sabine found herself in the awkward position of a new bride listening, from her own husband's mouth, to the confession of an unhappy love affair and the cruelty of her rival! There I was in the dramatic situation of a young girl discovering officially that she owed her marriage to the refusal of an aging blond! Having heard his account, I found what I had been seeking. "What?" you will ask. Oh mother dear, I have seen enough Cupids and Psyches on clocks and mantelpieces to understand what to do! Calyste ended his poem of reminiscences with the sincerest promise to forget completely what he called his madness. Any promise requires a signature. The happy hapless boy took my hand, carried it to his lips, and then held it between his hands for some time. A declaration then followed that seemed more fitting to our marital state than the first, though our mouths spoke not a word. I owed that pleasure to my spirited indignation over the poor taste of a woman foolish enough not to have loved my handsome captivating Calyste . . . .

I am being called to play a game of cards I have not yet mastered. I shall continue this tomorrow. To leave you in order to make a fifth at mouche could only happen in the depths of Brittany!

III How Fast, According to Scribe, Emotions Progress in a Coach *

May

I continue the course of my odyssey. The third day, your children no longer used the ceremonious vous, *but the lovers'* tu. *My mother-in-law, de-*

* Allusion to Scribe's play *La Tête-à-Tête ou Trente Lieues en poste.*

lighted to see us happy, tried to substitute for you, mother darling, and like all people who assume a role with the hope of eradicating previous memories, she was so charming she almost succeeded. Doubtless, she understood the heroism of my conduct, for at the outset of the trip she hid her anxiety too well, by her excessive discretion, to avoid making it apparent.

When I saw the towers of Guérande loom ahead I whispered to your son-in-law, "Have you really forgotten her?" My husband, now *my angel, was evidently unfamiliar with the treasures of a sincere innocent affection, for these few words made him almost wild with delight. Unfortunately, my desire to make him forget Madame de Rochefide carried me too far. What shall I say? I am in love. And after all, I am almost Portuguese, for I am more like you than my father.* Calyste took everything I had to offer, like a spoiled child, for he is an only child. Just between us, if I have a daughter, I would not want her to marry an only child. It is hard enough to keep one tyrant in check, but in an only son I see several. And so we reversed the roles and I played the devoted woman. There are certain dangers in a devotion from which one seeks to profit, one loses one's dignity. I consequently announce the collapse of this demivirtue. Dignity is no more than a screen*

* Sabine's mother was Portuguese, of the elder d'Ajuda branch. She became the mother-in-law of her cousin, the Marquis Miguel d'Ajuda-Pinto who married the Grandlieus' third daughter, Josephine, after the death of his first wife— Arthur de Rochefide's only sister. These interwoven genealogies appear throughout the *Comédie humaine* with frequent reappearance of the same characters, such as the Duchesse de Grandlieu, the Marquis d'Ajuda-Pinto, Claude Vignon, et al.

*set up by pride behind which we give free rein to
our fury. Oh mama, you were far away, and I saw
myself at an abyss. If I had maintained my dignity,
I would have suffered the frigid agony of some manner of fraternity that would surely have become
sheer indifference. And what future would I then
have had before me? My devotion bore the result of
making me Calyste's slave. Will I be able to cast off
this role? We shall see. For the moment, I am
enjoying it. I love Calyste. I love him with the total
irrationality of a mother who thinks her son can do
no wrong, even when he mistreats her.*

May 15th

*Until now then, mama dear, marriage has ap-
peared to me in its most delightful guise. I extend
all my affection to the handsomest of men who was
disdained by a fool for a croaker of songs, for that
woman is evidently a fool and a frigid one to boot—
the worst kind of fool. I am most charitable in my
legitimate passion, I cure wounds while inflicting
incurable ones on myself. For indeed, the more I love
Calyste, the more I realize that I would die of grief
if our present happiness were to end. I am, by the
way, adored by the entire family and by the society
that assembles at the du Guénics, all of them figures
in medieval tapestries, who have stepped out of
them to prove that the impossible exists. One day,
when I am alone, I will write you a full description
of my aunt Zéphirine, Mademoiselle de Pen-Hoël,
the Chevalier du Halga, the young Kergarouët girls,
and the rest. Even the servants—whom I hope to be
allowed to bring to Paris, Mariotte and Gasselin,
who consider me an angel descended from heaven*

*and tremble when I speak to them—all are figures
to be preserved under glass.*

*My mother-in-law solemnly installed us in the
rooms she and her late husband formerly occupied.
It was a touching scene. "I spent the whole of my
happy life here," she said to us. "May this be a happy
omen for you, my dear children." She then took
Calyste's room. That saintly woman seemed to want
to divest herself of the memories of her noble married life in order to bestow it on us.*

*The provincial life of Brittany, this town, this
family of antiquated mores, everything, despite the
derisive view that only we mocking Parisians share,
has something inexplicably grandiose about it, even
to its minutest details, that can only be defined by
the word* sacred. *All the tenants of the du Guénics'
vast properties, recuperated as you know by Mademoiselle des Touches, whom we must visit in her
convent, came in a body to greet us. Those good
people in their Sunday best, all of them expressing
intense joy over having Calyste as their master again,
helped me understand Brittany and feudal France.
It was a celebration that I would rather tell you
about than describe in writing. The terms of all the
leases were proposed by the peasants themselves.
The signing will take place after we make an inspection of* our *lands, mortgaged for the last hundred
and fifty years! . . . Mademoiselle de Pen-Hoël told
us that these chaps had kept accounts of the revenues
with an accuracy that no Parisian would believe. In
three days we are setting out on horseback for our
inspection tour. When we return, dearest mother, I
will write again. But what can I tell you if already
my happiness is complete? I will write then to tell*

you what you already know, which is how much I love you."

✳↩۞↪✳↩۞↪✳↩۞↪✳↩۞↪✳↩۞↪✳↩۞↪✳↩۞↪✳↩۞↪✳↩۞↪✳↩۞↪

IV BETWEEN NOVICES   LETTER II

From the same to the same
Nantes, June

After playing the part of the mistress adored by her vassals, as though the revolutions of 1830 and 1789 had never felled any banners, after long rides through woods, stops at farms, dinners on ancient tables with centenary linens groaning under homeric platters served on antideluvian dishes, after drinking exquisite wine in glasses like the ones used by jugglers, and rifle volleys served with the dessert, and deafening shouts of Vive les du Guénic, *and dances whose entire orchestra is a bagpipe blown for ten running hours, and flowers, and young couples come to be blessed by us, and the healthy exhaustion that finds its remedy in bed with a kind of sleep I have never known before, and delicious awakenings when love appears as radiant as the sun that shimmers with the myriad flies that hum in Breton dialect! And finally, after a grotesque stay at the du Guénic castle where the windows are carriage gates and the cows could graze on the prairies that have sprouted in the rooms, and our promise to restore and repair the castle in order to return every year was greeted by hurrahs from the du Guénic peasantry, one of whom carried our banner—ouf!— well, here I am in Nantes!*

Oh, what a day it was when we arrived at the du

Guénics! The rector came with his acolytes, all wreathed with flowers, to welcome us and bless us, and gave proof of such joy . . . tears come to my eyes at the memory. And my magnificent Calyste played the part of the lord like a character in Walter Scott. My lord accepted their homage as though he were still living in the 13th century. I heard girls and women saying "What a handsome lord we have!" like an operatic chorus. The elders discussed among themselves Calyste's likeness to other du Guénics they had known. Ah, noble sublime Brittany! What a region of faith and religion! But progress threatens it; bridges and roads are being built, ideas will soon follow, and goodbye to the sublime. The peasants will certainly not stay as free and proud as I have seen them, once it has been proved to them that they are Calyste's equals, should they choose to believe it. After that poem of peaceful restoration and the signing of the contracts, we left that ravishing district, now blooming now arid, now somber now gay, and came here to kneel before the benefactress to whom we owe all our happiness. Calyste and I both felt the need to thank the postulant of the Visitation. In her memory, he will quarter his shield with the arms of the des Touches which are: PARTY PER PALE ENGRAILED OR AND VERT. *He will take one of the silver eagles as supporter and place in its beak this charming feminine motto:* SOUVIÈGNE-VOUS! *And so yesterday, we were taken to the convent of the Ladies of the Visitation by the Abbé Grimont, a friend of the du Guénics, who told us, mama, that Félicité was a saint. She can be nothing less for him since her illustrious conversion promoted him to vicar-general of the diocese. Mademoiselle des Touches did not want to receive Calyste and saw only me. I found her somewhat changed, pale and thin. She seemed very pleased by our visit. "Tell Calyste," she said quietly, "that my not seeing him is an affair of conscience rather than obedience, for I had received permission. But I would prefer not to have this momentary happiness than to pay with months of agony. If you only knew how hard it is for me to answer when I am asked "What are you thinking about?" The mistress of novices cannot understand the extent and multiplicity of the ideas that tear through my mind like a whirlwind. At times I see Italy or Paris in all their spectacle while thinking about Calyste," she said in that wonderful poetic way of hers that you know, "who is the shining star of those memories . . . I was too old to be admitted to the Carmelites so I took the order of Saint Francis of Sales only because he said 'I will bare your head instead of your feet!' rejecting all those austerities that mortify the flesh. In fact, it is the head that sins. The saintly bishop did well to make his order austere toward the mind and ruthless toward the will! This is just what I wanted, for my mind is the true culprit. It deceived me about my heart up to the age of forty when one may be forty times happier than a young woman but fifty times more miserable later on. Well then, my child, are you happy?" she asked, visibly pleased to stop talking about herself. "You see me in the enchantment of love and happiness," I replied. "Calyste is as gentle and innocent as he is noble and handsome," she said with seriousness. "I have made you my heiress. In addition to my fortune, you possess the twin ideals of my dreams. What I have done fills me with joy," she continued after a pause. "Now my child, do not be misled. You caught hold of your happiness with ease; you had only to reach out for it. Now you must make sure to hold on to it. Had you come here only to carry away the counsel of my experience, your trip would have been worth your while. Calyste at the moment is experiencing a passion communicated by you but not inspired by you. To make your happiness lasting, you must try, my sweet, to add the one to the other. In your interest and his, try to be capricious, flirtatious, even a bit distant, if necessary. I do not advise ugly calculating, or tyranny, merely artistry. Between usury and prodigality, my dear, lies economy. Learn how to acquire a certain honest dominion over Calyste. These are the last mundane words I shall have spoken. I kept them in reserve for you, for in my conscience I trembled over having sacrificed you in order to save Calyste. Bind him to you well, give him children, make him respect their mother in you. And finally," she said with emotion in her voice, "see to it that he never sees Béatrix again! . . ." That name plunged both of us into a kind of stupor and we sat staring into each other's eyes, exchanging the same vague disquiet. "Are you going back to Guérande?" she asked. "Yes," I replied. "Well then, do not go to Les Touches. I should never have given you that property." "And why not?" "Child! Les Touches for you is Bluebeard's castle. There is nothing more dangerous than to awaken a sleeping passion."*

Mother dear, this in substance was our conversation. If Mademoiselle des Touches made me talk a lot, she gave me even more to think about, for in the intoxication of this trip and my captivation with Calyste, I had forgotten the serious mental state I spoke of in my first letter.

V WHAT QUARRELS LEAD TO DURING A HONEY-
MOON *After having thoroughly admired Nantes—
a charming and splendid city—and after having seen
where Charette gloriously fell on the Place Bretagne, we considered returning to Saint-Nazaire by
the Loire since we had already gone by land from
Nantes to Guérande. Most decidedly, a steamboat is
inferior to a coach. Public transportation is an invention of the monster of modernity, the Monopoly.
Three young and rather pretty ladies from Nantes
were misbehaving on deck, afflicted with what I call
Kergarouëtitis, a joke you will understand when I
have described the Kergarouëts to you. Calyste behaved admirably. Like a true gentleman, he had
made no public display of his bride. Though I was
satisfied with his good taste, I was like a child with
his first tin drum and thought this was a splendid
opportunity for me to try out the system recom-
mended by Camille Maupin, for it was the writer,
not the postulant, who made the recommendation.
I began to pout and Calyste very sweetly became
concerned. To the whispered "What is it?" I answered truthfully "Nothing!" And I fully realized
from this what little success is obtained by initial
truth. A lie is a decisive weapon when rapid action
is the salvation of women and empires. Calyste became very pressing and disturbed. I led him to the
foredeck amid a pile of ropes and there, in a voice
full of fears if not tears, I spoke to him of the sadness and terror of a woman whose husband is the
handsomest of men! . . . "Oh Calyste!" I exclaimed,
"Our relationship started out with a major defect:
you did not love me, you did not choose me! You
were not immobilized like a statue on seeing me for
the first time! It is my heart, my attachment, my*

tenderness that solicit your affection, and one day you will punish me for having heaped on you the treasures of a young girl's pure and unrestrained love! I ought to be nasty and coquettish, but I haven't the strength to use such weapons against you . . . If that horrible woman who rejected you had been here in my place, you would never have noticed those awful females from Nantes who by Parisian standards would be classed as cattle." Mother, Calyste had tears in his eyes and turned away to hide them. He then saw the Basse-Indre and ran to the captain asking him to put us ashore. One cannot resist such responses, especially when accompanied by a three-hour stopover in a rustic inn on the Basse-Indre where we lunched on fresh fish in a tiny room such as one sees in genre paintings, and where the bellowing of the Indret forges echoed across the shimmering expanse of the Loire. Seeing how the experience born of Experience turned out, I exclaimed "Ah, dearest Félicité! . . ." Calyste, incapable of suspecting the nun's advice and my duplicity, interrupted me with a delightful pun, "Shall we keep a remembrance of this? We should send an artist to capture the scene." Mother dear, I laughed to the point of upsetting Calyste and almost made him angry. "In my heart," I told him, "there is a picture of this scenery and this scene that can never be effaced and whose colors are inimitable!"

Oh mother, it is impossible for me to mix into my love the pretense of warfare or hostility. Calyste can do with me what he wants. Those tears were, I think, the first he gave me. Are they not worth more than a second declaration of our rights? A heartless woman would have gained total dominion after that scene on the boat, while I lost out for the second time. According to your system, the more womanly I become the more sluttish I make myself, for I am dreadfully cowardly about my happiness. I cannot hold out against one of my lord's glances. No, I am not abdicating to love, I am clinging to it as a mother clutches her child to her breast in fear of some mishap.

VI So Soon!   **Letter III**

From the same to the same

Guérande, July

Oh mother! To know jealousy at the end of three months! Now my heart is replete. It is filled with deep hate and deep love! How fortunate to have a mother into whose heart I can pour out my tears! To us women who are still somewhat girlish, it suffices to say "Here, among all the keys to your palace, is a key rusted with memories. Enter everywhere, enjoy everything, but take care not to go to Les Touches!" for us to go precisely there with feet racing and eyes burning with the curiosity of Eve. What temptation Mademoiselle des Touches injected into my love! But then why forbid me Les Touches? What kind of happiness is mine if it depends on a walk, a visit to some Breton hovel? And what have I to fear? Well, then, add to Madame Bluebeard's motives the craving that gnaws at any woman to discover whether her dominion is shaky or solid, and you will understand why I asked one day, with seeming indifference "What is Les Touches?" "Les Touches belongs to you," said my divine mother-in-law.

257

"Would that Calyste had never set foot in Les Touches!" exclaimed my aunt Zéphirine, wagging her head. "Then he would not have become my husband," I answered. "You know then what went on there?" my mother-in-law cagily replied. "It is a place of perdition," said Mademoiselle de Pen-Hoël. "Mademoiselle des Touches committed enough sins there to be asking for God's pardon now." "Isn't that what saved the noble woman's soul and provided the convent with a fortune?" exclaimed the Chevalier du Halga. "The Abbé Grimont told me she gave a hundred thousand francs to the Ladies of the Visitation." "Do you want to go to Les Touches?" my mother-in-law asked. "It is well worth seeing." "No, no!" I replied hastily. Doesn't this little scene strike you as a page out of some diabolical drama? It recurred under a dozen different guises. Finally, my mother-in-law said, "I understand why you do not go to Les Touches. You are quite right." You will admit, mama, that this knife thrust, unwittingly administered, would have decided you too to find out whether your happiness rests on such weak foundations that it must collapse under this or that ceiling. In all fairness to Calyste, I must say he never suggested we visit this charterhouse that is now his property. No sooner do we fall in love than we lose our wits, for one day, provoked by his reticence, I said: "What are you afraid of seeing at Les Touches that makes you the only one never to mention it?" "Let us go then," he replied. And so I was caught like all women who want to be caught, and who rely on chance to untie the Gordian knot of indecision. We went to Les Touches.

It is enchanting, done with great artistic taste, and I enjoy that pitfall which Mademoiselle des Touches so strongly warned me against approaching. All poisonous flowers are appealing—they were sown by Satan; for there are the devil's flowers and God's flowers, and we have only to look within ourselves to see that each of them created one half of the world. What bitter pleasures to be playing with ashes and not with fire! I watched Calyste to see if all the sparks were really extinguished, and believe me, I was on the lookout for drafts! I watched his face as we went from room to room, object to object, like children searching for some hidden thing. Calyste seemed pensive, but I thought at first that I had won out. I even felt strong enough to talk about Madame de Rochefide, whom I call "Rocheperfide" ever since that adventure on the rocks of Le Croisic. Finally, we went to see the famous box tree where Béatrix landed when he pushed her into the sea so that no one else would have her. "She must be very light to have remained up there," I said laughing. Calyste remained silent. "Let us respect the dead," I added. Calyste maintained his silence. "Have I angered you?" I asked. "No, but stop galvanizing that passion," he replied. What a remark! Calyste, seeing how distressed I was, doubled his attentions and tenderness toward me.

August

Alas! There I was at the bottom of the chasm, and like all ingénues in all melodramas, I amused myself by plucking the flowers I found growing there. Suddenly, a horrible thought galloped across my happiness like the horse in the German ballad.* I had the idea that Calyste's love grew out of his

---

* Allusion to the ballad *Lenore* by Bürger.

memories, that he transferred to me the throbbing passion which I revived in him by reminding him of that awful woman's caprices. How can anyone so unwholesome and cold, so stubborn and spineless— more like a mollusk or coral—dare call herself Béatrix! Already, mother dear, I am obliged to keep one eye on suspicion, while my heart belongs to Calyste. Is it not a catastrophe when the eye wins out over the heart, and suspicion is finally justified? This is what happened—one morning I said to Calyste, "I love this place, for I owe my happiness to it. And so I forgive you for taking me for someone else on occasion . . . ." This honest Breton blushed and I threw my arms around him; but I left Les Touches and will never return there.

As a result of that hatred that made me wish for Madame de Rochefide's death (good God! I mean of course from a pulmonary embolism or some kind of accident), I realized the extent and depth of my love for Calyste. That woman has now begun to disturb my sleep; I see her in my dreams. Does that mean I am destined to meet her? Ah, the postulant of the Visitation was right! Les Touches is a fateful place. Calyste's memories were rekindled there and they go deeper than the pleasures of our love. Mother dear, please find out if Madame de Rochefide is in Paris, for if she is I shall stay in Brittany. Poor Mademoiselle des Touches, who now regrets having dressed me like Béatrix the day of the contract in order to make her plan succeed, if she knew to what degree I am taken for our loathsome rival, what would she say? This is prostitution! I am no longer myself. I am mortified. I am gripped by the wild desire to flee Guérande and the sands of Le Croisic.

VII CONCLUSION

25 *August*

I have decided to return to the ruins of the du Guénic castle. Calyste, distressed over my distress, is taking me. Either he understands little of the world if he suspects nothing, or else he knows the reason for my leaving and does not love me. I tremble so at the possibility of finding the horrible certainty of this, should I seek it, that like a child, I cover my eyes in order not to hear the explosion. Oh mama, I am not loved with the same love I feel in my heart. Calyste is charming, it is true, but what man short of being a monster would not be as amiable and gracious as Calyste, receiving as he does all the flowers that bloom in the heart of a twenty-year-old girl, raised by you, pure and loving as I am, and whom many women have told you they considered beautiful . . . .

*Château du Guénic,
18 September*

Has he forgotten her? This is the only thought that echoes through my soul like remorse. Oh mama dear, have all women had to fight memories as I do? One should only marry innocent young men to pure young girls! But that is a utopian deception. It is better to have one's rival in the past than in the future. Oh pity me, mama, even though I am happy at the moment, happy as a woman is who is afraid of losing that happiness and clutches it! . . . a sure way of killing it, said the wise Clotilde.

I have come to realize that for the last five months I have been thinking only of myself, that is to say of Calyste. Tell my sister Clotilde that her depressing *wisdom often comes back to me. She is lucky to be faithful to the dead; she no longer has any rival to fear.* I kiss my sweet Athénaïs, with whom I gather Juste is madly in love. Judging by your last letter, he is afraid you will not let him have her! Cultivate that fear like a rare flower. Athénaïs will be the mistress, and I who trembled over not winning Calyste from himself, I will be the servant. A thousand kisses, mama dear. Oh, if my fears are justified, then Camille Maupin will have sold me her fortune very dearly. Affectionate regards to my father.*

※⤙⊕⤛※⤙⊕⤛※⤙⊕⤛※⤙⊕⤛※⤙⊕⤛※⤙⊕⤛※⤙⊕⤛※⤙⊕⤛※⤙⊕⤛※⤙⊕⤛

VIII In Which It Is Proven That J.-J. Rousseau in His System Did Not Consider the Dangers of Weaning These letters clearly explain the private relationship between husband and wife. Where Sabine envisioned a *mariage d'amour,* Calyste saw a *mariage de convenance.* In short, the joys of the honeymoon had not entirely measured up to the laws of matrimony. During the newlyweds' stay in Brittany, the decorating, arranging and furnishing of their town house in Paris had been undertaken by the noted architect Grindot, and supervised by Clotilde and the Duc and Duchesse de Grandlieu. With everything prepared for the young couple's return to Paris in December 1838, Sabine settled in at the rue de Bourbon with pleasure, less however to play the role of mistress than to see what her family thought of her marriage. Calyste, utterly apathetic, let himself be conducted through society by Clotilde and his mother-in-law, who were grateful to him for his acquiescence. He made a place for himself in that society which was befitting to his name, his fortune and his marriage. The social success of his wife, considered one of the loveliest, the distrac-

---

* Lucien de Rubempré, whom Clotilde would have married against her father's wishes, committed suicide in jail.

tions provided by high society, the obligations to fulfill, the entertainments of the winter season, all contributed to restoring some vigor to the happiness of the young couple by offering stimulation and intervals of repose. Sabine, adjudged happy by her mother and sister who saw in Calyste's coolness nothing more than his English background, relinquished her somber thoughts. She heard so many ill-mated young wives envy her marriage that she banished her fears to the realm of chimera. Finally, Sabine's pregnancy was the ultimate guarantee offered by this somewhat neuter union—an excellent augury in the eyes of experienced wives. In October 1839, the young Baronne du Guénic gave birth to a son and foolishly decided to nurse him, consistent with the logic of any young woman in her position. How can one not be a total mother when one has a child by a totally idolized husband? Toward the end of the following summer, in August 1840, Sabine was consequently about to wean her first child. During their two-year residence in Paris, Calyste stripped himself of the innocence which had served him so wonderfully when he first entered the realm of passion. Calyste—now a close comrade of the young Duc Georges de Maufrigneuse (also recently married to an heiress, Berthe de Cinq-Cygne), of the Vicomte Savinien de Portenduère, the Duc and Duchesse de Rhétoré, the Duc and Duchesse de Lenoncourt-Chaulieu, and all the habitués of his mother-in-law's salon—discovered the difference between provincial and Parisian life. Wealth has its moments of depression and boredom that Paris, more than any other capital, can while away with amusements, seductions, and diversions. Under the influence of these young husbands who desert the noblest and prettiest of creatures for the pleasures of cigars and whist, for the lofty conversations of their clubs, or the preoccupations of the track, many a domestic virtue came to be tainted in the young Breton gentleman. The maternal instinct in a woman who does not wish to bore her husband is invariably an accomplice to the dissipation of young husbands. A woman is always deeply proud of seeing return to her the man whom she has granted full freedom.

One evening in October of that year, to escape the screams of his weaning child, Calyste, whose troubled brow Sabine could not bear to see, went at her suggestion to the Variétés where a new play was being performed. The valet who was sent after an orchestra seat obtained one close to the stage. At the first intermission, while looking around, Calyste noticed in one of the stage boxes barely a few steps away, Madame de Rochefide. Béatrix in Paris! Béatrix in public! These two thoughts shot through Calyste like arrows. To see her again after nearly three years! How can one explain the upheaval that occurred in the heart of a lover who far from having forgotten her, had so successfully wedded Béatrix in his wife that his wife noticed it? To whom can one explain that the poem of a love lost and buried, but still alive within the heart of Sabine's husband, could obliterate the marital sweetness, the ineffable tenderness of his young wife. Béatrix was light, brightness, excitement, the unknown; while Sabine was duty, darkness, the foreseeable! In a single instant one became pleasure and the other boredom. It was a *coup de foudre!*

IX A FIRST ATTACK WITH SHARPENED TONGUE Prompted by loyalty, the first noble impulse of Sabine's husband was to leave the theatre. On his way out, he saw the door of the box ajar and was carried inside in spite of himself. The young Breton found Béatrix seated between two most distinguished men, Canalis and Nathan, one a political figure, the other a literary figure. During the nearly three years since Calyste had last seen her, Madame de Rochefide had changed considerably. Despite the metamorphosis that had taken its toll of the woman, she was bound to be all the more poetic and attractive to Calyste. Up to the age of thirty, pretty Parisians ask no more of fashion than that it provide a suitable covering; but once through the fateful portal of the thirties, they expect it to furnish weapons, seductions, and embellishments. Through fashion, they create all manner of gracefulness, finding in it the means to their ends, their characterization, and their rejuvenation. They analyze the subtlest accessories and ultimately pass from nature into art. Madame de Rochefide had played all the scenes of the drama which, in the social history of 19th century France, is called "The Abandoned Woman." Having been abandoned by Conti, she naturally became a great artist at dressing, flirting, and artificial flowering of every kind.

"How is it that Conti isn't here?" Calyste whispered to Canalis, after the frivolous greetings by which the most solemn conversations are always begun in public.

The erstwhile poet laureate of the Faubourg Saint-Germain, twice minister and for the fourth time aspiring candidate for a new ministry, placed his finger on his lips in a gesture that explained everything.

"I'm so happy to see you," Béatrix purred to Calyste. "I said to myself when I saw you sitting there, before you noticed me, that you would not repudiate me, not you. Oh my Calyste, why did you get married?" she murmured. "And to a little fool to boot!"

As soon as a woman begins whispering to someone who has just entered her box and has him sit beside her, sophisticated people always find some pretext for leaving her alone with him.

"Are you coming, Nathan?" asked Canalis. "Madame la marquise will permit me to say a word to d'Arthex whom I see with the Princesse de Cadignan. I must talk to him about tomorrow's agenda in the Assembly."

This tactful exit allowed Calyste to recover from his shock. But he managed to lose his presence of mind and his resolve on inhaling the delicious, though for him poisonous, fragrance of the poetic bouquet created by Béatrix.

X DEFINITION OF *JE NE SAIS QUOI* Madame de Roche-fide, now bony and stringy, her complexion almost gone, thinned out, dried up, rings under her eyes, had that evening resurrected her premature ruins with the most ingenious devices known to Parisian fashion. Like all abandoned women, she conceived of giving herself virginal airs, and with yards of white fabric tried to evoke the maidens in Ossian—so poetically depicted by Girodet—whose names end in *a*.* Her blond hair framed her long face in cascades of curls reflecting the stage lights captured by the perfumed oil on her hair. Her pale forehead sparkled. The rouge she had imperceptibly applied deceived the eye as to the dull pallor of her skin that was perked up with bran water. A shawl so delicate that one doubted human hands could have woven such silk was knotted around her neck, shortening its length, concealing it, and only partially revealing the jewels skillfully mounted above her stays. Her figure was a masterwork of composition. As to the general effect, a word will suffice: it was worth all the trouble she had taken to achieve it. Her thinned, hardened arms barely appeared beneath the calculated billowing of her sleeves. She was that mixture of artificial brightness and radiant silks, misty chiffon and crimped hair, vivaciousness, tranquillity and sweep that has been termed *je ne sais quoi*. Everyone knows the ingredients of *je ne sais quoi*. It is a blending of considerable amounts of wit, taste, and temperament. Béatrix was in effect a marvelously engineered stage set with changing scenery. The performance of these fairy tales, which includes brilliant dialogue as well, can drive honest men mad, for by the law of contrast, they experience a frenzied desire to play with illusions. It is all false and appealing, fabricated yet pleasing, and some men adore women who play at seduction the way one plays cards. And here is the reason: a man's desire is a syllogism that deduces from such external skills the secret

* Ossian, third century Scottish bard, sang of Morna, Frapela, Malvina, Galvina, Comala, etc.

theorems of sensuality. His mind argues, a woman who knows how to make herself so beautiful must have still greater resources when it comes to lovemaking. Which is true. Women abandoned by their lovers are those who love; the ones who keep their lovers know how to love. Though the lesson taught by her Italian had been hard on Béatrix's pride, she was of a nature too naturally artificial not to profit from it.

"It is not a question of loving you," she had been saying just before Calyste came in, "but the necessity of tormenting you when once we have caught hold of you. That is the secret of the women who want to hold on to you. The guardian dragons of treasures are armed with talons and wings!"

"A sonnet ought to be made of your idea," Canalis replied just as Calyste walked in.

XI A WOMAN WHEN SHE PRETENDS In one glance, Béatrix surmised Calyste's condition; she found, still fresh and raw, the marks of the collar she had put on him at Les Touches. Calyste, offended by her comment about his wife, hesitated between his husbandly dignity, his defense of Sabine, and a harsh word cast at a heart that evoked for him so many memories, a heart he thought was still bleeding. That hesitation was observed by the marquise who had only made the comment to see how far her empire over Calyste extended. Seeing him so defenseless, she hastened to rescue him from his dilemma.

"Well then, dear friend, you see me alone," she said when the two courtiers had left, "completely alone in the world! . . ."

"Did you never think of me?" Calyste asked.

"You!" she replied. "Aren't you married? That was one of my sorrows along with all the others I have endured since we last saw each other. I told myself, not only have I lost a love, but a friendship as well, and one I thought to be Breton. One gets used to everything. Now I suffer less, but I am broken.

This is the first time in a long time that I unburden my heart. Compelled to be proud in the presence of indifferent people, arrogant as though I had never erred in the eyes of the very people who flirt with me now, having lost my beloved Félicité, I had no one to whom I could cry out 'I am suffering!' And so now I can tell you what anguish I felt seeing you a few steps away without your recognizing me, and what joy I feel seeing you beside me. Yes . . ." she said in reply to Calyste's gesture, "it is a kind of fidelity! Oh, the unhappy people for whom a trifle, a visit, means everything! Yes, you loved me, you really did, as I should have been loved by the man who trampled all the gifts I laid at his feet. And to my misfortune, I cannot forget, I love him still, and wish to remain faithful to a past that can never return."

While reciting this tirade, already improvised a hundred times, she used her eyes to heighten the effect of the words that seemed wrenched from the depth of her soul by the violence of this long pent-up torrent. Calyste, instead of speaking, let the tears flow down his cheeks. Béatrix took his hand and held it tightly, making him grow pale.

"Thank you Calyste! Thank you, sweet child. That is how a true friend responds to a friend's suffering! We understand one another. Go now, don't say another word. People are looking at us and your wife might be hurt if someone told her we had been seen together, however innocently in the presence of a thousand people. Goodbye, you see how brave I am!"

She wiped her eyes, thereby creating what in feminine rhetoric is called an antithetical action.

"Let me laugh the laughter of the damned with those indifferent people who amuse me," she continued. "I see the actors, the writers, the artists, all those people I used to know at Camille's, poor Camille. How right she was! To enrich the man you love and then disappear, telling yourself 'I am too old for him!' is to end as a martyr. And that is the best alternative if one cannot end as a virgin."

She began to laugh as though to erase the sad impression she doubtless left on her idolater.

"Where can I see you?" asked Calyste.

"I have hidden away on the rue de Chartres in front of the Parc Monceau, in a little house in keeping with my means where I stuff myself with literature, but only for myself, for my diversion. God preserve me from the mania of those lady writers! Go now, leave me. I don't want to become a subject for gossip, and what wouldn't people say if they saw us? Furthermore Calyste, to tell the truth, if you stay one more minute, I shall begin to cry in earnest."

Calyste withdrew after taking Béatrix's hand and experiencing for the second time the strange sensations of a double pressure filled with seductive thrills.

"My God! Sabine has never been able to thrill me this way," was the thought that struck him as he walked into the corridor.

During the remainder of the evening, the marquise hardly looked at him directly, but there were sideways glances that were just as soul-shattering for a man completely immersed in his first unfulfilled love.

→☙→→☙→*→☙→*→☙→*→☙→*→☙→*→☙→*→☙→*→☙→*→☙→

XII THE INCONVENIENCE OF NAIVETÉ When the Baron du Guénic returned home, the splendor of his surroundings made him think of the mediocrity inferred by Béatrix, and he began despising his fortune for not belonging to the fallen angel. On learning that Sabine had retired much earlier, he was happy to find himself in possession of a night to spend with his emotions. He then cursed the intuition that love bestowed on Sabine. When a man happens to be adored by his wife, she can read his face like a book, she understands the slightest tremors of his muscles, she divines the source of his tranquillity, she investigates every trace of sadness wondering if she is responsible, she examines the expressions of his eyes; for her, his eyes are colored by the prime concern—they are or are not loving. Calyste knew himself to be the object of a cult so deep-rooted, so naive, so possessive, that he doubted he could compose his features sufficiently to conceal the change that had taken place in him. "How will I manage in the morning?" he thought as he fell asleep fearing the inspection he would have to pass under Sabine's scrutiny. First thing in the morning, and often during the day, Sabine would ask him "Do you love me?" or "You're not bored with me?"—charming queries, varied according to a woman's character or intelligence, that serve to hide her genuine or feigned anxieties.

Agitated by emotional storms, mud will rise to the surface of even the noblest, the purest of souls. And so, the following morning, Calyste, who surely loved his son, trembled with joy when he learned that Sabine, fearing croup to be the reason for the baby's coughing, would not leave little Calyste's side. The baron, on the pretext of some business, went out before breakfast. He made his escape like a prisoner, reveling in his freedom of movement, delighted to walk across the Pont Louis XVI * and up the Champs-Elysées to a café where he enjoyed a bachelor breakfast.

XIII SERIOUS QUESTIONS What is it then about love? Is it that nature balks under the social yoke? Is it that nature wants the vital force of the lifespan to remain spontaneous and free, to be the racing of a bubbling torrent propelled by the boulders of repression and seduction, rather than a tranquil stream flowing between the shores of the town hall and the church? Is there any design behind the volcanic eruptions nature brews and which may perhaps give rise to great men? It would be hard to find a young man more piously raised than Calyste, more wholesome in his way of life, less sullied by waywardness,

* Now the Pont de la Concorde.

yet he leaped toward a woman far inferior to him though radiant good fortune had given him in Sabine a young girl of truly aristocratic beauty, exquisitely refined intelligence; pious, loving; and totally devoted to him of angelic tenderness made even sweeter by love, by a love as passionate, despite its legality, as his for Béatrix. Perhaps in even the greatest of men there is a residue of clay; mud still attracts them. The less imperfect creature would then be woman, in spite of her faults and follies. Yet Madame de Rochefide, with all her poetic pretensions and pretenders, and despite her transgression, was of the highest nobility, was of more ethereal than earthy stuff, and concealed the courtesan she proposed to be under the noblest exterior. Consequently, this explanation cannot account for Calyste's strange passion. Perhaps the reason can be found in a vanity so deeply buried that moralists have not yet discovered this face of vice. There are men as noble as Calyste, as handsome, rich, distinguished and well-bred, who become bored, even unconsciously, with marriage to women of similar natures, men whose own nobility is unimpressed by nobility in another person, who are left cold by dignity and refinement always commensurate with their own, and who seek in inferior or tainted natures the confirmation of their own superiority, though they are not in search of praise. The contrast between the degenerate and the sublime intrigues them. Purity gleams in the presence of filth. It is an enticing comparison. Calyste had nothing to protect in Sabine, she was irreproachable; all the unused energy in his heart could be galvanized by Béatrix. If great men in the past have played the role of Jesus raising up the adulteress, why then should ordinary men be more prudent?

XIV   The Nest of the Fallen Angel   Calyste survived until two o'clock by dwelling on the thought "I am going to see her!"—a thought that has often compensated thousand-league trips! He walked with slackened pace to the rue de Courcelles, recognized the house though he had never seen it, and was kept waiting at the foot of the stairs—he, son-in-law of the Duc de Grandlieu, as rich and noble as the Bourbons—by an aged valet who asked: "Who shall I say is calling?" Calyste understood that he must allow Béatrix her freedom, and looked out at the garden and at the walls rippled black and yellow by the rains of Paris.

Madame de Rochefide, like all great ladies who break their bonds, had fled leaving her fortune to her husband; she had been unwilling to ask for alms from a tyrant. Conti and Camille had spared Béatrix from all material concerns, and from time to time, her mother had sent her money. Now that she was alone, she was reduced to an economy that was rather severe for a woman accustomed to luxury. So she climbed to the top of the hill where the Parc Monceau stretches out, and took refuge in a small town house formerly occupied by a nobleman, situated on the street but with a charming little garden in back and a rental of less than eighteen hundred francs. Nonetheless, waited on as she was by an old valet, a chambermaid, and a cook from Alençon, all of whom had remained faithful during her misfortune, her misery would have seemed opulence to many an ambitious bourgeois. Calyste climbed a staircase whose stone steps had been sanded and whose landings were decorated with flowers. At the first floor, the old valet led Calyste through a double door of padded red velvet, red silk quilting and gilded studs. Silk and velvet upholstered all the rooms through which Calyste passed. Deep-toned carpets, draped windows and doors, the whole interior contrasted with the shabbiness of the exterior which the owner neglected. Calyste waited for Béatrix in a drawing room of sober style in which luxury assumed the character of simplicity. This room, hung with garnet-colored velvet contrasted with pale yellow silk, a dark red rug on the floor, and windows so massed with flowering plants that it looked like a conservatory, was so faintly lit that Calyste could barely distinguish the two celadon vases between which gleamed a silver chalice, attributed to Cellini, that Béatrix had brought from Italy. The gilded furniture upholstered in velvet, the magnificent consoles on one of which stood a strange clock, the table covered with a Persian rug—everything attested to a former opulence whose vestiges had been tastefully arranged. On one small cabinet, Calyste noticed some jewelry, and a book on whose open pages rested a jewel-encrusted dagger used as a paper cutter, a symbol of criticism. On the walls were ten splendidly framed watercolors showing the bedrooms of the various houses she had occupied, which provided the measure of her supreme impertinence.

XV THE FIRST NO MEANING YES The rustle of a silk gown announced the luckless lady who appeared in a studied outfit that would certainly have indicated to a seasoned wencher that he was expected. Her gown, cut like a dressing gown to reveal a bit of alabaster bosom, was of pearl-gray moiré with bell sleeves over puffed undersleeves whose billows were segmented by straps, finished off with lace frills. Her lovely hair, frizzed into fullness, escaped from a lacy flowered cap.

"So soon? . . ." she said smiling. "A lover would not be so precipitous. You must have some secret to tell me, isn't that so?"

She sat down on a love seat, inviting Calyste with a gesture to sit beside her. By a coincidence—perhaps intentional, for women have two memories, one angelic, the other demonic—Béatrix was wearing the same perfume she used to wear at Les Touches when she met Calyste. The first whiff of her perfume, the contact with her gown, the expression in her eyes which, in that half-light, seemed to attract and refract the light, everything conspired to inebriate Calyste. The same violence that once before had almost killed Béatrix was reawakened in him, but this time the marquise was at the edge of a love seat instead of the ocean and got up to ring, putting her finger to her lips. At that, Calyste, called to order, controlled himself. He realized that Béatrix had no bellicose intentions.

"Antoine, I am at home to no one," she said to the old servant. "Put some wood on the fire. You see Calyste, I treat you like a friend," she said with dignity when the old man left, "don't treat me like a mistress. There are two things I should like to say to you. First, I would not play silly games with a man I loved, and second, I have no desire to belong to any man ever again, for I thought, Calyste, that I was loved by a kind of Rizzio * whom no obligation could bind, a man utterly free, and you see where that involvement led me. You, on the other hand, are bound by the saintliest of obligations, you have a young, lovable, delightful wife and are furthermore a father. It would be inexcusable for either of us and madness for both of us . . . ."

"My dear Béatrix, all your reasons collapse before one fact: I have never loved anyone but you, I was married against my will."

"A trick played on us by Mademoiselle des Touches," she said smiling.

Three hours passed during which Madame de Rochefide kept Calyste within the strict limits of his marital bonds by imposing the horrible ultimatum of a complete break with Sabine. Nothing less, she said, would reassure her given the horrible situation in which Calyste's love would place her. She moreover regarded the sacrifice of Sabine a minor matter; she knew her well!

"My dear boy, she is a woman who fulfills all the promise of her girlhood. She is indeed a Grandlieu, as dark as her Portu-

* David Riccio or Rizzio, an Italian singer, was the lover of Mary Stuart, under whose eyes he was assassinated by order of her husband, Darnley.

guese mother, if not as orange and dried out as her father. To be truthful, your wife will never be at a loss, for she is a strapping boy and can manage on her own. Poor Calyste, is that the wife for you? She has lovely eyes, but such eyes are commonplace in Italy, Spain, or Portugal. What kind of softness can one have with such boyish lines? Eve was blond. Dark women stem from Adam, but blonds stem from God whose hand marked Eve with his final thought once creation was completed."

❋↝۞↝❋↝۞↝❋↝۞↝❋↝۞↝❋↝۞↝❋↝۞↝❋↝۞↝❋↝۞↝❋↝۞↝❋↝۞↝

XVI THE SECOND NO MEANING YES   Toward six o'clock, Calyste, despairing, took his hat prepared to leave.

"By all means go, poor dear, don't give her the displeasure of dining without you!"

Calyste remained. He was so young, he was easily taken in by his weaknesses.

"What, you would dare have dinner with me?" said Béatrix, pretending insidious surprise. "My meager table would not frighten you away, and you would be independent enough to give me the pleasure of this little proof of affection?"

"Just let me write a note to Sabine, otherwise she will wait for me until nine o'clock."

"Here, this is the table I write on," said Béatrix.

She lit the candles herself, and brought one to the table in order to read what Calyste was writing.

"My dear Sabine . . . ."

" 'My dear!' Your wife is still dear to you?" she said throwing him an icy glance that froze the marrow of his bones. "Go! Go have dinner with her!"

"I am having dinner at a restaurant with some friends . . . ."

"A lie! Shame! You don't deserve to be loved by her or by me! All men are scoundrels when it comes to us! Go on, monsieur, dine with your Sabine!"

Calyste fell back in his chair and turned deathly pale. Bretons have the kind of courage that makes them stubborn in adversity. The young Breton straightened up, planted his elbow on the table and his chin in his hand, and glared at the implacable Béatrix. He was so superb that any woman from the north or the south would have fallen on her knees saying "Take me!" But Béatrix, born on the dividing line between Normandy and Brittany, came from Casteran stock; desertion had developed in her the truculence of the Frank and the spitefulness of the Norman. What she needed was some cataclysmic vengeance. She did not yield to his sublime gesture.

"Dictate what I must write, and I shall obey," the poor boy said. "But then . . . ."

"All right, I will, for then you will love me again as you did in Guérande. Write: 'I am dining in town, do not wait for me!' " *

"What else?" said Calyste, expecting more.

"Nothing. Sign it. Good," she said pouncing on her quarry with concealed delight. "I will have a messenger take it."

"Now then . . ." exclaimed Calyste rising with satisfaction.

"Ah, I believe I still have my freedom of choice!," she said wheeling around midway between the table and the fireplace where the bellpull hung.

"Here Antoine, have this note taken to this address. Monsieur is dining here."

❋❖❋❖❋❖❋❖❋❖❋❖❋❖❋❖❋❖❋❖❋❖❋❖❋❖

XVII THE SCHOOL FOR FALSEHOOD Calyste returned home toward two in the morning. Sabine had waited until past midnight and then gone to bed exhausted. She managed to sleep although she had been deeply hurt by the laconic tone of her

* In the French, "ne m'attendez pas"; the sudden use of the *vous* form would have been enough to make Sabine suspicious.

husband's note. However, she sought to explain it. A woman truly in love always begins by explaining everything to the man's advantage. "Calyste was rushed," she told herself. The next morning, the baby was well, the mother's fears were allayed. Just before breakfast, Sabine came in with little Calyste in her arms, laughing and saying the silly little things young mothers say, to present him to his father. This little domestic scene gave Calyste a chance to collect himself. He was charming toward his wife, all the while thinking what a monster he was. He played with his son, monsieur le chevalier, too well—in fact, he overplayed his part. But Sabine had not yet reached that level of distrust which enables a woman to distinguish such delicate shadings.

Finally, at breakfast, Sabine asked, "Well then, what did you do yesterday?"

"Portenduère kept me for dinner and we went to the club to play a few hands of whist."

"What a foolish waste of time, Calyste dear," replied Sabine. "The young men of today ought to think about regaining what their fathers lost. It is hardly by smoking cigars, playing whist, idling away your idle hours, limiting yourselves to sarcasms addressed to the social climbers who are usurping your position, detaching yourselves from the masses for whom you should be mind, soul, and providence, that you will survive. Instead of being a faction, you will be no more than an opinion, as de Marsay said. If you only knew how much my thinking has broadened since I have your child. I should like the ancient name of du Guénic to make history!" Then suddenly, gazing into Calyste's eyes, she said, "Admit that the first note you ever sent me was a bit curt."

He had been listening to her thoughtfully and answered, "I only thought of notifying you when I got to the club."

"But you wrote on a woman's stationary. It smelled of perfume."

"Oh those club directors are so funny! . . ."

The Vicomte de Portenduère and his wife, a charming couple, had become such intimates of the du Guénics that they shared a box at the opera. The two young wives, Ursule and Sabine, had formed their close friendship over the pleasant exchange of advice, concerns, and confidences regarding their children. While Calyste, a novice at lying, was telling himself "I must warn Savinien," Sabine was thinking "I was sure that writing paper had a coronet!" The thought flashed through her mind like lightning and Sabine reproached herself for it. But she promised herself to look for the note which, in the midst of her preoccupation the day before, she had tossed into her letter box.

❋→✧✦❋→✧✦❋→✧✦❋→✧✦❋→✧✦❋→✧✦❋→✧✦❋→✧✦❋→✧✦❋→✧✦❋→✧✦❋→

XVIII BUT HORSES DO NOT LIE After breakfast, Calyste went out telling his wife he would return shortly, and climbed into one of those low one-horse carriages that were beginning to replace the cumbersome cabriolet in use until then. In a few minutes he raced to the rue des Saints-Pères, where the vicomte lived, and begged him to do him the favor of covering for him in case Sabine should question the vicomtesse, promising to return the favor whenever needed. Once outside, Calyste, having already requested the greatest of speed, raced in a few minutes from the rue des Saints-Pères to the rue de Chartres. He wanted to know how Béatrix had spent the rest of the night. He found the happy martyr just out of her bath, fresh, lovelier than ever, and eating with great appetite. He admired the grace with which this angel ate her boiled eggs, and marveled at the gold service that had been the gift of a music-loving English lord for whom Conti had written a few songs, for which his lordship had provided the ideas and which Conti published as his own. He listened to a few choice anecdotes told by his idol, whose primary aim was to entertain him, but who pouted and fretted when it came time for him to leave.

He thought he had stayed but half an hour; he returned home at three o'clock. His handsome English horse, a gift from the Vicomtesse de Grandlieu, was dripping with sweat. By the coincidence that always occurs with jealous women, Sabine was stationed at a window that looked out on the courtyard, impatiently awaiting Calyste's return and anxious without knowing why. The condition of the horse, who was foaming at the mouth, immediately struck her. Where was he coming from? This question was prompted by that power which is neither a demonic nor an angelic consciousness, but one which sees and feels and points out the unknown, and encourages a belief in metaphysical beings—creatures born in our brains, coming and going, living in the invisible spheres of the mind.

"Where are you coming from, my love?" she said to Calyste, going down to meet him on the first landing. "Abd-el-Kader is worn out. You were to have been out for a few minutes and I have waited for three hours."

"Oh well," thought Calyste, who was making progress in the art of dissembling, "I'll get out of this one with a present."

"Sweet little nurse," he answered loudly, putting his arms around her waist more wheedlingly than he would have were he not guilty, "I see it is impossible to keep a secret however innocent from the woman who loves you . . . ."

"One doesn't tell secrets on the stairs," she replied laughing. "Come."

⤙☺↰⤙☺↰*⤙☺↰*⤙☺↰*⤙☺↰*⤙☺↰*⤙☺↰*⤙☺↰*⤙☺↰*⤙☺↰*⤙☺↰*⤙☺↰

XIX ESSAY ON MENTAL TOXICOLOGY Crossing the antechamber to the bedroom, she saw Calyste in the mirror who, thinking himself unobserved, had stopped smiling and thus betrayed his fatigue and the true nature of his feelings.

"Now the secret!" she said turning to him.

"You have been such a heroic nurse, which makes the heir presumptive of the du Guénics even more precious to me, that

I wanted to surprise you with a gift, just like a bourgeois of the rue Saint-Denis. At this very moment, a dressing table is being finished for you that true artists have been working on. My mother and my aunt Zéphirine have contributed toward it . . . ."

Sabine threw her arms around him, hugging him tightly, nuzzling her head in his neck, and growing weak under the weight of her happiness, not because of the surprise, but because her first attack of suspicion had been allayed. It was one of those magnificent outbursts that can be counted in a lifetime and that even the most extravagant passions cannot be lavish with, for life would be consumed too quickly. At such moments, a man should kneel at the woman's feet in adoration, for it is a sublime phenomenon in which the powers of the heart and mind pour out like water from the tilted urns of fountain nymphs. Sabine melted into tears.

Suddenly, as though stung by a viper, she pulled away, flung herself on a couch and fainted; the chilling shock in her burning heart almost killed her. While embracing Calyste, her nose against his tie, utterly immersed in her joy, she smelled the scent of the writing paper! Another woman's head had nestled there, a woman whose hair and face had left an odor of adultery. Sabine had just kissed the very spot where her rival's kisses were still warm!

"What is it?" asked Calyste, after reviving Sabine with a cold compress.

"Go get my doctor and my obstetrician, both of them! Yes, I have, I feel it, a milk fever coming on. They will only come quickly if you get them yourself."

Her sudden use of *vous* rather than *tu* startled Calyste who, thoroughly alarmed, ran right out. As soon as Sabine heard the carriage door close, she sprang up like a frightened doe and began tearing up and down the room shouting, "My God, my God!" like a madwoman. These two words summed up all her feelings. The crisis she had announced as a pretext did in fact occur. Her hair began to pierce her scalp like so many needles reddened in the fire of neurosis. Her boiling blood seemed to be mixing into her nerves and trying to emerge through her pores! For a moment, she was blinded. She screamed, "I'm dying!"

・❀・❀・❀・❀・❀・❀・❀・❀・❀・❀・❀・❀・❀・❀・❀・❀

XX As Happens in Such Crises, the First Requisite is Light   Following this dreadful shriek of an assaulted wife and mother, when her maid had rushed in and she was carried to bed, once she recovered her sight and senses, her first ray of lucidity was to send this girl to her friend, Madame de Portenduère. Sabine felt her thoughts whirling in her brain like straws in a whirlwind. She later said, "I saw myriads of them all at once." She rang for the butler and in the midst of her fever, found the strength to write the following letter, for she was driven by one mania, that of knowing for certain:

To Madame la Baronne du Guénic

Dear Mama,

When you come to Paris, as you have led us to hope, I will thank you in person for the splendid gift with which you, Aunt Zéphirine and Calyste have wished to thank me for fulfilling my duties. I was already fully recompensed by my own happiness! I will not try to express the pleasure that charming dressing table gave me. I will tell you when we are together again. Be assured, when putting on my jewels before this jewel of a vanity, I will always think, like that Roman lady, that my most precious jewel is our darling angel . . . ." *

She then had her chambermaid post the letter to Guérande.

*   The reference is to Cornelia, mother of the Roman statesmen, Gaius Sempronius Graccus and Tiberius Sempronius Graccus.

XXI AND THERE WAS LIGHT! When the Vicomtesse de Portenduère came in, the chills of a dreadful fever had replaced Sabine's first paroxysm of madness.

"Ursule," she said, "I think I'm going to die."

"My dear, what's the matter with you?"

"What did Savinien and Calyste do last night after dinner at your house?"

"What dinner?" replied Ursule, who had not yet been instructed by her husband since he did not imagine the inquest would come so soon. "Savinien and I had dinner together and went to the opera without Calyste."

"Ursule, my dearest, in the name of your love for Savinien, don't tell anyone what you have just told me, or what I am about to tell you. Only you will know why I am dying. I have been betrayed, after three years of marriage, at the age of twenty-two and a half."

Her teeth chattered, her eyes were glazed, her skin had the greenish tinge of old Venetian glass.

"You? So beautiful? But who?"

"I don't know! But Calyste has told me two lies. Not a word! Don't pity me, don't be angry, pretend you know nothing. Perhaps you will then find out *who* from Savinien. Oh, that letter yesterday!" And shivering in her night gown, she ran to the little table and found the letter. "The coronet of a marquise!" she said, returning to bed. "Can you find out if Madame de Rochefide is in Paris? . . . Then I can weep and sigh to you! Oh, my dearest, to see one's hopes, one's ideals, one's idol, virtue, happiness, everything, shattered, withered, lost! . . . There is no God in heaven! No love left on earth, no life in the heart, nothing! I don't even know if it is day or night, or whether the sun still shines . . . In short, I am so miserable I don't even feel the dreadful pain that wracked my breasts and my body. Fortunately, the baby is weaned, or my milk would have poisoned him!"

At this thought, a flood of tears burst from Sabine's eyes, which had been dry until then.

The lovely Madame de Portenduère, holding the fatal letter that Sabine had sniffed once more, remained transfixed at the sight of this intense pain, overcome by this agony of love which she could not fathom despite the incoherent account in which Sabine had tried to tell her everything. Suddenly, Ursule had one of those flashes of illumination that only occur to sincere friends.

"I must save her," she said to herself. "Wait for me, Sabine," she cried, "I will find out the truth."

"Ah," sobbed Sabine, "you I will always love, even in my grave!"

❋↝❀↝❀↝❋↝❀↝❋↝❀↝❋↝❀↝❀↝❀↝❋↝❀↝❋↝❀↝❋↝❀↝

XXII A PIOUS DUCHESS' FIRST FALSEHOOD The vicomtesse went to the Duchesse de Grandlieu, requested absolute secrecy, and informed her of Sabine's condition.

"Madame," said the vicomtesse concluding, "don't you agree that to forestall some dreadful illness, or who knows, even madness, we should entrust the whole matter to a doctor and invent some fairy tale which, for the time being, would white-wash that awful Calyste."

"My dear child," said the duchess, who had been chilled to the marrow by these confidences, "friendship has granted you the experienced wisdom of a woman in my years. I know how deeply Sabine loves her husband, you are right, she could go mad."

"She could also lose her beauty, which would be still worse," said the vicomtesse.

"Hurry!" cried the duchess.

The vicomtesse and the duchess, most fortuitously, preceded by a few minutes the celebrated obstetrician Dommanget, the only one of the two doctors Calyste was able to find.

"Ursule has told me everything and you are mistaken," the duchess said to her daughter. "First of all, Béatrix is not in Paris. As to your husband, my angel, he lost quite a lot of money and doesn't know how to pay for your dressing table."

"And this?" Sabine asked, showing her mother the letter.

"Oh that!" exclaimed the duchess with a laugh, "that is the stationery of the Jockey Club. Everyone now writes on coroneted paper. Pretty soon even our grocers will be titled."

The prudent mother threw the blighted letter into the fire. When Calyste and Dommanget arrived, the duchess, who had previously instructed the servants, was notified. She left Sabine in the care of Madame de Portenduère and intercepted Calyste and the doctor in the drawing room.

"It is Sabine's life that is in danger, monsieur," she said to Calyste. "You have betrayed her for Madame de Rochefide . . . ."

Calyste blushed like a still-virtuous maiden caught in the act of sinning.

". . . and furthermore," the duchess continued, "since you are not yet adept at deception, you made so many blunders that Sabine guessed it all. However, I have repaired the damage. You do not desire my daughter's death, do you? All this, Monsieur Dommanget, sets you on the path of the true nature of the disease and its cause. As to you, Calyste, an old woman like myself may be able to understand your sin but not forgive it. Such forgiveness is bought with a lifetime of happiness. If you desire my esteem, first save my daughter's life. Then, forget Madame de Rochefide. She is only worth having once. Learn how to lie, acquire the courage and impudence of a criminal. I managed to lie successfully, I who will be forced into severe penitence for that mortal sin!"

She then recounted the falsehoods she had been obliged to invent.

XXIII The Magnanimity of a Woman When She Con-
siders Herself Loved The experienced obstetrician, seated at
the head of the patient's bed, was already determining from
the symptoms the means of effecting the cure. While he was
prescribing a treatment whose success depended on the rapidity
of its execution, Calyste, seated at the foot of the bed, kept his
eyes fixed on Sabine and tried to express deep tenderness
through his glance.

"So it's gambling that is responsible for the circles under
your eyes?" she said feebly.

These words made the doctor, the mother and the vicomtess
shudder as they surreptitiously exchanged glances. Calyste
turned red as a beet.

"That's what happens when wives are nursing," Dommanget
said with brutal wit. "Husbands get bored, they go off to their
clubs and gamble. But don't be upset over the thirty thousand
francs that monsieur lost last night."

"Thirty thousand francs!" Ursule exclaimed ingenuously.

"Yes, indeed," Dommanget replied. "I heard about it this
morning from the young Duchesse Berthe de Maufrigneuse.
You lost to Monsieur de Trailles," he said to Calyste. "How can
you play with a man like that? Frankly, Monsieur le Baron, I
can understand your embarrassment."

Seeing his mother-in-law, a pious duchess; the young vicomtesse, a happy wife; and the old obstetrician, a cynical egotist,
all lie like rug merchants, Calyste, decent noble Calyste, realized the extent of the danger to Sabine and shed two heavy
tears that completely fooled her.

"Monsieur," she said, sitting up and looking angrily at Dommanget, "Monsieur du Guénic can lose thirty, fifty or a hundred thousands francs if it pleases him, and no one need shake
a finger at him or teach him how to behave. It is far preferable
that Monsieur de Trailles won from him than for us to win
from Monsieur de Trailles."

Calyste stood up, took his wife's head between his hands, and kissed her on both cheeks whispering in her ear, "Sabine, you're an angel!"

⤙⊛⤚⤙⊛⤚*⤙⊛⤚*⤙⊛⤚*⤙⊛⤚*⤙⊛⤚*⤙⊛⤚*⤙⊛⤚*⤙⊛⤚*⤙⊛⤚*⤙⊛⤚

XXIV A LIE LIKE MANY OTHERS Two days later, the young woman appeared to be out of danger. The following day, Calyste was at Madame de Rochefide's seeking credit for his infamy.

"Béatrix," he told her, "I deserve to be made happy by you. I sacrificed my poor wife to you—she discovered everything. That fatal paper you had me write on with your name and your coronet that I never even noticed! All I saw was you! Fortunately, the monogram, your B., was somehow invisible. But the perfume you left on me, and the lies I got twisted into, betrayed my happiness. Sabine almost died. The milk went to her head. She has erysipelas and may carry its traces for the rest of her life."

Béatrix's expression, while listening to this speech, was so arctic the Seine would have frozen over had she looked at it.

"Oh, well, so much the better," she replied. "That may bleach her for you."

And Béatrix, turning as brittle as her bones, as uneven as her complexion, as harsh as her voice, continued in this vein, coining one atrocious epigram after another. There is no greater clumsiness than for a husband to talk to his mistress about his wife's virtue, unless it be to talk to his wife about his mistress' beauty. Calyste had not yet received this form of Parisian education which might be called the etiquette of adultery. He could neither tell his wife a lie nor his mistress the truth, two indispensable skills to master for handling women. And so he was obliged to use all the powers of passion to wring from Béatrix a pardon solicited over two hours time, denied by a wrathful angel who kept her eyes glued to the ceiling to avoid looking at the culprit, and who reeled off reasons peculiar to marquises in a voice broken by convincing little tears wiped on the lace of her handkerchief.

"The idea of talking to me about your wife practically the day after my downfall! Why not tell me what a pearl of virtue she is! I know, in her eyes you are beautiful because she admires you. That's what I call depravity! While I love your soul! For you ought to know, my dear, that compared to some of the shepherds of the Roman countryside, you are awful!" . . . and so on.

❋⇝⊛⤍❋⇝⊛⤍❋⇝⊛⤍❋⇝⊛⤍❋⇝⊛⤍❋⇝⊛⤍❋⇝⊛⤍❋⇝⊛⤍❋⇝⊛⤍

XXV   A Chapter for All Women to Meditate   Language such as the above may seem surprising, but it constituted a technique Béatrix had carefully thought out. By her third incarnation—for with each love affair a woman changes completely, she had become proportionately skilled in chicanery, the only word possible to describe the effects of the experience gained through such adventures. The marquise had taken full stock of herself in the mirror. Intelligent women never fool themselves about themselves. They count their lines, play midwife to the birth of their crow's feet and the blemishes on their skin, know themselves by heart, and even proclaim it too loudly by the immensity of their efforts at preservation. Furthermore, in order to contend with a splendid young rival, to carry away six victories a week, Béatrix had to seek her advantages in the craft of the courtesan. Without admitting to herself the foulness of her method, forced into the use of such means by her stubborn passion for Calyste, she had resolved to make him believe he was ungainly, ugly, badly built, and to treat him as though she loathed him. There is no more effective technique with men of a conquering nature. For such men, is not the vanquishing of this sophisticated disdain like the triumph of the first day repeated each successive day? Better still, it is flattery disguised as loathing which bestows grace and veracity on all the metamorphoses invented by sublime unknown poets. A man then says to himself, "I am irresistible!" or "I know how to love, for I can overcome her repugnance." If you deny this principle discovered by coquettes and courtesans of every social stratum, then you may as well deny the investigators of science, the seekers of secrets, kept at bay for years in their struggle with mysterious causes. Béatrix had doubled the dose of contempt used as a stimulant by perpetually contrasting her cozy poetic interior with the hôtel du Guénic. Every neglected wife who lets herself go, lets her house go as well because she feels so unencouraged. In anticipation of this, Madame de Rochefide began making insidious attacks on the luxury of the Faubourg Saint-Germain, which in her estimation was ridiculous. The scene of reconciliation, during which Béatrix made Calyste swear to hatred of his wife, who in her words was playing a comedy of spilled milk, took place in a veritable grove where she simpered in a setting of lush flowers and potted plants, all of rampant luxury. The art of little nothings, of fashionable trifles, had been pushed to the extreme by her. Having fallen into total disgrace by virtue of Conti's desertion, she wanted at least the glory to be gained from perversity. The misfortune of a young wife, a rich and beautiful Grandlieu, was to become a pedestal for her.

❋⤙☙⤚❋⤙☙⤚❋⤙☙⤚❋⤙☙⤚❋⤙☙⤚❋⤙☙⤚❋⤙☙⤚❋⤙☙⤚

XXVI A Little Treatise on Certitude From a Vantage Point Other Than Pascal's When a woman returns to normal life after nursing her firstborn, she reappears in society with heightened charm and beauty. If this phase of maternity can rejuvenate women past their prime, it gives younger ones resplendent freshness, energetic gaiety, a certain *brio,* if one can apply to the body what the Italians attribute to the mind. In her attempt to revive the delightful habits of their honeymoon, Sabine no longer found her former Calyste. The unhappy girl became an observer instead of a participant in pleasure. She was looking for the fatal perfume, and found it. She finally stopped confiding in either her friend or her mother who had so charitably fooled her. She wanted certitude, and certitude was not long in coming. Certitude is never niggardly; like the sun, one soon needs shades to keep it out. It is a repetition in love of the fable of the woodcutter calling for death; one asks of certitude that it blind us.

One morning, two weeks after the first crisis, Sabine received the following shocking letter:

To Madame la Baronne du Guénic

Guérande

My dear daughter,

My sister-in-law Zéphirine and I have been pondering over the dressing table you speak of in your letter. I am writing to Calyste about it and beg you to forgive our ignorance. You cannot question our hearts. We are piling up treasures for you. Thanks to the advice of Mademoiselle de Pen-Hoël on the management of your holdings, you will find yourselves in a few years in possession of considerable capital, without any diminution in your income.

Your letter, dear daughter whom I love as though I had borne you and nursed you with my milk, surprised me by its brevity, and above all by your silence over my dear little Calyste; you had nothing to tell me about my big Calyste, whom I know to be happy, nevertheless . . . etc."

❋⟐↷⟿⟐↷❋⟿⟐↷❋⟿⟐↷⟿⟐↷❋⟿⟐↷❋⟿⟐↷❋⟿⟐↷⟿⟐↷❋⟿⟐↷

XXVII A Pin-Thrust Against Steel Armour Sabine wrote across the letter: *Not all of noble Brittany can be telling lies!* and placed the letter on Calyste's desk. Calyste found the letter and read it. After recognizing the commentary and handwriting as Sabine's, he threw the letter into the fire resolved never to have seen it. Sabine spent an entire week in the kind of anguish known only to angelic or solitary souls untouched by the fallen angel's wing. Calyste's silence horrified Sabine.

"I who should be all sweetness and delight for him, have displeased him, offended him! . . . My virtue has become heinous, I have evidently humiliated my idol!" she said to herself.

These thoughts plowed deep furrows in her heart. She would have liked to ask his forgiveness, but certitude hurled new proofs at her.

Béatrix in her insolence dared write Calyste one day at his home. Madame du Guénic received the letter and handed it to her husband unopened. But she said to him, heartsick and in a broken voice, "My dear, here is a letter from the Jockey Club. I recognize the scent and the paper."

This time Calyste blushed and slipped the letter into his pocket.

"Why don't you open it?"

"I know what's in it."

The young woman sat down. She was no longer feverish or tearful, but in one of those rages that in gentle creatures engenders crime, placing arsenic in their hands either for themselves or for their rivals. Little Calyste was brought to her and she fondled him on her lap. The infant, recently weaned, sought her breast through her gown.

"*He* remembers!" she said under her breath.

Calyste went to his room to read the letter. When he had left, the pathetic young woman burst into the kind of tears women only shed when they are alone.

but remained at home! Sabine made herself caressing and humble, gay and witty.

"Why are you so distant, Calyste? Am I not a good wife? Is there something here that displeases you?" she asked.

"All these rooms are so bare and cold," he said. "You don't have any flair for that sort of thing."

"What is missing?"

"Flowers."

"Fine," Sabine said to herself. "It would seem then that Madame de Rochefide likes flowers."

Two days later, the rooms in the hôtel du Guénic had been totally transformed. No one in Paris could have prided himself on having more beautiful flowers than those that decorated this house.

One evening after dinner some time later, Calyste complained of the cold. He kept twisting around in his chair to see where the cold air came from, and seemed to be looking for something behind him. Sabine was at a loss to guess what this new caprice meant, for this house of hers had a furnace that heated the stairs, the anterooms and the hallways. Finally, after three days of meditation, she figured out that her rival probably surrounded herself with a screen in order to obtain that half-light so flattering to declining beauty; and so she too acquired a screen, but mirrored and of oriental costliness.

"Which side will the storm come from this time?" she wondered. She had not yet reached the end of his mistress' oblique attacks against her. Calyste when home ate in a manner that drove Sabine to distraction. He let the servant remove his plates after two or three barely nibbled mouthfuls.

"Isn't it good?" asked Sabine, despairing on seeing wasted all the trouble she had condescended to by consulting with her cook.

"I didn't say that, my angel," Calyste replied unruffled. "I'm simply not hungry, that's all."

A woman devoured by a rightful passion who fights in this

way, subjects herself to a rabid fury to get the better of her rival and often goes beyond her objective, all the way to the secret recesses of marriage. This combat, so cruel, so raging, so incessant, over the noticeable and so to speak exterior facets of their relationship, continued just as arduously in affective matters. Sabine began to study her poses and her dress, even taking pains in the minutest details of love.

The matter of cuisine lasted nearly a month. Sabine, seconded by Mariotte and Gasselin, invented vaudeville gags to find out what dishes Madame de Rochefide served Calyste. Gasselin replaced Calyste's coachman, sick on command, and was thus able to make friends with Béatrix's cook. Sabine finally succeeded in offering Calyste the same food, only better, but then saw him fuss over some new thing.

"Is something missing?" she asked.

"No, nothing," he replied, looking on the table for something he could not find.

"Aha!" exclaimed Sabine the next day on awaking. "Calyste was looking for those crushed beetles,* those English ingredients that are sold in pharmacies in cruet bottles. Madame de Rochefide has accustomed him to all kinds of spices!"

She bought the English cruet and its burning contents, but she could not track down every preparation invented by her rival.

※↷◈↷※↷◈↷※↷◈↷※↷◈↷※↷◈↷※↷◈↷※↷◈↷※↷◈↷※↷◈↷

XXXI A CURABLE FORM OF RABIES This period lasted for a number of months, which is hardly surprising if one stops to consider the appeal that a struggle holds. It is life, and with all its wounds and pains is preferable to the somber shadows of disgust, to the poison of contempt, to the nothingness of abdication, to that death of the heart that is called indifference.

---

* Assumed to be among the ingredients of Worcestershire sauce.

Nonetheless, all of Sabine's courage left her one evening when she appeared dressed as women are when they are out to defeat a rival and Calyste said laughing, "Try as you may, Sabine, you will never be anything but a beautiful Andalusian!"

"Alas," she replied sinking on a couch, "I will never look like a blond, but I know, if this continues, I will soon look thirty-five."

She refused to go to the opera and decided to remain home all evening. Once alone, she tore the flowers from her hair and trampled them. She undressed, ground her gown and shawl and all her clothes under her feet, like a goat caught in its tether that only lets up the struggle when it feels death approaching. She then went to bed. When her maid came in, one can imagine her surprise.

"Oh! it's nothing," said Sabine. "It was monsieur."

Unhappy women are given to those sublime conceits, those lies in which, of two conflicting embarrassments, the more feminine wins out.

Under the terrible strain of this game, Sabine lost weight and was being worn down by chagrin. But she never stopped playing the role she had set for herself. Urged on by a kind of fever, her lips forced deep into her throat the bitter words that her pain provoked. She suppressed the fiery glances of her marvelous black eyes and made them gentle to the point of humility. Her dwindling health finally became apparent. The duchess, an excellent mother even though her piety had become increasingly Portuguese, thought she recognized some deadly cause behind the truly unhealthy state in which Sabine was luxuriating. She knew about the regularized intimacy between Béatrix and Calyste. She saw to it that her daughter came to stay with her in order to treat the wounds of her heart, and above all to pry her away from her martyrdom. For some time, Sabine maintained total silence regarding her miseries, fearing some intervention between her and Calyste. She insisted she was happy! . . . Having reached the limits of unhappiness, she rediscovered her pride and all her virtues! But after a month of her mother's and her sister's tenderness, she admitted her sorrow, confided her anguish, cursed her life, and declared she awaited death with delirious joy. She begged Clotilde, who wished to remain unmarried, to become the foster mother of little Calyste, the most beautiful child any royal family could desire for its heir presumptive.

XXXII   A Dithyramb to Matrimony   One evening, in the company of her family, seated between her younger sister, Athénaïs—whose marriage to the Vicomte de Grandlieu was to take place after Lent—Clotilde and the duchess, Sabine uttered the ultimate cries of an agonized heart, cries elicited by the excess of her most recent humiliation.

"Athénaïs," she said, seeing the young Vicomte Juste de Grandlieu leave towards eleven o'clock, "you are about to be married. May my example serve you well. Refrain, as though it were criminal, from exhibiting your qualities, resist the temptation of appearing in your best light in order to please Juste. Be cool, dignified and distant, weigh the happiness you give against the happiness you receive! This may seem infamous, but it is necessary. Don't you see, I am perishing because of my qualities! Everything in me that is beautiful, saintly, great, all my virtues are so many reefs against which my happiness has been dashed. I have lost my appeal because I'm not thirty-six! In the eyes of some men, to be young is to be inferior. There is no mystery in an open face. I laugh sincerely, and that is a mistake! To be seductive, one must know how to concoct that melancholy half-smile of fallen angels obliged to conceal their long yellow teeth. A fresh complexion is monotonous! Far more desirable is the waxen mask of a doll made of rouge, whale oil, and cold cream. I am straightforward while it is perversity that pleases. I am genuinely passionate, like any decent woman, while one should be wily, cheating, and fussy like a small-town actress. I am drunk with the pleasure of having one of the most charming men in France for a husband, I tell him naively how distinguished he is, how graceful, how handsome, while to entice him I should turn away in feigned disgust, dislike everything about lovemaking, tell him that his distinction is nothing more than a sickly look, the complexion of a consumptive; I should praise to the skies the shoulders of the Farnese Hercules, make him angry and defend myself, as though I were in need of a quarrel to hide some of those imperfections that can destroy love, at the very moment of happiness. I have the misfortune of admiring what is beautiful without any concern for my self-glorification by bitter, envious criticism of everything that emanates from poetry and beauty. I do not need to be told in prose and verse by Canalis and Nathan what a superior intellect I have! I am a pathetic, innocent child and know nothing but Calyste. Ah, if I had traveled all over the world, like *her,* if I could say *I love you* in all the languages of Europe like *her,* I would be consoled, pitied, adored, and could serve him the Macedonian feast of a cosmopolitan passion. One is only grateful for your tenderness if you contrast it with nastiness. In short, I, a pure woman, am obliged to learn all these impurities, all these lures of harlots! And Calyste is taken in by all these fakeries! Oh, mother! Oh, my dear Clotilde! I feel I have been mortally wounded. My pride is a deceptive shield, I am defenseless against suffering. I still love my husband like a lunatic, while to win him back I ought to have all the lucidity of indifference."

"Silly girl," Clotilde whispered to her, "pretend you are out to avenge yourself."

"I want to die without reproach, without even the illusion of guilt," Sabine replied. "Our vengeance ought to be worthy of our love."

"My child," said the duchess, "a mother should view life a bit more coolly than you do. Love is not the end but the means of married life. Don't try to imitate that poor little Baronne de Macumer.* Excessive passion is fruitless and fatal. God sends down our afflictions knowing full well what He is doing . . . . Now that Athénaïs' marriage is all arranged, I shall be able to look after you. I have already talked about the awkward situation you are in with your father, with the Duc de Chaulieu and with d'Ajuda. We will surely find a way to bring Calyste back to you . . . ."

"With the Marquise de Rochefide there is hope!" said Clotilde smiling. "She never keeps her admirers very long."

"You know, my angel, d'Ajuda was Monsieur de Rochefide's brother-in-law. If our dear confessor approves the little schemes we are forced into using to insure the success of the plan I have proposed to your father, then I can guarantee Calyste's return. My conscience rebels against resorting to such means, and I want to submit them to Father Brosette's judgment. We will not wait, my child, until you are *in extremis* before coming to your aid. So don't lose hope! Your unhappiness is so intense this evening that my secret has slipped out. However, I can't resist offering you some hope."

"Will this cause Calyste unhappiness?" Sabine anxiously asked her mother.

"Oh, my God! Will I be that silly?" Athénaïs naively exclaimed.

"Ah little one, you don't know to what baseness virtue brings us when it is influenced by love," Sabine replied, unaware in her grief of her inadvertent poetizing.

This line was said with such penetrating bitterness that the duchess, suddenly illumined by her daughter's tone, manner and facial expression guessed there was some still hidden misfortune.

* Louise de Chaulieu (in *Mémoires de deux jeunes mariées*), who first thought she would die of chagrin after her husband's death, commits suicide four years later out of jealousy, after marrying her lover.

"Children, it is midnight. Go now," she said to her daughters whose eyes were bright with curiosity.

"Even at thirty-six, am I still too young to stay?" Clotilde said teasingly. While Athénaïs was kissing her mother, Clotilde bent over Sabine and whispered, "Tell me tomorrow! I'll come and have dinner with you. And if my mother feels her conscience compromised, I will ransom Calyste from the infidel for you."

✻⤙⊛⤚✻⤙⊛⤚✻⤙⊛⤚✻⤙⊛⤚✻⤙⊛⤚✻⤙⊛⤚✻⤙⊛⤚✻⤙⊛⤚✻⤙⊛⤚✻⤙⊛⤚✻⤙⊛⤚

XXXII A COMPLICATION "Well then, Sabine!" said the duchess, taking her daughter into her bedroom, "what else is wrong now?"

"Oh mama, it's hopeless!"

"Why?"

"I wanted a victory over that horrible woman, and I got it. But now I'm pregnant and Calyste loves her so much I can foresee total desertion. For when she discovers his infidelity, *she* will be furious! Ah, I am going through more agony than I can bear. I know when he is going to see her, I can tell from his joyfulness; and his bad mood tells me when he has come back from her. It has reached the point where he no longer bothers to pretend; he finds me intolerable. Her influence over him is as nefarious as she is herself in body and soul. You'll see, she will insist on a public separation as the price of reconciliation, a rupture like her own, and she will take off with him to Switzerland or Italy. He has begun to find embarrassing his ignorance of Europe; I can guess what this is leading up to. If Calyste is not cured within the next three months, I don't know what will happen . . . yes I do! I'll kill myself!"

"Miserable child! What about your soul? Suicide is a mortal sin!"

"Don't you understand? She might have a child by him! And if Calyste were to become more attached to hers than to mine! Oh, that would be the end of my patience and my resignation."

She fell into a chair. She had handed over the innermost secrets of her heart and now found herself with no hidden sorrow. Sorrow is like the wire armature inside the sculptor's clay model; it is a support, a source of strength.

"Go now, go home, my poor darling. In view of all these misfortunes, Father Brossette will surely grant me absolution for the venial sins that the world's dishonesty forces us to commit. Now leave me, my child," she said going over to her prie-dieu. "I want to implore our Saviour and the Holy Virgin, especially on your behalf. Goodbye, my dearest Sabine, and above all do not forget your prayers if you want us to succeed . . . ."

"Even if we do mother, all we can save is the Family. Calyste has destroyed in me the holy fervor of love by surfeiting everything in me, even my capacity for pain. What a honeymoon that was, discovering as I did from the very first day the bitterness of retrospective infidelity!"

PART TWO

THE
SHADY SIDE
OF A
PIOUS WOMAN

I   A SPIRITUAL CONSULTATION   The next day towards one o'clock, one of the priests of the Faubourg Saint-Germain, the Abbé Brossette—one of the most distinguished members of the Parisian clergy who in 1840 was designated for one of the vacant bishoprics, a see thrice refused by him—was coming across the courtyard of the hôtel de Grandlieu with that particular walk that must be termed an ecclesiastical walk, because it personifies prudence, mystery, tranquillity, seriousness, the essence of dignity. He was a small thin man of about fifty, pale as an old woman, shrunk by the fasts of the priesthood, shriveled by all the suffering he espoused. Two black eyes burning with faith, but softened by an expression more mysterious than mystical, enlivened this apostle's face. He was almost smiling as he climbed the stairs, so little did he believe in the gravity of the circumstances that made his parishioner summon him. However, since the hand of the duchess was like a sieve when it came to alms-giving, she was well worth the time that her innocent confessions stole from the more serious problems of the parish. On hearing the priest announced, the duchess got up and took a few steps toward him—an honor she only accorded to cardinals, bishops, simple priests, duchesses older than herself, and persons of royal blood.

"My dear abbé," she said, offering him a chair herself and keeping her voice low, "I need the authority of your experience before embarking on a rather nasty intrigue which should, however, bear worthwhile results. I should like to know from you whether as a consequence, I will find thorns on the road to salvation."

"My dear duchess," the priest replied, "do not confuse spiritual matters with worldly matters, they are often incompatible. First of all, what is this about?"

"You know my daughter Sabine is dying of grief; Monsieur du Guénic is unfaithful to her with Madame de Rochefide."

"That is dreadful, and it is serious. But you know what our beloved Saint Francis of Sales said about that. And think of

Madame Guyon, who complained of the absence of mysticism in the manifestations of conjugal love. She would have been most happy to see her husband with a Madame de Rochefide."

"Sabine is as sweet as she could be and only too good a Christian wife, but she has not the slightest taste for mysticism."

"Poor girl!" said the priest mischievously. "And what have you devised to remedy this unfortunate situation?"

"I have committed the sin, my dear confessor, of thinking I might unleash against Madame de Rochefide a charming young man, strong-willed, practised in wickedness, who could certainly supplant my son-in-law."

"My daughter," he said stroking his chin, "we are not here in the confessional and I am not obliged to sit in judgment. From a mundane viewpoint, I admit this could be a decisive . . . ."

"It struck me as truly odious!" she added.

"But why? Of course, the duty of a good Christian is to remove a fallen woman from the path of perdition rather than prod her ahead. However, when one is as far gone as Madame de Rochefide, it is no longer the arm of man, but the arm of God that can rescue such sinners. They need a special kind of lightning bolt."

"Father," the duchess continued, "I thank you for your understanding. However, I also realized that my son-in-law is both brave and Breton. He was heroic during MADAME's illfated insurrection. Now then, if the young rascal who is to undertake the seduction of Madame de Rochefide were to quarrel with Calyste and a duel ensue . . . ."

"There you make a shrewd observation, Madame la Duchesse, which only proves that on such devious paths one always encounters stumbling blocks."

"I have discovered a method, my dear abbé, for doing a truly good deed which would divert Madame de Rochefide from her iniquitous ways, restore Calyste to his wife, and perhaps save from damnation a poor lost soul . . . ."

"In that case, why consult me?" said the priest with a smile.

"Ah!" replied the duchess. "I must engage in a number of rather foul acts . . . ."

"You are not planning to rob anyone?"

"On the contrary, it is I who will probably be spending a considerable sum of money."

"You will not engage in slander? You will not . . . ."

"Oh!"

"You will not harm your neighbor?"

"Hmmm, I am not too sure."

"Well then, let us hear your new plan," said the curate, whose curiosity was now aroused.

"If, instead of driving one nail with another—this is what occurred to me at my prie-dieu after imploring the Holy Virgin to enlighten me—I succeeded in having Monsieur de Rochefide send Calyste away by persuading him to take back his wife, then instead of soiling my hands to save my daughter, I would bring about one great benefit by means of another no lesser one . . . ."

The priest looked at his Portuguese parishioner and remained pensive.

"This is evidently an idea that has come to you from such remote inspiration that . . . ."

"That," said the kind and humble duchess, "is why I have thanked the Virgin and promised to offer, apart from a novena, twelve hundred francs to a poor family if I succeed. But when I explained my plan to Monsieur de Grandlieu, he started laughing and said, 'My word! I really think women of your age have a devil all their own!' "

"Monsieur le duc said in a husband's words what I was about to say when you interrupted me," said the priest, unable to suppress his amusement.

"Ah, Father, if you approve of the plan, can you also approve of the means to its achievement? What is involved is doing to a certain Madame Schontz—the Béatrix of the Saint-Georges quarter—what I had intended to do to Béatrix so that her husband would take her back."

"I am convinced that you can do no evil," said the priest slyly, unwilling to hear any more and satisfied by the necessity of the result, "and you can always consult me should your conscience begin muttering," he added. "However, instead of providing the lady of the rue Saint-Georges with a new cause for scandal, what if you provided her with a husband?"

"Oh my dear confessor, you have righted the one wrong in my plan. You deserve to be an archbishop and I trust I will not die before addressing you as Your Eminence."

"I see in this only one pitfall."

"And that is?"

"Suppose Madame de Rochefide continued with your son-in-law while returning to her husband?"

"I would see to that," the duchess said. "When one concocts few intrigues, one concocts them . . . ."

"Badly! Very badly!" the priest interrupted. "Experience is necessary in all things. Try to get hold of one of those rascals who thrive on intrigues, and use him without revealing yourself."

"Oh, monsieur le curé, if we make use of hell, will heaven be with us?"

"You are not at confession," replied the priest, "save your daughter!"

The good duchess, delighted by her curate, escorted him to the door of the drawing room.

❋↩☙✛↩☙✱❋↩☙✱❋↩☙✱❋↩☙✱❋↩☙✱❋↩☙✱❋↩☙✱❋↩☙✱❋↩☙✱❋↩☙✛

II THE ABANDONED HUSBAND As one can see, a storm was brewing over Monsieur de Rochefide, who at that moment was enjoying the greatest pleasure a Parisian could desire—he was as much a husband at Madame Schontz's as he had been at Béatrix's; as the duke shrewdly pointed out to his wife, it seemed impossible to disturb such a totally satisfying existence. This assumption demands a few details regarding the life led by Monsieur de Rochefide from the time his wife made him an *Abandoned Husband*.* It will then be possible to understand the enormous difference, created by our laws and customs, between the two sexes in the same situation. Everything that turns into misfortune for the abandoned woman becomes good fortune for the abandoned male. This striking contrast may perhaps encourage more than one young woman to cling to her marriage and fight it out, as did Sabine du Guénic, by utilizing at her choice the most murderous or most inoffensive of her attributes.

A few days after Béatrix's elopement, Arthur de Rochefide— sole heir by virtue of his sister's death (she had been the first wife of the Marquis d'Ajuda-Pinto and had died childless)— found himself in possession, first of all, of the Rochefide mansion on the rue d'Anjou-Saint-Honoré, then of an annual income of two hundred thousand francs left to him by his father. This munificent inheritance, added to the fortune Arthur already had at the time of his marriage, plus his wife's fortune, brought his income to one thousand francs per day. For a gentleman whose character Mademoiselle des Touches had sketched for Calyste in a few words, such a fortune was in itself immense happiness. While his wife concerned herself with love and motherhood, Rochefide took pleasure in his enormous fortune, which he did not squander any more than he squandered his wits. His overfed vanity, already satisfied by the label of "attractive," to which he owed a few successes and which he thought entitled him to look down on women, similarly granted him full privileges in the realm of intellect. Gifted with the kind of mind that must be called refractive, he appropriated the witticisms of others heard in the theatre or read in the newspaper, and seemed to be making fun of them; for they

---

* Allusion to Balzac's novel *La femme abandonée*.

were repeated in a tone of mockery and applied as critical formulas. In addition, his military verve (he had served in the Royal Guard) spiced his conversation so effectively that dull women declared him to be witty and the others dared not contradict. This system was used by Arthur in all things. He owed to nature the useful talent of imitation without aping; he could imitate with seriousness. Consequently, though totally lacking in taste, he was always the first to adopt and the first to drop the latest fashions. Accused of spending too much time on his dressing and of wearing a corset, he was the very model of the kind of person who, by constantly espousing the ideas and misconceptions of everyone, never offends anyone, and who, forever up to date, never grows old. These are the heroes of mediocrity. This husband then was pitied, while Béatrix was found unforgivable for having abandoned the nicest chap on earth, and so only the wife was scorned. A member of all the clubs, subscriber to all the inanities of misconstrued patriotism and party spirit, willing participant to anything which placed him in the front ranks of everything, this loyal, brave and very silly gentleman—of whom alas there are so many examples among the rich—naturally wished to distinguish himself by some fashionable occupation. His principal claim to fame lay in his sultanship of a four-footed harem governed by an old English groom, which ate up four to five thousand francs a month. His specialty was race horses, he became the protector of thoroughbreds, he subsidized a journal devoted to the study of horses, despite the fact he knew hardly anything about them, and from bridle to spurs depended entirely on his groom. All of which clearly indicates that this semibachelor had nothing of his own—neither wit, nor tastes, nor position, nor foibles; even his fortune came to him from his forebears. After tasting of all the displeasures of marriage, he was so delighted to be a bachelor again that he told all his cronies, "I was born lucky!" He was above all delighted to avoid the expenses of receiving at home, which befalls all married couples, and so his mansion, unchanged since his father's death, looked as though its masters were away on a trip; he was hardly ever there, never ate there, and rarely slept there. And here is the reason.

❋↝✥↝✥↝✥↝✥↝✥↝✥↝✥↝✥↝✥↝✥↝✥↝✥↝✥↝

III How the Rat, Accused of Destructiveness, Is on the Contrary, a Constructive Animal After a number of amorous adventures, followed by boredom with society women who are indeed boring and who set up far too many bramble hedges around happiness, he entered into a relationship, as we shall see, with the celebrated Madame Schontz—celebrated among women like Fanny-Beaupré, Suzanne du Val-Noble, Mariette, Florentine, Jenny Cadine, and others. This world—about which one of our cartoonists * cleverly remarked while pointing to the dizzying spectacle of an Opera Ball, "When one thinks how splendidly housed, dressed, and fed all that is, it gives one a damn good idea of mankind."—this pernicious world has already intruded into our history of mores through the characteristic figures of Florine and the illustrious Malaga in *Une fille d'Eve* and *la Fausse Maîtresse.*** However, to depict this world accurately, the historian would have to establish a ratio between the number of such individuals and the various endings to their singular lives—some in the most abject poverty, some by premature deaths, others in comfort, happy marriages, and still others in affluence.

Madame Schontz, first known by the name of Petite-Aurélie, to distinguish her from one of her duller rivals, belonged to the highest class of these women whose social usefulness cannot be denied by either the prefect of the Seine or by those

* Gavarni, whose cartoon, *The Opera Ball,* appeared in the May 1840 issue of *Charivari.*
** As with Louise de Chaulieu, Balzac frequently refers to characters in his other novels as though to historic personages or contemporary celebrities.

whose concern is the prosperity of Paris. The rat, held responsible for the destruction of what are often hypothetical fortunes, is in truth more the beaver's competitor. Without the Aspasias of Notre-Dame-de-Lorette,* fewer houses would be built in Paris. Pioneers of fresh plaster, they are carried along the hillsides of Montmartre on the waves of speculation, pitching their tents in the solitude of the sculpted rubble that lines the streets of Europe, be it Amsterdam, Milan, Stockholm, London, or Moscow—architectural steppes where the wind flaps innumerable signs attesting to the desolation all around: *Apartments for Rent!* The economic status of these women is determined by their housing in these apocryphal districts: if her house is in the vicinity of the boundary traced by the rue de Provence, the woman is assured a prosperous income; if, on the other hand, she sets herself up near the outer boulevards or toward the ghastly suburb of Batignolles, she has no chance. When Monsieur de Rochefide met Madame Schontz, she was living on the third floor of the only house standing on the rue de Berlin. She was thus right on the edge of misery and the boundary of Paris.

*~☙✦~☙✦~☙✦~☙✦~☙✦~☙✦~☙✦~☙✦~☙✦~☙✦~☙✦~☙✦~☙✦~

IV THE COMMON HISTORY OF DISTINGUISHED KEPT WOMEN
This unwedded wife was named, as you may have guessed, neither Schontz nor Aurélie! She concealed the name of her father, a veteran of the Empire, the perennial colonel who figures at the dawning of these feminine existences either as father or seducer. Madame Schontz had enjoyed the benefit of a free education at Saint-Denis where young girls are admirably brought up, but which offers them neither husbands nor opportunities on leaving this school, admirable creation of the Emperor with only one thing lacking—the Emperor! "I will be

* The district of well-kept women, formerly the 13th, now the 9th Arrondissement.

there to look after the daughters of my legionnaires," he replied to the observation made by one of his farseeing ministers. Napoleon also said "I will be there!" regarding the members of the Institut who were offered no stipend at all rather than 83 francs a month, which is less than many an office boy earns. Aurélie was very definitely the daughter of the stalwart Colonel Schiltz, a leader of those daring Alsatian partisans who almost saved the Emperor during the French campaign, and who died at Metz, pillaged, robbed and ruined. In 1814, Napoleon placed little Joséphine Schiltz, then aged nine, at Saint-Denis. Orphaned of both her father and her mother, homeless and penniless, the poor child was allowed to remain at the institution through the second restoration of the Bourbons, where she continued as an assistant teacher until 1827 when her patience gave out and her beauty took over. On coming of age, Joséphine Schiltz, goddaughter of the Empress, set out on the adventurous life of the courtesan, attracted to this uncertain future by the fatal example of some of her school friends, similarly destitute, who congratulated themselves on their choice. She substituted *on* for the *il* of her father's name and placed herself under the protection of Saint Aurelia. Vivacious, clever and cultivated, she made many more mistakes than her duller comrades whose misdemeanors were always prompted by money. After a few experiences with writers, poor but dishonest, witty but debt-ridden; after taking up with a few rich men as stingy as they were silly; after sacrificing security to true love and gaining experience in every school that offered it; one day of extreme misery while at Valentino's (Musard's first step to the top),* dancing in a borrowed dress, hat and shawl, she attracted the attention of Arthur de Rochefide who had come

---

* Valentino, former conductor at the Opéra, had opened a concert hall which later became a dance hall. Musard, conductor of the Opéra balls, had a concert and dance hall on the Champs-Elysées which became famous for the galop and other "scandalous" dances of the time.

there to see the famous gallop. Her brightness captivated this gentleman who no longer knew what interests to follow; and so, two years after Béatrix (whose brightness had often humiliated him) had left him, the marquis was in no way blamed for taking up with a secondhand Béatrix from the 13th Arrondissement.

❋↝✪↝❋↝✪↝❋↝✪↝❋↝✪↝✪↝❋↝✪↝❋↝✪↝❋↝✪↝❋↝✪↝❋↝✪↝❋↝✪↝

V THE FOUR SEASONS OF THE 13TH ARRONDISSEMENT

FIRST SEASON   Let us outline the four seasons of this happy relationship. It must be pointed out that the theory of marriage in the 13th Arrondissement is equally valid for the others. Whether forty-year-old marquis or sixty-year-old retired merchant, millionaire six times over or pensioner (see *Un début dans la vie*),* great nobleman, or commoner, the strategy of passion, except for the intrinsic differences of social spheres, does not vary. Passion and the pocketbook are always clearly related. You will therefore be able to estimate the problems involved in the execution of the duchess' charitable project.

One has no idea of the power of words in France over ordinary people, or of the harm done by the great wits who invent locutions. No accountant can estimate the sums of money that have remained unproductive, locked at the bottom of generous hearts and strongboxes, because of the ignoble expression, *Tirer une carotte!* . . . This expression, which means to be swindled or fleeced, has become so popular that it must be allowed to soil this page. Furthermore, in penetrating into the 13th Arrondissement, one has to accept the colorful local dialect. Monsieur de Rochefide, like all small minds, was always afraid of being *carotté*. The substantive became a verb. And so,

---

*   Cardot, in this novel of Balzac, a widower of sixty-eight, and man of considerable means, keeps Florentine at the outset of her career and experiences with her the four stages of extra-marital happiness discussed by Balzac here.

from the beginning of his passion for Madame Schontz, Arthur was on his guard and was extremely *rat,* to borrow another expression from the world of painters and prostitutes. The word *rat,* when applied to a young girl signifies the guest or game; but applied to a man, signifies a tightfisted host or hunter. Madame Schontz was too bright and knew men too well not to build great hopes on such a beginning. Monsieur de Rochefide gave her an allowance of five hundred francs a month, cheaply furnished a third-floor apartment for her on the rue Coquenard at a rental of twelve hundred francs, and set himself to studying Aurélie's character; she provided him with a character to study as soon as she became aware of his espionage. Rochefide was overjoyed to discover a girl with such a fine character, but saw nothing remarkable about it—her mother had been a Barnheim of Baden, a very proper woman indeed! Furthermore, Aurélie had been so well educated. With her knowledge of English, German, and Italian, she had full command of foreign literatures. She could compete very honorably with second-rank pianists. And most significant, her attitude toward her talents was that of well-bred people—she never talked about them! She could pick up a brush at a painter's studio, make a few strokes for the fun of it and turn out a jolly good head to the amazement of all present. Out of lassitude during her stint as assistant headmistress, she had begun dipping into the sciences, but her life as a kept woman had covered over these good seedlings with a blanket of salt; naturally, she gave her Arthur credit for the blossoming of these precious seeds, recultivated for him. Aurélie began by being as unmercenary as she was voluptuous, which permitted this fragile corvette to sink her grapnels into that highmasted vessel. Nonetheless, toward the end of the first year, she began to make terrible rackets with her clogs in the hallway, seeing to it that she came home just when the marquis was already there waiting for her, and hiding in a way to show it off best, the disgustingly muddied hem of her dress. Finally, she so artfully convinced her *big daddy* that her sole ambition after so many ups and downs was a decent middle-class existence that, ten months after their first meeting, the second season was ushered in.

→✦→✦→→✦→*→✦→*→✦→*→✦→*→✦→*→✦→*→✦→*→✦→*→✦→

VI SECOND SEASON   Madame Schontz then acquired a handsome apartment on the rue Neuve-Saint-Georges. Arthur, no longer able to conceal his wealth, gave her splendid furniture, a complete set of silverware, twelve hundred francs a month, a little one-horse carriage—rented however—and even graciously agreed to a liveried groom. La Schontz was not the least grateful for all this generosity, having discovered the motives behind her Arthur's behavior and recognized the calculating maneuvers of a *rat*. Fed up with restaurants where the food is most often execrable, where the simplest gastronomic meal costs sixty francs for one and two hundred francs if one has three guests, Rochefide offered Madame Schontz forty francs a day for his dinner and a friend's, wine included. Aurélie accepted. After cashing all her moral letters of credit, drawn for one year on the habits of Monsieur de Rochefide, she was favorably received when she requested an additional five hundred francs a month for clothing, in order not to embarrass her *big daddy* whose friends were all members of the Jockey Club.

"How would you like it if Rastignac, Maxime de Trailles, d'Esgrignon, La Roche-Hugon, Ronquerolles, Laginski, Lenoncourt and the others, found you with a Madame Everard? * Furthermore, you can trust me, old boy, you only stand to gain!" Aurélie, in fact, managed to reveal hitherto unseen virtues during this period. She undertook the role of housewife of which she acquitted herself admirably. As she put it, she brought the two ends of the month together on 2,500 francs without debts, something never seen before in the Faubourg

* Well-known character of a housekeeper trying to marry the master.

Saint-Germain of the 13th Arrondissement. She served dinners infinitely superior to Nucingen's, and exquisite wines at ten and twelve francs the bottle. Rochefide, overwhelmed and overjoyed to be able to invite his friends often to his mistress' house while saving money, would say as he held her by the waist, "You're a treasure!" Before long, he rented a third of a box for her at the opera, and ended up by taking her to all the openings. He began to consult his Aurélie, having recognized the soundness of her advice. She allowed him to borrow the witticisms she was constantly inventing, which, being unknown, furthered his reputation for cleverness. Ultimately, he acquired the certainty of being loved, and for himself. Aurélie refused the five thousand-franc-per-month offer of a Russian prince in exchange for his happiness.

"You are a lucky man, my dear marquis," exclaimed old prince Galathionne, finishing up a game of whist at the club. "Yesterday, when you left us alone, I tried to steal Madame Schontz away from you. But she said, 'My dear prince, you are no handsomer, but you are older than Rochefide; you would probably beat me, while he is like a father to me. Can you give me one good reason for leaving him? I don't feel for Arthur the wild passion I had for some of those patent-booted cads whose debts I used to pay, but I love him as a respectable wife loves her husband.' And she showed me the door."

This little speech, which sounded perfectly sincere, resulted in the prodigious encouragement of the state of neglect and decay into which the hôtel de Rochefide had fallen. Before long, Arthur moved his entire existence and all his pleasures into Madame Schontz's and stumbled on a gold mine, for in three years he found himself with four hundred thousand francs to invest.

VII THIRD SEASON The third phase began. Madame Schontz became the tenderest of mothers for Arthur's son; she picked him up at boarding school and brought him back herself; she showered him with gifts, and treats and pocket money, this child who called her his "little mommy" and who adored her. She entered into the management of Arthur's fortune, making him buy up securities when the market was low just before the famous Treaty of London which overthrew the government of March the first.* Arthur made two hundred thousand francs, and Aurélie did not ask for an obol. Gentleman that he was, Rochefide invested his six hundred thousand francs in Bank of France bonds, and put half of them in the name of Mademoiselle Joséphine Schiltz. A small house rented on the rue de La Bruyère was handed over to Grindot, the great architect of small dwellings, with instructions to turn it into a delicious candy box. From then on, Rochefide no longer kept accounts with Madame Schontz who received his revenues and paid his bills. Having become his wife, in effect, she repaid his trust by making him happier than ever. She had come to know his caprices and gratified them as Madame de Pompadour had humored the fantasies of Louis XV. She was in every way the acknowledged mistress, the absolute mistress. Consequently, she permitted herself to become the patroness of some enchanting young men, artists and writers newborn to glory who repudiated both the ancients and the moderns, and tried to acquire great reputations by doing very little. Madame Schontz's line of conduct should provide a clear indication of her masterful tactics. To begin with, ten or twelve young men entertained Arthur, supplying him with epigrams and subtle judgments of everything, and never cast doubt on the fidelity of the mistress of the house; in addition, they considered her an eminently intelligent woman. As a result, these walking ad-

* On March 1, 1840, Thiers became premier. The Treaty of London, signed on July 15, defeated Thiers' aggressive policy in the Middle East.

vertisements, these talking reviews, claimed she was the most delightful woman known on the boundary separating the 13th from the other twelve arrondissements. Her rivals—Suzanne Gaillard, who since 1838 had the advantage of a legitimate marriage over her, the pleonasm serving to denote a solid marriage; Fanny-Beaupré, Mariette, Antonia—spread rumors a bit more than amusing on the beauty of these young men and the indulgence with which Monsieur de Rochefide received them. Madame Schontz, who could far outwit the combined wit of these ladies, one evening at a supper given by Nathan at Florine's after an Opéra ball, having described her luck and her success, flung them a "Can you do as well? . . ." that has not been forgotten. Madame Schontz made Arthur sell the horses during this time, doubtless utilizing arguments she owed to the critical mind of Claude Vignon, one of her habitués.

"I can understand," she said one evening after having whipped the horses with another one of her sarcastic tongue-lashings, "how princes and wealthy men might take horse-breeding seriously, but for the good of the country, not for the childish satisfactions of a gambler's pride. If you had stables on your property and raised twelve hundred horses, if everybody raced the best horses in his stables, and all the stables of France and Navarre competed at every solemn occasion, that might be impressive. But you buy individual race horses the way booking agents buy acts. You demean an institution until it is reduced to a mere game; you have created a leg market as though it were a stock market! It's revolting! Are you really interested in spending sixty thousand francs just to read: *LÉLIA, owned by Monsieur de Rochefide, beat by one length FLEUR-DE-GENET, owned by Monsieur le duc de Rhétoré* . . . ? You would do better to give this money to poets who could assure you immortality through prose or poetry like the late Monthyon!"

By dint of her taunting, the marquis acknowledged the pointlessness to racing and made an economy of sixty thousand francs. The following year, Madame Schontz said to him, "Arthur, I no longer cost you a penny!" Many rich men envied the marquis his Madame Schontz and tried to lure her away, but like the Russian prince, they were wasting their old age trying.

"Listen to me, my dear," she had said two weeks earlier to Finot who had become very rich, "I am sure Rochefide would forgive me some little infidelity if I fell for someone, but no one would leave a good-natured marquis like him for a social climber like you. You couldn't keep me in the position Arthur has given me; he has made me an almost-honest woman, something you couldn't do even if you married me." This was the last rivet in the chaining of the contented convict. These words reached the absent ears for which they had been intended.

✻✦☺✦✻✦☺✦✻✦☺✦✻✦☺✦✻✦☺✦✻✦☺✦✻✦☺✦✻✦☺✦✻✦☺✦

VIII FOURTH SEASON The fourth phase had already begun, the phase of *habit,* the crowning victory of the battle plan that allows women like this to say "Now I have him!" Rochefide, who had just bought the little town house on the rue de la Bruyère in Joséphine Schiltz's name—a bagatelle of eighty thousand francs—had reached the stage, when the duchess began formulating her plans, of taking real pride in his mistress whom he named Ninon II in tribute to her rigorous honesty, her exquisite manner, her wit, and her culture. All his faults and qualities, his tastes and his pleasures were centered around Madame Schontz. He was now at that juncture in life where out of lassitude, indifference, or principle, a man no longer seeks variety and limits himself either to his wife or his mistress.

One can evaluate the importance acquired by Madame Schontz over the last five years by the fact that one had to be proposed far in advance in order to be presented at her house. She refused to receive rich bores or people of ill repute; the only exceptions she made were for great aristocratic names.

"They have the right to be dull," she used to say, "because they are *thoroughly respectable.*" Ostensibly, her personal fortune consisted of the 300,000 francs that Rochefide had given her and that a *dear little stockbroker*—Gobenheim, the only one she accepted in her house—was investing for her; however, she was manipulating all by herself a private little fortune of 200,-000 francs amassed from savings on her allowance over the last three years and from earnings on her perpetually reinvested 300,000 francs, this last being the only amount she ever admitted possessing.

"The more you make, the less you keep," Gobenheim said to her one day. "Water is so expensive," she replied.

The undeclared fortune was augmented by jewelry and diamonds that Aurélie wore for a month and then sold, and by sums of money given to her for fancies that had passed. When she was called wealthy, Madame Schontz replied that at the current rate of interest on investments, 300,000 francs yielded 12,000, which she had already spent during the harder times of her life when she was in love with Lousteau.

❋⤳☉↝❋⤳☉↝❋⤳☉↝❋⤳☉↝❋⤳☉↝❋⤳☉↝❋⤳☉↝❋⤳☉↝❋⤳☉↝

IX A FINAL WORD ON DISTINGUISHED KEPT WOMEN All of this indicated a plan, and Madame Schontz did indeed have one, you can be sure of that. Jealous for the last two years of Madame du Bruel, she had been stung by the desire to be married before church and state. All social positions have their forbidden fruit—some little thing magnified by desire to the point of being big as life. This ambition was necessarily accompanied by the ambitions of a second Arthur whom no amount of espionage could uncover. Bixiou thought he discerned the favorite in the painter Léon de Lora; the painter thought Bixiou was the one since he was now over forty and had to assure his future. Suspicion also fell on Victor de Vernisset, a young poet of the Canalis group, whose passion for Madame Schontz had reached delirium; the poet accused the sculptor Stidmann of being his lucky rival. This artist, a handsome young man who worked for goldsmiths, bronze dealers, and jewelers, projected himself into a resurrected Cellini. Claude Vignon, the young count de La Palférine, Gobenheim, Vermanton the cynical philosopher, and other habitués of this vivacious circle were successively suspected and found innocent. No one could catch Madame Schontz, not even Rochefide who suspected her of a weakness for the witty young La Palférine. She was virtuous by design and thought only of making a good marriage.

The only man of questionable repute one saw at her house was Couture, who more than once had caused havoc in the stock market. But Couture was one of Madame Schontz's oldest friends, and she alone remained faithful to him. The false alarm of 1840 swept away the last holdings of this speculator who had believed in the astuteness of the Thiers government. Aurélie, observing his unlucky streak, had made Rochefide, as we saw earlier, play the opposite game. It was she who named the final misfortune of this inventor of dividends and corporations, a *découture.** Delighted to have a standing invitation at Aurélie's, Couture—to whom Finot, that clever man, or if one prefers, that luckiest of parvenus, gave an occasional thousand-franc note—was the only one shrewd enough to offer his name to Madame Schontz who considered it, wondering whether the daring speculator would have enough power to make a career in politics, and enough gratitude never to abandon her were she to become his wife. Couture, a bachelor of about forty-three but considerably worse for wear, did not redeem the bad ring to his name by his genealogy; in fact, he rarely mentioned his background. Madame Schontz was lamenting the dearth of capable men, when Couture himself introduced a provincial who happened to be equipped with the two handles by which

* Pun on *couture,* a seam, and *découture,* a ripped seam.

women take hold of such vessels when they want to hold on to them.

An outline of this individual will amount to a portrait of a certain segment of today's youth. Here the digression is a matter of history.

❋↦☙❋↦☙❋↦☙❋↦☙❋↦☙❋↦☙❋↦☙❋↦☙❋↦☙❋↦☙❋↦☙❋↦☙❋↦

X ONE OF THE DISEASES OF THE AGE In 1838, Fabien du Ronceret, son of a judge of the royal court in Caen who had died the preceding year, left the town of Alençon, resigning the magistracy with which his father had forced him to waste his time, and came to Paris with the idea of making a sensation —a Norman idea of difficult achievement, since his income was barely 8,000 francs a year, his mother being still alive and the recipient of the income from some valuable real estate in the center of Alençon. This young man, during his earlier trips to Paris, had already tested his balance on the social tightrope, and recognized the great flaws of the social replastering of 1830 which he intended to exploit to his own advantage, following the example of the middle-class profiteers. This requires a rapid review of one of the effects of the new order.

Modern egalitarianism, developed in our day beyond all proportions, has, within private life as paralleled by political life, necessarily developed the three major divisions of the social Self—arrogance, conceit, and vanity. Fools pass themselves off as men of wit, men of wit take themselves for men of talent, and men of talent want to be considered geniuses. As to the geniuses, they are the most reasonable, content to be no more than demigods. This attitude of current public thinking, which makes manufacturers envious of statesmen and statesmen envious of poets, leads fools to denigrate intelligent men, intelligent men to denigrate talented men, talented men to denigrate those who surpass them however slightly, and demigods to threaten all institutions, the monarchy, in short anything that does not worship them unconditionally. As soon as a nation unpolitically breaks down the barriers of recognized superiority, it opens the dam over which is hurled a torrent of second-rate ambitions, of which the last would be the first. According to the democrats, the aristocracy was the disease of the nation, but it was diagnosed and under control. Now it has been replaced by ten armed and competing aristocracies, which is the worst of conditions. By proclaiming the equality of all, there has been a *declaration of the rights of Envy*. We are now wallowing in the orgies of Revolution transplanted to the apparently peaceable domains of culture, industry and politics. It would seem today that a reputation gained by hard work, service rendered, or talent is a privilege granted at the expense of the masses. Soon the agrarian law will be extended to the field of glory. Never before in history has one attained public prominence for lesser reasons. One distinguishes oneself at any cost for ridiculous causes—for pretended devotion to the Polish cause, the penal system, the future of paroled convicts, juvenile delinquents above and below the age of twelve, or any social misery. These diverse preoccupations create artificial dignitaries —presidents, vice presidents, secretaries—of societies whose number in Paris surpasses the number of social ills they seek to remedy. The great society has been demolished only to be replaced by a thousand little ones created in its defunct image. Are these parasitic organizations not an indication of decomposition? Are these not worms crawling out of the corpse? All these societies are daughters of the same mother, Vanity. This is not the path of Catholic Charity or true Benevolence, which examines the lesions on the wounds and heals them, instead of perorating in chorus on their maleficent symptoms for the sake of perorating.

XI A SPECULATOR IN FOOLISHNESS Fabien du Ronceret, though not a superior individual, had guessed, through the exercise of that sense of avarice peculiar to Normandy, the advantages to be gained from this public disease. Every age has its characteristic which clever men exploit. Fabien's only concern was to make himself known by being talked about. "My dear friend, one must get oneself talked about if one wants to be somebody!" he said to du Bousquier, a friend of his father's and the prime mover of Alençon. "In six months, I will be better known than you!" Fabien thus interpreted the spirit of his time; he did not dominate it, he yielded to it. He had made his début in Bohême, a region of the moral topography of Paris (see *Un Prince de la Bohême,* in *Scènes de la vie parisienne*), where he was known by the name of *The Heir,* because of his anticipated affluence. Du Ronceret had profited from Couture's extravagances toward the lovely Madame Cadine—one of the younger actresses credited with the greatest talent in second-string theatres—for whom he had purchased during his ephemeral opulence a charming garden apartment, on the rue Blanche. It was through this that du Ronceret and Couture became acquainted. The young Norman, desirous of ready-made luxury, bought all the furnishings and all the decorations that Couture was obliged to leave in the apartment—a kiosk for smoking, and a gallery of rustic wood curtained with Indian mats and decorated with pottery, which was used to reach the kiosk in bad weather. When The Heir was complimented on his apartment, he called it *his lair.* The provincial made a point of not mentioning that Grindot had put all his skill into decorating it, as had Stidmann in the sculptures and Léon de Lora in the paintings, for his greatest defect was the kind of conceit that lies even in its quest for aggrandizement. The Heir rounded out these luxuries with a greenhouse that he had built along a south wall, not because he loved flowers, but because he hoped to attract public attention with his horticulture. At that moment, he had almost reached his goal. Having become vice president of a garden club presided over by the Duke of Vissembourg, brother of the Prince of Chiavari, son of the late Marshal Vernon, he was now sporting a ribbon of the Legion of Honor on his vice-presidential uniform, following a flower show whose opening address, purchased from Lousteau for five hundred francs, had been boldly delivered as his own creation. He was awarded a prize for a flower, *given* to him by old Blondet of Alençon, the father of Émile Blondet, which he showed as having been raised in his greenhouse. But this success meant nothing. The Heir, who wanted to be considered a man of many parts, had formulated the project of associating with celebrities in order to reflect their glory—a difficult project to carry out given the fact that he had only eight thousand francs available for its execution. Consequently, Fabien du Ronceret had turned successively and unsuccessfully to Bixiou, Stidmann, Léon de Lora to be presented to Madame Schontz and to participate in this menagerie of every kind of lion. He staked Couture to so many dinners that Couture categorically proved to Madame Schontz that she had to acquire this character, were it only to use him as one of those elegant unpaid valets whom ladies of leisure send on errands unsuitable for servants.

❋⤝☙➶❋⤝☙➶❋⤝☙➶❋⤝☙➶❋⤝☙➶❋⤝☙➶❋⤝☙➶❋⤝☙➶❋⤝☙➶❋⤝☙➶❋⤝☙➶❋⤝☙➶

XII A Not So Gullible Gull Within three evenings, Madame Schontz had seen through Fabien and said to herself, "If Couture turns out to be unsuitable, I am sure of bagging that one. Now my future stands on two legs!" This fool, derided by everyone, thus became the favorite, but for a purpose which made that favoritism insulting, and this choice escaped all conjectures by its very improbability. Madame Schontz inebriated Fabien with her stolen smiles, and little scenes played over the threshold when Rochefide spent the night and he was the last to leave. She often invited him to join her and Arthur in her box at the opera and at first nights; she explained this by saying she had no other way of repaying him for this or that service. Men share the same foolish conceit as women, that of believing they are loved exclusively. Of all flattering attentions, there is none more prized than that of a Madame Schontz for the man she designates her heart's darling as opposed to her other attachment. A woman like Madame Schontz, who played the role of *grande dame,* and whose true value was even greater, should have been and was in fact a source of pride for Fabien who was so taken with her that he always appeared before her in full dress—patent leather boots, yellow gloves, embroidered ruffled shirt, a vast array of waistcoats, in short all the externals of total devotion.* A month before the discussion between the duchess and her confessor, Madame Schontz had confided the secret of her birth and true name to Fabien who understood nothing of this confidence. Two weeks later, Madame Schontz, amazed by the Norman's lack of perception, exclaimed to herself, "My God! Am I silly! He thinks he is loved just for being himself!" And so she took him off on a ride through the Bois in her tilbury, for as of the last year she had a tilbury as well as a phaeton, and during this public tête-à-tête, she brought up the question of her future and declared her desire to be married.

"I have seven hundred thousand francs, and I can assure you that if I met a man of ambition able to give me the kind of understanding I desire, I would change my present state. For do you know what my dream is? I would like to be a simple woman, married to a man of good family, and make my husband and children thoroughly happy!"

The Norman was eager enough to be singled out by Madame Schontz, but to marry her seemed quite another matter to this young man whom the July revolution had made a judge. Seeing his hesitation, Madame Schontz aimed all her barbs, her

* The panoply of the dandy of the day.

mockeries and her contempt at the Heir and turned to Couture. Within a week, the speculator, who had gotten a whiff of her bank account, offered his heart, his hand and his future, three things of equal value.

Madame Schontz's maneuvers were at that stage when Madame de Grandlieu began inquiring into the life and leanings of this Béatrix of the rue Saint-Georges.

❋↝⊕↝❋↝⊕↝❋↝⊕↝❋↝⊕↝❋↝⊕↝❋↝⊕↝❋↝⊕↝❋↝⊕↝❋↝⊕↝

XIII THE IMPORTANCE OF SOCIAL POSITION Following the Abbé Brossette's advice, the duchess asked the Marquis d'Ajuda to bring her the king of political knavery, the celebrated Maxime de Trailles, archduke of Bohême and youngest of its young men despite his fifty years. Monsieur d'Ajuda arranged to have dinner with Maxime at a club on the rue de Beaune, and proposed a game of three-handed whist with the Duc de Grandlieu who had been taken with an attack of gout before dinner and was alone. Although the duke's son-in-law, who was also the cousin of the duchess, had every right to present him at a house where he had never before set foot, Maxime de Trailles was not misled by the invitation and assumed the duke or the duchess had need of him. It is not an insignificant aspect of today's mores that one plays in one's club with people one would never receive at home.

The Duc de Grandlieu did Maxime the honor of appearing to be in pain. After fifteen hands of whist, he went to bed leaving his wife alone with Maxime and d'Ajuda. The duchess, encouraged by the marquis, communicated her plan to Monsieur de Trailles, requesting his collaboration while appearing merely to be asking his advice. Maxime heard her out to the end without comment, waiting to speak until the duchess had outrightly requested his cooperation.

"Madame, I quite understand," he said after giving her and the marquis one of those glances—clever, intense, astute and pervasive—with which these seasoned connivers compromise their interlocutors. "D'Ajuda can tell you, if there is anyone in Paris who can carry out this kind of double duplicity, it is I, and without involving you or even having my presence here discovered. However, before going any farther, let us establish the preliminaries of Leoben.* What are you prepared to sacrifice?"

"Whatever is necessary."

"Very well, madame la duchesse. As the price of my intervention, you will do me the honor of receiving me and offering your conscientious patronage to Madame la Comtesse de Trailles . . . ."

"Since when are you married, old boy?" exclaimed d'Ajuda.

"I am getting married in two weeks to the heiress of an extremely rich and extremely middle-class family—a sacrifice to public opinion! I am entering into the very principle of my government! I want to make a fresh start. Consequently, madame la duchesse will understand the importance to me of my wife's acceptance by her and her family. I am certain of becoming a deputy after my father-in-law resigns his functions, and I have the assurance of a diplomatic post in keeping with my new-found wealth. I do not see why my wife should not be as well received as Madame de Portenduère in the circle of young women illuminated by such stars as Mesdames de la Lastie, Georges de Maufrigneuse, d'Lestorade, du Guénic, d'Ajuda, de Restaud, de Rastignac and de Vandenesse! My wife is pretty, and I take it upon myself to *un-middle-class* her! . . . Is that acceptable to you, madame la duchesse? You are a pious woman; if you agree, your promise, which I hold sacred, can do a great deal to change my life. You will be doing still another good deed! Alas, I have been the king of

---

* Leoben is an Austrian town where the Treaty of Campo Formio was signed in 1797 between France and Austria, granting Belgium and the Ionian islands to France as a consequence of Bonaparte's Italian victories.

knaves for a long time; but now I wish to end my life with honor. After all, our coat of arms—*azure with chimera or spouting fire, carrying gules and scaled vert, chief counter-ermine*—dates back to Francis I, who thought it necessary to ennoble the valet of Louis XI, and we have been counts since Catherine de Medici."

"I will receive and protect your wife," the duchess solemnly declared, "and I give you my word, no one in my family will turn his back on her."

"Ah, madame la duchesse," exclaimed Maxime, visibly moved, "if monsieur le duc were also willing to be indulgent toward me, I promise you, I will carry out your plan with little cost to you. However," he added after a pause, "you must promise to carry out my instructions to the letter. This is the last intrigue of my bachelorhood, it must be all the more successful given the benevolence of its purpose," he said smiling.

"Obey you?" asked the duchess. "Then I will be revealed behind all this?"

"Ah, madame, I have no intention of compromising you," exclaimed Maxime, "and I have too much esteem for you to ask for guarantees. You have only to follow my advice, so that, for example, du Guénic must be carried off by his wife like a holy relic; he must be kept away for two years, and should be taken to see Switzerland, Italy, Germany, in short, as many countries as possible . . . ."

"Ah, I see you share my confessor's concern," the duchess naively exclaimed, remembering the priest's judicious objection.

Maxime and d'Ajuda could not repress a smile at the thought of this concordance between the sacred and the profane.

"To make certain Madame de Rochefide does not see Calyste again, we will all travel," she added. "Juste and Athénaïs, Calyste and Sabine, and I. I shall leave Clotilde with her father . . . ."

"Let us not sing victory hymns too soon, madame," said

Maxime. "I foresee tremendous obstacles, but I expect to over-come them. Your esteem and your protection are a prize that forces me into a great deal of dirty work, but it will be . . . ."

"Dirty work?" asked the duchess, interrupting this latter day *condottiere,* with a grimace as full of revulsion as surprise.

"And you too will be soiled, madame, since I am your pro-curer. But are you unaware of how blind your son-in-law has been made by Madame de Rochefide? I have heard about it from Nathan and Canalis, between whom she was hesitating when Calyste hurled himself into the mouth of that lioness! Béatrix was able to persuade this worthy Breton that she never loved anyone but him, that she is virtue itself, that Conti was a purely intellectual infatuation in which her heart and the rest played a very small part, in other words a musical affair! As to Rochefide, that was duty; all of which, as you can see, makes her a virgin! And she certainly proves it by not remem-bering her son whom she has made no effort to see in over a year. In fact, the little count will soon be twelve and finds in Madame Schontz an all the more motherly mother since, as you know, motherhood is the great passion of such women. Du Guénic would hack himself to pieces, and his wife as well, for Béatrix. And you think you can easily retrieve a man from such depths of credulity? Why Madame, an Iago would be wasting all his handkerchiefs on an Othello like him. One thinks that Othello, or his younger brother Orosmane, Saint-Preux, René, Werther, and other renowned lovers represent love! Not one of their coldhearted begetters had an idea of what total love means, except for Molière who had an inkling. Love, madame la duchesse, does not mean loving a noble woman, a Clarissa—great achievement indeed! No, love means telling oneself: 'The woman I love is vile, she has deceived me before, she will deceive me again, she's a harlot, she reeks of hell-fire,' running to her and finding in her arms the azure of heaven and the flowers of paradise. That is how Molière loved, that is how we love, we disreputable types; during the great scene in *Arnolphe,* I weep! * That is how your son-in-law loves Béatrix. It will not be easy to separate Rochefide from Madame Schontz, but Madame Schontz will probably cooperate; I will study her carefully. As to Calyste and Béatrix, it will take an axe to cleave them apart, and first-class treachery, and infamy so base that your virtuous imagination could not sink so low, unless your confessor gave you a helping hand. You have asked the impossible, and you will have it. But despite my determination to use fire and sword, I cannot promise success. I know lovers who are not deterred by the most dreadful disillusionments. You are far too virtuous to understand the power that women who are not can hold over a man...."

"Do not undertake these infamies until I have spoken with Father Brossette so that I know to what degree I am your accomplice," exclaimed the duchess with a candor that betrayed how much egotism there is in piety.

"You will remain totally unaware of it, dear mother," said the Marquis d'Ajuda.

❋✧❀✧❋✧❀✧❋✧❀✧❋✧❀✧❋✧❀✧❋✧❀✧❋✧❀✧❋✧❀✧❋✧❀✧

XIV THE IMPORTANCE OF SOCIAL RELATIONS AS WELL AS POSITION While waiting for the marquis' carriage on the stairs

* Arnolphe, in Act V, Scene IV of Molière's *L'Ecole des Femmes,* talking about unfaithful women says:

Leur esprit est méchant, et leur âme est fragile;
Il n'est rien de plus faible et de plus imbécile,
Rien de plus infidèle; et malgré tout cela,
Dans le monde on fait tout pour ces animaux-là.

Their mind is malicious, their soul is so fragile;
There's nothing more feeble, there's nothing more puerile,
There's nothing less faithful, yet despite all these features,
There's nothing that one does not do for such creatures.

outside, d'Ajuda said to Maxime, "You frightened the worthy duchess."

"But she doesn't realize the difficulty of what she's asking. Shall we go to the Jockey Club? I have to get Rochefide to invite me to dinner tomorrow at La Schontz's, for tonight I shall have my strategy worked out, and selected on my chessboard the pawns who will open the game I intend to play. In her brighter days, Béatrix was unwilling to receive me. Now I will settle my account with her and will avenge your sister-in-law so cruelly she may find herself too well avenged."

The following day, Rochefide told Madame Schontz that Maxime de Trailles was coming to dinner. This was a warning to her to put out all her finery and prepare the most exquisite dishes for this eminent connoisseur, feared by all women of Madame Schontz's class. She consequently went to as much trouble over her appearance as over the preparation of her house to receive this dignitary.

In Paris there are almost as many crowned heads as there are diverse arts, intellectual specialties, sciences or professions, and the most gifted among the practitioners has a majesty all his own. He is appreciated and respected by his peers who understand the difficulties involved and whose admiration is gained by the one who easily surmounts them. Maxime, in the eyes of the courtesans and the men who kept them, was an extraordinarily powerful and competent man, for he had known how to make himself enormously liked. He was admired by everyone who knew how difficult it is to live on good terms with one's creditors in Paris; in fact, the only rival he ever had in elegance, bearing, and wit was the illustrious de Marsay * who often used him for political missions. This suffices to explain his meeting with the duchess, his prestige in the eyes of a Madame Schontz, and his authority during the

* Typical Balzacian reference to a character of his own invention treated as though he were a public figure; appears in *Une Ténébreuse affaire.*

meeting he planned to have on the boulevard des Italiens with a young man, already famous though a recent member of Parisian Bohême.

The next day on arising, Maxime de Trailles heard Finot announced. He had called for him the day before and now asked him to arrange a luncheon at the Café Anglais * where by coincidence Finot, Couture, and Lousteau would be chatting within his hearing. Finot, who was in the same relation to the Comte de Trailles as a second lieutenant to a full general, could hardly refuse; furthermore, it was too dangerous to provoke this lion. So when Maxime came to lunch, he saw Finot and his friends already seated and their conversation already directed to Madame Schontz. Couture, cleverly maneuvered by Finot and by Lousteau, his unwitting accomplice, informed Maxime of everything he wanted to know about that lady.

Around one o'clock, Maxime was chewing on his toothpick while talking to du Tillet on the steps of Tortoni's ** where a miniature stock exchange was held among speculators preliminary to the real one. He seemed concerned with business matters but was in fact waiting for the young Comte de La Palférine to pass by. The Boulevard des Italiens is today what the Pont-Neuf was in 1650—all the important people go by at least once a day. In fact, after ten minutes, Maxime released du Tillet's arm and nodding to the young Prince of Bohême said to him with a smile, "I'd like a word with you, count! . . ."

<hr>

XV BETWEEN DUSK AND DAYLIGHT The two rivals, one a declining star, the other a rising sun, sat at a table outside the

---

* A famous restaurant which by day catered to the world of high finance and politics, and by night to the demimonde.
** A well-known café on the corner of the boulevard des Italiens and the rue Taitbout which was a meeting place for Parisian celebrities.

Café de Paris.* Maxime took care to keep a certain distance from the little old men who, from one o'clock on sat spread out to dry their rheumatism. He had very good reasons for distrusting these venerables (See *Un homme d'affaires, Scènes de la vie parisienne* **).

"Do you have any debts?" Maxime asked the young count.

"Would I be worthy of succeeding you if I had none?" La Palférine replied.

"When I ask a question like that, I am not questioning the fact but merely asking whether the total is respectable and whether it runs into five or six," replied Maxime.

"Six what?"

"Six figures! Do you owe 50,000 or 100,000? I once owed as much as 600,000."

La Palférine doffed his hat in mock respect.

"If I had the credit to borrow a hundred thousand francs," the young man replied, "I would forget my creditors and settle in Venice with great paintings all around, the theatre in the evening, beautiful women at night, and so on."

"And at my age what would become of you?" asked Maxime.

"I wouldn't get that far," replied the young count.

Maxime returned the compliment to his rival by raising his hat slightly in a gesture of comic seriousness.

"That is another point of view," he said as one connoisseur to another. "You owe then . . . ?"

"Oh, a trifle not worth confessing to an uncle; if I had one he would disinherit me for this miserable sum, six thousand!"

"One is more bothered by six than by a hundred thousand," said Maxime sententiously. "La Palférine! You have a plucky

---

* Meeting place of the aristocracy on the boulevard Montmartre.

** Balzac's own note referring to a character in the cited novel, Cérizet, disguised as an old man who tricks Maxime into paying up an old debt.

kind of intelligence, but your intelligence is even greater than your pluck. You could go very far, become a statesman. See here, of all those who have ever embarked on the career I am now ending and who tried to vie with me, you are the only one I ever liked."

La Palférine was so flattered by this admission, made with gracious candor by the lord of Parisian adventurers, that he blushed. This response of his vanity was an avowal of his inferiority and it offended him. But Maxime anticipated this offended reaction, easy enough to foresee in such an intelligent individual, and he immediately soothed it over by placing himself at the young man's discretion.

"Would you do something for me, now that I am retiring from this olympic arena into a handsome marriage? I will do a great deal for you," he added.

"You do me a great honor. This is the enacting of the fable of the lion and the rat," said La Palférine.

"I will begin by lending you twenty thousand francs," Maxime continued.

"Twenty thousand francs? . . . I knew if I continued wandering up and down this boulevard . . ." La Palférine said parenthetically.

"My dear boy, you have to be on the right footing," said Maxime smiling. "Don't stand on two feet, stand on six. Do as I do, I have never stepped down from my tilbury."

"But you may be asking something beyond my powers."

"Not at all. Just make a woman fall in love with you within two weeks."

"A tart?"

"Why?"

"That would be impossible. But if it is a respectable woman, highly intelligent . . . ."

"It is a famous marquise."

"Are you after her letters?" said the young count.

"Ah! . . . You delight me!" exclaimed Maxime. "No, it's not that."

"You mean really love her?"

"Yes, in the true sense . . . ."

"If I have to go outside the realm of esthetics then it's out of the question. You see, with regard to women, I have a certain integrity. We may cheat them but not . . . ."

"Clearly I have not been misled about you," exclaimed Maxime. "Do you really think I am a man to propose some cheap little villainy? No, you must go, bedazzle, and conquer. My collaborator, I will give you twenty thousand tonight and ten days to succeed. Until tonight then at Madame Schontz's."

"I'm having dinner there."

"Good," said Maxime. "In the future, should you need me, monsieur le comte, you will find me available," he added in the tone of a monarch making a pledge rather than a promise.

"Has the poor woman really done you such harm?" asked La Palférine.

"Don't try to fathom my depths, little one, and let me assure you that should you succeed, you will discover such powerful protection that like me you will be able to retire with a splendid marriage when you become bored with the life of Bohême."

"Does one ever become bored with having fun, with being nothing, with living as free as a bird, with hunting in Paris like a savage and laughing at everything?" asked La Palférine.

"Everything becomes boring, even Hell," answered Maxime laughing. "Until tonight!"

***

XVI First Reward for Valor The two rogues, the young one and the old, got up. Climbing back into his tilbury, Maxime said to himself, "Madame d'Espard can't stand Béatrix. She will help me . . . To the hôtel de Grandlieu," he called to his driver, noticing Rastignac pass by.* "Is there any great man without some weakness?"

* Rastignac, in *L'Interdiction*, had hopes of becoming Madame d'Espard's lover.

Maxime found the duchess, Madame du Guénic and Clotilde in tears.

"What has happened?" he asked the duchess.

"Calyste has not come home. This is the first time and my poor Sabine is beside herself."

"Madame la duchesse," said Maxime, drawing the pious lady into the embrasure of a window, "in the name of God who will judge us, you must keep the secret of my devotion to you carefully hidden, and must make d'Ajuda do the same. Calyste must never know anything of our schemes or we will end up in a death duel. When I told you this would cost you little, I meant that you would not be spending exorbitant sums. I now need twenty thousand francs; the rest is my concern. It may be necessary to procure some important posts, perhaps a ministerial position."

The duchess and Maxime went out. When Madame de Grandlieu returned to her daughters, she heard a fresh tirade from Sabine embellished with details even more painful than those that ended her domestic bliss.

"Calm yourself my child," the duchess said to her daughter. "Béatrix will pay heavily for your tears and your suffering. The hand of Satan will fall on her and she will suffer ten humiliations for every one of yours!"

Madame Schontz sent word to invite Claude Vignon who had often expressed the desire to meet Maxime de Trailles. She also asked Couture, Fabien, Bixiou, Léon de Lora, La Palférine, and Nathan, the latter having been requested by Rochefide on Maxime's account. Aurélie thus had nine guests, all of first caliber except for du Ronceret. However, the Heir's Norman vanity and crass ambition were on a par with the literary prowess of Claude Vignon, the poetry of Nathan, the subtlety of La Palférine, the financial acumen of Couture, the wit of Bixiou, the cunning of Finot, the profundity of Maxime and the genius of Léon de Lora.

Madame Schontz, eager to appear young and beautiful, had

dressed herself with the artistry that such women possess. She wore a point lace cape of web-like delicacy over a blue velvet gown with an opal-buttoned bodice, and her hair was combed into bands of gleaming ebony. Madame Schontz owed her reputation as a beauty to the brightness and freshness of a complexion as honey-toned as a creole's, a face of enchanting characteristics and firm cleancut features, whose most noted and most unaging example was the Comtesse Merlin, which may be peculiar to southern types. Unfortunately, the diminutive Madame Schontz tended to plumpness ever since her life had become happy and tranquil. Her neck, seductively rounded, had begun to thicken along with her shoulders. In France a woman's face is such a principal source of delight that lovely heads can vouchsafe long life to spoiled figures.

"My dear," said Maxime kissing Madame Schontz on the forehead as he entered, "Rochefide wanted me to see your establishment, which I had not yet visited. Why, it is almost in keeping with his income of 400,000 francs. Well then, he had fifty thousand less when he met you, and in less than five years you have helped make what another woman—an Antonia, a Malaga, a Cadine or a Florentine—would have spent."

"I am not a tart, I am an artist," said Madame Schontz with considerable dignity. "And I hope to end up, as they say in comedies, by founding a proper family."

"It's discouraging, we're all getting married," Maxime replied sinking into a chair near the fire. "Here I am on the eve of creating a Countess Maxime."

"Oh, I should like to see her!" exclaimed Madame Schontz. "Allow me to introduce Monsieur Claude Vignon. Monsieur Claude Vignon, Monsieur de Trailles."

"So, you're the one who made Camille Maupin, literature's innkeeper, go off to a convent!" Maxime exclaimed. "After you, God! I never received such an honor. Mademoiselle des Touches made you into a Louis XIV, monsieur."

"You see, that is how history is written!" replied Claude

Vignon. "Didn't you know that she used her fortune to recuperate Monsieur du Guénic's estates? If she knew Calyste had fallen into the clutches of her former friend . . . (Maxime nudged the critic's foot and gestured toward Monsieur de Rochefide) . . . she would leave her convent to snatch him away."

"You know, Rochefide, old friend," said Maxime, seeing that his warning had not stopped Claude Vignon, "if I were in your place, I would give my wife's fortune back to her so that people didn't think she latched on to Calyste out of need."

"Maxime is right," said Madame Schontz looking at Arthur who had turned bright red. "If I have helped you make a few thousand extra francs, you couldn't use them more wisely. I will then have made both husband and wife happy. How is that for a distinction!"

"I hadn't thought of it," replied the marquis, "but it's true, one is first of all a gentleman, then a husband."

"Leave it to me to tell you when to be generous," said Maxime.

"Arthur," said Aurélie, "Maxime is right. You see my dear, our generous actions are like Couture's transactions," she said looking at the mirror to see who was arriving, "one must know when to invest."

Couture was followed by Finot. A few minutes later, all the guests were assembled in the handsome blue and gold drawing room of the *hôtel de Schontz,* as it was called by its artistic habitués since Rochefide bought it for his Ninon II. Seeing La Palférine come in last, Maxime went up to him and handed him the twenty banknotes.

"Above all, my boy, don't hang on to them," he said with roguish charm.

"There is no one like you for doubling the value of what you seem to be offering . . ." replied La Palférine.

"Have you decided?"

"Evidently, since I'm taking it," replied the young count with ironic dignity.

"Fine! In two days time then Nathan, who is here, will present you to the Marquise de Rochefide," Maxime whispered.

La Palférine was taken aback on hearing the name.

"You must not fail to declare your mad passion for her, and to avoid any suspicion, get yourself good and drunk. I am going to tell Aurélie to seat you beside Nathan. And now, my boy, we must meet every night on the Boulevard de la Madeleine, at one in the morning—you to report on your progress, I to give you your instructions."

"I will be there, master," said the young count bowing.

❋✦⊕➔❋✦⊕➔❋✦⊕➔❋✦⊕➔❋✦⊕➔❋✦⊕➔❋✦⊕➔❋✦⊕➔❋✦⊕➔❋✦⊕➔

XVII SCHOOL FOR DIPLOMATS "Why do you make us dine with a character dressed like a headwaiter," Maxime asked whispering to Madame Schontz as he indicated du Ronceret.

"Have you never seen the Heir before? Du Ronceret from Alençon."

"Monsieur," said Maxime to Fabien, "you must know my friend d'Esgrignon?"

"It has been some time since Victurnien chose not to know me any longer," Fabien replied, "but we were very close as boys."

It was the kind of dinner that is only given in Paris, and by these great gold diggers whose elaborateness surprises even the most demanding people. It was at a similar dinner, given by a rich and beautiful courtesan like Madame Schontz, that Paganini declared he had never eaten such food in any royal palace, nor drunk such wines with any prince, nor heard wittier conversation, nor seen such tasteful luxury.

Maxime and Madame Schontz were the first to leave the table at about ten o'clock, leaving the other guests who no longer veiled their remarks and were boastfully comparing their masculine prowess, their greasy lips glued to liqueur glasses they were no longer able to empty.

"So my little one," said Maxime, "you were not mistaken. Yes, I am here for your lovely eyes, and it has to do with a very important matter: you will have to leave Arthur. However, I take it upon myself to get him to give you two hundred thousand francs."

"And why should I leave him, the poor old dear?"

"To marry that imbecile who came from Alençon for that very reason. He has already been a judge; I will have him appointed president * in Blondet's place, who is nearing eighty-two. And if you know how to steer your ship, your husband can become a deputy.** You will figure among the important people and can thumb your nose at Madame la Comtesse de Bruel." †

"Never!" said Madame Schontz. "She is a countess."

"Is he the stuff that counts are made of?"

"Come to think of it, he has a coat of arms," Aurélie said, rummaging through a handsome bag that hung from the mantelpiece for a letter which she handed to Maxime. "What does this mean? There are combs on it."

"His shield is *halved with chief argent and three combs gules; chief and base intertwined with three bunches of grapes purpure stemmed and leafed vert; base azure four plumes or laid in fret,* with SERVIR for motto and a squire's helmet. It doesn't amount to much. They were ennobled under Louis XV. There must have been some haberdasher grandfather, the maternal line made money in wine, and the ennobled du Ronceret must have been the town clerk. But if you succeed in

* *Président,* presiding judge or chief magistrate of a court of law.
** Elected member of the Chamber of Deputies (French legislative body).
† A former ballerina at the Opera, Tullia, who appears in *les Comédiens sans le savoir.*

getting rid of Arthur, the du Roncerets will be barons at the very least, I promise you my little doe. You understand, my child, you will have to spend five or six years embalmed in the provinces if you want la Schontz to be buried Madame la Présidente. The little fool looks at you with very clear intentions, you have him hooked."

"Hardly," replied Aurélie. "At the offer of my hand he remained, like brandies in the securities listings, 'very stable.'"

"I will see to it that he makes up his mind . . . if he is drunk. Go see what they are up to."

"It's not worth going. All I hear is Bixiou who is putting on one of his acts with no one listening. But I know my Arthur. He thinks he has to be polite toward Bixiou and even with his eyes closed is probably still looking at him."

"In that case, let's go back."

"Tell me, in whose interest will I be working, Maxime?" Madame Schontz suddenly asked.

"In Madame de Rochefide's," Maxime candidly replied. "So long as you have a hold on Arthur it is impossible to reconcile them. She has to be head of the household and dispose of the four hundred thousand francs income."

"And all she offers me is two hundred thousand? If it's for her, I want three hundred. How dare she! I took care of her brat and her husband, I took her place in every way, and she would haggle with me? In that case my dear, I ought to get a million. With that and your promise of the presidency of the court in Alençon, I will be able to play the role of Madame de Ronceret."

"Agreed."

"Will I be bored in that town!" Aurélie exclaimed philosophically. "I have heard so much about that place from d'Esgrignon and la Val-Noble, it's as though I had already lived there."

"And if I could assure you the backing of the nobility?"

"Oh Maxime, do you mean it? . . . Oh, but the gull won't take wing."

"And he's pretty ugly with his dark skin and bristles for sideburns; he looks like a boar, although he has the eyes of a vulture, but he will make the finest president ever. Don't worry! In ten minutes, he will sing you Isabelle's aria from the fourth act of *Robert le Diable:* 'Je suis à tes genoux,' but you must get Arthur back to Béatrix."

"It's not easy, but with all of us working together, we'll make it."

Around 10:30, the guests came into the drawing room for coffee. Given the situation Madame Schontz, Couture and du Ronceret were in, it is easy to imagine the effect produced on the ambitious young Norman by the following conversation that Maxime had with Couture in a half-whisper so as not to be overheard, but which was heard by Fabien.

"My dear friend, if you were sensible, you would accept the office of Tax Collector in some remote district that Madame de Rochefide can obtain for you. Aurélie's million will allow you to put up the collateral, and by marrying her you will be dividing the property. You will become a deputy, if you know how to maneuver things, and all I ask for having saved you is your vote in the Chamber."

"I will always be proud to serve in your troops."

"Ah, old boy, if you knew how close you came to missing out! Can you imagine, Aurélie took a fancy to that Norman from Alençon and wanted him made baron, president of the court of Alençon, and officer of the Legion of Honor, and this idiot never realized her worth, so you owe your good luck to spite. And don't give that clever girl time to think it over. As for me, I'm going to put the irons in the fire."

Maxime left Couture beside himself with joy and said to La Palférine, "Can I take you somewhere, my boy?"

XVIII STILL ANOTHER REWARD At eleven o'clock, Aurélie found herself between Couture, Fabien and Rochefide. Arthur was dozing in an armchair; Couture and Fabien tried to get rid of each other, but unsuccessfully. Madame Schontz finally put an end to the contest by saying to Couture, " 'Til tomorrow, my dear?", which he took with good grace.

"Mademoiselle," said Fabien very softly, "if I seemed vague when you made me your indirect offer, believe me it was not out of any hesitation on my part, but you do not know my mother. She would never consent to my happiness."

"You are no longer a minor, my dear," Aurélie insolently replied. "And if you are afraid of mommy, then you are not for me."

"Joséphine," said the Heir tenderly, daring to put his arm around Madame Schontz's waist, "I thought you loved me."

"What of it?"

"Perhaps we can appease my mother and gain more than her consent."

"How is that?"

"If you were willing to use your influence . . . ."

"And make you baron, officer of the Legion of Honor, president of the court, is that it, my boy? Look here, I have done so many things in my life that I am also capable of virtue! I can be a good wife, a faithful wife, and I can tow my husband very far. But I want to be loved by him so that I am never robbed of even a thought or a glance, not even wishfully . . . Does that suit you? Don't rush into this, it's your whole life that's at stake, my dear."

"With a woman like you, it's a deal with my eyes closed," said Fabien, as intoxicated by her glance as by the rum.

"You will never regret this decision, my love; you will be a peer of France . . . As for that poor dear," she added looking at the sleeping Rochefide, "from today on it is T-H-E E-N-D."

It was so sweetly and so cleverly said that Fabien took hold of Madame Schontz and kissed her in a surge of passion and delight in which the twofold inebriation of love and wine gave way to happiness and ambition.

"Remember, dear love," she said, "from now on, you must treat your wife with respect and not behave like a lover. And now, let me get out of this mess as gracefully as I can. Hah! Couture, who saw himself rich and a Tax Collector!"

"I can't stand that man," said Fabien. "I hope never to see him again."

"I won't invite him any more," replied the courtesan prudishly. "Now that we are agreed, Fabien my dear, go; it's one o'clock."

❋⤙۞⤚❋⤙۞⤚❋⤙۞⤚❋⤙۞⤚❋⤙۞⤚❋⤙۞⤚❋⤙۞⤚❋⤙۞⤚❋⤙۞⤚❋⤙۞⤚

XIX HOW TO START ON THE WAR PATH WHILE COOLING ONE'S HEELS This little scene gave rise, in the hitherto blissful relationship of Aurélie and Arthur, to a phase of domestic warfare, provoked within all relationships by the hidden motives of one of the partners. The very next morning, Arthur woke up alone in bed and found Madame Schontz as cool as women like that can make themselves.

"What happened last night?" he asked, looking at Aurélie while having his breakfast.

"That's how it is in Paris," she said. "One falls asleep while the streets are wet, and the next day they are so dry and frozen that it's dusty. Would you like a brush?"

"What's the matter with you, darling?"

"Go find your maypole of a wife . . . ."

"My wife?" exclaimed the poor marquis.

"Don't you think I guessed why you brought Maxime here? You want a reconciliation with Madame de Rochefide who probably needs you for a bastard brat. And to think that I, whom you call so clever, advised you to give her back her fortune! Oh, I see right through you! After five years, my lord is tired of me. I am well-rounded, Béatrix is well-hollowed.

It will be a change. You're not the first man I know with a taste for skeletons. Furthermore, your Béatrix dresses well and you're one of those men who like clothes horses. In addition, you would like to get rid of Monsieur du Guénic. What a triumph! Won't you look great, and won't everybody talk about it. You'll be a hero!"

By two o'clock Madame Schontz had not yet exhausted her supply of sarcasms despite Arthur's protestations. She said she was invited to dinner. She advised her "faithless one" to go to the opera without her; she was going to opening night at the Ambigu-Comique to meet a charming woman, Madame de La Baudraye, Lousteau's mistress. As proof of his eternal attachment to his little Aurélie and his aversion to his wife, Arthur proposed leaving the very next day for Italy and living with her as husband and wife in Rome, Naples, or Florence, at her choosing; he also offered her a gift of sixty thousand francs yearly.

"That's all eyewash," she answered. "That won't prevent you from patching things up with your wife, and you should."

Arthur and Aurélie took leave of each other, after this formidable exchange, he to play cards and dine at his club, she to dress and spend the evening alone with Fabien.

Monsieur de Rochefide found Maxime at the club and poured out his distress like a man whose happiness was being ripped out of his heart by the roots that clung to every fiber. Maxime listened to the marquis' lamentations as polite people do while thinking of something else.

"I'm just the man to give advice on such matters, my friend," he said. "You are making a mistake by showing Aurélie how much she means to you. Let me introduce you to Madame Antonia—now there's a heart up for rent at the moment. You'll see la Schontz come begging. She is thirty-seven, your Schontz, while Madame Antonia can't be more than twenty-six, and what a woman! And her cleverness is not all in her head, that one! Furthermore, she has been trained by me. If Madame

Schontz then remains on her high horse, you know what that means."

"I'm afraid I don't."

"It means she probably wants to get married, in which case nothing can stop her from leaving you. After a six-year contract, the woman has every right . . . But if you want to listen to me, you can do better than that. Your wife today is worth a thousand times more than all the Schontzes and all the Antonias of the Saint-Georges district. It is not an easy conquest, but she is not intractable and now she would make you as happy as Orgon! * In any event, if you don't want to look like a fool, you must come to supper tonight at Antonia's."

"No, I love Aurélie too much. I don't want to give her any reason to reproach me."

"Ah my dear chap, you're preparing an awful life for yourself."

"It's eleven o'clock; she must have returned from the theatre," said Rochefide leaving.

And he roared out to the coachman to get to the rue La Bruyère at full speed.

Madame Schontz had given precise instructions, and monsieur was able to come in as though he and madame were on the best of terms. But madame, informed of monsieur's arrival, made a point of slamming the door to her dressing room as doors are slammed when women are taken by surprise. Then, Fabien's hat, deliberately left lying on a corner of the piano, was clumsily snatched away by the maid as soon as monsieur and madame began conversing.

"You didn't go to the theatre, my love?"

"No, my dear, I changed my mind. I spent the evening at the piano."

"Who came to see you?" asked the marquis openly on seeing the hat carried off by the maid.

"Why, no one."

* The undeserving husband in Molière's *Tartuffe*.

After that blatant lie, Arthur could only bow his head as he passed through the Caudine Forks * of submission. True love is given to sublime cowardice of this sort. Arthur was behaving toward Madame Schontz like Sabine toward Calyste, and Calyste toward Béatrix.

❀↝✿↝✿❀↝✿❀↝✿❀↝✿❀↝✿❀↝✿❀↝✿❀↝✿❀↝✿❀↝

XX A NEW HISTORY OF MUTATIONS   In one week, a metamorphosis from larva to butterfly took place in the clever, young and handsome Charles-Édouard, Comte Rusticoli de la Palférine, hero of *Un Prince de la Bohême* (see *Scênes de la vie parisienne*), which dispenses me from drawing his portrait or describing his character here. Until then, he had lived miserably, making up his deficits with Dantonesque audacity. Now he paid off his debts; then, following Maxime's advice, got himself a tilbury; was admitted to the Jockey Club and the club on the rue de Grammont; became singularly elegant; and finally, published in the *Journal des Débats* a short story that in a few days netted him a reputation such as successful authors of numerous works rarely obtain. For in Paris, nothing creates more of a furor than that which is destined to be ephemeral. Nathan, convinced that the count would never publish anything else, praised this charming, unorthodox young man so highly to Béatrix that, titillated by the poet's accounts, she indicated a desire to meet this young king of high-class delinquents.

"He will be utterly delighted to come here," replied Nathan, "for I know he is so taken with you he would commit any folly."

"But I have heard he has already committed them all."

"All, no," replied Nathan. "He has not yet committed the folly of loving a virtuous woman."

* Pass in southern Italy where the Roman army capitulated in 321 B.C. signifying, as a locution, any humiliating concession obtained from a loser.

A few days after the plot was hatched on the Boulevard des Italiens between Maxime and the seductive young count, this young man whom nature had ironically endowed with a deliciously melancholy face, made his first eruption into the nest of the dove on the rue de Chartres and was received one night when Calyste was obliged to escort his wife. Should you meet La Palférine, or get to *Un Prince de la Bohême* in Book Three of this long history of modern mores, you will fully understand the success achieved in a single evening by such sparkling wit and singular verve, especially if you consider the skill of the mahout who assisted him during his first performance. Nathan was a real comrade; he made the young count shine the way a jeweler, showing off a necklace, makes the diamonds shimmer. La Palférine discreetly left first leaving Nathan and the marquise together, assured of the famous author's collaboration which was superb. Seeing how impressed the marquise already was, he set her heart afire with certain innuendoes that aroused in her a curiosity she had not known she possessed. Nathan let it be understood that it was not so much La Palférine's wit that was responsible for his success with women as his superiority in the arts of love, which he exaggerated out of all proportion. This would be the moment to point out another effect of the Law of Contrasts which determines so many of the crises of the human heart and explains so many of its aberrations that one is sometimes obliged to refer to it and to the Law of Similarities as well. All courtesans—taking in the whole of the female sex that is baptized, debaptized, and rebaptized every quarter century—cultivate at the bottom of their hearts a budding desire to recapture their freedom and discover a pure, saintly, generous love for a man to whom they would sacrifice everything (see *Splendeurs et Misères des courtisanes*). They experience this contradictory desire with such intensity that it is rare to come across a woman of this kind who has not aspired to virtue through love on more than one occasion. They remain undaunted even after atrocious disappointments. On the other hand, women hemmed in by their education and their rank, chained by their family dignity, surrounded by opulence, haloed with virtue, are often tempted, secretly of course, by the tropics of love. Both of these highly contrasting feminine natures thus have deep down a hidden yearning, one for virtue, the other for debauchery which J.-J. Rousseau had the courage to point out before anyone else.* In one it is the last ember of the divine spark as yet unextinguished, in the other, a residue of our primeval clay. This slumbering beast was aroused, this hair of the devil was plucked with consummate skill by Nathan. The marquise seriously questioned whether she had not until then been the victim of her intellect and whether her education was really complete. Vice . . . is perhaps the desire to know everything.

❋↬◈↬❋↬◈↬❋↬◈↬❋↬◈↬❋↬◈↬❋↬◈↬❋↬◈↬❋↬◈↬❋↬◈↬❋↬◈↬

XXI SOCIETY TAKES REVENGE The following day, Béatrix saw Calyste for what he really was: a devoted and perfect gentleman, but with neither verve nor wit. In Paris, a man considered witty is someone from whom wittiness flows like water from a fountain; for, sophisticated people on the whole, and Parisians in particular, are witty. But Calyste was too filled with love, he was too preoccupied with loving to notice the change in Béatrix and to satisfy her by tapping new resources; he seemed very pale in the light of the preceding evening and provided not the slightest gratification to Béatrix's awakened appetites. A great love is an account from which such voracious

---

* In the preface to the *Nouvelle Héloïse,* Rousseau writes:

It would seem that at one stage or another the feminine sex must experience a season of licentiousness. It is a dangerous yeast that sooner or later ferments. In civilized societies it is the girls who are of easy virtue and the women who are severe; in societies without morals, it is the other way around.

withdrawals are made that bankruptcy is bound to occur. Despite the boredom of the day (the day a woman becomes bored with her lover!), Béatrix trembled with fear at the thought of a meeting between La Palférine—Maxime de Trailles' successor —and Calyste—a man of unswaggering courage. She consequently hesitated to see the young count again; however, this knot of indecision was cut by a decisive event. Béatrix had taken a third of a box at the opera in an obscure corner of the orchestra so as not to be seen. Over the last few days, Calyste, emboldened, had been escorting the marquise, seating himself behind her, and timing their arrival late enough to avoid notice. Béatrix was among the first to leave before the end of the last act, and Calyste followed her watching from a distance, even though the aged Antoine was always waiting with his mistress' carriage. Maxime and La Palférine observed this stratagem inspired by a respect for convention, by the need for subterfuges that characterizes the worshippers of Eros, and by the fear that weighs on all women formerly the constellations of society whom love has wrested from their zodiacal position. In such cases, humiliation is feared as an agony worse than death. This agony of pride, this affront, inflicted on the fallen by those still esconced on Olympus, took place in a most dreadful manner owing to Maxime's machinations. At a performance of *Lucia di Lammermoor* which ends, as we know with one of Rubini's greatest triumphs, Madame de Rochefide reached the lobby before Antoine called for her. Grouped at the bottom of the stairs or layered along the steps were lovely women awaiting the announcement by their servants of the arrival of their carriages. Béatrix was recognized by all eyes at once; whispers sprang up among the groups and rose to the volume of noise. Suddenly, the crowd parted leaving the marquise standing alone like a pariah. Calyste seeing his wife on one of the stairs did not dare keep the outcast company; Béatrix twice, but vainly, threw him tear-stained entreaties to come over to her. At that moment, La Palférine, elegant, imperious, charming, left two ladies and came over to greet the marquise.

"Take my arm and walk out proudly. I shall find your carriage," he said.

"Would you like to spend the rest of the evening with me?" she asked, climbing into her carriage and making room for him.

La Palférine told his groom, "Follow madame's carriage!" and climbed in beside her to Calyste's stupefaction. Calyste remained rooted to the spot as though his legs had turned to lead; it was precisely this pale staring face that had led Béatrix to invite the young count to ride with her. Every dove is a Roberspierre in white feathers.* Three carriages reached the rue de Chartes with lightning speed—Calyste's, La Palférine's, and the marquise's.

"So you know this gentleman?" Calyste asked Béatrix, fuming.

"Monsieur le Comte de La Palférine was introduced to me ten days ago by Nathan," replied Béatrix, "while you, monsieur, have known me for four years . . . ."

"And I am prepared," said Charles-Édouard, "to make Madame d'Espard, and all the way down to her grandchildren, regret having been the first to walk away from you . . . ."

"So! It was she!" cried Béatrix. "I will pay her back for that."

"In order to avenge yourself, you will have to get your husband back, and I can arrange that for you," the young count whispered to the marquise.

The conversation begun in this fashion continued until two in the morning, without Calyste, whose fury was constantly repressed by Béatrix's glances, managing to say two words alone to her. La Palférine, who disliked Béatrix, was as superior in his tastefulness, wittiness and grace, as Calyste was inferior. He sat writhing like a severed worm and on three occasions got up to slap La Palférine. The third time Calyste made a move toward his rival, the young count tossed out a "Are you in pain,

* Balzac's habitual misspelling of Robespierre.

baron?" that made Calyste sink into a chair and stay there as though pilloried. The marquise chatted away with the ease of a Célimène * and pretended to ignore Calyste's presence. La Palférine, with sublime deftness, took his leave with a parting remark of great cleverness, and left the lovers to quarrel.

This was how Maxime set the fire of discord aflame in the households of both Monsieur and Madame de Rochefide.

❋↝☺↝❋↝☺↝❋↝☺↝❋↝☺↝❋↝☺↝❋↝☺↝❋↝☺↝❋↝☺↝❋↝☺↝❋↝☺↝

XXII THE INCURABLES The very next day, learning of the success of his scheme from La Palférine at the Jockey Club where the young count was winning at whist, Maxime went to the hôtel Schontz on the rue de la Bruyère to see how Aurélie was doing.

"My dear," said Madame Schontz laughing when she saw him, "I have come to the end of my remedies; Rochefide is incurable. Now, at the close of my amatory avocation, I am discovering that cleverness is a curse."

"What is that supposed to mean?"

"To begin with, for a week, I kept my Arthur on a diet of kicks in the shins, the most hackneyed old maxims, and all the worst treatment known to our trade. 'You must be ill,' he said to me with fatherly tenderness, 'for I have done you nothing but good and I love you adoringly.' 'You have one fault,' I told him, 'you bore me.' 'Well then, don't you have the wittiest and handsomest men in Paris here to amuse you?' the poor man replied. I was stuck! It was then I felt I loved him."

"Ah!" said Maxime.

"What can I do? These things are more powerful than us; you can't resist treatment like that. So I changed my tack. I openly seduced that judicial boar, my betrothed, who is now as sheepish as Arthur. I sat him there in Arthur's chair and

* The very self-possessed heroine of Molière's *Le Misanthrope*.

found him utterly unexciting. Was I bored! But I had to have him there so that we could be discovered together . . . ."

"And then?" exclaimed Maxime. "Get to the point! So then, when Arthur found you with him . . . ."

"You'd never guess! Following your instructions, the bans have been published, the contract is being drawn up, and so Notre-Dame-de Lorette* can make no accusations. With a promise of matrimony, it is perfectly legal to make a down payment . . . Well, on finding us together, Arthur withdrew on tiptoe as far as the dining room and started coughing loudly and knocking over chairs. That great fool of a Fabien, to whom I can't tell the whole story, was frightened . . . So there, my dear Maxime, is where we are . . . Arthur, were he to find me with him in bed one morning, is capable of saying, 'Have you had a good night, little ones?' "

Maxime nodded his head and toyed with his cane for a moment.

"I know such characters," he said. "Now this is how you must proceed; there is no other way but to throw Arthur out of the window and lock the door. You will repeat the same scene with Fabien . . . ."

"That's really an ordeal! And after all, the sacraments have not yet blessed me with their virtue . . . ."

". . . and you will see to it that you catch Arthur's eye when he finds you together," Maxime continued. "If he gets angry, that's the end of it; if he starts coughing again, it's an even better ending."

"How so?"

"Evidently, you will get angry and will tell him: 'I thought I was loved and esteemed, but you feel nothing for me, not even jealousy!' You know all the lines: 'In a situation like this (bring me into it) Maxime would kill a man on the spot (and you start crying). Fabien whom I love, Fabien would pull out a dagger and plunge it into his heart. That's love! And so,

* The district is treated metaphorically as a court of law.

farewell, goodnight, take back your house, I am marrying Fabien. *He* will give me his name, he will trample his old mother to the ground!' In short, you know . . . ."

"I know, I know! I will be magnificent!" exclaimed Madame Schontz. "Ah Maxime! There will never be another Maxime, as there was only one de Marsay."

"La Palférine is superior to me," he replied modestly. "He is doing very well."

"He has a sharp tongue, but you have grip and backbone. How many men have you stood up to and how many have you knocked down?" replied la Schontz.

"La Palférine has everything. He is immensely cultivated, while I am ignorant," Maxime answered. "Now then, I have seen Rastignac who immediately arranged everything with the Keeper of the Seals; Fabien will be made president of the court, and officer of the Legion of Honor after a year in office."

"I will become pious!" said Madame Schontz with an emphasis intended to get a rise out of Maxime.

"Priests are worth more than we are," Maxime countered.

"Is that so?" asked Madame Schontz. "In that case, I shall have someone to talk to out in the sticks. I have already begun playing my role. Fabien told his mother that I had been illuminated by grace, and he enraptured the good woman with my million and the presidency. She agreed to our living with her, requested my portrait, and sent me hers. If Cupid were to see it, he would fall over . . . backward! Go now, Maxime. Tonight I am going to execute the poor man; it breaks my heart."

❊⌄☺⌃❊⌄☺⌃❊⌄☺⌃❊⌄☺⌃❊⌄☺⌃❊⌄☺⌃❊⌄☺⌃❊⌄☺⌃❊⌄☺⌃❊⌄☺⌃❊⌄☺⌃❊⌄☺⌃

XXIII   THE FORTUITIES OF LIFE   Two days later, meeting over the threshold of the Jockey Club, Charles-Édouard said to Maxime: "Success!" This word, embracing the whole of a dreadful, terrible drama often carried out for vengeance, made Maxime smile.

"We shall soon be hearing Rochefide's lamentations," said Maxime, "for both you and Aurélie have reached the goal at the same time. Aurélie has kicked him out and we must now warm him up. He has to give three hundred thousand francs to Madame du Ronceret and go back to his wife. We are going to prove to him that Béatrix is far superior to Aurélie."

"We still have ten days ahead of us," said Charles-Édouard archly, "and in fact it's not too much, for now that I know the marquise, the poor man is being robbed but good."

"What will you do when the bomb explodes?"

"One always has one's wits about one when there is time to collect them. I am singularly great when I am prepared."

The two gamblers walked in together and found the Marquis de Rochefide aged by two years, not wearing his corset, inelegant and unshaven.

"How are you, my dear marquis?" asked Maxime.

"Oh, my friend, my life is shattered . . . ."

Arthur ranted on for ten minutes and Maxime listened gravely while thinking about his wedding, to be held in a week's time.

"My dear Arthur, I offered you the only weapon I knew for keeping Aurélie and you chose not to . . . ."

"Which one?"

"Didn't I advise you to have supper at Antonia's?"

"That's true . . . But what shall I do? I am in love . . . you make love the way Grisier makes thrusts.*

"Listen to me, Arthur, give her three hundred thousand francs for her little house and I promise to find you something better . . . I'll tell you about the lovely unknown later. I see d'Ajuda wants to have a word with me."

And Maxime left the inconsolable man to meet with the representative of a family to be consoled.

"Maxime," d'Ajuda whispered, "the duchess is in despair; Calyste secretly packed his bags and took out a passport. Sabine

* Grisi was a well-known fencing master.

wants to follow the fugitives, take Béatrix by surprise and let her feel her wrath. She is pregnant, and this begins to take a murderous turn, for she publicly went out to buy pistols."

"Tell the duchess that Madame de Rochefide will not be leaving and that in two weeks it will all be over. Now then d'Ajuda, give me your hand! Neither you nor I have said nor seen anything. We will merely admire the fortuities of life!"

"The duchess has already sworn me to silence on the gospels and the cross."

"You will receive my wife a month from now . . . ."

"With pleasure."

"Everyone will be satisfied," replied Maxime. "However, advise the duchess that something will delay her trip to Italy by six weeks, something pertaining to Monsieur du Guénic—you will find out later."

"What is it!" said d'Ajuda looking at La Palférine.

"In the words of Socrates before he died: 'We owe a cock to Asclepius'; but your brother-in-law will get off with just the comb," replied La Palférine, straightfaced.*

❋⤙☙⤚❋⤙☙⤚❋⤙☙⤚❋⤙☙⤚❋⤙☙⤚❋⤙☙⤚❋⤙☙⤚❋⤙☙⤚❋⤙☙⤚❋⤙☙⤚

XXIV A GHASTLY LESSON For ten days, Calyste had been the victim of a fury all the more implacable in that it was forti-

---

* The allusions here are multiple, the component parts being:

    1) Socrates' last words were: "Crito, I owe a cock to Asclepius; will you remember to pay the debt." (Phaedo)

    2) Asclepius was the god of medicine to whom the serpent and the cock were sacred.

    3) An easily treated venereal disease, probably gonorrhea, was vulgarly called "crêtes de coq" (cock's comb).

Hence Calyste would seem to be getting off cheaply for his transgression.

fied by a genuine passion. Béatrix was experiencing the kind of love that Maxime had so brutally and accurately described to the Duchesse de Grandlieu. There is probably no well-balanced person who does not experience this tremendous passion at least once in his lifetime. The marquise felt dominated by a superior force, by a young man, unimpressed by her social position, who, fully as noble as she, examined her with a cool and penetrating eye, and barely responded with an approving smile to her most ingenuous feminine devices. She was oppressed by a tyrant who always left her in tears, wounded and feeling inadequate. Charles-Édouard was playing the same scene with Madame de Rochefide that Madame de Rochefide had been playing with Calyste for the previous six months. Ever since her public humiliation at the opera, Béatrix had persisted in the same argument with Calyste:

"You preferred society and your wife to me, consequently you do not love me. If you want to prove that you love me, sacrifice your wife and society. Leave Sabine and come live with me in Switzerland, in Italy, in Germany!"

Arming herself with this cruel ultimatum, she maintained the kind of blockade that women declare through cold glances, contemptuous gestures, and fortress-like demeanor. She thought she had finished with Calyste, believing he would never break with the Grandlieus. Leaving Sabine, to whom Mademoiselle des Touches had bequeathed her fortune, would mean exposing himself to penury. But Calyste, mad with despair, had secretly obtained a passport and begged his mother to send him a sizable sum. While awaiting the arrival of the money, he kept a close watch over Béatrix, suffering all the fury of Breton jealousy. Finally, nine days after the fateful report made by La Palférine to Maxime at the club, Calyste, having received thirty thousand francs from his mother, ran to Béatrix with the intention of breaking the blockade, dismissing La Palférine and leaving Paris with his placated idol. It was one of those horrible dilemmas through which women who have preserved a minimum of self-respect can either sink forever into the quagmire of vice or return to virtue. Until then, Madame de Rochefide had considered herself a virtuous woman who had chanced to know two passions; but to love Charles-Édouard and let herself be loved by Calyste meant the loss of her own esteem, for that is where mendacity and infamy begin. She had given Calyste certain privileges and nothing could prevent him from falling at her feet and showering them with his tears of total repentance. Many people are shocked by the glacial coldness with which women snuff out their loves, but if they did not completely extinguish the past this way, life would be without dignity for them; they could never refuse the fatal liberties they once granted. In the entirely novel situation in which she found herself, Béatrix might have been saved had La Palférine arrived in time; but old Antoine's quick thinking was her undoing.

Hearing a carriage stop at the door, she said to Calyste, "There is someone here," and ran to prevent a crisis.

Antoine, a prudent man, said to Charles-Édouard who had come in the hope of hearing these very words, "Madame has gone out."

When Béatrix learned from her old servant of the young count's visit and the reply made to him, she said "Very well!" and returned to her drawing room adding "I will become a nun!"

Calyste, who had taken the liberty of opening the window, saw his rival.

"Who is it?" he asked.

"I don't know, Antoine is still downstairs."

"It's La Palférine . . . ."

"It could be . . . ."

"You love him, that's why you find me inadequate; I saw him!"

"You saw him?"

"I opened the window."

Béatrix fell stricken onto a couch. She then tried to postpone things by ostensibly coming to an agreement, but put off the departure for a week on the pretext of business affairs, and swore to close her door to Calyste if she could mollify La Palférine. This is the kind of atrocious scheming and burning anguish that lies beneath these lives which have been derailed from the tracks of convention.

XXV Beatified-Béatrix   Once Béatrix was left alone, she felt so miserable, so deeply ashamed, that she went to bed feeling sick. The violent struggle that had been waged in her heart seemed to have caused a terrible reaction. She sent for the doctor, but at the same time had a letter delivered to La Palférine in which she took wrathful vengeance on Calyste.

"Dear friend, come to see me, I am in despair. Antoine sent you away when your arrival would have put an end to one of the worst nightmares of my life by delivering me from a man I loathe and whom I hope never to see again. I love only you in all the world, and I will never love anyone but you, even though I have the misfortune of not pleasing you as much as I should like . . . ."

She wrote four pages which, having begun in this fashion, ended in an exaltation far too poetic to be set into type, but in which she compromised herself to such a degree that she ended by saying, "Am I sufficiently at your mercy? I would pay any price to prove to you how much you are loved." And she signed her name, something she had never done for Calyste or for Conti.

The following day, when the young count came to see the marquise, she was having her bath: Antoine asked him to wait. He in turn sent away Calyste who, love-starved, had come early and whom he watched from the window as Calyste despairingly climbed back into his carriage.

"Oh, Charles!" said the marquise coming into the drawing room. "You are the cause of my undoing!"

"I am fully aware of that, Madame," La Palférine calmly replied. "You swore to me that you loved only me, you offered to give me a letter in which you would put down all your reasons for committing suicide so that in the event of your infidelity I could poison you without risk of prosecution, as though superior people needed poison to avenge themselves. You wrote: *I would pay any price to prove to you how much you are loved!* . . . Well then, I see a contradiction between the words *You are the cause of my undoing* and the ending of that letter . . . Now I will know whether you had the courage to break with du Guénic . . . ."

"In that case, you are avenged in advance," she said throwing her arms around his neck, "and in view of that, you and I are bound to each other forever . . . ."

"Madame," replied the Prince of Bohême coldly, "if you wish me for your lover, I am amenable, but on certain conditions . . . ."

"Conditions?"

"Yes, the following ones: you will become reconciled with Monsieur de Rochefide, you will recover the honors of your position, you will return to your splendid house on the rue d'Anjou, you will reign there as one of the queens of Paris. And you can accomplish all this by making Rochefide go into politics and by making yourself as skillful and persistent as Madame d'Espard. That is the position required for the woman to whom I do the honor of giving myself . . . ."

"You seem to forget that Monsieur de Rochefide's consent is necessary."

"My dear child," replied La Palférine, "we have him all prepared; I gave him my word as a gentleman that you were worth all the Schontzes of the Saint-Georges district put together, and you owe it to my honor . . . ."

XXVI In Which It Is Shown That the Almavivas Are
Always Shrewder Than the Figaros * For eight days Calyste
went daily to Béatrix's where he was denied entrance by Antoine who announced with great formality: "Madame la marquise is seriously ill." From there, Calyste ran to see La
Palférine whose valet replied: "Monsieur le comte is out hunting." Each time, the Breton left a letter for La Palférine.

On the ninth day, Calyste, convoked by a note from La
Palférine, found him at home but in the company of Maxime
de Trailles, to whom the young rake doubtless wanted to show
off his diplomacy by making him a witness to this scene.

"Monsieur le baron," said Charles-Édouard in full possession
of himself, "here are the eight letters you did me the honor of
addressing to me; they are unopened. The seals are unbroken
because I already knew their contents, having learned that you
were looking for me everywhere, ever since the day I saw you
through the window when you were at the door of a house at
whose door I had been the day before with you at the window.
I thought it wiser to ignore unwarranted provocations. Quite
frankly, you are a man of too much taste to be vindictive toward a woman because she no longer loves you. It is a very
poor stratagem to try to win her back by challenging your
rival. However, in the present circumstance, your letters were
vitiated by a radical error—null and void, in legal terminology.
You are far too sensible to hold a grudge against a man for taking back his wife. Monsieur de Rochefide felt the marquise's
position was undignified. You will no longer find Madame de
Rochefide at the rue de Chartes, but at the hôtel de Rochefide
in six months—by next winter. You threw yourself headlong
into a reconciliation between husband and wife which you
yourself brought about by not rescuing Madame de Rochefide

* Traditionally, Figaro (here Maxime de Trailles) is the
wily factotum who handles all the scheming for Count
Almaviva (here La Palférine)—viz. Beaumarchais' *Le
Barbier de Séville.*

from the humiliation she suffered at the opera. Upon leaving that night, Béatrix, to whom I had already transmitted several friendly overtures on her husband's part, took me into her carriage and at once said to me, 'Go find Arthur!' "

"Oh my God!" exclaimed Calyste. "She was perfectly justified; I failed her."

"Unfortunately, poor Arthur was living with one of those dreadful women, la Schontz, who for some time had been seeing herself on the brink of desertion. Madame Schontz, who, on the basis of Béatrix's pallor, had been nurturing the illusion of one day becoming the Marquise de Rochefide, became furious on seeing her castles in Spain crumble, and decided to avenge herself on both husband and wife with one stroke. Such women, monsieur, will pluck out one of their own eyes if they can pluck out two of their enemies' eyes; la Schontz, who has just left Paris, managed to pluck out six! And if I had been imprudent enough to make love to Béatrix, that Schontz woman would have plucked out eight. You must have become aware of your need for an occulist . . . ."

Maxime could not refrain from smiling at the altered expression on the face of Calyste who turned pale as he suddenly understood his own predicament.

"Would you believe that that ignominious woman is marrying the man who provided the means for her vengeance? Oh, women! You can understand now why Béatrix has shut herself up with Arthur for a few months in Nogent-sur-Marne where they have a delightful little house; they will recover their sight there. During their absence, their house in Paris will be completely redone; the marquise intends to live in princely splendor. When one sincerely loves a woman as noble, as great, as gracious as she is—a victim of conjugal love just as she finds the courage to return to her duties—the only role open to those who adore her as you do, who admire her as I do, is to remain her friends, since we can no longer be anything else . . . You will forgive me for having thought it necessary to ask the

Comte de Trailles to witness this explanation; but I was very eager to be utterly candid about all this. As for me, let me assure you that if I admire Madame de Rochefide as a mind, I find her supremely distasteful as a woman."

"So that is how our cherished dreams, our celestial loves, end!" said Calyste, overwhelmed by so many revelations and so many disillusionments.

"All fizzed out!" exclaimed Maxime, "or worse yet, in a bath of mercury.* I don't know of a single first love that did not end stupidly. Ah, my dear baron, all that is heavenly in man is nourished in heaven alone! That is what justifies rogues like us. I have delved into that problem very deeply, monsieur; as you see, I was married yesterday, I shall be faithful to my wife, and I urge you to return to Madame du Guénic . . . however . . . in three months. Do not regret Béatrix; she is a paragon of conceit, lethargy, and vain flirtatiousness; she is a Madame d'Espard without her keen sagacity; a heartless, mindless woman, irresponsible in her mischief. Madame de Rochefide loves no one but Madame de Rochefide. She would have irreparably estranged you from Madame du Guénic and thrown you over without remorse. In short, she is as wanting in vice as she is in virtue."

"I don't quite share your opinion, Maxime," said La Palférine, "she will be the most charming hostess in Paris."

Calyste did not leave without shaking hands with Charles-Édouard and Maxime de Trailles, and thanking them for having exised his illusions.

❋↷☙↷❋↷☙↷❋↷☙↷❋↷☙↷❋↷☙↷❋↷☙↷❋↷☙↷❋↷☙↷❋↷☙↷

XXVII How Much is Explained by the Fables of La Fontaine One morning three days later, the Duchesse de Grandlieu, who had not seen her daughter since the morning this meeting took place, came by and found Calyste in the bath-

---

* Mercury was a common treatment for venereal diseases.

tub * with Sabine beside him knitting little things for the new layette.

"So my children, what news have you to tell me?" asked the good duchess.

"Only good news, mama dear," replied Sabine, raising eyes to her mother that radiated happiness. "We have acted out the fable of the two pigeons! That is all." **

Calyste took his wife's hand and pressed it tenderly.

---

* Presumably a therapeutic bath for his "affliction."

** La Fontaine's fable tells of two pigeons who loved each other dearly, one of whom, bored at home, was mad enough to undertake a distant voyage. After many mishaps, he returned home half-dead and limping. La Fontaine then asks:

> Lovers, fortunate lovers, would you travel?
> Let it be no further than the nearby shores.
> Be for each other a world always beautiful,
> Always different, always new.
> Be everything for each other, consider the rest as nothing.

AFTERWORD

Compared with the symphonic masterworks of the *Comédie humaine, Béatrix* is like a tone poem in which the technique and art of the composer can be observed, the leitmotifs singled out and linked with the recurring themes of the other works. It also allows one to admire the master with cooler objectivity because of its smaller scope. Even the imperfections of *Béatrix* —the multiple styles, the lack of structural unity, the overly-descriptive beginning, the tacked-on ending, the chronological discrepancies, the pathetic hero—contribute to a greater appreciation of Balzac.

The idea for *Béatrix* sprang full-grown from a thirty-six hour visit with George Sand at Nohant in February 1838. From five in the afternoon to five in the morning, for three nights running, Balzac listened to the fascinating accounts of George Sand's early years, her disappointing affair with Jules Sandeau, her triangular relationship with Marie d'Agoult and Franz Liszt who had been her guests at Nohant the previous spring.

Jules Sandeau, a talented writer but weak, lazy, and self-indulgent, was well-known to Balzac. For the two years following Sandeau's rupture with George Sand, Balzac had subsidized him in exchange for his unfruitful assistance in one of Balzac's many playwriting projects. Countess Marie d'Agoult was also known to Balzac, having already been described in 1835, the year of her scandalous elopement with Liszt, in a letter to Mme Hanska.* As for George Sand, Balzac had long admired her and had been a frequent visitor to the garret apartment where she lived with Sandeau.

---

* Countess Eveline Hanska, to whom Balzac wrote hundreds of letters (collected in *Lettres à L'Etrangère,* 4 vols., Calmann-Lévy, Paris) during the nineteen years he waited for her to become a widow, finally became Mme Honoré de Balzac five months before his death.

The characters were thus all assembled, and the plot formulated from Marie d'Agoult's own words to George Sand: "Is this love affair anything but the sublime falsehood of two people who would like to offer each other a happiness in which neither believes any longer?" And so *Les Galériens* (the convicts) was announced to Mme Hanska in a letter dated March 2, a few days after leaving Nohant: "It was on the subject of Liszt and Madame d'Agoult that she provided me with the plot for *Les Galériens* or *Les Amours forcés* which I am going to write, for in her position she cannot." *Her position* referred to George Sand's highly prized friendship with Liszt (the aftermath of an earlier love affair that never soured, or the outgrowth of her rejection of his ardor?—both were widely rumored, but we will never know for certain). It also referred to her equivocal relationship with Marie d'Agoult, who was understandably irritated at seeing her lover's name constantly linked in European newspapers with her putative rival, and whose skittish nerves made her see in every pleasant exchange between the two artists an attempt on the part of George Sand to spirit him away.

Those three nights in Nohant in fact engendered more than one offspring. The first was a sketch for a short story set in Paris entitled *Les Amours forcés,* which subsequently furnished material for three novels, *Béatrix, Une fille d'Eve,* and *Mémoires de deux jeunes mariées.* The second was a rough draft of *Béatrix,* situated in Brittany, which ultimately provided the opening pages of the present novel. The first three parts of *Béatrix* (under the sub-title *Les Amours forcés*) appeared in serialized form in 1839. The novel was not to be completed until 1844, during which time Balzac published fifteen other novels.*

The biographical aspects of the novel are of interest only in

* For a complete history of the novel, see the excellent prefatory essay, and critical appendices, by Maurice Regard in the Classiques Garnier edition of *Béatrix,* Paris, 1962.

terms of literary genesis, in keeping with Balzac's own theory that "to invent in all things is to die a slow death; to copy is to live." And so Félicité des Touches, the most detailed literary portrait we have of George Sand, is a composite of a number of models. She has George Sand's literary genius, singular upbringing, masculine tastes, and temperamental characteristics. The maternal yet sensual love, and intellectual stimulation she offers the hero are an echo of Mme. de Berny.* Her literary beginnings are borrowed from Prosper Mérimée, and her face and figure from the celebrated actress, Mlle. George. Félicité des Touches, the woman, is then provided with a sexless mask —her pen-name, Camille Maupin—behind which all her feminine unfulfillment is hidden.

Other portraits from life are Gustave Planche in the character of Claude Vignon (another of the few first names in French equally suited to either sex, and in both cases applied to characters who never attain fulfillment). Like his model, Claude Vignon is a vituperative critic, the nemesis of all writers, rendered emotionally and artistically impotent by his hyper-intellectuality. Béatrix de Rochefide begins as a physical and moral portrait of Marie d'Agoult, but in the second section of the novel (The Honeymoon) undergoes a Dorian Gray-like degeneration. Her willowy slenderness has turned bony, her earlier pathos has become vengeful and meretricious, her subtle seductiveness has altered to cheap immorality. She is put together like a piece of costume jewelry, showy and fake. Her lover, Gennaro Conti, has Liszt's physical traits and musical genius, with Sandeau's character defects.

Balzac could not have offered a greater tribute to his friend-

* Laure de Berny became Balzac's first mistress, and first great love, when she was forty-five and he twenty-three. During the fourteen years of their relationship, she was always called La Dilecta. She provided him with a mother's affection, a sybarite's passion, a mentor's guidance. She was his first champion and his most devoted editor.

ship for George Sand than this novel of revenge which she dared not write. But beyond the unflattering portrait of Marie d'Agoult and the fictional justice meted out to this cold, egotistical woman, Camille Maupin is a dithyramb to George Sand's talent and intelligence, wit and generosity, which may perhaps, in some small way, have compensated for her loneliness as a woman.

Still another character drawn from life is the delicate Irishwoman, Mme. du Guénic, the hero's mother, whose fair beauty and nickname, Fanny, were borrowed from Sarah Guidoboni-Visconti, to whom the book is dedicated—the English enchantress whose sexual appetite and generous purse made her one of Chance's greater gifts to Balzac. Mme. du Guénic's indulgent understanding and devoted patience were yet another tribute to Laure de Berny, whose passion and tenderness provided the underside of the relationship between Mme. du Guénic and her son, Calyste, with its unavowable yearnings and natural affection.

Here the chronicle ends and the novel begins.

What Balzac has created from the threads of biography is a tapestry of the faces of love. At first one sees the noble faces: the old Baron de Guénic's love of God and country, family and friends; Fanny's exquisite attentions to her aged husband; Zéphirine's blind devotion to her brother and his family; the love and understanding shared by Fanny and Calyste; the loving concern of old friends. But soon the innocent smiles fade. Hidden beneath the quixotic exterior of the Chevalier du Halga is the aching memory of his clandestine affair with the wife of his commanding officer and best friend, a love he continues to mourn long after her death. Fanny has never known passionate love, and all the frustrated exuberance of her generous nature has been transferred to her love for her son, through whom she discovers all the missed nuances of jealousy, duplicity, anxiety, compassion, and tenderness. Calyste even makes her a declaration of love, her first, when he promises to be for her all the loves she never had. However, Calyste's emotional Eden becomes a stifling hothouse once he discovers the lighter air of Les Touches. The scene now grows more somber as the chain gang of love's condemned assembles.

Félicité des Touches (or Camille Maupin, as she is more often called in the novel), the forty-year old writer who from childhood understood more than she felt, and later willed herself to feel what she understood, discovers in Calyste who is twenty years her junior the first true passion of her life. Despite his ardor, she rejects him as a lover, preferring to awaken his intellect, and tries to distract him with the glittering Béatrix. She in turn tries to distract herself with Claude Vignon, whom she wants to love for reasons hardly flattering to him. Claude could serve as a barrier against her almost incestuous love for Calyste; he could provide her with an *oeuvre de vieillesse* in her desire to mold and promote this unlovable but brilliant man; he could shield her from the loneliness that otherwise awaits her. But Claude, already impotent because of his destructive intellect, is emasculated by the magnitude of Camille's love for Calyste. There is nothing left for them to discover together; he is merely the instrument of her salvation. Able to envision a realm of love they can never attain, they are condemned to perpetual solitude; they have gone beyond the limits of human understanding, and for their hubris are meted out the punishment of Tantalus.

Béatrix appears on the scene with her lover, Conti, whom she is doomed to endure. Although flattered by Calyste's anguished pleas, she remains unresponsive since she feels no self-respecting woman can permit herself more than one transgression. Already on the margin of society because of her abandonment of husband and child, she has no choice but to remain with Conti and graciously overlook the infidelities with which he lightens the burden of his committment to a woman who has sacrificed everything for him. These two are condemned to each other out of pride: she to protect the poetry of her own martyred image, he to flaunt this testimony to his charms. Though eager to be rid of her, he would never allow her to leave him. And she, for fear of being abandoned, will make any concession.

The final pair of love's prisoners are Calyste and Sabine. Though Calyste is the hero, and the plot is woven around the vicissitudes of his sentimental education, he is the least dynamic of the lot. Throughout the novel he is carried along by the forceful energies of the other characters. A literary relative of Félix de Vandenesse and Fabrice del Dongo, he shares with them only their capacity for idealized love and their irresistible appeal to women. When Calyste tells Béatrix he has no other gift but that of love, he is not underrating himself. Calyste's penance is multiple, but his inertia inhibits our compassion. Out of filial respect to his dying father, and out of gratitude to Camille, he agrees to the marriage arranged and enriched by her. Camille's sublime sacrifice of her love and her fortune have made him both her victim and her beneficiary. But his marriage bonds do not loose the fetter of his passion for Béatrix.

Sabine consequently suffers the torment of serving as a perpetual stand-in. Though delicately put, so delicately that in our present-day style of bare sex and bald language it might be overlooked, we are given to understand that between the conjugal sheets it is Béatrix, not Sabine, to whom Calyste makes love. The otherwise cloying sweetness of Sabine's long-suffering nature is mitigated, and highlighted, by another biographical tidbit. Balzac's close friend, the young, beautiful and intelligent Delphine de Girardin became the victim of Marie d'Agoult's autumnal charms when in 1841 her husband was smitten by that great heroine of love's misfortunes. The novel thus avenges two women: George Sand in the first part, and Delphine de Girardin, even more ferociously, in the second.

Here, whether out of irony or haste on Balzac's part, we see a pair condemned to a happy ending. Sabine has won a doubtful victory—the strategy was not her own and the prize leaves much to be desired. Calyste may remain faithful to her in the future, but he has undergone no real change. He has not renounced Béatrix; she has been taken from him. Nor does Sabine excite him any more than she did. She is too much like him. As Balzac explains in an intervention on contrasts (*The Honeymoon,* Chapter XIII) nobility in others is taken for granted by noble souls. Its absence is noticeable, and most often titillating. These two victims are thus condemned to each other; Sabine to a handsome but ineffectual husband, a man compliant out of lethargy, or delinquent out of weakness, not wisened by time, merely chastened by life's cruelty and his own incompetence. Calyste in turn is condemned to Sabine's excessive attentions, to an emotional death by smothering—a curious repetition of the stifling atmosphere of his family's love. For him there is no escape. His course has been ineluctably set on a return voyage to childhood.

Although a number of eloquent male voices are heard in this disquisition on love—Calyste's adolescent, tearful odes to Camille, his wracking lamentations to Béatrix; Claude Vignon's penetrating aria on the splendors of the mature woman; Conti's ingenious cadenzas on the entanglements of bachelorhood; Maxime de Trailles' sardonic analysis of sensual enslavement to the Lilith-woman—*Béatrix* is primarily an oratorio to the glory of women with the major solo parts distributed among female voices. It is the companion piece to *Adolphe,* a corrective to Benjamin Constant's one-sided masculine view, magnified by a multiple mirror technique achieved through references to Camille's fictional novel on the same theme, constant allusions to Constant's real novel, discussions on the subject of a woman's suffering in love between Camille and Béatrix, Sabine's letters on marriage, along with Balzac's analytical interventions on behalf of women in general. Far more than a penetrating and understanding balance to the "insistently male approach" of

Balzac's "pontifications on the proper destiny of woman" *
Béatrix is an outright apologia, a feminist treatise, that places
all the burden of guilt on a male-oriented society. Camille's
ultimate sacrifice—and Balzac goes to great pains to applaud
and justify her equal status and masculine mores—is not a deserved punishment for breaching society's rules, but the tragic
dénouement of a singular character. Even the much-maligned
Béatrix is justified in large measure by Balzac's comments on
the abandoned woman, whether by husband, lover, or her own
choice ("tout ce qui tourne en malheur pour une femme aban-
donnée se change en bonheur chez un homme abandonné").
The homilie that follows ("ce contraste frappant inspirera à
plus d'une jeune femme la résolution de rester dans son ménage
et de lutter . . .") is not to be construed as a recommendation
because it is desireable, but because society offers no quarter to
the "unattached" woman; she is besmirched with contempt or
condemned to loneliness. Even the professionally unvirtuous
Madame Schontz is painted in glowing pastels. Victim of a
society that cultivated her mind and manners but offered her
neither the opportunities of suitable marriage or suitable em-
ployment, she is finally obliged to buy herself a fool for a husband with her carefully saved wages of sin in order to achieve
respectability.

Every disadvantage known to woman is heaped on this celeb-
ratory pyre: the plight of the nursing mother whose husband
wanders off out of boredom, the destruction of twenty years'
loving care once the child grows up, the compulsory abdication
from reigning queen to lonely matron, the hopelessness of finding lasting love once the gates of hell swing open at forty.
Perpetually a vassal of society or a victim of her own sensibility,
she can never take but must wait to receive, and often gets little more than crumbs. Where the older woman may enjoy the
fragrant blooms of a short season, the young girl often waits
through a long winter for a meager nosegay. Poor Sabine in

* Hemmings, F.W.J., *An Interpretation of La Comédie humaine,* p. 78, Random House, New York, 1967.

her youthful innocence is defenseless against the sophistication of the ripe Béatrix, who at least has the satisfaction of knowing Calyste embraces her entirely for herself. Irony of ironies, when Sabine finally gets Calyste back, it is to knit beside him while he sits in a tub curing the gonorrhea he contracted from Béatrix.

Out of all this emerges one of Balzac's central themes—sacrifice in love. Sacrifice of pride, of happiness, of wealth of health, even of life: Père Goriot, Louise de Chaulieu, Madame de Mortsauf, Félicité des Touches . . . the list is too long to be catalogued here, all make their total sacrifice out of love, and most often they are women. Throughout his writing, Balzac's glorification of the sacrifices of womanhood is not the confirmation of a divine ordinance. It is first an apotheosis and second an attack. The first bears testimony to the quality of the man, to his good fortune and gratitude for having received the love of extraordinary women—his sister, the first Laure of his life; Mme. de Berny, the second Laure, a woman whose essence pervades all the noble women of the Balzacian personae; the Countess Guidoboni-Visconti, his fiery Sarah-Fanny; Mme. Hanska, his long-awaited and considerably idealized love whom he did not live long enough to enjoy. The second reveals the modernity of the critic whose diatribes against the societal ills of the 1830's are singularly apposite in the 1960's.

As an early champion of feminism (in *Béatrix,* a woman of genius like Camille Maupin is admired by the brightest of her male peers, while criticism of gifted women comes from fools like Arthur de Rochefide), he was already aware of the high price of emancipation. The standards are still double—in morals, professional opportunities, salaries, and the cost in personal happiness has remained exorbitant. Other ailments in Balzac's pathology of society also appear in *Béatrix* and are surprisingly up to date. One need only list them to recognize how many still pullulate today. Post-revolutionary France, in which the aristocracy of blood was replaced by an aristocracy of money, saw a collapse of standards and values. The old gods were dead and new ones, other than Mammon and Envy, had not yet been found. In the vulgarity of this nouveau-riche society, the easy success of a parvenu was taken for granted, immorality was normal in an amoral milieu, any notion of excellence was abandoned in favor of notoriety, materialism was rampant and consumption conspicuous, egalitarianism had promoted an illusion of parity of achievement, the younger generation held its elders in contempt, and any new idea or cause, however flimsy, was by definition significant as a victory over the old order. With only the lightest of editorial pencils, the chapter entitled "One of the Diseases of the Age" in the present novel, could be slipped into any contemporary text without suspicion of anachronism.

Béatrix, seen in the light of key Balzacian themes,* is truly a summa, which accounts for both its defects and its interest. Familiar characters from the myriad pages of the *Comédie humaine* flit in and out of its chapters, sometimes with major speaking parts, sometimes merely as supernumeraries; the plot at times centers around and at other times gives way to the constant preoccupations of the other novels; the construction of the novel, though loose, utilizes the same technique, today the primer of the movie camera—a traveling shot of the town moving in on the buildings, penetrating the houses, lingering over architectural and decorative details, followed by close-ups of the characters engaged in a pantomime of habitual movements, used today as a background for credits. Then suddenly the action begins. The tedious narrative gives way to fast-paced dialogue, and the whole plot is set up, leaving only the ending as a surprise. It is somewhat like a murder mystery: the reader is given all the clues but has to wait for the master sleuth to reveal how he solved the case.

Beth Archer

* Marceau, Félicien, *Balzac et son monde,* Gallimard, Paris, 1955.